ALSO BY DOUG MAGEE

Never Wave Goodbye

DARKNESS ALL AROUND

DOUG MAGEE

A TOUCHSTONE BOOK
Published by Simon & Schuster
New York London Toronto Sydney New Delhi

For Tim, Joey, and Jack—all my love, guys

Touchstone
A Division of Simon & Schuster, Inc.
1230 Avenue of the Americas
New York, NY 10020

This book is a work of fiction. Names, characters, places, and incidents either are products of the author's imagination or are used fictitiously. Any resemblance to actual events or locales or persons, living or dead, is entirely coincidental.

First Touchstone trade paperback edition June 2012

TOUCHSTONE and colophon are registered trademarks of Simon & Schuster, Inc.

For information about special discounts for bulk purchases, please contact Simon & Schuster Special Sales at 1-866-506-1949 or business@simonandschuster.com.

The Simon & Schuster Speakers Bureau can bring authors to your live event. For more information or to book an event contact the Simon & Schuster Speakers Bureau at 1-866-248-3049 or visit our website at www.simonspeakers.com.

Designed by Renata Di Biase

Manufactured in the United States of America

10 9 8 7 6 5 4 3 2 1

The Library of Congress has cataloged the hardcover edition as follows:
Magee, Doug.
Darkness all around / By Doug Magee.—1st Touchstone hardcover ed.
p. cm.
"A Touchstone book."
I. Title.
PS3613.A3425D37 2011
813'.6—dc22

2011011933

ISBN 978-1-4391-5402-1
ISBN 978-1-4391-5404-5 (pbk)
ISBN 978-1-4391-6010-7 (ebook)

ACKNOWLEDGMENTS

I'd like to thank my most potent nightmare, the one in which I am guilty of murder and realize I will live the rest of my life in the shadow of my guilt. And, equally, I'd like to thank whatever forces allow me to wake from this horror to the sunshine of innocence.

This book began years ago as a seed idea having to do with a sobriety drug. I'd like to thank Rick Leed for supporting that idea and Trish Grader for helping me reorient and expand the story. An encounter with Oliver Sacks's account of a brain-damaged patient who recovered memories of a murder confirmed the plausibility of what I had imagined.

A shout-out to the unsuspecting citizens of Berwick, Pennsylvania. I spent a very instructive afternoon in their company and hope my imaginings of their lives are somewhat close to their reality.

Early readers of the manuscript were most helpful. Thanks to Linda Esposito, Mary Hedahl, Stacey Weaver, and Jim Thomsen.

Andrew Nagorski helped me round out some of the cultural background of my imagined town.

The Title Posse at ARLA, Ann, Penn, and Peri, came to my rescue at a very crucial juncture.

My editor, Sulay Hernandez, once again forthright and supportive, helped greatly in the production of this book. And thanks to Lauren Spiegel for her help in the final stages.

All praise to Ann Rittenberg for being as helpful to a sophomore as she was to a freshman. Her combination of faith and acumen got me through the bad days and helped me celebrate the good ones. Many, many thanks.

And Mary, without you there would be no books.

As consciousness grew clearer, so memory, full memory, a now terrible memory, came with it. . . . *The murder, the deed, lost to memory before, now stood before him in vivid, almost hallucinatory detail.* Uncontrollable reminiscence welled up and overwhelmed him—he kept "seeing" the murder, enacting it, again and again. Was this nightmare, was this madness, or was there now "hypermnesis"—a breakthrough of genuine, veridical, terrifyingly heightened memories?

Oliver Sacks, "Murder,"
in *The Man Who Mistook His Wife for a Hat*

Showed me light out of the tunnel
When there was darkness all around instead.

Van Morrison, "Tore Down a la Rimbaud"

1

It's a body. That's all I know."

The woman's voice coming through the phone was still new to him. He had met her only once, after she had hired him, in a rushed introduction to the central offices of the paper in nearby Docksport. She had been uninterested in him, insisted on calling him Hank when he said he preferred Henry, said he really didn't need to know anything about the central office in "this fucking computer age," hacked up a gob of phlegm that she then swallowed and would probably chase with a cigarette as soon as she could, and dismissed him swiftly when news came that a school supply storage shed in Upton had burned to the ground. He could barely remember her name: Doris Whiting.

"You got a car yet?" she asked now.

"Not yet. I'm . . ."

"Well, pedal your ass out there and let me know what's up. Find the sheriff. Armey. Jack Armey. Townies are going to be standing around fucking lost. Jack's a Nam vet. He's seen a dead body or two. And don't take any 'no comment' shit from him. Get him to grunt something. That cell phone we gave you might not work out there. Go to The Ding Dong and ask Walt if you can use his phone."

She hung up. He looked out the gable window of his single-room apartment over the Rumskis' one-car garage and saw that a gray day had dawned. He was cotton mouthed and hungover, and shuffled through a couple of crushed beer cans to his cramped half bathroom, thinking he was going to throw up. But after standing in front of the toilet for a couple of minutes he realized he wasn't going to heave then. That would come later, he guessed. When he saw the body.

He was pedaling hard uphill against a light wind, a little spitting rain blurring his vision, when he realized he didn't have his helmet or his notebook. Or a pen. He looked down at himself to make sure he was actually wearing clothes. He had covered mock murders before, mock accidents, one just weeks ago, before graduation, but this was the real thing. What kind of real thing, he didn't know. "It's a body." A body in a wooded area off a two-lane country road. Doris had said there were some details on the scanner, but she didn't trust them. She wanted eyes and ears on the ground. A week and a half on the job, a couple of nights getting shitfaced with a new friend. Was he ready for this?

He crested the hill and saw a long flat stretch of road and a cluster of cop cars and an ambulance in the distance, about a quarter of a mile before The Ding Dong, the roadside tavern he'd helped close down two or three nights ago. What was the sheriff's name? He fished a piece of paper out of his pants pocket. Armey. The light rain stained the writing. Hadn't there been some kooky congressman from this part of Pennsylvania named Armey?

He put the paper back in his pocket and realized he had a pen after all. He braked quickly when he saw a flattened paper bag by the side of the road. He was ready now. He had his tools.

After he got off his bike and moved in the direction a couple of cops were heading, a trooper held out his hand. Henry showed his newly minted press ID and the trooper scowled, looking down at his parked bike.

"You workin' on a reporter merit badge or something?"

"I'm new."

"You goin' up there to see the body?"

"Yes."

"You won't be new for long."

He had folded the paper bag and stuffed it in his back pocket, hoping when he had to take notes he could do so surreptitiously. He caught up with the cops, who he thought were town cops, introduced himself, asked for Armey. Both of them were close to his age and looked as nervous about what they were about to see as he was. They said Armey had gone up about five minutes earlier. He asked what the cops knew as they tramped through brown weeds and then brush leading to a stand of hardwoods. They shrugged, not with indifference but with something like fear.

A trooper surprised them, running out of the woods, barking into a walkie-talkie. They parted and he ran through them without acknowledging their presence. The younger of the two cops stopped and shook his head, giving his partner a defeated, pleading look.

"He said we didn't have to do this. I ain't gonna do it."

"Don't pussy out on me. This is real shit."

"You take the nightmare. I got enough."

He turned and walked back down the incline. The other cop had a moment of decision, flipped his cohort the bird, and kept walking. He was mumbling and about to say something coherent when they looked up to see a small gaggle of troopers and cops in a clearing ahead.

Though the cop with him slowed at the sight, Henry kept moving. In the days and months later, when he told the story, when he wrote about it, he couldn't say what it was that hooked fingers in his nostrils and hauled him forward, that made him think he wasn't going to throw up, that had him reaching for his flattened-out paper bag notebook. A reporter's curiosity? The clarity that comes when a hangover lifts? A sense of duty? He didn't know, he didn't care. He simply went up to a spot where he could see all as the technicians and the ME and the cops hovered and worked and photographed and jabbered. He stood with his pen and his paper bag, but he made no attempt to take notes.

"Who the fuck are you?"

Henry had not yet glimpsed the body when the gravelly voice barked at him. He turned to see a man in his fifties, wearing a faded Eagles T-shirt over a sizable paunch, shorts, flip-flops, and a seed cap that said SHERIFF on the front. Henry held out his ID.

"Henry Saltz. I'm the new—"

"Yeah. Don't touch anything, okay?" He started to walk away.

"Sheriff?"

"What?"

"Can I get a comment from you?"

"Sure. Tell Doris to lay off the fucking exclamation points and report the fucking facts. I guess that goes for you too, Wet-Behind-the-Ears."

"Okay. What are the facts?"

Armey gestured toward the body. "Take a look." He moved away.

Henry waited until the ME and a photographer weren't blocking his view. He then took a couple of steps forward, as if he were approaching a casket at a wake. He heard a voice to his right say, ". . . waitress at The Ding Dong." Henry knew then what he was looking at. But he didn't make a note as he took another step. Then as he came close to the body, as he saw its features, something kept him from seeing the corpse as dead. He both lost focus and saw things with utter clarity. He looked through the body to something deeper.

She had been pretty and alive, but that had been days ago, when she walked and laughed. Now she was part of the earth, a fallen log across the trail, gravity and the elements working to make her one with the soil. She was no longer whole, but she was recognizable, her hacked, cubist features hinting at the woman she had been. He could see that woman in sunshine, with white teeth and shiny legs, with glistening hair curving over an ear. He could see how untouchable she had been, a perfect specimen of grace and form. The more he looked, the deeper he went. He knew her now, in a way no one could ever have known her in life. To the cops she was a broken body, a case, a puzzle, but to him she was elemental existence. Whatever had happened had closed off one thing, closed off time and space for her, but it had opened him to new life. As contradictory as all this was to any rationality, he didn't question it. He felt it with ever more assurance. The cops were looking at an endpoint. He was looking at a commencement.

There was a small commotion and a trooper came into the circle gingerly holding a curving machete between his latexed thumb and forefinger. The blood-caked metal made sense to the cops. They could see how it had been used, how it explained the beauty pageant ribbon of open flesh from her shoulder to her hip. But to him it was an intrusion, an ugly mechanism that explained nothing, that was all surface. He would write about it, but in the first flush of its appearance it had the effect of pulling him back from the fuller picture. He wanted to stay in the presence of this creature, lifeless as she was, to know in his bones and his heart that all was over for her, that all was over for him. These weren't things you could write about. You could barely feel them. But here they were now. He only wanted to stay.

Then the sheet came over her, and as it fluttered down on what he would later call the remains, it was as if a curtain had been dropped on a stage, on a play. The end. That's all, folks. He raised the flattened paper bag, but he knew he had nothing much to write. He didn't need to make notes. He would never, ever forget any detail of what he saw.

Nor could he ever write the strange yet certain sentence forming in his head now, billowing like blood from a wound, giving him finality and assurance despite the almost depraved incongruity of the words. He fought against letting the sentence have life, but the battle only agitated him more. Blood soaked through the sheet and he saw again the macheted flesh. Henry was at war with himself now, working to keep the sentence at bay. But finally it burst through from nascent words to something whole. Then, as if the sentence were a physical manifestation, Henry turned, took two steps back, and covered a photographer's open camera bag with a spray of vomit. But that couldn't stop the words from surfacing. As the photographer protested, Henry only looked back at the draped body.

"Whatever happened to her," he said to himself, "maybe she deserved it."

2

The drunk would remember nothing of what was about to happen to him. But that wasn't unusual. He couldn't say who he was, couldn't say where he came from. When strangers asked, he'd simply nod or mumble or give any answer he thought might get him away from them, with enough money for a bottle.

He woke this morning with the hunger, the ever-present hunger, competing with a biting cold for his attention. When he was upright and able to make out shapes in the frozen, brick-strewn basement, he could see his fingers as bluish blobs at the ends of his hands. Some primal instinct launched him out of the basement, out into a wind-whipped street. Those bluish fingers meant something, like storm clouds to a farmer. There was some danger lurking. He had no memory, but his brain stem could still react.

Subway. Warmth. He tried to move his feet, but they seemed foreign, rooted, blocks of ice. Then they began to move, as if on their own. People wrapped tightly against the wind rushed by him. He tried to follow them, something told him to follow them, but he couldn't keep up and the wind blared in his face.

Then suddenly there was a hole in the ground and stairs and legs and feet running up and down the stairs and sounds of scraping metal in the hole. He limped down the stairs, one agonizing step at a time, until he was at the bottom and out of the wind. There was a ticket booth and the ratchet noise of turnstiles. Something gigantic, an express train, filled the cavity of the station with a deafening thrum for a full minute before it disappeared.

He was able to fling open a door between him and the platform. An alarm sounded, a scratchy loudspeaker voice shouted at him. He shuffled toward the tracks and the warmth as people on the crowded platform parted for him. He heard a sharp voice, saw the woman cop's blue uniform stretched over large breasts. Knowing this sign as he knew the blue in his fingers, he turned to walk the other way, but the turning was too much. The platform tilted heavily to the right, though the passengers waiting were unfazed. He tried to right himself, but then the platform fell out from underneath him and he dropped to the hard bed of rails and ties.

He was still conscious, but the screaming that was going on above meant little to him. The metal his hand rested on was warm, the ties not uncomfortable. Maybe this had been his destination after all, not the train car with the angry eyes where all moved away from him, but the tracks. He would rest. He closed his eyes.

Then the screaming became the screeching of brakes, and a piercing light grew in his head. Sure hands yanked his collar, choking him, rolling him to the center gutter of the tracks. The screeching became unbearable, drowning the woman's voice in his ear. He fought to get her off him. She flailed at his wild arms. He got his head off the concrete, and as he did, a huge shadow raced over them, sparks from the rails showering the undercarriage, giving him a brief glimpse of the strut that clobbered him into oblivion.

The blow set off a riot of change in the drunk's brain. Massive subdural hematomas exploded on both sides of his frontal lobes, cascading blood and swelling and destructive pressure to the tissue and gray matter beneath. The synapses and neurons in memory centers began winking out like city lights in a fast-spreading blackout. Childhood, adolescence, and yesterday shut down as the nerves that carried their messages became pinched and blood soaked. Then one by one the major, never-to-be-forgotten memories, the ones grooved so deeply they could never be touched, were found by the flooding brain and engulfed. The birth of his son went. His father's limp, hanging body. His wife's shining eyes.

And then the last one, the one he had spent years trying to poison out of his brain. It was the dark, bleak vision of a lifeless body, only a foot from his face, almost unrecognizable as a body. And with this came a close-up of the unmistakable instrument of that body's destruction: a curved, bloody, murderous machete.

And then nothing.

3

"Warren, I've gotta close up for a few hours. You're going to have to go outside."

Warren Mastic, still dapper, still firmly planted in his spot at the bar, still twirling the glass of club soda in front of him, looked across the polished wood at Risa Tuvic and smiled the smile of the lost.

"Peggy?"

"That was my mother," Risa responded, knowing most of the lines that would follow.

"You've got great legs."

"Should have told her that when you had the chance, Warren."

"It might rain."

"It might, but not likely. Look outside. Hot day. No clouds. Perfect weather for Scrimmage Day. It's Scrimmage Day, Warren. Everybody's over at the stadium. I've gotta close up. Your daughter's coming to get you. I'm going to put you on the bench outside."

Warren smiled and sipped his club soda. He was the last patron left in The Kitchen, a large, light-filled one-room bar-restaurant Risa's father had opened forty years earlier, a place Risa had, reluctantly at times, called home her entire thirty-nine years. A thin woman with sandy hair, calm cheekbones, and green eyes that were both inviting and watchful, she had been a town darling since the days she, as a six-year-old, used to waitress for her father and mother, taking a good five minutes to precariously get a glass of ice water to a table without spilling it.

"I'll just have another," Warren said, indicating his club soda, which was only half empty.

Risa looked at the clock. It was three forty. No matter how much she rushed it, she was going to be late. She looked at Warren and in a second the urgency that had been pushing her the last hour, the need to get the afternoon's loose ends tied up, to get The Kitchen closed, drained from her, and she wanted nothing more than to refill Warren's glass and stay where she was.

In a few hours, after the high school football scrimmage that gave the day its name, The Kitchen would be packed. Laughter would bounce off walls clotted with photographs, proclamations, ribbons, flags, and plaques. Over the years the homey space had been not only a bar and restaurant but also a union hall, a political club, and a common ground for the Poles, Greeks, and Ukrainians whose parents had come to dig coal and stayed to work in the postwar factories. Risa's father, Sim, had been a uniter, a man whose goodwill and charm made people flock to his restaurant, to him, and to rub elbows with people of other ethnicities their parents had warned them about.

The crowd that would fill The Kitchen would be buzzing about the football team, but it was a far cry from the days when local politicians would be holding court in one corner, a Greek Orthodox priest would be accepting a dinner from his parishioners, and news that the Top-Co plant was expanding yet again had diners wondering just how big the truck parts manufacturer could get.

"I got back from Korea in 19 and 53," Warren said, as if Risa had asked him.

"That's right." Risa knew she shouldn't be standing there, that she should be going, but something had her rooted. Voices from the last few hours, the "see yas" and "can't waits" and "this is going to be greats" hung in the slanted light coming through The Kitchen's front windows along with the dust motes. Every one of those heartfelt salutations had made her wish that her presence was not required at Bulldog Stadium.

"And when you came across the old bridge," Risa said, finishing Warren's usual recitation, "you kissed the pavement on Market Street and said you'd never leave Braden again."

Warren smiled. "Peggy?"

He didn't resist being led out the front door of the restaurant. He sat on the slatted bench that accommodated the overflow on Friday nights. Warren's daughter had asked Risa to tie Warren to the bench with a dish towel so he wouldn't wander away, but something in this went against Risa's nature. She was not the type to tell people what to do, and the role of jailer certainly didn't fit. She thought maybe she'd just sit with Warren until his daughter showed up. But that was foot dragging too, and after a few minutes she secured Warren's forearm to the armrest and patted his shoulder.

"She'll be right here, Warren."

"Peggy?"

"That was my mother, Warren."

"Sim around?"

"Not really. He's up at the cemetery."

"What's he doing up there?"

"Resting. I gotta go. See you tomorrow."

Warren looked straight ahead and Risa backed away, watching to see if Warren would chafe at the dish towel shackle. He didn't, and when she reached the corner of Third and Williams, she turned and walked forward. Now, with Warren behind her, she had to confront the problem that had been growing all afternoon. What was she afraid of? Why did she dread walking into Bulldog Stadium when anyone in her right mind would see such an entry as triumphal? BENSON FOR CONGRESS signs that shouted out her husband's name from every shop on Third should have made her glow with pride, but they only widened the bubble in her stomach. The Bulldog souvenir shop, closed for the afternoon, of course, had the same effect, though it too should have made her swell with affection for her town, for her son.

What was going on? Whatever it was hadn't just suddenly come to her. The whole summer had been fraught, anxious, the flooding on the Susquehanna more like something she was feeling than river water overflowing its banks. For a time she thought it was the campaign, the appearances, the handshaking and plastered smiles she knew Alan and all around her expected. That wasn't her, but she made it seem as if it were. Was she paying the price for that sort of playacting? No, that was not fun, but it didn't have the same sort of ominous quality as this other, inchoate feeling.

She had one foot off the curb crossing Market when the sharp blast of a bus horn made her jump back. A rush of hot wind, metal, and glass swept past her as the bus blew by. She saw her reflected image distort and wobble on the brown surface of the bus's flank. She caught her breath and watched the incongruous machine slow and make its wide turn onto Fifth Street. She didn't have to see the destination sign on the front to know the bus was from New York.

She looked to her left, where the bus had come across the bridge into town, down to where it left when it was heading east into the city. The valley below, the scruffy hills beyond were hazy in the late afternoon sun. That view, down Market Street to the bridge and beyond, had always been a loaded one for Risa. It was the escape route to all the things Braden wasn't. She had taken it once, into Philadelphia for drawing classes, for the excitement of the city, for a clichéd but loving affair with a teacher. And she wished now she could be on a bus for anywhere rather than going to the stadium.

She crossed Market, shaking off any thought that what she was feeling had to do with the world outside Braden. It wasn't that. In the middle of the block she pushed open the door to the Benson for Congress headquarters and felt the icy air within. She had strongly suggested to Lilly Barkin, Alan's campaign manager, that a warmer temperature in the storefront, a former Verizon showroom, would save money and show the candidate to be ecofriendly. Lilly had ignored her. Risa had let it go. Now Lilly, a fiftyish country club doyenne, working hard to have her picture next to the word "imperious" in the dictionary, came toward Risa in full screech.

"What are you doing here? It's almost four. We're doing all the press before, Risa, before. Didn't Alan tell you?"

"He told me."

"Well, hop, skip. Have you got your car?"

"No."

"Mine's on Market. Let's go."

"I'm gonna walk."

"Oh, no you're not." Lilly was texting as she talked. "I can get things delayed a little. I told Coach there might be a few glitches. He's going to"—pause for sending something on her BlackBerry—"he's going to pull Kevin out and we'll do sort of a family hug kind of thing, you know, the 'go get 'em, son' shtick with the team in the background running around."

Though it was the myth that every soul able to walk in Braden ringed the field for the storied Braden Area High School football team's annual rollout known as Scrimmage Day, Risa suspected that Lilly and her ilk rarely left their tanning chaises to inspect the Bulldog squad at close range, to ooh and ahh over the newcomers, to tsk at Coach's early season decisions. If she had, she would have known that a family hug, even for a popular politician in the middle of a fairly tight race, was a no-no. The warriors parading before the town weren't to be thought of as mortals on Scrimmage Day. They were in the clean slate portion of their schedule, and for this afternoon they were on pedestals with no space for families.

"I'm going to walk, Lilly," Risa said, turning toward the door. "And I wish you'd turn the air down in here."

Lilly bobbed her head up from her BlackBerry, prepared to physically escort Risa to her car. But Risa was gone.

In more ways than one. She took a quick turn up Columbia Street to avoid Lilly running after her and kept her head down as she trudged the little incline that would lead to Saffron Park and then the stadium. Kevin, she knew now, was at the center of her dread. Fifteen, about to enter his sophomore year, his name had been buzzing around The Kitchen for weeks. "This year we're going to have some defense," was the consensus, and the reason most often given was that Alan Benson's stepkid, Risa Tuvic's son, had hefted up over the winter and looked like he was going to be a linebacker the likes of which hadn't been seen in Braden since Rick Staussen broke heads two decades earlier. Alan had treated all this cracker-barrel chatter as an adjunct to his campaign, making it clear to anyone who hadn't noticed that it was he who had raised Kevin from his sixth year on, that it was he who had drilled him in the basics from Pee Wee ball to middle school, and even over the winter. And he made sure that Kevin's touted toughness was seen by all as an echo of Alan and his political philosophy.

Risa hadn't seen Kevin play football in years. The last time she had seen him, in a middle school game on a frozen November Saturday morning, he had been involved in some wild scrum over a fumble and had cracked his left index finger. She had broken all the rules by going out onto the field and helping him off, something the coaches had strictly warned the parents not to do. The finger, dangling from the second knuckle, was an image she carried with her still. Those watching the game had carried something else away. Kevin Collins, his finger clearly snapped, had asked to go back in.

Risa had made excuses since then, saying she had too much to do at the restaurant, making sure her class in Philadelphia met on fall weekends, even once feigning sickness. She heard much about Kevin's progress from Alan and from customers and from Kevin himself, enough that she felt she knew how things were going. She knew, for instance, that Coach had deliberately kept him off the traveling team the year before, made him run opposition plays in practice, in order to "make him hungry," according to Alan. That strategy seemed to have worked.

But in other ways he was still the gentle Kevin she had given birth to seven months after graduating from college. He was a considerate kid, thinking of others often, a good science student who also appreciated the art his mother made. When he grew taller than Risa he was fond of looping an arm around her shoulder, a gesture of affection as well as a very visible sign that he was becoming a man.

Risa entered Saffron Park as a breeze rippled the leaves of the neatly planted ginkgos, the late afternoon sun brushing the tops of the trees. She stopped, even though she knew she should be storming through the park to get to the stadium. Saffron, only a few blocks from The Kitchen, had been her refuge as a child. Instead of doing her homework at a back table in the restaurant, she would bring her books to the small, green oasis and be calmed by the little patch of nature. She wished she could sit now and just watch the dancing leaves. But she could hear the drums of the marching band coming from the stadium, and she knew she had no recourse but to go there and play her role. Kevin, that morning, had made sure she would show up by literally taking her aside, as he left for the morning practice, and guiding her into the kitchen, looking her in the eye and telling her how much the day meant to him.

"You're not going to flake on me today, are you, Mom?"

"Of course not."

"Dad's counting on you too."

"Kevin, come on. I wouldn't miss this for the world."

Kevin had cocked his head and given her a look that said he didn't quite believe her. "I'm starting now, Mom. We've got all the elements in place. That's what Coach says. And I'm one of the elements. Do you know what that means?"

"Hey, I've lived in this town a lot longer than you have."

"Yeah, but—"

"I was a cheerleader. You haven't forgotten that, have you?"

"No, but I still don't believe it." An old joke between them.

"Believe it. And you just wait. Those girls they've got out there now, they've got nothing on me. You'll hear me loud and clear."

She gave him a fist bump to the biceps. He pretended this hurt him, smiled, and took off. Now as she left Saffron Park, as the horns of the marching band kicked in and she could hear the buzz coming up from the ancient stadium, that mother-son moment seemed far away, hard to recapture. What was gnawing at her?

She crossed Eleventh Street and went through the open gate onto the track surrounding the football field. She couldn't see the field itself because every inch of space around it was taken up by Bulldog supporters, an impressive crowd all clad in the blue and white school colors. She panicked for a second, wondering if she had remembered to wear blue, looked down quickly and remembered that she had slipped a Bulldog T-shirt over her white blouse. She visored her eyes with her right hand against the slanting sun and looked for Alan. Candy Simmons, a truly obnoxious little twit of a high school student who had wormed her way into Alan's campaign, appeared out of nowhere.

"Risa, there you are. I'm supposed to take you to Alan. He's waiting."

"I can find him. Thanks, Candy."

"No. I have orders. Find Mrs. . . . uh . . . Risa and get her here."

"Who told you that?"

"Lilly."

Risa gave in. She didn't want to make an issue of Lilly and being hauled to her husband. She had caught a glimpse of bobbing helmets above the heads of the crowd, and her stomach had dropped. She wanted to get to a place where she could see the team, see Kevin. With Candy she moved around to the west side of the field and got hellos from several friends. They had to stop as the crowd parted and the band, all blaring and pounding, left the field and congregated in front of them to finish the Bulldog fight song, which was really the Notre Dame fight song with new words. The stomping band had raised dust, and for a minute the scene in front of Risa was hazy and spectral. Someone tapped a microphone and blew into it, and she was hit with the sound from a nearby speaker. She wasn't sure she could continue.

But Candy was there and motioned her to follow around the back of the band and down the rows of onlookers. The high school principal was speaking about the beginning of a new era and getting little bursts of applause. Coach Martin, the young head coach who had taken over the team from a legend only three years ago, was given a rousing welcome as he made some mumbling predictions about a return to greatness. Candy pushed Risa through the people near the microphone at the fifty-yard line, and Risa found herself at Alan's side.

He was in the tense seconds before he was going to speak, gave her what Risa had come to see as his campaign smile, the subtext of which was, "Where the hell have you been?" Coach finished and Alan took the microphone, his polished, booming voice almost a rebuke to Coach's ramblings.

"I'm so glad Dave and Jim asked me to speak to you today. Isn't this a wonderful time in Bulldog history?" Risa jumped when the stadium filled with "yeses!" and applause. "I come to you today not as your state senator, not as your next congressman"—he smiled and laughed at the applause that followed this—"but as a very, very proud father." More applause now as he settled into his timing. "But I want you to know that we're all proud parents here today. These wonderful kids, these sons of Braden, are not only terrific athletes, they are the future of our fair city on the Susquehanna. We are proud of them now for what they are about to accomplish on the field of battle, but we will be even more proud of them for what they will become as men and leaders in our community. To the team I say, we are with you all the way. Fight, Bulldogs, fight!"

As the choreographed roar went up and Alan raised his right arm, pulling Risa to him with his left, Risa worked a wan smile and caught the eyes of friends nearby. A couple, she could tell, saw the question mark behind the smile, but most saw only what they wanted to see, the perfect Braden couple in a moment of triumph.

Then Risa felt a rumble in the ground and with everybody else looked to the south goalpost to see the sixty-six padded gladiators charge down the field to the roar of the crowd. For most, Risa knew, this was a heart-stirring moment, one of pumping thighs and churning arms, but for her it was as if some dreaded event had come to pass. This must be what she had feared all day, this show of force, this atavistic charge, and what might be unleashed. She didn't look for Kevin. She could see only the unity of the army, hear the hysteria of the supporters. Her heart sank even as Alan, hooting next to her, pulled her closer.

At the fifty-yard line the squad split like precision jet pilots, with those in home white jerseys going to one sideline, those in away blue jerseys going to the other.

"Go, Kevin!" Alan shouted, pumping his fist.

"Which one's Kevin?" Risa asked. Alan turned to her to see if she was kidding. He gave his head a little shake.

"Defense is in blue. You know his number, don't you?" He could see she didn't. He pointed. "There. Number fifty-four."

Risa looked past the white jerseys massed in front of them to the blue jerseys on the other side of the field. It took her a minute to find 54, but when she did there was no sense of recognition. There was nothing about Kevin that looked much different from the others. He seemed as solid, maybe a little taller, but, as he did little warm-up bursts of sprinting, pounded another player's shoulder pads, had his pounded in return, there was no sense of Kevin beneath the round plastic of his helmet. Risa tracked him as best she could through the players standing on her side of the field and the distance between them. The crowd noise swelled as the opposing halves of the team lined up for a play at midfield, without a kickoff. Risa felt Alan look at her, but she didn't want to take her eyes off Kevin, fearing she might lose him in the crowd of other players.

"It's a proud day, isn't it, hon?" Alan said. Risa was forced to turn to him. He was sincere and Risa thought she saw a tear forming. He was right, she thought. Think of all that was happening in front of her from Kevin and Alan's perspective. All those games of catch she had witnessed in the backyard, the ones that could choke her up when she thought about what a saint Alan had been with Kevin. Why had she been so reluctant to come to Alan's side today? Her son, she knew from the buzz at The Kitchen, was being cradled in the town's arms, and he, in return, was giving the town hope in these bleak days. Alan might have been exploiting that for his campaign, but he had earned it, hadn't he?

A cheer went up as the first play began. Risa whipped her head around to find Kevin. But all she saw was a blur of armored bodies receding, the play ending on the opposite sidelines.

"Yeah, Kev!" Alan shouted. Risa wanted to ask what had happened, but she didn't want to get that disappointed look from him again.

She kept her eyes on the blue jerseys, found 54, then lost him when players in front of her obscured the field.

"I can't see with these guys—"

Alan, hearing this, took a step forward and raised his voice to the players on the sidelines. "Hey, guys, down on one knee." The players obeyed without looking back. Risa's vision improved, but something about the lockstep way these kids blindly obeyed Alan was unsettling to her. And then the dread returned. She could see the field now, spot Kevin through the huddles and the pileups. But she couldn't shake the sense that something dark was about to happen.

"See that?" Alan said to her and those close by, but Risa didn't know what he was referring to. She had been staring for a couple of plays, trying to sideline the dread by losing focus, letting the blur of the action filter through her artist's eyes, changing the specifics of bodies and pads to line and form. The next play developed to her side of the field and she had to snap back to the reality in front of her.

A thin, quick blade of a ballplayer in white, cradling the ball, had outrun a couple of tacklers and looked like he'd make the corner, be able to turn his graceful body upfield along the sidelines. The players in front, on one knee, shuffled back some, cheering. And then Risa caught sight of 54. Miraculously he seemed to be moving as fast as if not faster than the player with the ball, and just as the ball carrier was ready to make his move, 54 plowed through him like he was a stick.

The play was so close to the sidelines that Risa could not avoid seeing Kevin's eyes through the bars of his helmet, steely and hungry, his balled fists pumping just before impact, the grunt of his voice as he sent the ball carrier's body backward, whiplashing his neck. The pop of the pads was a sickening thud followed quickly by the hollow sound of the ball carrier's body slamming on the turf. Kevin had so completely leveled the running back that he didn't even land on him, and when the football popped up and rolled on the turf, he was the first one to pounce on it.

Risa's vision froze. She couldn't take her eyes off the running back, now squirming on the ground as a pile of players scrambling for the loose ball threatened to trounce him again. Through his mask she could see he was Jimmy Robich, two years older than Kevin, a tough kid whose mother had complained to her just a week earlier that she didn't know how to control him. He didn't look like any uncontrollable kid now. He was in deep pain, his shoulder clearly not sending the proper signals down to his flopping arm.

Risa looked away from this to see Kevin rise from the pile with the ball and wave it triumphantly. It was then sound came back into Risa's world and that sound was deafening. Alan beside her was screaming Kevin's name over and over. Coach came jogging up to Kevin, put his hand on the upraised ball as if Kevin had just won in a KO, blew his whistle, and signaled that the scrimmage was over. In seconds the field was swamped. Jimmy Robich struggled to a sitting position, then succumbed to the pain and lay back down as trainers and coaches surrounded him.

Alan rushed the field with the others, but Risa was rooted, pinned by the image of her son, his eyes ablaze, ramming through another human being. "It's a game, Mom," Kevin had said once when she voiced reservations about the violence, about the possibility of permanent damage. But what she had just witnessed seemed far from a game. Her instant replays, run in slow motion, highlighted all the ferocity, the raw desire to . . . to what? Not just tackle. To . . .

"He killed him, man!" she heard from someone nearby, as if completing her thought. Killed him? She looked over at Kevin. He and Alan had their arms around each other's shoulders and were facing a cameraman from Channel 3. Other players were trying to get in the shot. The cheering around them made it seem as if they'd just won the state championship. Alan's eyes swept the crowd, found Risa, and motioned her to come to them. She moved slowly, and when other players crowded in front of her, she stopped and let them. Alan, being interviewed by Debbie Fins now, didn't realize she hadn't arrived.

She may have told herself before the play that she worried for Kevin's safety, but now she was fearful of the opposite, of his ability to wound, maybe maim. Where had that look in Kevin's eyes come from? Do they coach that? she wondered. She was no stranger to football. You couldn't have grown up in Braden and not known about the culture of pads and toughness, of broken bones and Super Bowl dreams. What did they say to a kid like Kevin, a soft kid, to make him bear down on a fellow player and stab him with his helmet, run over him, ignore him as he dove for the coughed-up ball? Or did the game just bring out something in Kevin she and probably he had not been aware of yet? Was he at heart a violent person?

This thought chilled her. Had something been unleashed in Kevin, something genetic, inherent, something they could do little about? And then Sean Collins rose before her. Kevin's father, gone eleven years, declared dead, half dead before he left, forgotten by Kevin. Not an overtly violent man but certainly violently self-destructive. Son of a suicide. Was he behind Kevin's murderous eyes on the field? He hadn't even played high school football. Had the gene skipped a generation?

She looked back at the field, the jubilant crowd having raised a scrim of dust, the late summer light giving the celebration a buttery glow. The scene that would have raised a lump in many a throat only served to deepen her sense of confusion and sadness. And her feeling of dread. The scrimmage hadn't put any questions to rest. The dark premonition that something lay in wait for her had only increased.

"Risa, got a minute?"

She turned to see Henry Saltz, the local reporter for *The Statesman*, the regional paper. He was in his early thirties, still fresh faced and smiling. He had been a staple in the community for more than a decade, and Alan saw him as vital to the election. Henry had been trying to do an "in-depth" interview with Risa for weeks now.

"Not really, Henry. I gotta get back."

"Great play, huh?"

"Yeah."

"I noticed you didn't go out on the field."

"Didn't want to get my new sneakers dusty."

Henry actually looked down at her old sneakers before looking back up, smiling, then turning serious.

"Could I talk to you, like, later, maybe at The Kitchen?"

"Come on. You know what it's going to be like over there tonight."

"Can I call you later?"

Risa stopped walking and looked at him. "Henry, what is it?"

Henry shook his head. "Not here. I'll catch up with you later." He gave her a look that puzzled her. He seemed to have left the scrimmage and the campaign behind and was looking out from some deeper pool, asking a question at the same time he was itching to tell her something. He turned and walked into the buzzing crowd leaving the stadium, and Risa had the sinking feeling that whatever Henry had on his mind wasn't going to be good news.

She took another look back at the field, but this time she saw a snowy night years ago, when she was in college, when she and Sean Collins had finally realized they were in love, and he stood in the knee-deep drifts and yelled to her, "This touchdown's for you, Risa Tuvic." Then he'd made her laugh as he zigzagged and leaped and rolled and ran toward her, an imaginary football under his arm. He dove into the snowbank end zone, jumped in triumph, arms raised, much as Alan and Kevin had just done. And then he came close, his cheeks rosy, his smile dazzling in the soft light, his happy, dancing blue eyes trumpeting his love for her, his warm kiss a promise of future beauty.

A lie. That promise had been drowned in sorrow and booze. She would have given anything to rewind to that night, to have it all play out differently. But the past, she knew, the could-have-been, was as dead as Sean Collins.

4

The woman had gotten on the bus in Stroudsburg when it was crowded and sat in the aisle seat next to Sean. She was in her fifties, never introduced herself but talked nonstop, her knitting needles keeping time. In her blunt confidence and imperious manner, she reminded Sean of his sixth-grade teacher, Mrs. Ostrowski, a woman who had scared the bejesus out of him. When the bus nearly emptied in the Poconos, she stayed where she was, pinning Sean to his seat. He didn't move.

He had only half listened to her patter, his thoughts on his destination, Braden, and what he was going to do there. When the bus left Route 80 and paralleled the Susquehanna, when he began to recognize points in the landscape, his stomach knotted and the woman's voice faded. Until she addressed him directly.

"You're married, aren't you?" Sean thought about this long enough that the woman took his silence for an answer. "Course you are. Handsome, pleasant guy like you. Easy to tell you're married. My son-in-law, one I told you about, one I'm going to see, him, you couldn't tell. He doesn't have that pleasant face like yours. My daughter thinks he does, but she's in love. I've got the gift, though. I can tell things about people."

Sean wondered if her gift had an expiration date. He had been married. He wished in the deepest part of him that he was still married. But he knew that his legal marriage had ended seven years earlier, when he had been declared dead.

"Sorry. I'm not married."

The woman stopped her knitting and gave him a withering Mrs. Ostrowski look over her reading glasses. "I don't believe that. I told you, some things I know."

"Maybe you're right."

The woman watched him for another few seconds, to be sure he wasn't taking her lightly, then went back to her knitting. "What I see is the inner stuff. Maybe you were married and that got called off somehow, but you're still married. It's all there to see. Now don't bother me here. This is tricky. I gotta count these stitches."

Sean turned to look out the window. As he did, the road curved north and the sun shone full on him, his reflected image on the window glass superimposed over the flat hills to the south. He stared at his own face and tried to calm himself. The image was that of a man in his late thirties with a full head of hair, a lined, street-hardened face that had soft touches around the eyes, and an almost invisible scar on his right temple.

Maybe she was right. Maybe he hadn't let the marriage go. He knew Risa and Alan were married now, that Alan had adopted Kevin, and while that all made perfect sense on paper, he couldn't quite understand it deep down, maybe down where this woman and her gift hung out.

"You get married right, you stay married," she said. Her ball of yarn rolled onto the floor and Sean retrieved it for her. "Thank you. Right, and you stay married through that kid too."

He hadn't said anything about Kevin, had he? He'd been thinking about him the whole trip, off and on, about the Facebook picture he'd seen that had surprised him, but had he said anything? No. He hadn't.

"You're a good man. I can tell that. And don't think I'm buttering you up or nothing cause I've had others right there, in a seat like you, right there and I could see they were no good and I said so. Told them to shape up."

Sean wished he could change the channel. Though he prayed

that she was right, wished in his deepest being that what he was about to do in Braden might prove her right, he knew in his horrified and guilty soul that she was wide of the mark. A good man doesn't leave his wife and kid. A good man doesn't . . .

"You have seizures, don't you?"

Sean turned from the window and looked at her. She kept her head down as if maybe she hadn't even asked the question. One of the doctors had called what Sean was going through "like seizures."

"Seizures?" he asked, but she didn't say anything. "Yes, something like that."

"I knew it."

He looked back at his image and wondered if it was the scar at his temple that allowed her to guess right. Or was she some sort of oracle?

He had been, as one doctor said, kicked in the head by a train, and for months after he had survived that kick, his amnesia had been almost complete. He had gone from a coma to awareness, to fully returned speech and motor functions, and to a semblance of peace that came with drying out completely and knowing who he was, where he had lived, whom he had married, who his son was. It was for a while a blissful reawakening. But that peace was shattered one bright spring morning, after he had left the hospital, when he was cleaning up an apartment he had been given for his transition to independent living.

It wasn't a dream or a nightmare or a vision. It was a memory, but much, much more than a simple recollection. It flew at him unbidden. It made him sit down and pinned him to the chair. For over an hour it came in bits and pieces, disparate images that begged to be put together like a simple child's jigsaw. There was a face at first, at least the semblance of one, seen from a very close distance in dim light, hacked by some knife. Then a limp hand, also slashed. Then the blade of a machete so close to his face he could almost feel the glistening blood on it, almost stick out his tongue and lick it. And then he saw his own hand holding that machete, making it clear who had done the damage to the body.

The doctor he first told about this a day later thought for sure Sean had replayed some horror film he'd seen years ago. But that didn't wash with Sean. He was no horror film fan and the memory was too real. When, two weeks later, on a bus going down Lexington Avenue, the same horrible scene hit him so hard he had to get off the bus to breathe, he knew what he was seeing was something from his life. Far from fading, the second appearance of the memory was even sharper than the first, high-def, a heightened vision that clung like napalm for long, searing minutes.

Another doctor took a sanguine approach to these horrific "reminiscences," as he called them. They were evidence the brain was healing, that it was finding ways to bring back memories, slowly finding ways to compensate for memory pathways that had been destroyed in his injury. But Sean lived in terror of their return. And he was nearly paralyzed by the unavoidable conclusion that this scene, in which he was clearly a participant, not an observer, was one of murder.

The fourth time the memory struck, he realized that he knew the woman whose mangled features were the centerpiece of the horror. She was a close high school friend named Carol Slezak. For days he tried to deny this, telling himself he was mixing up old friends with this daytime nightmare. Finally, after nights of little sleep, he approached Sandy Perez, his caseworker, and asked her to help him do computer research. It didn't take them long to find out that Carol Slezak had been killed eleven years earlier, the murder weapon a machete.

Because Sean had no memory of leaving Braden, Sandy urged him not to jump to conclusions. He might have heard about the murder and incorporated it in his memory as if he had been there. He read what he could about the killing, and for a day or so found some relief in the fact that G. G. Trask, a dishwasher at a bar-restaurant on the outskirts of town, The Ding Dong, had confessed to the crime. But once Sean went deeper, remembered G.G.'s simple, gentle mind, read his so-called confession, and read too that a lawyer was convinced the confession was false, Sean was back to square one.

On a late spring Saturday, with rain keeping him indoors, the horror came and wouldn't leave. Though the light in the memory was low, almost dark, Carol's face was clear and the machete that he held had clearly done the horrible damage, the image of which roared up at him with a fury he couldn't blunt.

And with it came a deep, tormenting guilt. He had obviously killed in the middle of an alcoholic blackout, but that excuse, if you could call it that, the reason he had taken a lethal blade to Carol, made no dent in his self-incrimination. The casual drinker goes too far and wakes up the next morning being told he did something silly or embarrassing and he may not remember it, but he gets over it. But to realize that you have committed the ultimate sin while blacked out, that you ended the life of a woman you liked very much, that there is no way to undo what you have done, is a devastating hell.

Sean made it through the weekend, but he couldn't get out of bed for work Monday morning. He had come to the realization that only killing himself would put an end to the horrible guilt he was living through. He climbed the stairs to the roof of his eight-story building and went to the low-lying wall overlooking an empty lot. He was standing in puddles left by the weekend rain. The street in front of his building was bustling as always. He knew asking for forgiveness was useless, that his sin was too deep. He was drawing shallow breaths as he imagined his plunge, the brief terror of it, then the welcoming darkness. He put one foot on the wall and waited for courage to well up and send him flying out.

Had the horror returned then, he would surely have jumped

to flee it. But another horror filled his vision instead. A man, his father, hanging lifeless from a joist in a darkened garage. He stepped back from the wall as if that body had been right in front of him. He was about to follow in his father's footsteps, he realized. And really, hadn't he been told this would happen? Didn't he know suicides run in families? Hadn't everybody told him when he started his heavy drinking that he was killing himself? His father's suicide wasn't going to stop him. It was his destiny.

This warped logic took him back to the wall. He would dive headfirst and make certain there was no chance he could survive. Survival in, say, a mangled shell of a body, with mind and memory intact, would be even worse than the vise-grip vision and guilt that now plagued him. He leaned forward and heard a baby somewhere crying. Tears came as he thought the last sounds he would hear would be those of a baby crying. A baby like his sweet, beautiful son. He put enough weight on his forward foot to stand on the wall, but the baby's crying became physical to him, a hand pushing on his chest. He couldn't move forward, couldn't make the leap.

One word, Kevin, was all that came to him. At first he thought it was only knowing that he was never going to see his son again that was stopping him. He wiped the tears that were blurring his vision and moved forward. But then he knew it was something deeper that held him. Kevin would be the son of a suicide, grandson of a suicide, a link in a chain of self-destructive men and a very likely candidate for bridge jumping or wrist slashing himself. Sean saw that he could jump to his own sweet oblivion, but by doing so he would be holding a loaded gun to his son's head.

He stepped back and sat heavily on the wet roof. His tears became sobs. His stomach began to ache with the crying. He felt himself to be a shell of a man and that his future was going to be one long black night of unremitting guilt and recrimination for the death he had caused, darkness all around, and one titanic struggle to save his son from an almost certain fate.

Once she saw and heard what was happening to him, Sandy, a fiery chica who had a soft spot for Sean, let him have it.

"You're gonna take your own life because you think what you see is something real? And all this time I been telling you how your brain is this crazy fucking video game after it got knocked silly by that train. Sean, don't make me go ape on your ass. You're the sanest, nicest, cutest client I got. Don't weird out, huh?"

Unusual therapeutic language, but it did make some rough sense to Sean. When he was in the grip of the memory he knew, without a doubt, that he had committed murder. But that belief didn't completely carry over to other times. He prayed for the relief one feels waking from a nightmare in which you've committed a horrible, irrevocable crime and realize it was all in your head. He had to test his hypothesis.

He got in touch with a reporter in Braden who had covered the murder and had seen Carol's body. He could verify the details of Sean's memory. He made an appointment to see him. Sandy covered for him, not letting the staff and doctors know the real reason he was going back home.

The bus took the ramp onto the bridge into Braden. Sean shaded his eyes against the sun, which was now pouring in his window. The Susquehanna, wide as a football field and running slow in the August heat, flowed under the bridge and the bus. The flat roofs of downtown Braden were hazy and ill defined on the bluff above the water. He clutched his backpack and thought that he was going to be sick. He told himself that he didn't have to get off the bus. He had his return ticket. He could just stay on the bus and go back to the city.

He panicked briefly when he thought he might not have his pills. He had been, since his hospital stay, enrolled in a clinical trial of a new sobriety drug. He took his one pill a day faithfully though he thought it was pie in the sky to think some drug could keep you from drinking. Yet it had been over six months, he had had no desire for even a beer in all that time, and he was now dependent on the pill.

His anxiety deepened as the bus huffed up Market Street. The buildings were a blur. The bus driver blew his air horn and tapped his brakes. The bus jounced and Sean tensed. He looked to the right side of the bus and saw the top of a blond woman's head as she stepped back to the curb, as the bus flew past her. She looked like she could be Risa. It probably wasn't her but it reminded him he didn't want to see her now. Nor Kevin. Maybe, please, please, if this reporter told him he'd gotten the details all wrong, if he acquitted himself of the crime, he could face them. He'd still have the humbling embarrassment of his absence to deal with, but that would be almost a joy compared to the searing guilt he felt now.

A block later the bus turned right and after half a block stopped in front of a small candy store. The woman picked up her ball of yarn and fixed him with her over-the-glasses look.

"You're going to do what's right, aren't you?" It wasn't really a question.

Sean hadn't quite thought of it that way. He didn't know what he was going to do. He was going to listen to the reporter and then . . .

"I know you are 'cause you've got something tells me you're going to."

She was really scaring him now, the way Mrs. Ostrowski had years ago. Sean looked left, to a five-story pile built early in the last century, its vertical HOTEL sign rusted and hanging like a tooth ready to be pulled. The building was boarded up, the plywood still fresh, as if someone had slapped it on that morning.

Sean looked back, ready to ask the woman to let him out, but she was gone. He looked to the front of the bus, but she wasn't there, nor in the back of the bus either. He was certain she had been real. Where did she go?

Sean got his backpack and went down the aisle, the only passenger getting out in Braden. The driver was standing on the sidewalk, looking at a ticket a fifty-something woman had given him. Sean didn't recognize the woman and she gave him only a cursory glance. Sean spoke to the driver.

"Did a woman just get off the bus?"

The driver shook his head no. Sean looked back into the bus. Had he manufactured that whole conversation? He didn't know, didn't think it could be, but he realized he'd have to be careful. His brain was still recovering. He was on the ground now, his feet once again on Braden pavement. He had to be able to trust himself in what he was about to go through.

"How long has the hotel been closed?" he asked the driver.

The driver looked up, as if this was news to him.

The woman getting on gave the question some thought. "Month. Month and a half."

The hotel had still been listed online, but he hadn't made a reservation. As the bus left he went into the candy store. The place looked as if it were going out of business. Shelves were half empty. A soda cooler didn't appear to be cold. The older woman behind the counter, with thick glasses, her hair done in tight curls, looked as if she were going to sell off what she had left and abandon the eyesore. He couldn't remember even being in the store.

"Hotel's closed, huh?"

The woman stood up from the stool she was sitting on and gave him a long look. He didn't recognize her.

"Yeah. I guess so. Put them boards on it."

"Where do people stay, then?"

"Stay?"

"Get a room."

"Hazelton. They got motels over there."

He was about to ask how far it was to Hazelton when he remembered that Hazelton was a good thirty miles away.

"Nothing closer? I just got off the bus. I don't have a car."

"That's usually the way it works, isn't it?"

"The way what works?"

"You're takin' the bus, you usually don't have a car. Or you don't have a car so you take the bus."

Sean ignored this, wondered if he was making this women up as well, and went back outside. His knotted stomach was still with him, but being on the ground, talking to people, had calmed him some. The street was empty and the traffic practically nil. He thought he heard a marching band far in the distance, but it could have been a radio playing out a window. He looked at the street, at the defunct hotel, and then realized that the landscape was festooned with campaign posters. The name Benson was everywhere, and when he turned to look at the curio shop next to the candy store, he was confronted with the smiling face of Alan Benson himself. Unlike his own reflected portrait in the bus window, this face was familiar, this face hadn't changed much over the years. He had known Alan since the sixth grade, had been close friends with him until they both left for college. Moving now to get a better look at the poster, he could see the sixth-grade Alan, beefed up a little, his hair tamed, but with the same thin-lipped smile that had confidently invited him to a Pac-Man duel.

This smiling politician was Risa's husband and father now to his son. Sean wanted to feel something about those facts, anger for having been replaced as a husband, gratitude for being replaced as a father, but Alan's eyes kept warning against any sort of feeling. His vote-for-me gaze did its work well, holding you without letting you in, staying on the surface, almost telling you to keep any thoughts of anger or even gratitude to yourself, to unload the negative ones on his opponent.

The marching band noise in the distance came to him

again. It was clearly not a radio. He remembered a sign he had glimpsed without recognition from the bus, SCRIMMAGE DAY SALE, and put two and two together. He started toward the sound, certain now it was coming from the stadium. He didn't think he'd get close, just stand across the street. He didn't want to plow into a situation in which many might know him. He didn't want any *Night of the Living Dead* moments.

At the corner of Market, the scene morphed for him. It was no longer summer. The sidewalk was shoveled and small patches of hard-packed, dirty snow lined his way. He was pushing a stroller and he could see the stroller weave one way, then the other, but every time he tried to correct the drift, the wobbling worsened. He stopped and looked over the top of the stroller. His son, bundled but without mittens, two years old, waited for the stroller to move, then looked back.

"Go!"

The stroller began to move again, and Sean could see he still didn't have much control. A woman passing the other way on the sidewalk gave him wide berth and a withering look.

And then he was back on the summer street, stopped, gathering the threads of this memory piece as he'd learned to do, looking it over, seeing if he could put names to faces, seeing if he could possibly date the occurrence. Nothing much more came, but when he replayed the boy's turning face, full of question and trust, he was certain of what he was seeing.

"Kevin."

The blocks he walked after that were a struggle against self-recrimination. The visceral weaving of the stroller, the look on his son's face trumped rehabthink. Yes, he had been in the grip of a disease then. Yes, he had been buffeted by forces he had no control over. But in daylight, with the supreme responsibility riding in a stroller at the end of his arms, he had been derelict, drunk, weaving, drawing the irate glare of townspeople. He knew all this was mild compared to the horror he had come back to deal with, but this taste of the past made him realize things would be different in Braden. Back in New York he viewed the returning memories as if he were outside a movie theater, watching them through the door. Now he was inside, in a front row seat, unable to escape what was on the screen.

Sean reached the stadium gates. The music had stopped and words were echoing out of the loudspeakers. He stood there, heart pounding, head swiveling like a wary point man, everyone in the crowd a potential danger.

The next half hour was a blur more than a catalyst for memory. He had thumbed his nose at the norms in high school, not played football, not attended more than one or two Scrimmage Days, so there was no nostalgia and few moments of deep remembrance. He did recall one gorgeous snowy night with Risa in the days after they realized they were in love. But that was a far cry from Scrimmage Day.

Then a whistle blew, the scrimmage was over, and people turned and headed for the gate. He knew he should turn himself, get ahead of them, file out and try to find a place to stay for the night. But he was rooted to the spot, irrationally certain he was invisible. As the crowd shuffled by, he felt his memory flex. He began to recognize some faces clearly: Mrs. Worth, the Spanish teacher he had hated when he was a student, liked when he had taught with her; David Ball, a kid who had forged his working papers and started at McDonald's when he was thirteen. Glen Dolski, a handyman who had painted his father's house once, looked right at him, smiled affably, but smiled as you would to a stranger asking directions.

And then, to his right, moving with the crowd, he saw Risa. She wasn't coming toward him, so he could move to the side and watch her as she talked with people leaving the stadium. Sean had secretly hoped for something like this, an opportunity to see and not be seen. He had imagined peeking in a window, watching the family eat dinner. But this was much better.

He walked parallel to her, watching the low light cast a gold rim around her hair. She was listening to someone Sean didn't recognize, her head down, not responding. Then a smile, a forced one, it seemed to Sean, and then a man came and threw his arm around her. It took Sean a second to realize this was Alan. He was as ebullient as Risa was subdued. Sean was amazed at the way time collapsed, and he thought he was seeing a scene from high school, the proprietary way Alan hugged Risa, the seeming clash of their moods, Alan's rah-rah obtuseness, Risa's wide-eyed thoughtfulness.

Alan's gaze swept the crowd, and Sean thought at first he'd been spotted. He turned away and tried to meld into the crowd. He didn't look back. He didn't have to. His brief glimpse of Risa could be replayed over and over. She looked much as he had remembered her, and the moment with Alan fit his imagination of their marriage.

And then a hollowing feeling. He had been seen but not recognized, he had watched Risa and Alan as if he were behind one-way glass. He was viewing the world as he had always imagined the dead do. The dead. Was he really in Braden, home, returned? Or had that subway train put him away forever and all he was seeing now was the brain's afterburn, a final lap through his life before the void?

He felt a sting and touched his cheek. What he was seeing might be a dream, but his tears were real.

5

Alan Benson didn't want the moment to end, but when he saw he was losing his crowd, when the team had run back to the locker room and a lot of the people on the field were filing out of the stadium, he knew it was time for him to go as well, to walk with the others, to lead them, even. He had, for weeks now, been practicing what his father had preached to him—use every event as an opportunity to show your strength, your leadership abilities, your forward thinking.

He fell in step with Father Vubich, the young pastor of St. Cyrillic's, the dwindling Ukrainian Catholic Church.

"Your boy made a great hit there, Alan."

"He's coming along."

"Good to see the team starting to get back on its feet."

"Say that again. I haven't seen this kind of optimism in years. Reminds me of the golden days back in the nineties."

"I wish I'd been here."

"It was truly something." Alan paused as they shuffled behind the bottlenecked crowd leaving the stadium. "Did you get your tax situation taken care of?"

"Not yet. We've got a couple more hurdles. It all takes so much time."

"Who's representing you?"

"Nick Colsus."

"Isn't he retired?"

"Yes, but he's working for us for free, so . . ."

Alan took out his BlackBerry and made a note. “I’ve got a guy up in Scranton who might be able to move things along for you. What’s your number, Father? I’ll give him a call, then let you know.”

“Thanks, Alan, but you don’t have time for that sort of stuff now, do you?”

“That sort of stuff, Father, is what any good community servant is supposed to do. Right?”

He gave Alan his number.

“Great. You people got enough to think about. You don’t need these worries.”

Alan saw Risa ahead of him, excused himself from Father Vubich, and started toward her. Suddenly he was in high school again, on the team but not playing, and Risa, lovely Risa, was a cheerleader. He remembered how just being with her made everything right with the world. His mother had told him time and time again not to “let that one get away,” and he had obeyed. Alan wasn’t lacking in self-confidence, but with Risa, in the orbit of her gorgeous green eyes, he was king. He caught up with her, putting his arm around her lovingly, in part for all those around to see but really in celebration of all she meant to him.

“Is Kevin okay?” Risa asked.

Alan looked to see if she was joking. She wasn’t.

“He’s fine. But I don’t think that Robich kid’s going to have a great night.” Alan turned and nodded to an acquaintance. He was about to turn back to Risa, to question why she didn’t come on the field, when a face caught his eye. About ten yards ahead of him he saw a man turn, scan the crowd, then turn back. Alan wanted to move faster, to get an angle on whoever it was, but a voice turned his head.

“We’re going to need to make some tracks. I’ve got my car out here. We can do a swing by at The Kitchen and then head out.” It was Lilly Barkin at his side. Alan turned back but the man was gone. Sean. The man had looked a lot like Sean Collins. Couldn't be. Just a coincidence, a thought following his thoughts of the young Risa. He kept walking, replaying the image.

It couldn't have been Sean himself. You don't disappear like that and just waltz back into town. If Sean had somehow returned, he would have gotten in touch with Risa and Risa would have told him. And if there were someone in town, someone new perhaps, who looked a little bit like Sean, he might not have seen him before this. He'd been away from Braden a lot lately. He dismissed the whole episode as a nostalgia-induced mirage and turned his attention to what Lilly was saying.

Risa didn't know how she was going to get through the Scrimmage Day dinner at The Kitchen. She thought about burying herself in cooking, but she knew Teddy Noyce, the longtime near-deaf cook who always spoke loud enough to be heard in the dining room, would inadvertently out her scheme by yelling about how he could take care of the orders.

So she braced herself as she approached the restaurant. Bell Richards, Risa's cousin on her mother's side, had come back from the stadium early and opened. The place would be humming by the time Risa entered and she would have to be on, ready for the team's triumphant entry. She would have to make a public show of hugging Kevin. Alan, she imagined, would want a picture of that. But she kept seeing the look in Kevin's eyes through his face mask, Jimmy Robich's dangling arm as he was carried off the field.

She nodded to some people about to go into The Kitchen with her and then looked over at the bench where she had deposited Warren earlier. He was gone. The dish towel shackle was still there, still tied, as if Warren had slipped his bony arm through it and taken off. This looked promising. If Warren had in fact taken off, she would have to go looking for him.

Bell, the IndispensaBell, as Risa once called her, had the ritual dinner in full swing. The tables were full already, with one long one near the window empty, waiting for team members to arrive. Bell's arthritis had her gimping around, but she managed to put on her usual show of good cheer, all-too-truthful recommendations ("Stay away from the roast beast tonight, something off with the seasoning"), and, of course, this being Scrimmage Day, her usual prediction that this was the year the Bulldogs were going all the way. She met Risa near the door.

"Hey, Mother of the Day. Aren't you proud?"

"Yeah."

"Boy, I kept thinking Uncle Sim's up there in heaven smilin' his ass off."

"I bet. Did somebody come and pick up Warren?"

"Not that I seen. I got here about twenty minutes ago, had to kick Teddy in the butt about the oil, but I didn't see him leave. Why? He wanderin' again?"

Risa took out her cell, dialed Warren's daughter, got voice mail, and left a message saying she was going to look for Warren. It was a flimsy excuse to get out of the celebration, but it had plausibility. She went back out through a thickening crowd at the door, putting on the Wife's Face, telling everyone she'd be right back.

When she got outside and was just about to turn toward Market, Alan and Lilly got out of Lilly's Lexus and came toward her. Alan, knowing they were onstage in front of those people going into the restaurant, gave Risa a big hug and spoke loudly.

"Wasn't that something, hon?" Risa nodded as she left the hug. "What have you got planned for the team?"

Risa couldn't remember for a second. "Pierogis."

"Hmm. Great. Look, is there anything we can do to make Kevin's special?"

"Like what?"

"I don't know. Put a little flag on it, something like that?"

Risa could feel Lilly watching the two of them, judging probably, and she pulled Alan away from her a few yards down the block.

"Alan. I don't want to single him out. I don't want to celebrate that."

"That?"

"That tackle. That's what you're talking about, isn't it?"

"Well, that, and, I mean, this was his debut."

"Wasn't it other kids' too? Rick and Larsen and—"

"What's the matter with you? I saw it at the stadium. What's going on? You were late, you didn't seem like you were into the scrimmage, didn't come out on the field."

"It wasn't like it was some official campaign stop." Risa knew this was not what she was supposed to say.

"What? What difference does that make. It was your son. It was his moment, and you were just this sour face over in the corner."

"I'm sorry, but it bothered me."

"You know what things like this mean, Risa? Buzz. I bet you dollars to doughnuts I'm over in Scranton tonight and somebody's going to come up to me and say, 'Heard about your kid. Hope he makes it up to State before Paterno retires.' That's how it happens. Buzz. Kevin knows it. Kevin wants it. Are you going to try to trip him up because you're worried about some second-string scrub getting his shoulder dislocated?"

"No." She didn't have the energy for the fight. Alan's prediction of buzz and a bright future had made what she had seen even more ominous. She gave him a long look. He was a good man and had been all the years she'd known him. She knew his ambitions often clouded his thinking, but she could forgive him that, knowing she herself had nowhere near the drive he had. He wanted Washington and more. She wanted to paint. The campaign had put his ambitions in overdrive, but she still knew he meant well. And she knew his pride in Kevin was the sort any male growing up in Braden would have. But the image of the hit and the dark foreboding she had carried around all day made her wish things were different, that Kevin was small and frail, that Alan was content with his law practice. "I'll be back," she said, turning.

"Where are you going?"

"Warren's missing."

"He's always missing. Somebody will get him home."

"I'm responsible," she said, moving away. She heard Alan huff and Lilly say something to her, but she had escaped and she kept walking. She got to Market and stopped, remembering the bus that had ripped by her earlier. She looked both ways before she crossed. She wasn't really thinking about Warren or even looking for him. She was thinking about what Alan had said, about Kevin going to Penn State. Even in its bad years Braden always sent a couple of players to State College. They left spindly, graceful athletes and returned seventy pounds heavier, with no necks and all the grace of a Hummer.

She heard footsteps behind her, someone calling her name. Alan? She turned to see a red-faced Henry Saltz catching up.

"Whew. You walk fast."

"Where's your bike?" Henry was known around town for biking everywhere, even though he owned a car. The regulars at the restaurant bar had started calling him Wheeler when he first came to Braden. He didn't mind.

"I saw you walking away from the restaurant. I didn't think I'd need a bike to catch up."

"You want to do an interview right here?"

"No. Not now. I mean I want to do an interview sometime soon, but I just wanted to tell you something else."

"What?"

Henry looked around as if someone on the street might be overhearing them. There was nobody on the street and only a few cars. When he turned back, his face had gone slack with a gravity Risa had rarely seen in him.

"I had a call a couple of days ago and I want to tell you about it."

"A call?"

"A phone call. It wasn't an e-mail. It was a phone call."

"Okay, Henry, you're stretching this out. Who called? What's up?"

"It was your former husband, Sean."

"Collins?"

"Yes."

"He's dead, Henry."

"Legally."

"No, Henry, we tried everything. He must be . . . How do you know it was him?"

"Well, he said he was and—"

"And you checked?"

"What was I going to check, Risa?"

"I don't know. A telephone number, something like that?"

"Maybe, if there was a reason. But why would anyone call me and say he was Sean Collins when he wasn't?"

Risa could feel a sheen of sweat on her forehead, the night suddenly muggy. She couldn't imagine why Henry or someone else would play this kind of trick on her. It had been six or seven years now since she had made peace with Sean's disappearance, truly treated it like a death, had come to believe in fact that it must have been a death.

"What did he want?"

"To talk to me."

"About what?"

"I don't know. We're supposed to meet tomorrow."

"Tomorrow?"

"At my office."

"He's going to be in town?"

"I think he already is."

Risa couldn't help herself. She looked quickly up and down the street as if Sean might be trailing right behind Henry.

"Why do you think that?"

"I saw him a couple of times before he left, when I was first here, at The Ding Dong. I think I saw him today. I think he might have been at the stadium."

"Just now?"

"Yes."

Risa was struggling to stay vertical. "What else did he say?"

"Nothing much."

"He just called to say he wanted to see you? Did you know who he was, how long he'd been missing?"

"Not at first. I mean the name didn't really click in. He told me."

"What did he say?"

"He said he'd been in New York, that he had been sick, that he was in treatment, and that he had some questions for me."

"Questions for you? He doesn't know you."

"He said he had read some of my reporting."

"About what?"

Henry balked. "About Carol Slezak's murder."

"Carol's . . ." A thought hit Risa. "Was he drunk?"

"He didn't sound it."

"Are you sure?"

"He said he was in rehab. The caller ID was some clinic. It was the first time I'd ever heard his voice, but he sounded sober to me."

"Carol's murder. What about Carol's murder?"

"I don't know. That's what we're supposed to talk about tomorrow."

"Why couldn't he talk to you over the phone?"

"I don't know. It was a very short call."

"When?"

"I think it was Monday."

"No, when are you meeting him tomorrow?"

"At ten. Do you want to—?"

Risa shook her head slowly. She didn't know what she wanted except for Henry to vanish, for his assault to be a figment of her imagination, for Sean to be where he had been for years, silent, gone, lost.

"Why did you tell me this?" she asked finally.

"I thought you should know."

"Why? You can't be sure it's him. You don't know what he wants. Maybe this is a hoax. Alan. Maybe somebody's trying to get at Alan. A campaign trick or something."

"I'm sorry."

"Did you tell Alan?"

"No. I thought you'd want to know."

"He's dead, Henry. Somebody's fooling you and now . . . You should have checked things out. You haven't told anybody else, have you?"

"No."

"Good. Don't. If this guy shows up tomorrow, you get to the bottom of this. Does he want you to write something about him?"

"He didn't say that."

"Maybe he will. Maybe that's his goal. Alan helped get Sean declared dead. Maybe this guy's pulling a hoax to disrupt the campaign."

"Maybe. I'll be careful. But what if he's for real?"

"He can't be. Can't be."

Risa turned and continued walking down the street. She didn't want to look back to see if Henry was watching her. She wanted him and his information to disappear. She came to the corner of Market and Third and hesitated before rounding the bank building. What if Sean were around the corner? In the beginning, when he was simply gone for longer than usual, she had feared every such corner, the clutch of anxiety overshadowing her desire to have her husband back. Now she felt the grip of that anxiety again, even as she worked feverishly to dismiss Henry's news.

There was no Sean around the corner. She plowed ahead, oblivious to the street, Carol's name battering her thinking. Why would someone go that far with a hoax? Sean didn't have anything to do with Carol's murder. Was this hoaxster trying to hurt Alan or her? Carol was with her again, laughing in the cafeteria, behind the wheel of her mother's pickup. Risa didn't want to think of her as the victim she ultimately became. But somebody was forcing her, pushing her nose back in it. After half a block she looked up and realized she was only feet away from a man staring into the window of Monty's Bait and Tackle. In her frenzied thinking she stopped, fearing it was Sean. A second later she realized it was the wandering Warren.

6

Kevin and many of his teammates were already at their table when Risa led Warren through the front door. Kevin got up and came to her, beaming his blue-eyed smile under his shock of thick dark hair. Risa had always loved her son's face. Even in the darkest of times, when that face and his gestures so often reminded her of Sean, she would get lost in its welcome. For a brief moment he won her over again, coming to her with his arms wide. They hugged to the aahs around them.

"You see it, Mom?"

"I did, Kev. I'm real proud of you." This was for the benefit of those nearby who had turned to watch the moment.

Flashes popped all over the room as parents snapped their kids. Alan made a big show of having Kevin and Risa stand with him under Sim Tuvic's smiling portrait. Risa endured this, even managed to put on the Wife's Face, but she was sure she hadn't covered up all the turmoil behind the mask. When the picture taking was over and she felt the eyes in the room leave them, she lowered her voice and spoke to Kevin.

"How's Jimmy?"

"Jimmy? Oh, Jimmy. Yeah. He's okay."

"He looked hurt."

"Dislocated. He's out for the season." Kevin wasn't insensitive to his mother's concern. He paused a second, then rushed ahead. "What about the defense, huh? We were awesome, weren't we?"

"You were. Uh, how many guys have you got with you?"

Kevin clearly wanted more adulation, but he turned and counted. "Twelve and I think there are maybe three more on the way. What have you got?"

"What do you think?"

"Broccoli?"

"With brown rice."

"Yummy. Serious, what kind of pierogis?"

"Surprise."

Risa caught a glimpse of Alan leaving the restaurant, shaking hands with everyone in line waiting to get in. She stopped Kevin as she was going back to the table.

"Do you know where Dad's going?"

"No. Great for his campaign, right?"

"What, tonight?"

"No, Scrimmage Day. Jeez, Mom. They said it's going to be on Channel Three at eleven. I don't know what they got. Derek got a cool vid of my hit. We're going to put it on YouTube tonight."

"Really, you want that?"

"Mom."

He gave her a look that questioned her sanity and then went back to the table of teammates. Risa stared for a while as they bellowed, slapped one another fives, and generally put on the show the townspeople hoped for, boys becoming men, celebrating their warrior status for the elders. Kevin, it seemed, was at the center of it all, but as Risa watched his beaming face, heard his put-down that sent the table into gales of laughter, she found it impossible to erase the image of him about to run through Jimmy Robich, the hot fury in the slice of eyes and teeth she could see through his face mask. She turned away. She didn't want to think of Kevin like that, didn't want to see him slapped on the back for that violence. Was it just a game? Or was it something else?

The next few hours didn't give her much time to think about

any of this. Bell was crippled by a flare-up in her hip and called her son to come pick her up.

"Risa, I'm sorry as sorry can be. I love this day and I'm so happy for you. Maybe that's it. Maybe I get too happy and my body says, 'Slow down there, Missy.' You sure you're going to be able to handle this? I hear there's gonna be another rush in an hour or so, when the overtime boys show up."

"I can handle it. Take care of yourself. I'm guessing you never called that guy in Scranton, right?"

"No. They can't do nothin' for what I got."

"Alan told the guy exactly what you've got, and he said, 'Send her over. We can help.'"

"God bless that husband of yours. He's always lookin' out for everybody."

"It's his job."

"Bull. He don't have to do all the stuff he does."

Risa let this be the last word as she directed traffic, pulled beers, cleared plates, filled glasses, joked with customers, gave the team members the ritual fake bill for a thousand dollars, which they ceremoniously tore up in front of her to the applause of the other diners.

But all the activity was a dodge, a feint, an attempted end run around Henry's news. She hadn't fooled herself with talk of some hoax, somebody trying to foul up Alan's campaign. Sean was alive and either on his way to Braden or already here. As she walked home up Heights Road the all too familiar houses seemed inky black and shuttered to the announcement of Sean's return. Patchy clouds muted the moonlight. The gnawing dread of the day, Risa knew now, hadn't been due to football or campaigns or violence, but rather some preternatural connection she had with her lost husband. She had, over the years of his disappearance, felt him from time to time as a phantom limb in her life, one she could rationalize and ignore. But this was different. Henry had just made clear what her whole being had been trying to tell her all day. Sean was near. Had there been any clues? She couldn't remember any. Maybe it all was deeper than clues, something she simply would not be able to understand.

The part about Carol and her murder somehow seemed tacked on to the news, a fillip to the true shocker. But that dimension of the story was real as well. And it was, finally, all too much to absorb. She decided to keep it to herself, at least until the morning, when the clouds and the moon were gone and the houses lit and the world became normal again.

At home, as she climbed the stairs to the second floor, she could hear the thump of bass from Kevin's room and then loud talking from more than one teenage boy. Kevin's room wasn't often the meeting place, but she guessed his celebrity made it so now. Instead of turning around, she stood on the stairs until she adjusted to the sounds coming through the bedroom door, until she could distinguish words. Derek Evans was there, she could tell that. And there were maybe two others. They seemed to be working on something together. The music stopped and started, rewound and started again.

"That's it. Right there. Now start the music when the ball's snapped."

A loud cheer made her jump and she heard hoots and high fives being slapped. She could imagine some video cruelty they were cooking up at Jimmy Robich's expense. She didn't want to use her parent capital to try to halt them. As she walked back downstairs, she had a thought she hadn't had in years. If Sean had still been here, would something like this gathering in Kevin's room be going on?

Even from across the street, Sean could tell that Risa no longer lived in their old house. Through the wide front window he could see a room of floral prints and knickknacks on shelves. Risa liked stark bold colors and artwork on the walls, hers half the time. Standing in the shadows as the streetlights came on, he could see that the shrubs and the trees in the front yard were the same ones he'd grown up with, but now, of course, they were almost unrecognizable in their height and fullness. A sugar maple near the corner of the lot, one he had nearly ruined trying to climb when it was not much more than a sapling, was now too big to get his arms around.

He saw a figure walking up Heights Road and decided he didn't want to be seen lurking on the sidewalk. He turned at the next corner and headed back toward the center of town, toward Saffron Park. Since leaving the stadium he had avoided talking to anyone but the girl at McDonald's. He had picked up an information brochure at a kiosk in front of the Chamber of Commerce building and found that indeed there was no motel or accommodation of any kind in Braden. He had decided he would spend the warm night in Saffron Park, on the benches back away from the streetlights, see the reporter in the morning, catch the two thirty bus back to New York.

As he walked toward Saffron Park, he remembered clearly nights when his drinking had been hard but not out of control, nights when he and Risa would be at each other and all he wanted to do was take a bottle and be alone. On those nights he would feign an errand or a task out of the house, pick up the Smirnoff hidden in an evergreen bush beside the garage, and take it to the park, returning later and later as the years went on, until nights when he never returned at all.

In group he had been challenged to say why it was he cradled that bottle instead of the baby back in the house. He found answers that satisfied the members of the group, the leader, but they all seemed watery to him. Yes, of course he'd had problems with his father's death, and, sure, he had thwarted ambitions, but, shit, who didn't? He drank because there was some worm inside him needing to be stilled. That was as close as he could come. Some worm.

There was a group of teenagers at the south end of the park

as Sean entered. Their rituals probably weren't all that different from the ones he and Risa and Alan and sometimes Carol had gone through. They'd snag a twelve-pack, maybe a joint, and meet after dark so their drinking wouldn't be completely obvious, hide their stash in the shrubs, sweet-talk the occasional cop who stopped his cruiser and swept his side light over them.

Sean went to a bench near a small Korean War veterans' monument and sat. He quickly felt the weight of the day. He had been up half the night before and now his bones felt like dumbbells and his back melded into the ancient slats of the bench.

He could remember very little of the decade he'd spent on the street, the blackout amplified by the brain injury at the end, but he knew from things he'd been told and the few things he could recall that he'd slept in every contortion the human body was capable of. Most of the things he could remember were moments of waking up, in some doorway, under some cardboard, sitting up on some hard surface, in a frozen hallway, in a rat-infested brick pile. Saffron Park was a paradise compared to those places, and a soft breeze lullabyed him to sleep.

He hadn't been asleep long when a dog's nose poked his leg, and he woke with a start.

"Can't sleep here," someone said, and Sean followed the leash to a man standing nearby, his features in shadow.

Sean stood quickly, grabbing his backpack, some vestige of his street existence telling him not to protest. Still half asleep, he walked aimlessly for fifteen minutes until he turned onto Market and was face-to-face with the boarded-up hotel. He had been in the place only a few times. He remembered it as small and musty-smelling, a faded elegance in the little sitting room off the lobby. He crossed the street and started to circle the hulking building, stopping to look at the way the plywood was nailed to the window frames.

Suddenly he felt as if he were watching himself probe the seams of the plywood, find a weak one, push and yank until the nails in the half-inch board squawked and a piece of wood ripped away from the sheet. Was this a memory? In the dark, in his near sleep, he didn't know. He put a foot on a stone outcropping and shimmied through the hole in the plywood.

There was no light in the room. He fell over a couch draped with sheets. He stood listening for sounds that would indicate someone else was there. He could feel having done that before, finding himself in an abandoned building, maybe, antennae out for danger. But there seemed to be no danger in this draped sitting room. He lay down on the couch. He heard a car go by. And as he had been doing for months now, when he could tell sleep was near, he steeled himself for an assault by the horror. But it didn't come this time. Instead there was the golden portrait of Risa, coming out of the stadium. In the moments before sleep, this image seemed something otherworldly, something he had imagined. Maybe that was true, he thought, maybe that was true.

Alan called at ten. Kevin and his friends had come out of Kevin's room earlier to get something to eat in the kitchen, but Risa had been in the den, staring at the TV, not even registering what she was watching, and didn't want to see them. She saw it was Alan on the caller ID and picked up quickly.

"Alan?"

"Hey. How's it going? I've only got a minute. We're having a meeting with the brain trust here. We've had some feelers from Joe Tomlin's people. There's a chance he might make a trip here. How does that sound?"

"Tomlin?"

"Senator from Virginia?"

"Oh, right. Good."

"Tape the eleven o'clock on Channel Three, will you? We're gonna watch it here but I want to look at it when I get home. Marty's got an idea for a spot and we might be able to cut in some of that footage."

Risa listened to this rush of words and decided she had to tell Alan about Sean's return. She didn't want him to hear it from somebody else.

"Okay. Alan. Give me a minute. This is important. I think somebody's playing games."

"Who?"

"I don't know."

"What games?"

"Henry Saltz says he got a call from someone who said he was Sean Collins."

"Sorry. There was something in the background here. What? Did you say something about Sean?"

"Henry Saltz got a call from a guy who said he was Sean."

There were a long few seconds of silence, and Risa couldn't tell if the call had been dropped or if Alan was just absorbing the news. "Couldn't be," Alan said finally.

"I know. That's what's disturbing."

"Why'd he call Henry?"

"I don't know. Maybe he's looking for publicity. He said he had read Henry's reporting and wanted to talk to him."

"Henry's reporting? On what, the campaign?"

"On Carol's murder."

"What?"

"On Carol's murder. Henry's reporting."

"What did Henry tell him?"

"They're going to meet tomorrow."

"Meet tomorrow? Where?"

"At Henry's office. At ten. Henry said he thought he saw him today at the stadium."

"That, uh. That couldn't be, right?"

"No. He's . . . gone."

"I'll call Henry, see what this bullshit's all about."

"I don't think he knows."

"Did you tell anyone else?"

"No."

"Kevin?"

"God, no."

"If this is some sort of campaign trick, it's a real fucking lousy one."

"I know. I don't get it."

"I'll call Henry. I gotta run. Tape the news, okay?"

"Alan?"

"What?"

"He might be alive."

"Bullshit, Risa. Bullshit. You don't disappear for what, now, eleven years, something like that, then show up out of the blue. Don't you think he would have called you first?"

"Maybe."

"I'll get to the bottom of this. Don't worry. Love you."

"Love you. Bye."

Risa hung up no better off than when she started the conversation. Alan would get to the bottom of things. He was very good at that. But it was the bottom of things that bothered her.

She heard Kevin's friends leave and waited a few minutes before going to Kevin's room. She decided to say as little as she could, a quick good night. His door was ajar. She knocked and poked her head in.

"Kev?"

He was at his computer and turned to her with a pleased, proud face.

"Look at this, Mom. Look."

Risa stood behind Kevin's chair as he clicked around YouTube and pulled up a video.

"We did slow-mo on Derek's shot."

The video took a couple of seconds to load and then rap music, the words of which Risa couldn't get, came up as a scene from Scrimmage Day faded in. The camera seemed to be close to where Risa had been standing. The last play of the day began in regular speed, but when Jimmy Robich took the pitchout and began to run with the ball, the video slowed to almost a standstill, as if he'd run into quicksand. Jimmy continued to be the only one in the frame for a few seconds until, like a predator in a nature video, Kevin's helmet and then Kevin appeared in the frame. Risa couldn't see Kevin's eyes, but she didn't have to. She knew what they had looked like.

When the hit came, when Kevin's helmet slammed into Jimmy's right shoulder, the music shifted from a thumping bass to something that sounded like a raucous laugh and made the contact seem like an explosion. Jimmy's head bobbed forward and, even in slow motion, quickly whipped back, the football popping up like some fountain of leather. Then the camera must have moved because the scene went blurry and faded out. A title came up, "The Hit," and then Derek's name followed. Kevin paused it.

"Cool, huh Mom?"

Risa had all she could do to keep from crying. She bent over Kevin's head and kissed the soft waves of his hair. From his days of infant baldness to his middle school years of gelled dos and on she had loved nothing better than kissing that head. Now she wanted the kiss to work a magic, to bring her sweet son back from this . . . this what? This violence. She wanted him to look at that explosion with different eyes, to see what he'd done to another kid. But she had no hope in such magic. He was floating away from her.

"Cool, Kev."

He let her kiss his head again and started to replay the video.

Alan told his advisers to start the meeting without him and called Henry Saltz. He decided he would challenge the notion that it was actually Sean who had called Henry, even though he knew now it must have been Sean he had seen in the stadium. Alan didn't know why he hadn't told Risa he thought he had seen Sean. It was probably because he felt like something was happening outside his control. He didn't know what the fuck Sean wanted.

"Henry," he began without introduction, "Risa told me. What's this shit about Sean Collins calling you?"

"He called a few days ago. He—"

"You don't believe it was him, do you?"

"I don't know."

"Well, Jesus, Henry. Risa's pretty upset. Don't you think you should have made sure, seen some ID, done some background before telling her."

"I was going to, but then I thought I saw him at the stadium this afternoon, and I . . . I wanted to warn her."

"What's this shit about Carol Slezak's murder?"

"That's what he said he wanted to talk about."

"He was gone by the time she was murdered."

"Yeah. Maybe he's just catching up."

"So you think he's in town now, tonight?"

"I guess so."

"Where's he staying?"

"Hazelton, I guess. Unless he's got friends."

"What are you going to say to him, Henry?"

"I don't know. I don't know what he wants to talk about."

"Call me as soon as he's gone, okay? You've got my cell. I've got a factory tour at eleven, but you can call me. Don't call Risa, got it?"

"Maybe he won't want me to call anybody."

"Fuck him. Henry, I need to protect Risa and Kevin. He left them high and dry. He can't just waltz back in and screw things up. Not now especially. You understand the situation?"

"I do."

"Good man. Call me soon as he's gone. See ya."

Alan went down the motel hall to the meeting room and motioned to an intern, a young girl named Terry, never got her last name, and took her out to the hall.

"Top secret mission, Terry. Call all the motels around Braden and see if they have a Sean or an S. Collins registered for tonight."

Terry scratched this in a steno book. "There are only three, right? Two in Hazelton and—"

"Yeah. Go wider if you have to. And check the B and B in Braden. Annie's place. What does she call it?"

"I don't know. I didn't know there was a B and B in Braden."

Distracted, Alan started into the meeting. "Top secret. You don't tell anybody what you're doing and you report to me only. Got it?" Terry nodded and Alan went back into the room hoping she had success. He could take off later, find Sean, cut him off at the pass. That's what it felt like, the Old West, the ghostlike figure coming back to town to mess up the good order, settle scores. Alan couldn't stand for that. He'd be like Kevin today. Knock Sean on his ass before he turned the corner.

The two glasses of wine Risa drank to put her to sleep didn't work. She lay in bed unable to tame her runaway thoughts. Sean was this strangely benign man, the Sean of the wintry night in the stadium. Kevin was no longer sweet and simple. Alan was receding somehow, even though the night before they had made love for the first time in a long while. And over all the jumble was Carol's calm, concerned face.

Risa couldn't shake the feeling she was being asked to do something. She didn't know what it could possibly be, but she felt the burden anyway. Be more of a politician's wife? Get fully behind Kevin's passion? Welcome Sean with open arms? It was Scrimmage Day, the calendar's highlight for her father. Would she ever be able to see the day again as anything but the day a hole opened in her life? Or might it be forever circled as the day Sean returned from the dead?

7

Street noise and some pinhole light shafts in the sitting room finally woke Sean. He had woken several times during the night and all had been calm, the room still dark, few sounds. He had dreamed he was at Risa's parents' house for their traditional Polish Christmas Eve dinner. He wasn't sitting with the rest of them; he was standing for some reason. Risa's father, Sim, was about to start the Oplatki ceremony, taking a piece of the wafer, holding it in front of his mouth. Then he looked up at Sean and gestured toward the plate set for no one, in remembrance of Joseph and Mary having no place but a stable on the first Christmas Eve.

"But that's for a stranger," Sean kept saying, and Sim, round-faced, charming, gregarious Sim, just kept gesturing.

This angered Sean for some reason and he kept trying to tell Sim he was Irish, that he didn't want to sit. Then the dream wisped away.

Sean's eyes were crusted and he rubbed them until he saw the room more clearly. A bigger shaft of light came through the opening he had made in the plywood. He realized he was going to have to go back out the way he had come in, but in daylight. He got up, looked through the hole, and saw that it faced an empty lot, not the street. There was enough light in the room now so that he could see the landscape. He found a janitor's closet off the lobby and was surprised when he turned on the faucet and water spurted into the slop sink.

He washed there and managed to shave. In the middle of his shaving he remembered his sobriety pill. For a brief second of panic he couldn't recall where he'd put his pills, if he'd packed them at all. He went to his backpack and started to unzip pouches. In the third pouch he found the pills and grabbed the bottle as if it might float up out of his reach. He went back to the sink, put the pill on his tongue, and cupped his hands under the faucet. When he leaned down to drink, the pill popped out of his mouth and landed on top of the drain. He grabbed it quickly, threw his head back, swallowed hard, and the pill went down. But when he looked back down he saw bits of the pill disintegrating in the drops of water. He tried to scoop them up, but it was too late.

Had he gotten a full dose? He began to obsess about this, then realized he was just trying to deflect his anxiety. He was about to get the answer to a horrible question. The pill was enough. He packed up, slithered through the plywood hole without being seen, he thought, and headed for Henry's office. Braden in daylight gave him strength. He'd had the balls to come here. That was the hard part. All he had to do now was ask a couple of questions and leave.

Henry's office was in a small room above the Dollar Store. The door to the stairway was open and Sean climbed the creaking steps quickly. The frosted glass door to the office had a card with *The Statesman* logo on it and Henry's name underneath. Sean tried the door knob and it turned. Henry was there, his desk so close to the door Sean wondered if he was going to be able to get in. Henry stood, opened the door wider, and held out his hand.

"Sean, I'm Henry Saltz."

"I'm early. Am I . . ."

"No. Come on in. Take any chair." Henry forced a grin to underline his joke.

Sean had known Henry was young, but he wasn't prepared for the youthful shock of hair Henry sported, the smooth, almost beardless, cheeks. He had imagined someone wise beyond his years, scowling, judgmental.

"I don't have coffee here, but I can go out down the street and get us some."

"None for me, thanks."

Sean couldn't imagine putting anything in his sour stomach. He sat with his backpack in his lap, until he thought this looked too much like some schoolkid in the principal's office, and he put it on the floor.

"Thanks for seeing me. I won't take up a lot of your time. I've just got a few questions."

"Fine. I've got a couple of questions for you first."

"Yeah?"

Henry picked up a minirecorder from his desk. "Mind if I tape our conversation?"

"Why?"

"Habit. In case there's anything you or I might want to go back to later."

"No. I don't want that. Not now. I'm just asking some questions."

"Then let me ask you this: Why couldn't you just ask me over the phone, or by e-mail?"

"I just wanted to do it this way. I think you'll see it's not something for the phone." Sean used the tone he'd used when he was substitute teaching and wanted to let a new class know he meant business.

Henry stared hard at Sean now, a glassy look Sean couldn't read.

"On the phone you said you had been in New York since you left here."

"I'd rather not talk about that. It's embarrassing. I . . ."

"Okay. Just a little background." Henry consulted a

notebook. "Born in Philadelphia, raised here, graduated from Penn State, taught at BAHS, and—"

"That's enough, isn't it? Do you need to see ID?"

"No. Just one more. How did you get to New York?"

"I don't know." Sean looked down. His nerves were starting to make his hands shake. He didn't want to talk about New York, but he feared what he was about to find out. "You saw Carol Slezak's body, didn't you?"

Henry tapped a manila folder on his desk. "Yes."

"I need to ask you some tough questions, specifics. Is that all right?"

"I got hold of the crime scene photographs." Henry started to open the folder.

"I don't want to look at those. Do you remember what you saw?"

"I could never forget her."

Sean looked down again, blinking. Henry's use of the word "her" instead of "it" or "the body" made personal what Sean had been struggling for weeks to keep at some objective distance. In forming his questions, he had always used "the body." But he knew that wasn't the whole truth. They were talking about Carol Slezak, a woman he had loved.

"There was more than one . . . wound, from the machete, wasn't there?"

"There were a few, yes."

"There was one big one that went this way, from left to right, right?" Sean drew the index finger of his right hand from his left shoulder, across his chest to his right hip. *Please say, no, Henry. Please.*

"Yes. That was the biggest one."

Sean felt light-headed and couldn't get words out for a long minute.

"Her right arm had been almost cut off up here." Sean put

the fingers of his right hand on his left biceps. Henry only nodded this time. Sean rushed through his last question. "And one here, a deep one." He drew a line from his forehead to his right jawbone.

"Yes."

The word echoed for Sean and the room dropped away. His mother's voice from his childhood bloomed in his ears. "Sean, Sean, what have you done now?" The relief he had longed for blew away. An oily swamp of condemnation rose all around him. He stood.

"I can show you," Henry said and flipped open the manila folder. Sean caught a glimpse of the black-and-white photograph on the top before he reached over and quickly closed the folder.

"No."

"How did you . . . ?"

"Thank you," Sean said, reaching for his backpack.

"How do you know this? You saw photographs?"

Sean shook his head. He reached his hand out and Henry shook it. Sean then bolted for the door and was out and down the steps before Henry could stop him.

Sean's eyes were so tear-filled that he could hardly navigate the steps to the street. He made it to the door and stopped. He wiped his eyes with his sleeve, but he couldn't wipe away the atrocious images that seemed to leap through the door's glass and grab him by the throat. He had called up the horror himself this time. The obscene blade of the machete loomed in front of his face in the pale wash of a milky moonlight. It turned and exposed its murderous knife edge, running with blood. Then the machete dropped out of sight and Carol's carved body screamed up at him.

Sean rocked back, lost balance, and sat heavily on the stairs. He heard Henry call from above.

"Are you all right?"

Sean stood up quickly, got the door open, and forced himself out into the hot morning sun.

Henry stared down at the slammed door. He tried to make sense of what had just happened. He too could not shake the horror. He sat at his desk staring for a long minute. Then he reached out and turned off the minirecorder that had been running the whole time.

8

Risa. I'm gonna come right out and tell you. People say they seen Sean around town. I tol' em that can't be. It can't, can it?"

Bell was calling as Kevin was wolfing down pancakes and bacon on his way out to the morning practice.

"Just a minute, Bell." Risa spoke to Kevin, "Are you coming home for lunch?"

"I don't know. I've got money." He grabbed a duffel and left.

"Bell?"

"Sorry, honey. I opened up an hour ago an' I heard from three, four people he's in town. Lynn Kasivich says he seen him on a bench in the park last night when he was walking his dog. Told him he couldn't sleep in the park. Thought the guy looked familiar an' about a half hour later realized it was Sean. I don't know, but Lynn ain't no dreamer."

"There were others, others who saw him?"

"Yeah. Couple said they saw him at the stadium yesterday."

"I heard about that."

"And this is the weirdest. April said she was takin' a shortcut past the hotel this morning and this guy with a backpack comes squirmin' out of a hole in the plywood they got there. She didn't know what to make of it. But when she heard the talk about Sean she went, 'Oh, my God. That was him.'" Risa didn't say anything in response. "Jesus. So it's true?"

"I guess."

"But wasn't he supposed to be dead? Sorry. Why'd I say that?"

"'Cause he was. Legally."

"He tried to get in touch with you?"

"No. He's come to talk to Henry Saltz."

"Henry. What for?"

Risa couldn't go further. "I don't know."

"When are you coming in?"

"I'll do lunch. How's your hip?"

"Same old, but I can take lunch if you need time or somethin'. This is kinda weird, isn't it?"

"Yeah. I'll be all right. See you later."

Bell's was the second call she'd had that morning. Alan had woken her at six thirty, a half hour after she had fallen back asleep. He had said that Sean wasn't registered in any area motels and now, after Bell's call, Risa guessed that he had slept in the boarded-up Braden Hotel. Alan said he wanted to go to Henry's office when Sean was there, but he couldn't break his morning schedule. He asked if Risa wanted to go and she said she didn't. Then he asked if Risa had seen Kevin on the news last night and she realized she had forgotten to tape it. She had apologized to Alan, but he hadn't really accepted the apology.

She looked at the clock: nine thirty-six. She had told Alan she didn't want to go to Henry's office, to intercept Sean, but now, after Bell's call, she did want to see him. Everybody else in town had. Henry's office was ten minutes away. She could make it in time to see Sean go in perhaps. Did she want to do that? What would people think if they saw her, lurking around on Fifth? She couldn't exactly hide herself. But she could go in the Dollar Store, hang out pretending to get something, talk to Elda or whoever was working.

She went in the half bathroom off the kitchen and looked in the mirror. Her lack of sleep showed. She didn't have time to get made up. She splashed water on her face, went back in the kitchen, grabbed her keys and cell phone from the counter, and left the house.

She turned the corner onto Fifth slowly, not knowing which direction Sean might come from going to Henry's office. There were a few people on the sidewalk. The bank clock, reliably unreliable, said it was five thirty. Risa opened her cell phone and saw that it was nine fifty-one. She crossed at the light and made it to the Dollar Store having to nod hello to only one acquaintance. She yanked the door hard but it didn't yield. She looked at the hours sign and found, to her surprise, that on Tuesdays and Thursdays the store opened at ten. She peered in and saw Elda Kuzinski coming toward the door, keys in hand. Risa looked nervously up and down Fifth but saw no one who could have been Sean.

"Hi, Risa," Elda said, smoothing the old-fashioned smock she wore. She was only in her forties but always seemed to affect the airs of an old lady. Maybe, Risa had always thought, it was the name she had been saddled with.

"Elda. What's this ten o'clock opening?"

"I don't know. Gene did some sort of calculation with that computer of his and said we're losing money opening early. Ask him. Don't ask me."

"I will."

"Whatcha lookin' for?"

"I don't know. Haven't been in for a while. Thought I'd just snoop around, see what's new before I went on to work."

"Help yourself. If you need anything, let me know. I'll be in the back trying to figure out Gene's inventory nonsense. Used to be real simple. Now he's got all these tags with bar codes and a damn machine that works about half the time."

She walked away and Risa looked quickly out to the street. She moved along the big front window until she could see the door to Henry's office. She inspected a set of heavy, cheap goblets very, very carefully.

Fifteen minutes later she was still examining the goblets. One other customer, a new teacher at Rhodes Elementary whom Risa hadn't met yet, came in and went to the back, engaging Elda, allowing Risa to maintain her post. But with every check of her cell phone Risa realized that Sean either hadn't shown or had gone into the building before she got there.

The schoolteacher was winding up his talk with Elda, and Risa looked back to see if Elda was going to come to the front with him, if she had to examine something other than the goblets. The teacher came out from the back by himself, smiled at Risa, and went out the door.

Risa turned with him, watched him leave, and saw him sidestep quickly as he almost ran into another man. The other man nodded to the teacher's pardon but kept his head down. It took a couple of seconds for Risa to realize the other man was Sean.

The goblet slipped from her hand and clattered on the table. She kept her eyes on Sean. Through the glass, between signs and displays, she could see clearly it was he, even though something was off. He shouldered a backpack that made him look like he was back in college, but his face, the profile she could see, anyway, was slightly distorted from what she had remembered and his features were aged, creased. He wiped his eyes as he walked, his thick head of wavy hair, like Kevin's, bouncing, his lanky stride unmistakable to Risa.

And then he was gone. Risa craned her neck to watch him but another sign obliterated her view and she looked quickly down at the goblet, rolling toward the edge of the table. She caught it and stood frozen for a second as Elda came from the back.

"What was that?"

Risa thought she was referring to Sean at first, then realized it was the goblet.

"Oh, sorry. I dropped this. Glad it didn't break."

"Have to drop from the Empire State Building to break those. You okay, Risa?"

Risa nodded, put the goblet down, worked a reassuring smile into her exit, mumbled something about how she'd be back, and left. Outside the store she stopped again and looked to her left.

Sean was gone. Del Cronin was coming toward her, only a few yards away, smiling his big banker's smile.

"Risa, Risa. How're you doin'? Sorry I didn't make The Kitchen last night. I had a crazy day. I saw Kevin on Channel Three. You must be real proud."

"Yeah. Excuse me, Del."

Risa wasn't thinking now. It had been him. It wasn't some apparition, though it seemed as if it were. She had to follow to make sure. She walked as fast as she could without running and reached the corner quickly. He was heading down Market, crossing in the middle of the block. Risa stayed on her side of Market and walked behind him. She passed a couple of people but ignored them, keeping her eyes on Sean. She had the feeling that if she looked away he might disappear.

Sean had to stop for traffic at Front Street, then he crossed and headed for the open area beside the bridge ramp. Risa hesitated. If she followed and he turned around, she would be too exposed. She waited at the corner of Front Street and watched him walk beside the ramp, then take the pathway that led down the riverbank to the water. Risa waited, thinking he might go halfway down and then come back up. There was nothing at that part of the river but an old concrete abutment and the bridge pilings. A horn honked and she looked up to see her beer supplier, Howie Francis, waving from his Bud truck as he came off the bridge. Risa waved, and when she looked back down the pathway to the river, Sean was gone.

Walking away from Henry's office, Sean felt the full weight of his guilt press down on him until he thought he wasn't going to be able to get a breath. He walked, made turns, headed blindly toward the river, and wiped away the stinging tears. He was a killer.

The word pounded. The small flame of hope that he was wrong about the horror had been blown out, and he knew that nothing in his lifetime would ever absolve him. He was a killer and always would be. Only death could free him from that guilt.

He found himself by the bridge, going down the pathway. It didn't make any difference where he went. He could never escape. He was supposed to go back to New York in a couple of hours, but that would change nothing about what he had just learned. He saw the lazy waters of the river and wanted desperately to dive in and never come up for air.

He put his backpack down and stared out, seeing nothing but his own obliteration. And then it hit him that he had to turn himself in as quickly as possible. He had to be in the open, punished, in some place where he couldn't take his own life. Prison would be a piece of cake compared to the cage his bones made for him now.

Suddenly he didn't want to be near the river. He picked up his backpack and turned, aware there was somebody coming down the pathway toward him, hoping he could just walk past whoever it was.

"Sean?"

He lifted his head to see Risa standing above him, her eyes wide with questions. He didn't believe she was really there. Had he willed this apparition into being just as he had conjured up the woman on the bus? It didn't seem so. She spoke again.

"Sean? It's me."

In all the darkness that had engulfed him since he first realized he had killed Carol, the only sliver of light had been an imagined Risa, her listening eyes drinking in the depths of his guilt and still forgiving him. He wanted this ideal woman to hold him and soothe all the raw hurt. And he wanted to open himself to her in a way he hadn't been able to when he had spiraled into drink and despair.

But the Risa standing in front of him was flesh and blood, someone he had hurt deeply, the last person he wanted to see now. He opened his arms wide, a gesture of surrender, a man about to be frisked by questions. "Are you real?" he finally managed to get out, though he knew the answer.

"Am I real? Are you kidding? Are *you* real?"

Sean started up the pathway. "I'm going to walk past you and . . ."

Risa blocked his way, and when he was close enough, put a hand to his chest to stop him. It was as if she had completed a circuit. They both stepped back, jolted.

"Risa, dammit, I didn't want this. Didn't want to see you."

Risa glared at him. "Sean Collins, look at me. I don't know what the hell's going on, or where you've been, or where you're going, but if I've just got this one time, I want to tell you something. I tried to let you go. I tried to kill you in my head. But I couldn't. You were never really dead to me."

Sean's eyes crinkled ever so slightly. "So you were the one saving my ass time and time again, huh?"

Risa caught the hint of humor, the smidgen of the old Sean. Her eyes filled. "Yes, that was me, and now you owe me."

"No. Not if you mean I should tell you what I'm doing here, tell you where I've been. No. Later. Some other time. I'm leaving in a couple of hours. I'll be in touch."

"Uh-huh. You stay right where you are. I beat you up once. I can do it again."

"We were eight."

"Yeah. I'm stronger now. My son's a big football star. Try me."

The mention of Kevin stopped them both for long seconds. Sean finally got his breath back.

"Ris, really. I mean it. I'm not ready. I just got hit with a two by four and I can't think straight. How did you find me down here?"

"This is Braden, remember? Remember how we hated everybody knowing everybody's business? Remember we were going to get out and . . ."

"Stop. I don't remember much but that . . . You're killing me, Risa. Let me go."

"Why are you asking Henry about Carol?"

"I told him not to say anything."

"I repeat, this isn't New York. Maybe people there rise from the dead and nobody thinks twice about it. But you've lit up the switchboards, Sean. I wouldn't be surprised to turn around and see a welcoming committee behind me. Now what's this about Carol?"

"Nobody's going to welcome me. You don't know what you're looking at. I'm sick. I was sick when I left and I'm sick now."

"You're sober."

"For now. I had an accident. My brain's all scrambled. Don't take advantage of me in this state. Let me go and I promise I'll fill you in soon."

"Fill me in? This isn't some office memo, Sean. What accident? What about Carol? You can't expect me to turn away, go back to my life with all these questions in the air."

Sean caught the full intense beauty of Risa's green eyes and suddenly she was the imagined, hoped-for Risa who would understand and forgive. He opened the door he'd been holding shut.

"I killed her, Ris. I killed Carol."

Risa recoiled as if she'd been slapped. She searched Sean's face to see if this was some joke, if she'd heard him right. "Is this part of your sickness?"

"No. I mean, it was. I was sick and . . ."

"G.G. Trask killed Carol. He confessed. He's in prison. You remember G.G.?"

"Yes. But he didn't kill her. I did. Now I've told you, so just let me go and I promise I'll . . . well . . . You're right. It's Braden. I guess you'll hear about it."

Risa's anger flared. "I don't want to hear about it. That's why I followed you. I want you to tell me! You've been gone eleven years. You owe me a few complete sentences. Where are you going? Do you have to be somewhere?"

"Well, no, but I told them I'd be back."

"Who's them?"

"I'm in rehab, counselors."

"Well tell them you're staying overnight. We've got an empty apartment over on Front Street. Come on." She went to him and started to take his arm, tug him forward. He pulled his arm back and stood where he was.

"I'm not a drunk now. I don't have to be led like a child. I'll stay, but don't expect me to spill my guts, tell all, whatever. I'm just working this out for myself. I'm a basket case at times. I need to think, figure things out. I'll stay if you promise to give me time, space."

Risa softened. He wasn't a child anymore. This wasn't the run-up-the-driveway-arms-wide-open homecoming she had often imagined. There was a crazy, demented darkness to this one, but Sean was right, he was no longer the drunk, a child. She didn't say anything in response. She nodded.

Sean stood still. It was Risa in front of him, the old Risa, not the one he had to lie to about his drinking, but the one who had held him and loved him. She had worked her magic. Now he wanted to talk.

"I was a drunk on the streets in New York all that time. You oughta know that."

"Okay."

"The accident was a subway. I fell on the tracks, got hit in the head. I don't remember leaving Braden, most of the years on the street, nothing. All wiped out so far."

"So far?"

"Some of it's coming back. They say there'll be more."

"Good."

"No. It's horrible. One of the first things that returned was this . . . I don't know . . . horror show. I see myself killing Carol, alone, with G.G.'s machete. And it's like it's happening right now, and all I want to do is kill myself. I came close to doing that, but . . ."

"But?"

"Kevin. Suicide runs in families. I didn't want him to inherit . . . I just couldn't pass that on to him the way it was passed on to me. That's why I'm going to have to do something, get myself safe from me. So there. Do you still want to put me up in your apartment?"

Risa barely heard the question. Sean had gotten to her. It was as if an eclipse had darkened the noonday sun. Carol. G.G. Doubts from the past floated up. Kevin vulnerable to suicide. Sean, gentle Sean? She knew her silence betrayed her shock, but she couldn't get words out right away. In sickness and in health? Was that it?

"Yes. I still want you . . . in the apartment. I can't believe . . . You left days before she was killed. You must have heard about it, read about it, and it seemed like a memory."

Sean shook his head no. "I didn't hear anything, read anything. The reporter just confirmed . . . I was there. I did it."

Risa realized she shouldn't challenge this unburdening, but she couldn't help herself.

"Memory is tricky. And if you got hit in the head . . ."

"No. It's as vivid to me as Kevin's birth."

"You remember that?"

"Yes."

There was nothing more to say. Risa turned and started up

the pathway. Then she stopped and turned back. Sean was still standing there, as if he were waiting to be invited again. Risa tried a smile.

"Simon says come with me."

Sean obeyed.

They moved awkwardly around the light-filled one-bedroom apartment, Risa showing him the closets as if she were a real estate agent, both avoiding eye contact, both wary of the intimacy of the small space. When she said she had to get to work, she told him about her father dying suddenly eight years ago, about her mother not being able to handle the restaurant, and that she had taken over "very reluctantly," keeping the restaurant after her mother's death because Alan urged her to do so and Bell needed the work

"We had you declared dead, Sean."

"I know. They told me that as soon as they found out who I was."

"You didn't know who you were?"

"Not at first. That was probably the head trauma. I had an ID that said I was Wallis Corning."

Risa tried to imagine a state of living that completely obscured the past, including your name. But it eluded her. She said she wouldn't tell anyone that he was in the apartment, would say he had left if asked, "but you know you can't keep a secret in this town." She told him that Alan knew he was here, but Kevin, as far as she knew, didn't know. Sean said he wasn't ready to see Kevin, but had seen on his Facebook page that he was some sort of football star.

"Obviously not my genes," he said.

Risa wanted to tell him about the scrimmage, about the hit and how that affected her. But there was too much else in the room, in her head, and she only nodded. Then, standing only a couple of feet from Sean, Risa had the overwhelming feeling that he was back to stay, that she could touch him again, talk to him as much as she wanted. She knew it was wrong, too much, impulsive, but she couldn't stop herself. She put a hand on his shoulder, reached up, and brushed a kiss over his shaved cheek. She felt Sean's lips brush her ear. It was for her a welcome deeper than some hug or wild fuck could ever be. Her heart pounded in her chest until she pulled back, said a quick goodbye, and went out the door.

She headed down Front Street, feeling as if she should have exacted a promise from him not to leave. She wished she could have barred the door, maybe chained him to the radiator. She knew she should be dialing Alan's number as she walked, but she left her cell phone in her pocket. She started to think about Sean staying for good, about telling Kevin. When she passed the bridge she replayed their first moments of reunion and was taken aback a second time with how solid Sean seemed despite what he said was a sickness, despite his impossible claim.

And then she stopped dead in her tracks. It had happened. Sean had come back. That was a reality now. She had looked Sean in the eyes when she thought she never again would. She had spoken to him, listened to him. And yet throughout, she realized now, she hadn't shed a single tear.

9

For a long time after Sean left, Henry sat in his office staring at the bike helmet on his desk. Sean had clearly seen what Henry had seen, but how could that have been? Henry knew without having to go over old notes that there had been conclusive evidence that G. G. Trask was the only one on the scene, a lone killer. Sean said he hadn't seen the police photos, but maybe he was lying.

Henry called Alan Benson as he said he would, gave him an airbrushed view of the conversation, not saying he couldn't figure out how Sean had known the details. Alan fumed about shenanigans, swore Henry to secrecy, and hung up. Henry wondered why Alan wasn't celebrating the return from the dead of one of his old friends, and then it hit him that there were political implications to the reappearance lurking. The current DA, John Stallings, who had prosecuted G. G. Trask, was in a tough little battle for reelection. He wasn't going to be happy about this case resurfacing now. Alan had married the "dead" man's wife after working with Risa to have Sean declared legally dead. How was that going to look in his campaign? And Sheriff Armey, in both a reelection contest and a battle with colon cancer, was not going to want to have the only murder in his time in office regurgitated in either the press or the rumor mill.

Henry played the Sean tape as he let his answering machine take calls. Then he opened the manila folder with the crime scene photographs. After he had gotten them from the sheriff's office, he hadn't looked at them. The photos had been taken with film and printed on paper using chemicals. The fixer hadn't been applied evenly, and there were a couple of browning spots on the black-and-white images. But the full gore of the horrible scene was intact. The flat, monochromatic images were nowhere near as vivid as his memory, but when he imagined the photographer leaning over the body to get his shot, he remembered his own turmoil then, the time-out-of-time feeling he had, the vomit, the jumbled thoughts, and the repeated internal question: Who could have done this?

He shuddered and put the photographs away. Things would right themselves as they had back then. Time and distance would prevail. Maybe Sean was already on a bus back to New York. His reappearance would be just a blip on the screen and Henry could get back to covering the elections, the Water Board's hearing, a Boy Scout ceremony.

Then he remembered where he was, what the town's rumor mill was like, and, most important, how tuned in Doris Whiting was to everything happening anywhere in the county. He could put that photograph back in its folder, but he couldn't keep his foul-mouthed boss from jumping down his neck. He was caught.

Risa was close to The Kitchen when Alan called on her cell phone. She decided to talk to him even though she wasn't sure what she was going to say.

"Hi."

"Risa. Where are you?"

"Near the restaurant."

"You weren't home. I talked to Henry. He saw Sean about an hour ago." Risa waited. "He said Sean was strange, asked some questions about what Carol's body looked like and then left. He may be walking around somewhere. Henry said he left in a hurry."

"I saw him." Risa said, knowing it was useless to keep this from Alan.

"Saw him? Where?"

"He was leaving Henry's."

"What were you doing—?"

"I wanted to see him. I followed him down to the river. We talked."

"You talked to him?"

"Yes."

"What did he say?"

"A lot. Maybe we should talk about it later, when you're home."

"No. I want to know now. What was all this business about Carol's murder? He just wanted to find out what happened to her?"

"He said he thinks he was the one who killed Carol."

"What?"

"You heard me, Alan. He thinks he killed—"

"That's nuts."

"That's what I said. He said something about recovered memory, about seeing Carol's body. He can't remember much about anything from the past ten, eleven years, but he said he can see this one, I don't know what you'd call it . . . scene."

"But everybody knows G.G. did it."

"I told him. He wouldn't listen to that. I think he may be brain injured. He fell on some subway tracks and was nearly killed."

"Yeah. Henry said that."

"He just wanted to get back to New York. I don't know what he's planning."

"So he's gone?"

Risa knew that she had gone too far now, that she had to tell everything. "No. I put him up in the Front Street apartment."

"Why?"

"He's not right, Alan. I couldn't let him go back and, I don't know, turn himself in, do himself harm. I had to do something."

"How's that going to look?"

"How's what going to look?"

"Us taking him in after all these years. He abandoned you, Risa. You and Kevin. And now he's back saying he killed Carol. We shouldn't have anything to do with him."

"Why?"

"Well, uh, excuse me, but one of us is a public figure in a tight race for office."

"What's Sean got to do with that?"

"Come on, Risa. Don't be fucking naïve. You can't keep something like this quiet for long. What's it look like to, like, voters in Scranton? They open their papers, turn on their TVs, and hear about me harboring some drunk who claims to be a murderer."

"But that's a good thing. I mean, helping him. We're . . . we're showing kindness. He's sick, Alan. He was sick when he left."

"Let's not go through that horseshit again. Being a drunk might be a disease, but leaving your wife and kid in the lurch isn't. And I don't want to have to go to every goddamn debate and forum and campaign stop in the next three months and have to explain my ass on this one. You can be kind to puppies and widows and the working poor, but not to some asshole who just pops up after eleven years. Jesus, if I didn't know what an idiot Errol Roberts is, I'd think he planted this to fuck me up."

"Well, he's there for tonight. I'll take care of it. You don't have to be involved."

"I've gotta go to this goddamn factory tour. I'll be home late this afternoon. Do me a favor, huh? Come to your senses. Think about me. Put him on a bus and wash your hands of the whole thing."

"There isn't another bus today. How can you . . . ? We were all together. We—"

"Not now, Risa. Later."

He hung up, and Risa pocketed her cell phone. In the space of ten minutes or so she had spoken with Sean and Alan. It was like old, old times, high school maybe, when she'd be in class with one and see the other in the hallway. Sean might have cornered her with some new interest, like cargo ships you could book passage on, and she would pass this on to Alan, who, of course, would shake his head and ask if Sean had been toking up between classes.

Risa hadn't told Alan about Kevin, about Sean's saying he was doing what he was doing for Kevin. That was too unsettling for her to think about. How can you even imagine your son committing suicide? But then she realized that only the day before she had seen a violence in Kevin she could never have imagined. Did one have anything to do with the other? It couldn't. No. Sean was sick and deluded. Stay with that. He's alive and Kevin's going to be fine. She went into The Kitchen steeling herself, ready to deal with questions and sidelong glances. She knew her ex-husband. She knew her son. That would get her through.

For a good fifteen minutes after Risa left the apartment, Sean sat motionless on the mattress, stunned by her appearance under the bridge. He could feel her lips on his cheek, and that brushed kiss replayed like a repeated absolution. She had interrupted his planning and now he didn't know whether to stay in Braden or go back, to go directly to the DA in the morning or to return later to turn himself in. Both the city and where he was now held dangers for him. He couldn't think, couldn't get past the searing guilt, the soothing kiss. Stay. Go. He couldn't decide.

He checked the bus schedule, saw there was the bus at two thirty, thought a trip back to the city would at least give him some time to think, even if he turned right around and came back. His eyelids wouldn't stay open. He took off his jeans and lay down for a nap. He woke once thinking he heard a knock on the door but didn't wake fully and was back asleep quickly. When he did wake up for good, he heard a thunderclap and looked out the window to see a cloud bank building to the west. His watch said two ten and he started to dress. Then he noticed a paper bag just inside the door to the apartment. He opened it to find a hamburger, lukewarm, cold fries, a milk shake, and coleslaw, all in containers with The Kitchen's logo on them.

As he ate, he checked the schedule again, read the fine print explaining an asterisk, and realized that the two thirty was only a weekend bus. There were no more buses out that day. He thought he might hitchhike, go over to the bridge, catch some trucker going into the city. He had done that once, going in the opposite direction, when he hadn't been able to find a ride back to college.

A half hour later, the storm broke over Braden and rain clattered like birdshot against the flimsy windows of the apartment. Sean was glad he hadn't gone to the bridge. He would be soaked. He wondered how many times in New York he had been out in such rain. He thought he could remember the feel of soggy, unlaced shoes and soaked, foul-smelling clothes. But he had no more specifics than that.

He was taking a piss in the bathroom a few minutes later when he heard a thump and wondered if the rain had turned to hail. He was coming out of the bathroom when he realized the thump was a knock, the door handle was turning, and the door was opening.

"Risa?"

"No, it's me, Alan."

Even more than his campaign poster, the Alan who came through the door reminded Sean of the boy who had been one of the first to befriend him in sixth grade. New to the school, Irish, not Ukrainian or Polish or Greek, Sean had kept to himself for a week or so before Alan, big smile, formal, offering a handshake for chrissake, pulled him into some game, brought him out of his shell.

"Alan," Sean got out as Alan came toward him, hand out again, and Sean took it. Alan brought him into an awkward hug and then the two just stood looking at each other for what seemed to Sean an inordinate time.

"Risa told me."

"That I was here?"

"And why you're back."

"Oh. I didn't want to see her. I didn't call or anything. She . . ."

". . . followed you. She said. I guess she couldn't believe her eyes. Frankly, neither can I. We tried everything we could think of."

"Everything?"

"I mean to find you, to find out what happened to you."

"Before you got me declared dead?"

"Right. Everything, Sean. I must have talked to every agency in every big city on the Atlantic seaboard. You were way, way, way under the radar, my friend."

"Yeah."

"Risa says you don't remember any of it."

"No. Little bits and pieces are coming back now that I'm . . . now that I'm off the juice."

"Kicked it, huh?"

"So far. You're always recovering."

"I hear that," Alan said.

They stood awkwardly as the rain outside tapered off.

"You're running for Congress."

"Yup."

"Following in your father's footsteps, huh?"

"He never made it past county manager. I'm hoping to one-up him. That's what kids are supposed to do, right?"

This might have been a line Alan had used countless times. Sean nodded but could only think of how he had definitely failed in that regard. He looked down at the floor, then back up.

"Thanks, Alan. For taking care of Risa, Kevin. When they found out Risa was remarried and it was you, I was glad. That was the way it was supposed to be anyways, right?" Sean tried to give this a light touch, but there was a hitch in his voice. Alan caught it.

"We were young. Who knew anything then?"

"Yeah."

"Risa always says I was the one who left our threesome when I went east."

"Ivy League. You just wanted that Ivy League."

"Trust me. Yale wasn't worth it."

"All worked out for you, huh?"

"So far. Politicians are always recovering too."

He smiled and they laughed nervously.

"Bet that's a tough drug to kick."

Alan walked over to the window, looked out, nodded to someone on the street, then turned back.

"What's this business about you having something to do with Carol's murder?"

"Risa told you?"

"And I talked to Henry Saltz. He said you were asking questions about Carol, the way her body looked, her wounds, that sort of thing. Risa said you think you killed her."

"Know, Alan. I know I did."

"Didn't you say you don't remember anything from all those years ago?"

"Yes, but this is different. They tell me there are some

traumas that shut off memory and some that keep things open forever. It's one of those. I can see myself right there over her body and I've got G.G.'s machete."

"G.G. would dispute you on that. He confessed, hasn't recanted a word. Something else must be going on with you."

"I wish. I'd like nothing better than for someone to prove me wrong, but G.G.'s no proof. You know he's always been just a stutter away from retarded. If they told him to say he was the king of England he'd show 'em his throne."

"John Stallings and Jack Armey would not appreciate the implication of that. You come to them with this sort of flimsy stuff and you'll get a good definition of the word 'stonewall.'"

"It's not flimsy to me."

"All right, but it's fucking tissue paper to them." Alan's tone sharpened. "Don't you think for the good of all concerned you should just drop this, go back to the city?"

"I'm planning to go back. But I can't drop it. You can't imagine what living with these . . . these pictures is like."

"Pictures fade, Sean. Everything's raw to you right now. Go back, let things settle."

"I'm going to. First bus out tomorrow."

"Fuck the bus. My driver. I got a guy for the campaign. He's outside. He can run you into the city, have you there in two and a half tops."

Sean at first thought this would be a good solution, but when Alan turned to him with an anxious, false grin, Sean smelled something he didn't like. Why the hustle?

"I bought a round trip," he said.

"Oh, for chrissakes. Come on. You've been on the fucking streets for eleven years. Indulge yourself."

"I'm going to have to come back to give myself up."

"Jesus, Sean. What the fuck is this, an episode of *Lives of the Saints*? They're not going to let you give yourself up. This isn't fucking playtime. Even if you had a video of you killing Carol they would tell you to get lost. You've gotta get back in the real world here. Pack up. Come on. Guy's a good driver, got some great stories from Iraq."

Sean found himself coming quickly back to Alan's real world. All those campaign posters started chattering at him. Alan didn't care about the horrors that would pounce on Sean without warning. Horror for Alan was bad press, a bad vote count. Did he think that Sean being in town was going to affect that count? Sean remembered Risa standing above him on the pathway, beckoning him to come with her, asking him to stay in Braden. His choice was a no-brainer.

"I'll catch the bus in the morning."

"Shit, Sean. Haven't you done enough to Risa?"

"She wants me to stay."

"That why she asked me to come over? Who do you think thought of using my car?"

They stared at each other, Sean gaining confidence by the second. He didn't challenge the lie.

"I'll be out of your hair tomorrow."

"It's not my hair you should be worried about. It's your ass."

"I know that. I'm willing to take what's coming."

"Oh, right. Cagney now. 'Top o' the world, Ma!' You think you're still in some bubble, sucking down your pint on the street? You do what you say you're going to do and you're going to hurt some people."

"Can't help it."

"Fuck that. You can't help it, somebody's going to help it for you."

"Alan, that sounds like a threat."

"And what do you think your I'm-going-to-the-cops horse-shit sounds like?"

"A threat? To who? You?"

"Yeah, me. 'Cause I'm thinking about Kevin and what this is going to do to him."

"Well, great minds think alike 'cause that's precisely why I'm standing in front of you and not a suicide in the morgue."

Alan had no response to this. He shook his head, started to say something, went to the door, and turned back.

"You better be the fuck out of town tomorrow morning."

Sean didn't say anything. Alan left without closing the door. A minute later Sean heard a car door slam. Hard.

10

Risa had taken a hamburger over to the apartment around one o'clock and found Sean asleep on the mattress. He was wearing boxers and a T-shirt, his long legs curled in, his sleep heavy. She felt there was something not right about standing there, looking at him, but she didn't move. She remembered that body, its almost bony feel, and she remembered too that heavy sleep. After he had lost control of his drinking, there were nights when he just barely made it home before he passed out and slept beside her, an inanimate object hardly breathing.

The afternoon at the restaurant was lost. Bell and a few others who spoke to her about Sean understood. Bell told her to go back to the office and do the books, that she would handle up front. Risa did as she was told. But she didn't do the books. She spent the whole time seeing Sean's face under the bridge, hearing him say he had killed Carol, replaying this over and over. He said he was getting help, but what kind of help would lead him to that ludicrous conclusion?

Kevin called after his last practice of the day.

"Where were you at lunch, Mom?"

"Here. At the restaurant."

"I thought you said you were going to be home. There wasn't much in the fridge."

"I need to shop. You got something?"

"Yeah. Good practice. He put the depth charts up today."

"Yeah?"

"Do you want to know?"

"Know what?"

"Where I am on the depth chart?"

Risa had heard Kevin and Alan talking about depth charts. She had misheard it at first as "depth charge" and wondered what the hell they were talking about. They explained it to her but she couldn't remember now.

"Yes. Of course. Where are you?"

"Number one strong side and number two middle. He said he might think about using me at middle linebacker depending on the team we were playing and how Stevie does. Where's Dad?"

"I don't know. Scranton? He had some factory tour, said he'd be home late in the afternoon."

"He's going to be blown away."

"Why don't you come here for dinner tonight?"

"Guys are meeting at Subway. I've got money."

"That food, Kevin. You need something better than that."

"Mom, come on. You should see the veggies I pack in."

"I bet. Don't be out late. What time's practice tomorrow?"

"Usual."

Risa suddenly pulled herself back from this entirely normal conversation and realized that Kevin's father, his real father, a man he says he barely remembers, was sleeping in his boxers and T-shirt only a mile or so away from Kevin. She was dying to tell him this, but she knew how badly Kevin might be thrown by the surprise and she knew she didn't want Kevin to see Sean when he was spouting nonsense about killing Carol.

"Mom. You there?"

"Yeah. Home early, okay?"

"See you. I'm going to try Dad again."

They hung up and Risa stood as if she were going to leave the office, but then she sat again with a new thought. If news of Sean's reappearance was buzzing around Braden, how could she shield Kevin from it? There were only ten thousand people in the town. News and rumors didn't need any Internet to spread virally.

She heard Alan's voice as he walked toward the office, probably talking to Kevin on the phone.

"We'll talk about it more at home. See you."

He appeared at the office door and Risa jumped to a conclusion.

"You told Kevin about Sean?"

"What? No?"

"I just heard you say you'd talk about it at home."

"His practice. Jesus, Risa." He huffed, staring at her. "I just saw him."

"Who?"

"Sean, who else?"

"You said you wouldn't."

"I don't think I said that. How could I not?"

"What did you talk about?"

"Talked about the weather, old times, you know. Tried get him to go have a beer with me but it seems he's off the juice."

"Stop that."

"What?"

"You know. What did you talk about?"

"I want him to leave, Risa. I told him Frank could drive him back to New York."

"And?"

"You know, I think he was ready to hightail it, but that fucking stubborn Irish streak kicked in. 'No, I'll take the bus tomorrow.' Shit."

"You don't want him messing with your campaign."

"Our campaign. Remember? *Our* campaign. We're in this together."

"Not with this."

"You want him to waltz in here and fuck things up?"

"I didn't ask him to come."

"No, but you can ask him to leave."

"You realize the cat's out of the bag, don't you? Bell called me first thing this morning. He's not dead anymore, Alan. And he's here."

"Yeah, well let's put the cat back in the bag or scare him up some fucking tree. Braden's one thing. The rest of the district is another. We can keep this local. But we can't if you're going to play Florence Nightingale, cure him of his goddamn delusions."

"Why wouldn't you want him cured? That would solve part of your problem, wouldn't it?"

"Eleven years, Risa. He's gotta be hard-core loony."

"Did he sound that way to you?"

"You don't have to sound loony to be loony."

"And you don't have to sound cruel to be cruel. Alan, he's nuts with this murder thing, but look at what he's trying to do. He's trying to make amends, make things right."

"Bullshit. He's trying to get some demons out of his head, some vision shit. He's no saint."

"I didn't say he was a saint. I said he was, well, he wasn't out to get you."

"I don't care what he was out to do, he's doing it. Or he will if he stays around here."

Alan was still filling the door with his frame, Risa pinned in the closet-sized office. She felt she had been ambushed; she hadn't figured out what to do, and yet she was being asked to come up with some solution other than the one Alan proposed. She decided to shift gears.

"We have to tell Kevin."

"Kevin. Why?"

"He's going to find out. He ought to find out from us."

"See, that's another reason to get his ass out of town. We corral this thing, maybe we can keep it from Kevin."

"Get your head out of the sand, Alan. Consider it done.

The only question is whether he's going to hear it from us or from . . . from who knows."

A voice came to them. "Alan. I'm sorry. I really need to speak to you."

Lilly Barkin, BlackBerry in hand, appeared behind him.

Alan turned to Risa. "Don't do anything until we talk again."

He left and Risa sat for a minute, feeling oddly as if Alan had jilted her for his campaign manager. Why hadn't he told Lilly to wait? She got up and walked into the bar side of the restaurant. She could see Alan and Lilly on the sidewalk outside, Alan with his BlackBerry to his ear, smiling as he carried on an animated conversation, charming someone, Risa imagined.

Just like his father. Risa looked over at the table Marty Benson used to call his "branch office." He was in The Kitchen most lunches and a lot of dinners brokering whatever deals he had going. Alan tagged along with him often, and he and Risa, who was at the restaurant practically every night, started occupying their time together, doing homework in the office, "helping" the cooks, playing out in the alley. When Sean's father became the principal at the high school, he, with a sick wife who couldn't cook, began coming regularly and held a court of his own, answering parents' questions while he and Sean had dinner. Alan brought Sean into his playgroup with Risa, and the three, all only children, spent many, many hours together in grade school and middle school.

They were close away from the restaurant as well. All three were, in the ways of Braden, children of royalty, and as such often shut out of some social circles. So they leaned on one another. *The Three Amigos* movie came out when they were sixteen. Before they'd even seen the film they'd adopted the title for themselves. Though they weren't constant companions, they relied on one another the way you might rely on a brother or sister. They told one another things they would tell no one else, confessions, crushes, insecurities, and experiments.

They took different paths through high school. Sean, the quintessential principal's kid, underachieved in class and underparticipated outside of class. His father had insisted on him taking piano lessons because his mother had been a fine pianist, and Sean kept up his studies to honor his mother. His father wasn't happy when Sean found jazz and went with that passion, but at least he was still playing the piano. Alan was a model student and made it onto the football team, though he played little. Risa sat somewhere between the two of them. She actually liked her studies and did well; she became a cheerleader, though she wasn't as bubbly and rah-rah as most of the others, and she was active in the Polish Catholic youth group, at least until her senior year.

As they navigated high school, the three never dated one another, though they got teased often about their "love triangle" and asked what a threesome's like. But there seemed to be an assumption among them that somewhere down the road Alan and Risa would marry, settle in Braden, and Alan would enter politics, follow in his father's footsteps. Sean, who had spent the first ten years of his life in Swarthmore, loved going into Philadelphia, spent the summer between his sophomore and junior years in a small town in Spain, and seemed destined to travel after college, see the world.

Alan had known for years that he wanted to go to an Ivy League school and set his sights on Yale early. His father had been the first in his family to go to college but always felt that his own career in politics was dragged down by the lack of pedigree of Mercyhurst, the Catholic college he had attended, and wanted Alan to "go for the gold." Alan was accepted early decision at Yale. A friend two years older than Risa was going to Allegheny College in Meadville, a very good little liberal arts school. Risa applied, it was the first acceptance she got, and she made her decision on the spot. Sean's father had to pull a few strings at the last minute for Sean to go to his alma mater, Penn State.

College not only changed them individually but also altered the dynamics of the Three Amigos. Alan would come home on vacation and talk about things like networking that meant little to Risa and Sean. In her sophomore year, Risa took a studio course in drawing and got hooked, changing her major to fine arts despite her father's pleading with her to do "something useful." Sean found it easier to get interested in studies in college, but he also used the time to, as he used to say, "freak a little." He dropped acid. He played keyboards in a protopunk outfit that was more about getting roaring drunk in front of a crowd than the shitty music they played. Always a good athlete but never interested in varsity sports in high school, Sean took a dare, went to the walk-on tryouts for the Nittany Lions, and made the team as a receiver. Alan, who had been cut from the Yale squad, couldn't believe Sean was going to play for Coach Paterno. As it turned out, he wasn't. Sean quit the team after a week of spring practice, telling the receivers' coach he didn't like all the yelling.

That story, when it made it back to Braden, a place where Coach Paterno was right up there with St. Nicholas, infuriated many but made Risa laugh. She had visited Alan at Yale a few times by then, enjoyed going with him to New York, but their relationship began to feel dutiful to her. Alan was angling for a job in Senator Hathaway's office in Washington and didn't notice Risa was losing interest in following him there. Sean didn't notice it either until Risa suggested she go visit him at State College. He had set up a room for her with a female friend of his, but they didn't use it. Sleeping together for the first time, even though fueled by way too many tequila shooters, didn't feel awkward. In fact, it felt like that had always been going on between them, though it hadn't.

Alan's senior year at Yale was like a sprint to a finish line, with much of his time spent on trips to Washington with his politico friends, trying to get their feet in the door. Risa and

Sean burned up the road between State College and Meadville, though neither Alan nor anyone else in Braden was aware of what was going on.

Only Carol Slezak kept tabs on the shifting relationships. She'd sometimes been labeled the Fourth Amigo, but in high school she didn't have time for much beyond her studies and her invalid parents. She and her sister had to do everything for them, and Carol agonized over her decision to go to college, which would mean leaving her sister with all the responsibility. A social worker from County Medical intervened in the knick of time, got round-the-clock help, and Carol went off to Syracuse.

Carol had gotten serious about political science and liked to jabber with Alan when they saw each other on vacations. Risa thought there might be something going on, something that would help her out of Alan's assumptions, but in her senior year Carol fell in love with a graduate student.

It was then Risa knew she had to have The Conversation with Alan. She and Sean had made plans to take off as soon after graduation as feasible, spend time in Seattle, and then go to either China or Indonesia. But Risa hadn't had The Conversation with Alan before she found out she was pregnant. That happened in April as serious senioritis had hit both Sean and Risa. She waited a week to tell Sean and was surprised when he burst into tears at the news. She had never seen him cry before and at first she couldn't tell if they were tears of joy or sorrow. They were in fact tears for his imagined future. He mumbled something about *It's a Wonderful Life*, and Risa assured him it wasn't going to be like that. She would abort.

They made it to within a mile of a clinic in State College when both of them, lapsed Catholics but not yet completely divorced from the church's teachings, realized they wouldn't be able to let go of the baby. They switched gears, revised their plans, decided to go back to Braden and have their child, and then hit the road. They knew couples who were doing just that. "Babies aren't anchors," was their mantra.

Telling Alan, in person, at Easter vacation was rough. Had he been completely honest with them, with Risa, he would have told her that he'd been having an affair with a Yaley who was going to Washington in the fall as well. He had seen that as "one before the wedding," but he said nothing about it at The Ding Dong the night Risa and Sean faced him across a table and told him the news. He was so blindsided he finished his beer, gave them weak hugs, and left.

Risa's father said he thought the church's abortion prohibition was "old school" and said you had to be ready to have children. "Parents, they should have a license." But her mother was appalled at what her husband was proposing and quickly jumped in. Sean's father, a widower and a single parent who fretted over Sean's plans to travel the world, was at a literal loss for words for minutes before he asked where they would live, how they would get by. Sean gave him a hug. "Always the practical one, Dad."

That may have been so, but it turned out his simple question must have had a mother lode of worry, anxiety, and sorrow behind it. Sean and his father drove back from Sean's graduation in separate cars, Sean leaving later to say goodbye to friends. When he pulled into the driveway, he thought it strange the garage door was closed. That almost never happened even when there was a car inside. Sean went into the house and found the note first, the one that wished him and Risa and the baby the best, the one that said he was leaving everything, the house and his small nest egg, to Sean so the family could get off on a good start. It ended with an apology "for what I'm doing" but said he missed Sean's mother too much not to be with her.

Sean walked slowly out to the garage, realizing his life was changing with each step. His father was still wearing the suitcoat and tie he had worn at the graduation. Sean knew there was no reason to call 911. He cut his father down with hedge shears.

"Risa? You okay?"

Alan was standing across the bar from her, a worried look on his face. She was still back in Sean's garage, at the house she and Sean had eventually moved into, wondering now for the ten thousandth time if doing that, moving into the house instead of selling it, had determined Sean's path. Seeing Alan's face she pulled herself back from that fraught time.

"What?"

"You look spaced out."

"I've got a lot to think about, Alan."

"Well, here's something else." He turned and motioned to Henry, who was sitting at the end of the bar. Risa hadn't even seen him come in, seen Alan come back in, or the two of them talking. "Come here, Henry. Tell Risa what you told me."

Henry came to them, subdued, wary of Risa's response.

"I'm going to have to do a piece on Sean, on his return."

"I said, 'Like hell you are,' right, honey?" Alan didn't often look for Risa's support of his opinions, but he seemed to be doing it now.

"It's not me, but I'm sure as soon as Doris hears Sean's back in town, she's going to want to do some sort of, excuse this but this is her way of framing things, some sort of back-from-the-dead story."

Alan seemed intent on replaying his conversation with Henry.

"How the fuck is she going to find out, that's my question. Right, Risa? She's over there at headquarters. You're her man here. You don't say anything . . ."

"Alan. Forty years at the paper. She knows what you had for breakfast. Or if she doesn't she can find out before you've digested it. I'm just kicking myself for not telling her first I heard from Sean. 'Cause when she does find out she is going to go up one side of me and down the other."

"A back-from-the-dead story," Risa said, almost to herself.

"That's not me. That's her. That's what she's going to say."

"What if Sean doesn't want that?" Risa asked.

"He was in my office, Risa. He came voluntarily. I've got a tape of the conversation. He asks questions about Carol Slezak's murder. Put yourself in my shoes. Or Doris's shoes. Instead of putting a two-car fender-bender on the front page you've got something like a back-from-the-dead."

"Did he agree to be interviewed, to be taped?" Alan asked.

Henry looked Alan in the eye. "Yes. Look, I might be able to get around the stuff about Carol's murder. I mean he just asked questions about it and left. He asked me because I saw the body. And I'll do an uplifting sort of number about his recovery."

"Bullshit, Henry. Bullshit. Doris's gonna want more than that. I can bet you. What if he doesn't want to talk to you anymore?"

"I've got enough, Alan. And tongues are wagging. Go into the restaurant now and I'll bet the news is all over the place out there."

Alan looked at Risa to see if she realized that Henry was missing a crucial piece of the story, that Sean believed he killed Carol. Risa, he guessed, from the way she returned his gaze, was thinking the same thing.

Alan turned to Henry. "When would you run this story?"

"Monday's the next issue. I don't know. I don't think this would be enough for one of Doris's occasionals."

"Gonna need a photograph, aren't you?"

"That would be good but not crucial."

"Well, it wouldn't be possible now."

"How come?"

"He's gone. Left a little while ago, probably halfway to the city by now."

Risa looked at Alan, at the ease with which he floated out this lie.

"I know. He said he was going right back. I thought I might go into New York and see what his life's like there."

"How are you going to find him?"

"He called me from his rehab program. I've got the number. Journalism 101."

Risa gave Alan a warning look before she turned to Henry. "Sean's still here, Henry. In Braden. He wanted to go right back but I urged him to stay for the night. Alan said he'd left because he wants to protect his old friend. But he's here. Let me talk to him tonight and I'll call you in the morning. You can wait that long, can't you?"

"Why don't we cut out the middleman? Tell me where he is and I'll go talk to him. Is he staying with you?"

"No," Alan said quickly. "And I'm sure he doesn't want to talk to any reporter."

Henry looked from Alan to Risa and back again, smelling something amiss.

"He already did. Staying the night. My guess is he's over at one of those apartments you guys have on Front Street."

"You guessed right," Risa said. "But Henry, please, stay away tonight. You saw him. He's not well."

"Looked fine to me."

"Fine?" Risa said, raising her voice. "He agreed to be taped? Not a smart thing to do. Either you preyed on a fragile guy, or he didn't really give you permission to tape and you're bluffing."

Henry stared at her for a second. "I'm going to let that pass, Risa. Those are my ethics you're talking about. And I'll give you tonight. But if I don't hear from you early tomorrow morning, I'll do what I can to see him."

Henry nodded as if he were about to leave. Alan, slipping into an avuncular mode, tugged on Henry's shirt to keep him from going.

"Henry, I want to make sure you know what you're doing. There are two ways people get their news around here. A friend calls them up, they bump into somebody at church, they overhear somebody who overheard somebody, and things get passed around. There's that. Then there's *The Statesman* and TV. Most of the time they've heard the news before you guys get hold of it, but when it's in print, on their computers, on the TV, it's somehow a little more real. Just remember that. You make things real. If people are kicking things around in here, over a beer, it's not as real. You've got a responsibility. You understand?"

Henry looked at Risa to see if she was buying this crap. She wasn't.

"You know, Alan, I've only been here eleven, nearly twelve years. I realize I don't speak the language like a native, but I'm learning. I think I can figure this one out, do what's right. But if I understand what you're saying correctly, I'm not going to be able to hold off on the story until after the election. Sorry."

He turned and left before Alan could respond. Risa and Alan watched him walk out, then turned to each other.

"Jesus, Risa. He believed Sean was gone. What were you doing calling me out like that?"

"It was a dumb lie. It wasn't going to get you anywhere, especially not when somebody was bound to have seen us go into the apartment, seen you there maybe. I'm going to take Sean dinner tonight. I'm going to warn him. Maybe he'll just stonewall Henry tomorrow. For 'our' campaign."

"Man. What's up here? Lies? It's strategy, Risa. Jesus. You can't leave your flank open. And for the record, I told Sean it was your idea to have my driver take him into New York."

"You did, huh? Why'd you want to make me the heavy?"

"It wasn't that. There's stuff between us. You, Kevin. I just thought it was better if he thought you wanted him to leave."

"After we had talked about it?"

"Risa. This isn't some small incident. And it's not just about us, about our relationship to him. Not even about Kevin. There are some things here that can affect thousands and thousands of people."

"The campaign again?"

"Right, the campaign, the future of Braden, maybe even the country. You can question that but think about it. The timing sucks. He's waited eleven years. He can wait a few more months, go back to New York, think about things."

There was something new in the way Alan made his argument, an exaggeration that didn't seem to fit his normally plodding, point-by-point explications. Risa realized there was nothing to be gained by keeping the argument going. "What's on your schedule tonight?"

"Rotary Club dinner in Hazelton."

"We'll see you late, then?"

"Yeah. Think about it, Risa. We just need to keep the lid on."

Risa nodded but couldn't picture a lid that was anything more than a lie. Had she been living under a stone these past few years, hearing and seeing only what she wanted to hear and see? Had Sean's appearance unearthed something new in Alan, or had it been there all along?

Alan left, unholstering his BlackBerry as he went out the door. With every footstep she watched, Risa grew less and less interested in what Alan thought about Sean. All she could see was Sean's face, under the bridge, looking up at her, telling her he'd killed Carol. That was her world now. That and Kevin. The campaign could flap off in the breeze and she wouldn't even know it was gone.

11

Most of the time when it happened it was as if you were listening to a radio station, something nice and soothing, classical or smooth jazz, then someone flipped the dial on you and suddenly, at deafening volume, some crazy-ass metal bullshit was bleeding your ears, but you couldn't find the dial, couldn't turn the motherfucker down.

But this time the horror came over Sean slowly. He had been in the apartment, making notes in a journal he was supposed to be keeping, when he realized what was happening. The room's oxygen was being replaced by the rotten-egg smell of the night and the vision. Sean worked against it, scribbled something as if his pen had become a sword and he could slash against what he knew was on the way. But the sword became a machete, broad and fine edged, and Sean knew there was nowhere to turn for relief. It had come to him again, this time with a tap on the shoulder first, then powerful fingers yanking his jaw away from the journal, then the full show filling the room with its blood and mangled body.

Sean's hands became clammy and he pushed back on the mattress as if he could get away from it physically. But that made no difference. Carol's one intact eye, lifeless but open, became his whole horrible world for a long minute. He thought he was going to throw up, as had happened before. But he didn't even get that relief. The soundtrack pounded, as it always did, with recriminations: *You did this, this was you, you used that blade on that body.*

He stood quickly, trying to jar the vision. He knew closing his eyes would have no effect. He went to a blank wall and jammed his forehead into the sheetrock, hoping the pain would do battle with this thing he couldn't destroy. But the pain was no match for the images that engulfed him now. The dim night, the blood-soaked body, all the product of some dark, vicious rage he had been in, crescendoed, layering snippet upon snippet of gore and guilt in the room until the pressure blew Sean out the door, down the hall, and into the soft, late summer evening.

The torment chased him as he half ran down Front Street, blind to everything around him. At Market he swerved south toward the bridge and found himself by the pathway above where he and Risa had met. The bridge curved out over the shallow water and seemed to call to him over the incessant din of the memory. The town daredevils used to jump off the old bridge in the spring and early summer when the water was high, but come August they knew they were asking for a broken leg or worse if they did so.

The new bridge, with its low sidewall, promised escape. He could pick a spot near the shallow banks and dive headfirst into permanent, everlasting relief. He could be rid of the horror forever. He walked onto the bridge, hugging the left sidewall as a car passed going into Braden. But there was no car for him, only the bloody blade and Carol.

Then something new, another piece, a further snippet. He flung the machete to his right and bent over Carol. That was all. Just that little bit more. But that was how the whole picture had come at first, in increments, devastating new pieces of a puzzle he didn't want to put together. There would be more, he realized now. This wasn't it. What else? Why was he leaning over Carol? Was he going to do her even more damage?

He gripped the sidewall and looked down. The bridge's shadow from a street light spread far out on the water. He picked out a little eddying pool near the bank by the stanchion. He could feel the cool of that water. He could feel the forever obliteration that would give him. He knew all would be over in an instant and he worshipped that instant as the perfect end.

Then suddenly the water's beckoning overtook the horror's howl. Had he jumped? Had it happened? Was he alive? Where was he? He looked down and saw his hand still gripping the sidewall. He heard the swoosh of a car leaving Braden. At the top of the bridge's shadow, bobbing in the river's current, he could see the shadow of his torso and head.

Kevin. Kevin came to him then. If he'd jumped, where would Kevin be? On the bridge behind him, ready to follow his father's lead? Sean whipped his head around as if this could be a real possibility. But no, Kevin wasn't there. There was no reason for him to be there. Sean hadn't jumped. Sean was alive.

Now the sidewall was a flimsy barrier between him and the ultimate fuckup. He stepped back and walked off the bridge. There were no cars, no noise, just the drumbeat of suicide still in his ears, the last wisps of the horror.

At the apartment, he flopped himself on the mattress, exhausted. He saw the woman on the bus asking him if—no, telling him he had seizures. He didn't even question how she had known, why she had asked, if she had been real. His brain had been hijacked by a fury the equal of an epileptic's, compounded by the now certain guilt.

But he hadn't jumped. There was a sliver of redemption in that. Kevin wasn't lining up behind him on the bridge. The light was low in the room. His bones ached. But he could salvage some sense of himself as alive, as able to withstand, and even as a guardian. He would live for Kevin.

And once he realized this, going back to New York seemed to be only a useless detour. He had to stay, to corral himself, to make the DA, Stallings, listen, to get himself where he belonged. The apartment creaked with age or wind or shifting temperatures, but to Sean it sounded like a voice telling him what the woman on the bus had told him. Do what's right.

12

Kevin was stuffed as he stood with Stevie and Ring Tone in the Subway parking lot. He had had a foot-long packed with every kind of cold cut they had and then gone back for a minimeal. It was early, only five o'clock. He knew he'd be hungry again before bedtime, but right now it felt as if he were trying to make his XL T-shirt into an XXL.

It had been a great day for him. His Scrimmage Day performance had given him a confidence he hadn't had before and he found himself running through drills as if he were a captain, yelling encouragement, angling for the front of the line, even in the dreaded one-on-ones against the tackles. Jimmy Robich had come to the practice with his arm in a sling, even though he was out for the season, and Kevin had gone to him, shook his left hand, told him he was sorry. Jimmy didn't say much and Kevin didn't feel all that sorry, really. It was a game. That was what his dad had repeated to him on the phone the night before. It was a game, and he, Kevin, played it hard.

"Yo, dog. One thousand four hundred and thirty-two hits," Ring Tone said, looking up from his BlackBerry. Ring Tone, aka Tom Smolinski, was a geek head who hung with the football players because he and Kevin had been friends since pre-K.

"The Hit?" Kevin asked, though he knew what Ring Tone was talking about.

"No, your first communion."

"That's not much," Stevie said. A year older than Kevin,

he'd been none too happy that Kevin was getting all the notoriety for one goddamn tackle when he knew he'd had one or two just like it in the scrimmage and he knew too that the way he had taken out Malloy had allowed Kevin room to make the Hit.

Kevin didn't know if fourteen hundred hits on YouTube was good or bad. He was about to join the conversation just for something to say when he saw a familiar battered Toyota pull into the parking lot. She'd come after all. He turned away, not wanting to be too obvious. Listening to Stevie and Ring Tone debate YouTube numbers, he was able to catch a glimpse of Ellen Baker's long, tanned legs preceding her out of the driver's seat. She was with two friends. Kevin had been expecting her, though her text earlier was ambiguous. She hadn't shown up by the time he finished his sub and so he had had the minimeal to stall. When she still hadn't shown up, he got Stevie and Ring Tone to hang, not telling them Ellen might show up.

Even though everybody knew everybody at BAHS, it wasn't easy to really get to know another kid unless you had some time alone. Kevin and Ellen had spent six weeks during the summer supervising play at a little water park for toddlers the town had set up. There wasn't much to do. The mothers or babysitters who brought their kids were required to stay with them. All Kevin and Ellen had to do was make sure the hoses were working, the makeshift bathroom was clean, and the place was opened on time. So they talked. A lot.

Ellen lived on a dairy farm a few miles outside of town. She and Kevin had been in Advanced Algebra together but had rarely said more than a few words to each other. Now, after the six weeks, Kevin felt as if he'd known her for a long time, and the more he got to know, the more he liked her. It didn't hurt that she was both willowy and funny.

As Ellen and her friends walked toward them, Kevin didn't know how to handle the situation. Kids at BAHS didn't date, pair off. They clumped. A clump of boys would have a connection to a clump of girls and, as might be the case now with Ellen coming to them, they would sort of meld. But first meldings were always a little awkward.

Ellen took control of this one. "Hi, Kev. You going in or coming out?"

"We're done."

"We're starved. We're going to get something to eat. Hang around, huh?"

"Yeah."

She smiled as she and her two friends passed, as Stevie and Ring Tone gave nonchalance a stab. When they'd gone into Subway, Stevie looked up quickly.

"You know she was going to be here?"

"Nope. Pure coincidence."

"Thanks, man. She was in front of me in Global. Got me through."

The door hadn't been closed more than a couple of seconds when two forty-something factory workers, hoarse-voiced, in work clothes, one with a mullet, came out and passed by Kevin. As they did, the one without the mullet, a man with piercing, cruel blue eyes, did a double take on Kevin and spoke to his friend, purposefully loud enough for anyone nearby to hear.

"Fuckin' cheap shot artist."

He stared at Kevin and kept moving. The stare, with its malice and grown-up hostility, froze Kevin. He looked away.

When the two men were out of earshot, Stevie spoke up. "That's Robich's uncle Frankie."

"Looks like an upstanding citizen," Ring Tone said.

The three of them broke up, their voices louder than they intended. Kevin looked over and saw Frankie stop and look back.

"Shut up guys."

Too late. Frankie handed his sandwich package to his friend and strode back to the group. Kevin had rarely been in anything resembling a fight, and his stomach knotted now as Frankie's stare lasered him from ten yards away.

"Somethin' funny over here?"

"Not about you," Stevie said, angling so his wide-body frame was between Frankie and Kevin. Frankie ignored him.

"I'm asking the fucking cheap-shot artist here. Anything funny I should know about?"

"No," Kevin said as Frankie continued toward him. Ring Tone, slight and not the least bit interested in pissing off this torpedo, backed away.

"Put my nephew out for the season when he had scouts lookin' at him. That hilarious?"

In fact it was. The only scout that might have interest in Jimmy Robich was of the Boy variety. Stevie could not suppress a grin. Frankie didn't catch it but Kevin did, and he must have had a pale reflection of it on his face because Frankie cranked it up a notch.

"Joke boy, huh? You want to spear me illegally like you speared Jimmy?"

"No."

"No? How come? No helmet?"

"No."

"What the fuck, then."

He was several inches shorter than Kevin, wiry and muscled. He'd clearly been here before. He lunged forward quickly with both hands and thumped Kevin on the chest, a provocation. The blow surprised Kevin, but he stood his ground. It reminded him of pregame warm-ups in the locker room, when you'd thump each other just to get the blood and adrenaline flowing. It certainly did that for Kevin now.

"No chance for a cheap shot here, huh, asshole? Want me to turn my back?"

Kevin didn't answer. They were standing very close now, cars and planters near the building hemming all of them in. Kevin couldn't hold Frankie's vicious stare and looked away, catching a glimpse of Ellen, in line inside Subway, looking out at him. He started to turn back to Frankie when Frankie caught him with a hard slap to the face.

It was all reflex then for Kevin. He didn't know how to punch, but he knew how to tackle. He dodged Frankie's second swipe, this one with a fist, lowered his upper body, drove forward with his thighs, buried his head in Frankie's now-exposed chest, wrapped his arms around him, then pulled up with his arms as he churned forward. Frankie left his feet much as his nephew had, his head whiplashing back. Forgetting he wasn't on turf, Kevin drove Frankie toward the pavement. But the force of his powerful, trained legs took them a few yards back, and as they came down Kevin heard Frankie's head hit the concrete rim of a planter.

Kevin sprawled over Frankie as the taut body went limp. He rolled off, his hand deeply scraped, and could see Frankie wasn't moving.

The next few minutes were chaos in slow motion for Kevin. Frankie's mullet friend rushing in, screaming, Stevie screaming back that it wasn't Kevin's fault, Ring Tone trying to get an ambulance, people pouring out of the Subway, cars on the street stopping. Kevin didn't know what to do. The whole thing felt like a good hit in practice, like a coach should be coming to him now and banging his shoulder pads. But there was a guy on the ground bleeding and inert. This wasn't right.

He looked over at the gawkers staring out of Subway and saw Ellen looking at him. She wasn't staring, wasn't accusing, but she wasn't neutral. She seemed to be searching, to be asking herself a question. Is that really Kevin?

13

Risa was about to cross Market, a take-out dinner for Sean in her right hand, when an ambulance blew past her and she stopped. It wasn't as close as the bus had been a day earlier, but she realized she was in a fog. She kept moving toward the apartment. As she turned down Front Street her phone buzzed a couple of times, but she let it go. Against her wishes, counter to what she felt, she had to tell Sean to leave early in the morning, to dodge Henry.

Sean was sitting on the mattress, back to the wall with no lights on in the room when Risa knocked and pushed open the door.

"Sean?"

He got up quickly but didn't come to her. He stood awkwardly and Risa could see that something was off.

"Are you okay?"

"Not really. I don't want you to see me this way."

Risa moved farther into the room.

"Mind a light?"

"Yeah. I do. Let's just . . . Is that dinner?"

"Yes. See you what way?"

"I went through the ringer an hour or so ago. A bad one. I don't know what I look like. I feel like shit. Thanks."

He reached out for the bags as Risa looked carefully through the dim light. He didn't seem all that bad, but it was hard to tell.

"What is it, Sean? Like a hallucination?"

"I wish. It's more real than real. I can't explain it. The only guy who really knows what I'm talking about is this guy in my group, a vet, who had half his brain blown off by an IED He knows the real I'm talking about."

"What can I do for you?"

"Nothing. This food will be good."

He remained standing, remained holding the bags, as if waiting for Risa to make a quick exit.

"Henry Saltz, the reporter, says he's going to come over tomorrow morning and talk to you some more. He thinks he's going to have to do an article on your return."

"You told him I was here?"

"He guessed or knew somehow. Word's probably out all over town. I think you should leave before he gets here, go back to New York."

"Alan wanted me to leave today, with his driver."

"I know. And that wasn't my idea."

"I didn't think so. That's part of the reason I stayed. He do that often now?"

"What?"

"White lies."

"Part of his profession, I guess. But now I do think you should go. You need to . . . to talk to people like that vet, people who know how to help you. Those things you see may seem real, Sean, but they could never be."

"I can't go back. I'm too afraid of what I might do there. I'm going to go to John Stallings's office tomorrow and turn myself in.

"Sean, please."

"I didn't want to see you, Risa. I didn't want to dump this all in your lap or Kevin's."

"Then why did you come back? You could have talked to Henry over the phone."

"You don't understand. I needed to be sure. I needed to see the look on his face, to know he was being honest with me."

"And you're sure now?"

"Yes."

"Why? Because what you think you saw was what Henry saw. You were in the hospital, you were, I don't know, drugged up, in shock, having surgery, and somebody came along and said, 'Oh, and we found out this and that about where you grew up and that one of your friends was murdered.' And maybe you didn't absorb it all until later."

"It didn't happen that way."

Risa tried a new tack.

"In these memories, is G.G. with you?"

"No. He had nothing to do with the murder."

"He confessed."

"It was a false confession. Very easy for the cops to get a false confession out of G.G. There's a lawyer in Pittsburgh. Hamilton. Charles Hamilton. Specializes in false confessions. He's been working on G.G.'s case. He's found this guy who was in jail over in Scranton with G.G. when they first arrested him. The guy said the cops came to him, gave him details of the murder, and had him pump G.G. full of the details."

"And he just repeated them?"

"Yup."

"Bullshit. Impossible."

"You knew G.G."

"Yeah, but they couldn't make him say that sort of thing."

"They could if they made him believe he actually did it. He knew how to wash dishes and clean floors. He loved to chop brush with his machete. That was his world. All they had to do was convince him he'd sleepwalked or something, maybe showed him pictures of the body and made him feel bad. They say you can hear him crying on the tape while he's confessing, quote, unquote."

Risa was about to reply when her cell phone buzzed in her pocket. She took it out, saw it was Alan, and didn't answer. She was pissed at Sean now, not for his abandonment, not for his reappearance, but for cutting into the delicate hold she had on the truth of what had happened to Carol. The murder had come at such a difficult time for her that she'd had trouble accepting it, grieving, and then reliving it all through the trial eight months later. But she had been helped by the certainty of the prosecution. G.G. had been a time bomb, John Stallings had said in his closing, and Carol had been a friend to him. G.G. just exploded and Carol happened to be in the way. It was tragic, but it was irrefutable.

Now Sean and some lawyer in Pittsburgh were coming in to stir that pot again. She couldn't have that.

"He was a time bomb. G.G."

"Stallings said that."

"But he was."

"Maybe, but he didn't go off with Carol. She was good to him."

Risa knew that ever since Carol had started to waitress at The Ding Dong, she and G.G. had been close. Carol had been able to make the sullen G.G. laugh in ways that were a surprise to all the regulars.

"Forget about G.G. You weren't around when Carol was murdered."

"I must have been. And they don't know for sure what day she was killed."

Both of these were true, Risa knew, though at the time it had been her assumption that Sean had taken off long before Carol was murdered. She had forgotten the exact dates now, willfully putting them out of her mind years ago, but she remembered last seeing Sean on a Saturday, getting none of the usual reports about him in one of his haunts or sleeping somewhere for over a week and then hearing about Carol's body being found.

Nobody really knew how long Carol had been missing either. She had been making three- and four-day trips to Syracuse to be with her boyfriend, and when people didn't see her they assumed she was with him. The boyfriend was a lab rat who would go days without communicating with Carol and so too he wasn't expecting to hear from her.

The upshot was that Carol and Sean could have been in Braden at the same time.

"There's something else," Sean said. "But I don't think you want to hear it."

"What?"

"This is hard. About a month after I got this news about Carol, you know, I'd been thinking about her a lot and everything, and memory started coming back of things before I left, I remembered very clearly, could see it all, that she and I slept together."

Risa flinched. Her cell phone buzzed again but this time she didn't even look at it.

"It was before things got really, really bad, maybe one of the last things I can remember. She would drive me home from The Ding Dong. One night we went to her house. I don't know why. I know her sister was there and her mother was like always, you know, in a fog. I remember something about me helping her, telling some asshole who was harassing her to get lost, but I'm not sure when that was. Maybe that night. I'm . . ."

"Don't say you're sorry." Risa, stung by both the revelation and the evocation of those dark days before Sean's disappearance, flashing on long talks with Carol about Sean, didn't know whether to turn heel or let him have it.

"Don't turn yourself in. Please."

"You don't know what I just went through, Risa. I have to get this done."

"You can't. It's too much. Not now."

"Have you heard me, Risa? Do you realize this is life or death for me? I was on the bridge a couple of hours ago trying to stop the pain by diving headfirst into the river. Kevin was the only thing that kept me from doing it."

"Get yourself committed."

"Maybe that's what they'll do with me."

"Just wait, will you?"

They were close now, but there'd be no kiss on the cheek this time.

"I'm too scared of what I might do. And I have to do what's right too. Don't I? For Carol? For G.G.?"

"For me? For Kevin?"

"You'll see. It's for you and Kevin too."

"Don't say that, Sean. Leave. Come to your senses. Please."

Sean drew in a deep breath and looked into the bags of food as if some answer might be there. But when he looked back up he could only shake his head no.

14

Risa's phone buzzed a couple of times on her walk home, but she was too tangled in her thoughts to answer. As she came close to her house she saw that Kevin's bedroom light was on. She was hoping he was out. She needed time to think, to figure out what she could do. She went up her driveway and into the house through the kitchen. Kevin was coming toward her from the living room as she reached the island, his face drawn and worried.

"Hi, hon. You're home."

"You talk to Dad, Mom?"

"No. He called but I didn't answer. I think he's in Hazelton."

"He's coming home." Kevin took a deep breath. "Mom, something happened."

"To him?"

"To me."

"To you? What?"

"I got attacked. By Jimmy Robich's uncle."

"Attacked?"

"He started saying things outside Subway. He shoved me, slapped me."

"My God. Are you all right?"

"Yeah, but he isn't."

"What do you mean?"

"I tackled him. Like in a drill. Just to stop him. It was instinct.

He went down and hit his head. They took him to the hospital. He's unconscious."

Tears welled in Kevin's eyes now, and Risa went to him, putting an arm around his waist.

"God, Kevin."

"Mom, I swear, you can ask Stevie, Ring Tone, he just came at me."

"I'm sure."

"I just wanted to get him away from me, you know. He was calling me a cheap-shot artist."

"And he hit you first?"

"Yeah. Twice."

They heard a car door shut in the driveway. Through the kitchen window, Risa could see Alan get out of the passenger side of his car and head for the garage. She saw his rage-filled face, his stride, and she steeled herself, ready to protect Kevin if Alan unleashed that fury on her son.

But Kevin didn't share this worry. "Dad knows. He said he'd handle it."

When Alan came into the kitchen he looked from Kevin to Risa, bull breaths heaving his chest.

"Why didn't you answer?" he hurled at Risa. She didn't respond but her silence told him to get to the business at hand. Alan slowed a little and turned to Kevin. "You all right?"

"Yeah."

"Mel said he'd handle things. They're not considering it a criminal case, but if this asshole wants to press charges they're going to have to do something."

"Like what?" Kevin asked.

"I don't know, Kev. They may have to arrest you, but it would be nothing, just a formality."

Risa reacted to this, leaving Kevin, heading toward Alan. "How is he?"

"Robich? He's in a coma. They think he's going to be all right."

"A coma?"

"It's not as bad as you think. They may even deliberately keep him in the coma for a day or so for some sort of healing reason, pressure on the brain, I don't know."

Risa turned to Kevin. He couldn't read her look.

"Mom, he just kept coming after me."

She went to him, but he was so much bigger than she now that her hug was awkward.

"Mel said the cops all know what happened, there are about ten witnesses who say just what Kevin said. We don't have to worry. It's just the timing of the thing. They're going to try to keep a lid on this, just call it a fight. He called Jack Armey at home."

Mel Carney was Braden's answer to a fixer. He was a lawyer with some sort of goods on most people of influence in the county. He was a DUI specialist, people joked that his office was on the ninth tee at Cresthill, he was divorced, and though he was in his fifties, had twenty-year-olds on his arm constantly. Risa thought of him as a cartoon. Alan had always agreed with her but said he was a necessary evil on the local landscape and a useful one at times. Risa now hated the thought of Kevin having anything to do with him.

"Can't you just handle this yourself, Alan?"

"Me? Are you kidding? First of all, you never handle your own family's cases. Second, why would I want to shoot myself in the foot by getting publicly involved with this?"

"Because he's your son."

"Right. And you know what Errol Roberts would do with that?"

"I don't care what Errol Roberts would do with that. He's your son. He needs a good lawyer."

"Trust me. Mel's the best at this sort of thing."

"What's that? Sweeping dirt under the rug? My son was attacked. He protected himself. I want everybody to know that."

"Stevie said he was going to tell everybody, Mom."

"Yeah, well, there's Stevie's everybody and then there's everybody's everybody. I want this out there, Alan. I don't want people whispering about Kevin."

"You want them shouting about me instead, huh?" Alan's chest began to heave again.

"Give me that choice and I'll take it, yes. But you're just scared. How's this going to affect your campaign? It was all right for your campaign when he hit Jimmy Robich, but this isn't all right?"

Risa regretted saying this in front of Kevin as soon as it was out of her mouth. But she didn't want to back down.

"Kevin, maybe you should let Mom and me talk about this alone."

"Okay, but there's one more thing. Just before you guys came back, I got a text. Some guy in Subway might have shot a phone video. I don't know if it's true or not. It might be one of those things that just flies around."

"That's not good."

"It may just be some bull, Dad."

"But it would help, wouldn't it?" Risa asked. "It would prove Kevin was innocent."

Alan grabbed a tumbler from the cupboard, went to the sink, drew a glass of water, and downed half of it.

"Just give us a moment, will you, Kev."

When Kevin was gone, Alan and Risa were quiet, staring for a moment. Then Alan started.

"We got word today that Joe Tomlin wants to do an event and it has to be next Wednesday. We've gotta get this thing and that other nonsense cleaned up before then. I don't want to be out there fielding questions about a fight and some crazy with one of the most powerful senators in the country standing next to me, rolling his eyes, wondering why this shit is getting play and his agenda's not."

"The crazy is Sean?"

"Of course."

"Well, maybe you ought to reschedule."

Alan snorted. "Yeah. 'Hi, Joe, love to have you come but could we put it off for a month or so?' Joe Tomlin's like fuckin' Vince Lombardi. He says sit you don't even look for a chair, you just sit."

"Don't count on Sean being gone."

"No? Why not? He said he'd be on a bus tomorrow."

"Not when I talked to him half an hour ago."

"Why did you talk to him?"

"I told you I was going to. I took him dinner. I asked him to leave."

"What'd he say?"

"He said he has to turn himself in."

"Good luck with that. See what I mean about crazy?"

"He sounds sane otherwise. Did you know there's some lawyer in Pittsburgh who thinks he can prove G.G. didn't kill Carol?"

"There's always some lawyer who thinks he can prove somebody didn't do something. Shit. What did he say new?"

"Sean? He definitely could have been around then. And he had these memories of seeing the machete and her body before he knew anything about the murder."

"That it?"

"He said he remembers Carol helping him." Risa couldn't go further with that. It was too raw. She didn't know how Alan would react. He might even say he knew Carol and Sean had slept together. That would be the worst.

"Shit, everybody helped him back then. He didn't chop them up. Sorry. I apologize. What makes you think he's going to stay around?"

"He said so. He said he wants to get things cleared up."

"Goddamn it. Stallings is going to throw his ass out in a

second, but if he starts bleating to Henry . . . I just gotta keep a lid on this till Thursday."

"Why do you think Stallings won't listen to him? He's the DA. Doesn't he have to listen?"

"He doesn't even have to meet with him if he doesn't want to. And trust me, he sure as shit doesn't want to meet with him."

"How do you know?"

"'Cause I talked to him, of course. Gave him a heads-up."

"And?"

"And, like I said, he probably won't even give him a meeting."

"Wait a minute, Alan. There's something else you're forgetting here. Carol's got a say in this. If Sean's right, then she hasn't gotten justice yet and G.G. shouldn't be where he is."

"Yeah, yeah, yeah. But not now."

"Hey, don't yeah, yeah, yeah this! Now you're sounding like that sleazebag Mel Carney. And by the way, I don't want him having anything to do with Kevin."

"Too late. He's the attorney of record."

"So change it." Alan was about to answer when his phone rang. "Is that Lilly? Tell her to get lost."

Alan ignored this and answered the call. He moved away from Risa, listening. She fumed. He said nothing but made a couple of grunts, then hung up.

"Father Vubich is at the hospital."

"My God. Last rites," Risa said with growing horror.

"Frankie Robich hasn't seen the inside of St. Cyrillic's since his baptism."

"Maybe his wife has."

"They said it wasn't life-threatening." Alan sounded worried now himself.

"In a coma? Did you see Kevin? He's shaken now. What if something worse happens?"

"It wasn't his fault." Alan turned his back on Risa, thinking.

"Well, Frankie Robich didn't trip."

"I know, but he pushed Kev."

Risa looked to make sure Kevin hadn't come back downstairs. "Right. But Kevin reacted the way he'd been taught, Alan. He said that. It was a drill. That's what he said. Only they didn't have pads and they weren't on grass. Nice lesson for a kid to learn."

Alan turned back. "Hey, I'm proud of him. He defended himself." Risa shook her head. Alan saw an opening. "Can't we work together on this, Risa? Go back to Sean. Get him to leave. I'll take care of all the shit with Kevin. I promise Mel won't play any tricks."

Risa was tired of words. She just wanted to go to Kevin, sit with him, make sure he was all right.

"I don't know if I can see Sean again right now."

"Get to him before Henry does. Take him up to Scranton if you have to. There are buses out of there all night."

"He's not going to go."

"Work him, Risa. For us. I want us all up on that stage Wednesday. You, me, and Kevin. There may be stuff flying around but we'll show them we're together on this. We get past that we can deal with the long-term."

Risa imagined driving Sean to Scranton, putting him on a bus to New York. She had taken those buses for escape, for pleasure in the city. She had often wondered if that was how Sean had disappeared. She wanted him to go now, to gather himself, to find out if what he was seeing was real. But she wondered if she could be the one to put him on that bus, to watch that bus leave the station. No, she wouldn't be the one to do that.

15

As predicted, Doris Whiting heard about Sean's return through her extensive network of informers and called Henry immediately. When she found out that Henry had been sitting on his information about the reappearance, she was, at first, surprisingly low-key. But when Henry told her that Sean was asking questions about Carol Slezak's murder, that Sean knew details without, supposedly, having seen crime scene photographs, Doris dropped any pretense of civility.

"Jesus fucking Christ on a stick. You taken up pot down there? What do you mean you don't know why he was asking those questions, what it means?"

"Well—"

"It means he was fucking there! And he wasn't there as a CSI, right? You didn't see him when you trooped out there with your goddamn paper bag." Doris had never quite gotten over the fact that she had sent a greenhorn to cover the murder.

"No, but why was he there?" Henry of course had an idea why he was there, but it didn't square with the gentle man who had come to his office.

"Okay. It's not pot. It's very early onset Alzheimer's, or a concussion. You been playing football without a helmet, Henry?"

"No, but he did, or something like it."

"So you said. He's got a brain injury like half the kids comin' back from Iraq. But he remembers what the Slezak girl looked like. Henry, think. He was practically begging for you to connect the dots. He's saying he killed her."

"That couldn't be."

"'Cause of G.G.?"

"Yeah."

Henry and Doris had gone round and round about G.G.'s guilt for years. Doris didn't believe the confession G.G. had made and tried to get Henry to dig into it, to see if there was any contamination, any tinkering, cajoling, any dirty business, but Henry hadn't done so. He stuck with the arguments presented in court, and Doris never found any source to back up her hunch.

"Fuck, Henry, let's leapfrog that shit, huh? Get your ass over to wherever he's staying and get him to tell you why he's here, why he's asking those questions, why he knows so much. Say he's got some legit case against himself. I can't imagine why the fuck he would come back. Maybe he knows Stallings and Armey wouldn't touch him with a ten-foot pole. Maybe he thinks he's got immunity or something. But shit, wouldn't you love to have a full confession from him and flap that in Jack Armey's face?"

That was the last thing Henry wanted. As he pedaled toward the Front Street apartment, this time armed with a minirecorder and a notebook, he carried his own guilt about the resolution of Carol Slezak's murder. He had been so young and so scared of screwing up his first big story that he hugged the shore. Sheriff Armey had put the fear of God in him at the time and he couldn't imagine running afoul of the big-bellied Vietnam vet.

Plus he was certain G.G. was guilty. Maybe G.G. was, as the defense tried to prove, mentally incapacitated, but that didn't alter the fact that he had killed Carol. Henry tried to remember what people had said over the years since the trial, what they'd heard. Wasn't there something about G.G. writing letters to Carol? That sounded right, but he drew a blank when he tried to recall specifics.

Sean was sitting on the front steps of the apartment building, wearing a Yankees ball cap, when Henry rode up. Henry didn't recognize him at first and started to go into the building.

"Risa said you were coming tomorrow morning," Sean said.

"Oh, it's you. The hat. Mind if I sit?"

"Nope. But if you're looking for an interview, I can't help you."

Henry sat and pulled his minirecorder out of his fanny pack. "Let's not call it an interview. A conversation. Mind if I tape this time?"

"What difference does it make? I said no the last time and you taped me anyway." Sean gave him an even look, and Henry realized he'd underestimated him.

"Sorry about that. So."

"So let me ask you. The machete. Where did they find it?"

"Off in the bushes."

"Like it had been thrown there? Not hidden?"

"I guess. Why?"

"Just wondered." Sean yanked at the bill of his cap and shook his head. Another detail corroborated.

Henry gave him a few seconds, then launched into the question he'd been rehearsing on the way over. "You were there, weren't you?"

Sean looked down at the sidewalk, then reached over and took the minirecorder from Henry's hand before Henry knew what he was doing. Sean turned the machine off but still held the recorder.

"I'm just going to tell you one thing. G.G. Trask didn't kill Carol. If I were you, I'd pursue that story or angle or whatever you call it."

"How do you know?"

"You'll find out soon enough, but let's just say I didn't get my information from a little birdie."

"You saw the real killer?"

Sean let out a long sigh but didn't respond to the question. He handed the recorder back to Henry and stood. "Interview's over. Is Doris Whiting still at the paper?"

"Yes. She's the one who sent me out here tonight. She thinks—"

"Say hello for me. She did me a favor once, when my dad died. Tell her I still remember that."

"Wait. G.G.? How do you—?"

"Sorry, Henry. Not now."

Sean didn't want to go back into the apartment. He feared the return of the horror, the night alone there. But he didn't want to sit with Henry. He didn't want to tell him what he was going to tell Stallings in the morning. He figured he'd wait for Henry to leave, then wander some, keep moving, get away from the room and the bridge. Make it through the night and in the morning get everything off his chest.

Doris Whiting. Even though everybody in town knew his father had committed suicide, Doris reported only that the death was under investigation. Doris and his father had been close, and when Sean saw Doris openly weeping at the calling hours, he wondered if they had been closer than he realized, wondered if she had been just as blindsided by the suicide as he had been.

He turned on the light in the apartment and through the window saw Henry pedal away. He had come close to telling Henry what he now knew as fact, but when the words began forming in his head, they seemed so foreign, even more so than they had when he had used them to tell Risa of his guilt. He held the machete, he threw it in the bushes, he had used it on Carol, but was that really him? He wasn't going to duck responsibility, say he was blacked out, say he was taken over by some evil twin. He'd be unequivocal about his own guilt.

But he couldn't imagine where the fury he'd used to kill Carol had come from. He'd never been in a fight in his life; the minor violence of football turned him off. Risa had loved that about him. That was probably why she was refusing to believe what he was telling her. But he believed it himself. That was all that was important. And he would make Stallings and Armey and all of them believe it too.

The flung kitchen chair shot across the room, doing a crazy lethal cartwheel before shattering the glass-front cupboard above the kitchen counter. Risa stood in heart-pounding horror as the chair snagged momentarily on the sink lip, then dropped to the floor. Sean lurched out the back door.

Risa stood transfixed. The memory echoed. It had come to her after Alan had left for the Rotary dinner in Hazelton. She was alone in the kitchen, and the moment, the height of Sean's violence as far as she could remember, had scared the hell out of her. He had never come close to hitting her, but the fury of the hurled chair had surprised her so much she couldn't scream, couldn't cry. Kevin, probably four at the time, had heard the breaking glass and had come down to see what happened. He found Risa sweeping up. She came to him quickly, turned him back, took him upstairs, and put him back to bed.

From then on, as the fights increased in frequency and intensity, Sean would stumble out the back door before his rage sent him groping for a chair, or worse. But the garage got its share of abuse, broom handles snapped, garbage cans thrown so hard the thick plastic cracked, the back window smashed.

Was this some sort of proof that Sean was capable of killing Carol? Maybe, but she still couldn't imagine Sean choking Carol, hacking her with a machete. Risa's cell phone buzzed, and she saw it was Lilly Barkin calling. Lilly was the last person she wanted to talk to then, but she worried that something might have happened to Alan and she answered.

"Lilly?"

"Risa, I've got to talk to you. Got a minute?"

"Yes," Risa answered reluctantly.

"You talked to Alan, right? You know we've got this golden opportunity dropped in our lap Wednesday, right?"

Risa could barely remember what Alan had said, something about Joe Tomlin coming.

"Yes."

"We've got five, six hours with him here and we want to make the most of it. This is Alan's chance to get some national exposure, and we think the best way to do that is with some photo op around Braden. We thought about going over to the stadium, setting something up there with Kevin and all, but that might not be a good idea right now."

"No," Risa said, expecting the conversation to turn to Kevin and his problem. But it didn't.

"So, what better than The Kitchen? Family business, heart of the heart of coal country, apple pie America, and yet a rich history of union involvement. We thought we'd get a cake made, decorate the restaurant, and serve Tomlin a special meal. We know you do a great job with that sort of thing. You can pull that together by Wednesday, can't you?"

"I don't know. Maybe Bell could—"

"No offense but we'd rather have you do it."

"Bell's very good and she could use the extra pay."

"Well, there won't be any extra pay from the campaign, and we really want to be able to highlight the wife." Lilly stopped herself, knowing she'd let fly the after-hours designation for Risa.

"The wife will have to think about it. I've got a lot going on."

"I'm sorry, Risa. I'm running around like a head with my chicken cut off. I'm sincere, though. It's your business and it is the heart of Braden. We can see great shots of you, Alan, and

Joe going out all over the country. We can get you help. Some kids from the community college. They can do the legwork."

"I'll see, Lilly."

"I'll call tomorrow morning, let you sleep on it."

"Okay."

They hung up and, as always after talking with Lilly, Risa wanted to punch something. Lilly obviously knew about Kevin's incident, but instead of mentioning it directly, maybe talking about it parent to parent, she had simply referred to it as some sort of impediment to the campaign. Get The Kitchen ready for some photo op, that was all Lilly cared about. Risa couldn't even begin to think about that.

Kevin came into the kitchen, his head buried in his phone, texting. He didn't look like the scared kid who had come to her earlier.

"How are you doing, Kev?"

Kevin didn't look up as he spoke. "I'm okay. Coach called."

"What did he say? Kevin. Will you stop texting while we're talking, please."

Kevin gave her his usual "chill, Mom" look but stopped his flying fingers.

"He said I don't have to practice tomorrow if I don't want to."

"That's good."

"But I'm going to go in."

"To practice?"

"Yeah."

"Why?"

"I'm on a team, Mom."

"But didn't you say it was the practice that made you react the way you did?"

"Yeah, but you heard Dad. I protected myself. So it was a good thing I had that practice, right?"

Risa saw the spin. His football training had saved him. That was going to be the party line now. A man lay in a coma but he had started the fight and Kevin had been able to protect himself. Kevin went to the refrigerator, got sandwich stuff, and started heaping meat on mayonnaised bread.

"Oh, Stevie says Robich was never in a coma. It's a concussion, like, big-time concussion."

"Is he conscious?"

"I guess so."

"Guess so?"

"I don't know. Stevie just said it wasn't a coma. I looked it up. You can get a concussion that knocks you out for a while."

Risa thought about calling Molly Nimmons, a nurse, to see if she could get any more information. She watched Kevin spreading more mayonnaise, making a ceremony of layering cheese, bologna, and ham. He felt her staring and looked up.

"What, Mom? You still worried?"

"Well, yes."

"It's gonna be okay. Dad's gonna take care of things. Coach wasn't worried."

"But this guy, Robich, Frankie."

"I know. I know what you mean, but he's going to be okay."

"I hope so."

Kevin put the sandwich fixings away, put his sandwich on a plate, and started back upstairs.

"You know what they're saying? When this gets out we're going to have some tough teams shaking in their boots."

"Who says that?"

"You know, guys, online, it's just a joke, you know?"

"No I don't, Kevin. Come back here just a second. This isn't just a joke."

"I didn't mean that."

"Yes, you did. What happened to you? I came home and you were practically in tears."

"Mom, I wasn't . . ."

"You were, Kevin. And now you're calling it a joke."

"I meant other teams shaking in their boots."

"Yeah, and why would they be shaking? Because you put some guy in the hospital? Because you're this, I don't know, badass brawler?"

"Mom, that was the first fight I've ever been in. There are guys—"

"I don't care about guys. I care about you."

"So what do you think? Think I'm some brawler?"

"That's going to be your reputation."

"No, Mom. I'm a football player. That . . . that thing was a one-time deal. That guy was off and way out of line. That won't happen again. Trust me."

Suddenly the hurled chair returned for Risa and scared her again. Sean's violence. Kevin's. Did she have her head in the sand? Was she denying some truth that was practically jumping up and down for recognition?

"Mom? I'm going upstairs. Anything else?

He tried to give Risa something like a reassuring look before he gestured with his plate toward the stairs. Risa wondered if this was the time to tell him about Sean's return. She had the words in the pipeline. Kevin seemed okay now, able to take the news. But she held back and Kevin left. She'd say something in the morning, when Alan was back and the three of them could talk.

She stood at the sink for a while before a knock on the window of the back door made her jump. She looked and couldn't at first make out who was behind the glass. Then the knocker leaned down and she saw it was Henry.

"Sorry to surprise you, Risa," he said, starting to come through the door. "I just talked to Sean. I wanted to talk to you."

Risa looked back to make sure Kevin had gone upstairs. She ushered Henry back to the door. "Let's talk outside."

A waning full moon was rising over the Susquehanna as they went a little ways down the driveway to Henry's parked bike. The moon would normally soothe Risa, but its slightly lopsided perch over the river was unsettling. It looked misplaced. She turned to Henry when she felt they were out of earshot of the house.

"You said you'd wait until tomorrow to see him," she began. "You lied, Henry."

"Doris called. I didn't have a choice."

"So what did he say?"

"He didn't say much. But he did say G.G. didn't kill Carol. I asked how he knew and he wouldn't really say. But you don't have to be a genius to figure it out. I guess he's saying he did it."

"Maybe."

"Yeah, but that can't be right. G. G. Trask murdered Carol, by himself. Period. That's why I'm here talking to you. I'm going to tell Doris he's sick, doesn't know what he's talking about, and that an article about him would be inappropriate, an embarrassment. I just want to make sure you are okay with that."

"Did he seem sick to you?"

"No."

"But what he's saying sounds sick, right?"

"Right."

"And it couldn't be true, could it?" Risa tried to give this conviction, but she couldn't hide her doubts.

"No. Doris wants to use this to embarrass Armey. I'm going to tell her we'd be the ones who would be embarrassed if we ran an article."

"Good." Risa looked up at Kevin's bedroom window. "Try to keep this quiet, will you? Until things get resolved."

"Sure."

As Henry rode away, Risa looked out at the jagged moon, higher and brighter now over the scarred coal hills south of the river. She felt as if the town's surface calm was giving way to dangers. Until things get resolved? What could relief look like now? The man she had loved, her son's father, a killer? Where was the relief in that? She took this sort of thinking as far as she could, but when she came to a certain point she stopped cold. She could never bring herself to wish Sean had, in fact, died.

16

Alan had made it to the Rotary Club dinner just as plates were being cleared. He apologized to his florid-faced host, made sure he swept through the kitchen to thank the Auxilary women for making what he was sure a great dinner, then took the podium to deliver a stump speech to the fifty or so attendees, mostly men in their sixties. He stumbled a few times in his talk. His mind drifted and he blew his cap-and-trade line, one that usually got some sort of reaction. He found his footing when he inserted a line about the Hazelton downtown renovation proposal, saying the plans, which he hadn't read himself, were the most exciting things happening in the whole district. He got applause for this, skipped a section on immigration that he knew was tricky in a town now dependent on Mexican laborers, and rushed to the finish. He was in the car and back on the road to Braden, with the Rotary Club a faint memory, before he knew it.

His driver, Frank Tartaglia, handed Alan his flask and waited until the first couple of swigs hit his boss before he spoke.

"Somethin' eatin' you tonight, huh?"

"It showed when I was up there?"

"Naw. I can just tell. I'm guessin' it's your buddy Sean just come back's got you twisted up."

"Yeah."

Twisted up is right. Like he'd been twisted up eleven, twelve years earlier, maybe even before that, when he saw what was happening to Risa, how things were coming apart for her. He had forgiven her the mistake she had made marrying Sean. He couldn't tell her directly then, but he had never stopped loving her. He did what he could to help her, but fucking Sean was always there to throw her off track. And now look at this. He's back pretending he's all better, making like this great, what, humanitarian 'cause he's going to confess to a crime. And Risa, lovely Risa, whom Alan had sheltered, kept from Sean's clutches, was being sucked back into his fucking loosey-goosey, aimless life.

"His father strung himself up, didn't he?" Frank asked. Alan looked over at Frank's bobbing, way-too-black-for-his-age walrus mustache.

"Yeah."

"Shitty thing to do to a kid, huh?"

Frank looked over for some sort of confirmation, but Alan was sunk in his own thoughts. The Johnnie Walker was working for him now, taking him from tender thoughts of Risa to a sour assessment of the current situation.

"Let me ask you this, Frank. You help a guy out years ago, save his fucking ass big time. Then you work like a dog to help people, to help the guy's wife and kid, and you're right there, you know, right where you want to be, and what happens? The shit shows up again like a fucking stink bomb in the classroom. Is that gratitude?"

"That's the shits. Over in the sandbox we would have taken the guy out for a good fuckin' talkin' to."

"You would have, huh?"

"Nothin' too nasty. Just a warnin'."

Another couple of silent swigs and Alan realized Frank was earning his pay that night.

"Say we're not in the sandbox. What?"

Frank looked over at him, saw it wasn't just the booze talking, curled his lower lip over his walrus, and cocked his head.

"What's good for the goose, you know."

Alan nodded. "Right. What's good for the goose. That's it. What's good for the goose."

Risa woke to soft talk coming from the kitchen, something that sounded like a buzz at first. She had been asleep curled up in the armchair in the den. She thought at first it was Kevin in the kitchen, but then she remembered he had said good night earlier. She cleared her head, stood, and walked barefoot toward the sound. It was Alan she was hearing, on his phone, faced away from her, listening. He didn't realize she was there.

"All right. All right. That sounds good," he said.

Risa was going to cough, move around, make her presence known, but something told her to wait.

"Fine, just make sure I'm not connected with it. Got that? Call me when it's done." Alan hung up, took a deep breath, and spun on the stool, nearly falling off when he caught a glimpse of Risa behind him. "Jesus!"

"Sorry. What was that all about?"

"What?"

"That you don't want to be connected to something. You sounded like some tough guy, like you were calling in a hit."

"You caught me. Roberts is going down tomorrow."

"No, seriously. What don't you want to be connected to?"

Alan went to the refrigerator and retrieved a beer. "You really want to deal with minutiae of the campaign? I thought you said you didn't."

"I don't, but I do want to know this."

"Why?"

"I don't know. The tone of it. Does it have something to do with Kevin and what happened to him."

"No, and the Robich guy never was in a coma. It was a concussion and he's going to be all right."

"If he's not paralyzed. Kevin told me."

"How's he doing?"

"Kevin? Good. Maybe too good."

"Why do you say that?"

"He may be denying what he did."

"Protecting himself?"

"Not what he did but how he did it. Couldn't he have just defended himself, not attacked in return?"

Alan came to her, beer in hand, put his other hand on her shoulder, and kissed her cheek. She could smell the scotch through the beer. She wondered if he was going to want to make love. A little booze was often the catalyst. She certainly wasn't into it. She had questions.

"I don't know, Risa. I've never been in a fight in my life."

"But you were cheering him on."

"Was I? I thought I was being a supportive father."

Risa knew she was dealing with Alan The Lawyer now and went back to the previous topic.

"So what don't you want to be connected to?"

"Damn, Risa. I can't even remember now."

"Bullshit."

"Why does this interest you so?"

"Because it sounds a little sleazy and because you can't think of a plausible lie to cover up what you were really talking about."

Alan puffed out a sigh, took a swallow of his beer, and gave Risa a long look.

"I take it you didn't get Sean on the bus in Scranton tonight."

"No, I didn't. He was busy."

"Busy?"

"Henry crossed us up and went and talked to him."

"So then you talked to Sean?"

"No. But Henry now knows what Sean's here for."

"Shit. That fucker. Why would Sean talk to him?"

"He didn't. Not directly. Just said that G.G. wasn't guilty and Henry took it from there. I guess he's determined to turn himself in."

"Yeah, well that's not going to happen."

"Because you talked to Stallings?"

"No. That phone call you were so curious about, seems there are a few people who don't want Sean around."

"But not you, right?"

"I want him out of here. What are you talking about?"

"You're not going to be connected, though."

"Right."

"Just what are these people going to do to induce Sean to leave?"

"Like I said, I'm not connected."

Risa pounded the countertop. "Jesus, Alan! What are you into here? And don't you dare say you're not connected. You were just setting something up. What is it?"

"Honestly, Scout's honor, I don't know."

"Well, how about some parameters? Are they going to kidnap him, ride him out of town on a rail? What? I don't like the sound of this at all."

"He's trespassing."

"Oh, good, brilliant. Bring the cops in and keep it all quiet that way."

"I'm just saying there are legal grounds."

"But I don't get the feeling that's what you were talking about on the phone."

Alan took a last swallow of beer, crushed the can, and tossed it in the recycling bin. He started out of the kitchen, stopped, and pointed an accusing finger.

"Would you please not sneak up on me again. I've got a lot of stuff going on right now and I don't want to have to look over my shoulder every minute I'm in the house, wondering if you're spying on me. You haven't been able to take care of this situation, so I'm going to have to do it myself. If you want updates, let me know. But don't sneak around. Okay?"

This was one of Alan's closing arguments that he expected to give without the other side rebutting. He started to walk away, then turned.

"I've got to be in Syracuse at ten. I'm leaving at seven thirty."

"Syracuse?"

"State Fair. I'm doing a tit for tat with John Engle. You want all the details of that too? He called me. I'm somebody from out of state he thinks can help his fucking rudderless campaign. I *am* going to be connected to that. Okay?"

He turned and walked away. A minute later, as Risa turned off the kitchen light, the chair Sean had thrown flew through the air again, headed for the glass-front cupboard. But it never made it, the memory swallowed by the dark.

17

When sunlight first came through the venetian blinds in the living room of the apartment, Sean was already awake, half rested from a few uninterrupted hours of sleep. He showered and then repacked all he had carried with him, put on his Yankees cap, picked up the backpack, and left.

He was almost out of the building when he remembered, with the same moment of panic that happened practically every day, that he hadn't taken his pill. He went back in the apartment, washed down the pill with a glass of water, and counted the pills he had left. Thirty-six. That would give him plenty should he be locked up right away. He wondered if he'd even need them in jail, but when he thought about prison hootch, he realized he would have to have those pills no matter where he was.

The day was bright, and the slanting morning sun at six thirty modeled the nondescript street and gave it a vibrancy. A powder blue pickup parked at the corner of Front and Market candied up the scene. Sean walked past the pickup and started to look inside. A woman in the passenger seat appeared out of the darkness of the cab and looked fully at him, as if she were waiting to see him. Sean turned quickly away, ducking his head so the bill of his cap hid him.

He walked to McDonald's, was happy to see there were few customers, got a sausage biscuit to go, and continued down Third Street. He was headed to Saffron Park, but he wanted to detour past the address of Stallings's Braden office on Euclid Street.

The office was a two-room storefront with an empty desk in front and a closed door to the room behind it. Sean shaded his eyes, peered in, and took a mental picture of the place. A little later, sitting and eating in Saffron Park, he used that image to place himself in the space, to see himself making his case.

It was then he remembered something about Stallings. He wasn't from Braden. Sean couldn't remember where he was from, but he did recall an article in the paper about him when he was a senior in high school in the area. Sean was a freshman at the time, confused about things like girls and sports, and so he read with interest the article about the kid with a 14–0 record pitching and a .410 batting average, who was recruited by the Pirates but who turned down a minor league contract in order to go to Dartmouth. That kid was Stallings, Sean now realized. He had looked up to him then as someone willing to buck the sports culture. He hoped he would look up to him after their meeting.

And then a moment of calm descended. For weeks, months, even, he had been knotted by the horrors he recalled and what they meant for him. The trip to Braden and his talk with Henry had been heroic and exhausting. What he was about to do would seal his fate for his lifetime. The certainty of that, the knowledge that he was doing all he could to right a wrong, gave him a peace he hadn't had in decades. Saffron Park came alive in the morning sun. All seemed bright and hyperreal to him; the soughing leaves on the ancient trees, nervous squirrels, day camp kids on the swings, a park employee with a leaf blower. He had made it back home and was, for these brief few minutes, free. Then he heard the church bell at St. Cyrillic's ring nine forty-five. He willed himself down from this blissful cloud, gathered his things, and left the park for Stallings's office.

He was surprised to see Stallings standing with two other

men in business suits in front of his office. Sean was walking toward them and didn't know whether to pass by and return when Stallings had gone into the office, or stop. There wasn't enough room to pass on the sidewalk comfortably, so he stopped.

Stallings, in shirtsleeves with a tie, a briefcase in hand, glanced at Sean, didn't recognize him, and turned back as one of the two other men finished a story. Sean didn't hear the words. There was blood pounding in his ears and he was running through his own speech, his story. Stallings laughed about something, mentioned some gathering he'd see them at, and shook hands with them as they walked away. He fished keys out of his pocket and was opening the door when he turned to Sean, standing where he had stopped.

"Can I help you?"

Sean got a "yes" out a little weakly, then indicated he'd tell Stallings inside.

The sun hadn't yet heated the nearly empty front room, and Sean stepped into the coolness, feeling it play on his sweat-misted skin.

"Do you have an appointment?" Stallings asked, putting his briefcase on the spotless faux-wood desk. Sean shook his head.

"No. My name's Sean Collins."

Stallings stopped at the name, and his expression changed from open faced, smile ready to wary.

"I have a ten o'clock coming in. Maybe we can set up an appointment for later in the week."

"I need to talk to you now. I used to live in Braden. And—"

"I know who you are. And I know why you're here."

"How do you know that?"

"It's my business to know when new people are in town making certain claims."

"I guess so."

"Right. So I don't think we really have anything to talk about."

"You know all you need to know?"

"Yes. I know you left Braden eleven years ago and you've come back now claiming to have participated in the murder of Carol Slezak."

"I did it. Yes. By myself."

"I've got to stop you right there, Mr. Collins. I'm sure you're aware we have convicted a man for that crime."

"Yes, but he didn't do it. He—"

"I've heard the arguments, a lawyer in Pittsburgh. It's hogwash. Gary Trask killed Carol Slezak and has admitted so. That case is closed. If you believe you had something to do with the murder, you're mistaken and should seek some help."

Sean had anticipated resistance, but he thought it might come with the particulars of his evidence. He was thrown off rhythm and stumbled long enough for Stallings to move to the front door and get it open.

"Give me fifteen minutes and I can prove to you I did it."

"I don't have fifteen minutes and I'm certain you can't. Do you need money to get back to New York?"

The condescension bit into Sean and made him plant his feet.

"Isn't it your sworn duty to investigate any claims of guilt, especially of a crime of this nature?"

"I don't know about sworn, but the only claims of guilt I'm going to investigate are credible ones."

"What makes you think mine is not credible?"

"You don't believe Gary Trask is guilty, for one. You're a newly recovered alcoholic whose memory, I'm told, was shot even before you got hit by, what was it, a train? And you're coming to me without a lawyer to defend you, to make sure you don't say something stupid like most of what you've been saying here now. Please leave."

He stood holding the door, a man about to sweep dirt out

onto the sidewalk. Sean scrambled to find some sort of leverage.

"There's going to be an article in the paper about my story. I think you're going to have to listen to me then."

"I doubt it."

"Doubt what?"

"That there's going to be an article in the paper."

"I've already done an interview with the reporter."

"Yeah, good luck with that."

The door was suddenly filled with Del Cronin smiling at Stallings. "Your own doorman these days, Johnny?" he said, winking at Sean.

"Come on in, Del." Cronin sensed the tension, dropped the wink face, and moved between Sean and Stallings into the office. "Del, this is Sean Collins. Sean, Del Cronin."

Del's eyes narrowed. He reached out and Sean shook his hand.

"Sean, wow. I heard you were back. Good to see you."

Sean looked from Del to Stallings. "Thanks."

"Movin' back?"

"It depends. I have some business to take care of first."

Stallings jumped in.

"Thanks for coming," he said as Sean moved forward.

"You're going to have to listen to me sooner or later," Sean said firmly. Stallings nodded, not wanting to prolong the parting. "You've got it wrong and I can prove it."

Again Stallings nodded and Sean glanced quickly at Cronin before he left. Stallings would have to tell Cronin what was going on. Maybe Cronin would stick up for Sean. But as he stepped out onto the sidewalk Sean realized Cronin wasn't going to be any help. He was going to have to force Stallings to listen to him. He could do that. He was over his nervousness. Now he was pissed.

Sean caught his reflection in the window of the Bulldog souvenir shop. He was surprised to see himself in his Yankees hat. He saw that he fit right in with the sweatshirts and T-shirts in the window. He looked inconsequential, silly even. He would have to change that and change his whole approach as well. He had been too tentative, too naïve, too much on his own. Stallings had been right about that. He should have had a lawyer with him, not for protection but to give weight to what he was saying. He continued walking and vowed to put the embarrassment of Stallings's office behind him.

When he got to Market, he realized he didn't know where he was heading. He hadn't thought he'd be leaving Stallings's office a free man. But here he was, able to hop a bus back to New York, able to stay right where he was. He kept taking rights, once through an alley, and after a few minutes he found his spot, the shaded rusty wall behind an abandoned bedspring factory near the rail spur.

He peeled off his backpack and slid to a sitting position against the wall. He had worked in the factory before it closed, one of a succession of jobs he'd had after being fired from his teaching job. He remembered hungover mornings at this very wall, the metal a silent rebuke. But the wall accepted him now, gave him some comfort. He faced an empty parking lot and tried to clear his thinking, come up with a strategy.

But nothing appeared and he found himself getting very sleepy. The adrenaline rush of meeting with Stallings and the anger that followed subsided and left Sean drained and drowsy. In minutes he was asleep, his Yankees cap sliding to the right.

"How's it going?"

The words woke him. He was still sitting against the factory wall, but instead of an empty parking lot in front of him there was a young, buff woman in jeans and a T-shirt, wearing sunglasses, standing over him, smiling down. Behind her, idling, was the powder blue pickup he'd seen earlier, the passenger door flung open, a man in the driver's seat.

"How's it going, Sean?"

Sean sat up and shaded his eyes.

"I know you?"

"Hope not. But we know you. You're sort of a celebrity."

If the woman was trying for sincerity or warmth, she missed badly. Sean stood and faced her. He didn't recognize her, and when he looked back into the shadows of the pickup cab he didn't recognize the man either. He did realize, though, that he needed to move, to get away from them. There was something primal in this feeling, as if he'd learned it on the street.

"Sorry. Guess I'm not supposed to be here?"

"Got that right, if by here you mean Braden."

Sean didn't like the tone of this at all. He picked up his backpack and started toward the street, away from these two.

The woman's voice turned him back. "Forgetting something?"

She stood holding out her right arm, Sean's pill bottle pinched between her thumb and index finger. She was grinning. Sean looked quickly down at his open backpack and then went to retrieve the bottle. The woman turned and tossed the bottle into the cab. Sean stopped.

"I need those pills. They're no joke."

"Roger that. You better go get 'em, huh?"

Sean went to the door of the cab and looked in. It took a couple of seconds for his eyes to adjust to the light. When they did, he saw a man in his late twenties, tightly shaved Fu Manchu, tanned, with arms full of four-color tattoos, and a Mohawk he was growing out. He reeked military. Sean turned and found that the woman was a little closer behind him. He realized she'd probably done a tour of duty herself.

When he looked back, Fu had put Sean's pill bottle on the seat, or so it seemed at first. Then Sean realized the bottle was balanced on a .45 lying on the seat.

"Pretty neat, huh?" Fu said, a toothy grin splitting the hair on his face. "Carrot and the stick all in one little pitcher." He held up the pill bottle. "This is the carrot." Wider grin.

"I need that."

"You were right, hon," Fu said to the woman. "He needs this bottle."

"Told you."

Fu turned back to Sean. "Hop in. I'll give it to you."

Sean shook his head. "Just let me have it, will you?"

"I can't do that. See, this is our carrot. You seen the pitchers where the farmer has the carrot on a string and the donkey keeps reachin' for it. That's what keeps the cart movin'. You don't see the farmer givin' the donkey the carrot until they get to where they're going, right?"

"Cut the shit. Where are we going?"

"Home, for you."

"New York?"

"Bingo."

"No thanks. Just give me the pills."

Fu looked up to see an SUV pass on the quiet street running beside the factory. He dropped his game quickly and picked up the .45.

"Get in the fuckin' car. You know how the stick works, right?"

Sean stared at the gun. It was huge in his vision, appalling even though it wasn't pointed right at him. He turned to see Hon edging even closer.

She spoke. "Come on."

"Why? What are you doing?"

"Let's just say we're a citizens' committee," Hon said. "Everybody in town took a vote and we don't want you around here anymore. You should have stayed gone, so we're going to take you back to where you were."

"Wait a minute. I've got a right to—"

"Stick!" Fu growled, and Sean turned to see the .45 now

pointed at him. It didn't bother him as much as he thought it would, but seeing Fu wrap a meaty hand around the pill bottle got to him. He climbed in the cab and sat. Hon pushed in after him and slammed the door shut. Fu handed the .45 to her across Sean's chest and stuffed the pill bottle in his pocket. He jammed the truck into gear and made gravel fly as he peeled out of the parking lot.

Alan had been up very early and out the door before Risa came downstairs. She didn't want to tell Kevin about Sean's reappearance without Alan around, so she got Kevin his breakfast and said little as he hoovered it and went out the door. She did manage to get a "Be careful" in before he was gone, but it sounded weak, almost insincere after what had happened to Kevin the night before.

Risa spent the next hour at the kitchen table in front of her laptop. About two years earlier Kevin had been embarrassed by her lack of computer skills and had taught her the rudiments of e-mail, Googling, Twitter, and Facebook. Risa had undergone the training just to please Kevin, but she soon got hooked on the machine when she realized how it could bring her into the art world, let her research painters and paintings. She had even put some of her own work online.

She normally didn't have much e-mail traffic, she got her news the old-fashioned way at The Kitchen, but now her inbox was stuffed. She glanced at some of the subject lines and realized many of the writers were people in town who were asking if she were okay, if she needed anything, and if it was true what they heard about Sean. She found this unsettling, realizing that there was a lot of buzz around town but nobody wanted to speak to her directly about it. She answered none of the e-mails.

It took her a while to find some New York newspaper accounts of a homeless man who had stumbled onto the subway tracks at the 116th Street station on the 6 line and had been saved by a hero cop, who had rolled the man into the gutter between the tracks and nearly been killed herself. One account said he was in critical condition and not expected to live. Another gave his name tentatively as Wallis Corning. Risa wondered if, had she read the accounts at the time, she would ever have connected Sean to the incident.

Googling "Carol Slezak" surprised her. Most of the first references that popped up weren't local accounts of the trial, as she had suspected, but Internet chatter about possible wrongful convictions. There seemed to be a small movement dedicated to freeing prisoners like G.G. whose cases weren't open and shut. Risa started following some of these threads, but then realized that a vote for G.G. was a vote against Sean. She closed the laptop.

She wasn't surprised to find that Sean had left the apartment, but she hadn't expected it to be completely empty, towels and sheets folded on the mattress, the bathroom sink cleaned. There was something final about the way the rooms looked. She hoped Sean had changed his mind and was leaving. Maybe his interview with Henry had opened his eyes, made him see things differently. She looked at her watch. If he were leaving by bus, the first one he could take would be in twenty minutes. She left the apartment and headed for the bus stop.

He wasn't there, and May Sargent in the candy store hadn't seen him. Risa waited until the bus came. No one got on or got off, and the bus U-turned back the way it had come. Then Risa's argument with Alan the night before returned. What had he done? What was he up to? She dialed his cell phone, got his voice mail, and told him to call her.

At The Kitchen, Bell said a couple of the early breakfast crowd had said they'd seen Sean walking the streets with a Yankees cap and backpack.

"People who knew him, like Junior and Cal, said it was like seein' a ghost."

"Don't say that, please."

"Sorry."

"I declared him dead, Bell, is all."

"You didn't have any choice, Risa. He'd been like he was dead for seven, eight years, right? You had to get on with your life. I remember those days if you don't. Remember how good you felt once that paper come through?"

"Yeah. I'm going to go out and clear my head."

"Okay. But, uh, news on Frankie Robich too."

"What?"

"Might have a little paralysis, but he's okay."

"Oh."

"And he ain't gonna press charges."

"How do you know that?"

"Lindy Georgevich, married to one of his cousins. Said Mel Carney scared him off plus he's got some problem with a fight he got into over in Bloomburg. She said he might go civil if the paralysis is bad."

Risa acknowledged this but had nothing to say. She walked out of the restaurant and decided to head to John Stallings's office first, thinking Sean might have tried to plead his case there after all.

Stallings was in the front room talking to Del Cronin. Neither saw her, and she turned back away from the office. She wondered if this ghost whom others had seen would appear to her. She spent the next few minutes walking the central streets of downtown. People nodded to her, but no one said anything. She imagined them running home and e-mailing her what they couldn't say to her face. She called Alan but again got his voice mail. She didn't leave a message this time.

When she had covered most of the main streets, she found herself a couple of blocks from the stadium and heard the boot camp sounds coming from the practice field behind the bleachers. She started for the hoots, whistles, and deep-voiced chants.

In the stadium, she climbed the bleachers and from the top could look down on the practice. The players were all wearing either blue or white tunics over their jerseys and but for that they all looked the same to Risa. They were spread out at various stations, blocking sleds, tires laid out on the grass, cone mazes snaking off to the right. The activity made no sense to Risa, and she became increasingly frustrated that she couldn't spot Kevin.

Every time she heard the crunch of pads and helmets, she flinched and looked to see if Kevin was involved, but she could never tell if it was him or not. Shouldn't she be able to tell her son from others, even with those mounds of pads and a helmet covering him? When a small, slight player caught a pass, turned, and was flattened by a defensive back, Risa looked anxiously to see if it was Kevin who had bulldozed the kid. She couldn't tell, but an assistant coach came over and clapped the defensive back's shoulder pads and said, "Solid hit, Pete. Solid hit."

The word "solid" leaped up at her. She'd always thought of Alan as solid, a man navigating a world he knew and was confident in, and she liked that about him. Sean had been a different kind of solid. He was a dreamer and a seeker who had little real understanding of the way things worked in the world. And yet he always seemed to Risa somehow solid, maybe solid in his soul. Not now, however. Not in his quixotic reappearance. But she could remember a time when she understood the difference between Alan and Sean, when she preferred the questioning Sean to the certain Alan.

Risa looked out over the squat buildings of downtown and wondered where Sean was. From her perch, the past two days seemed small and fading, the monumental nature of Sean's return somehow flattened. She thought about times when Kevin was very young and she'd take him to the busy little playground behind the grade school. She'd be talking to another mother, look around for Kevin, not see him at first, be quickly engulfed in panic, but then, when she spotted him, regain the confidence that he wouldn't just wander off. She felt that now with Sean. All the tragedy of his disappearance was over. He would never be gone for good again. She walked down the stadium steps, feeling as if she were going back into the fray. She didn't have to know exactly where Sean was now. He was alive and they were reconnected. That was enough.

18

Fu and Hon turned out to be into heavy, heavy rap. Loud heavy, heavy rap. Their decade-old truck was tricked out with a state-of-the-art sound system that sent bass notes plunging into Sean's chest until he thought he was going to puke. He couldn't understand a word of what was being rapped other than the "fucks" and "suck my dicks" and "bitches."

Fu had started out talking over the din, narrating the trip out of Braden, over the bridge, down the state road past the cooling towers as if he were catching Rip Van Winkle up on all he'd missed. About the fifth time Sean said he knew there was a nuclear plant on the river, knew the bridge had been redone recently, knew the Wise Potato Chip factory was still going strong, Hon gave Fu a look as if to say, "Shut up, you're ruining the music," and he went silent.

The cab, unfortunately for Sean, was the opposite of silent, and the trip down Route 80 to the Delaware Water Gap was a torture that had his ears bleeding. He didn't have to pee, but he asked to stop just to relieve himself of the cacophony.

Fu went into the rest stop bathroom with him and said something as they stood a stall apart. In the echoey tiled place Sean's ears rang and he couldn't understand what Fu was saying.

"Huh?"

"Your kid's quite the killer, huh?"

Sean heard what he said but didn't want to have a

conversation about Kevin with this guy in the bathroom. He started out of the bathroom when Fu stopped him.

"Hey, cleanliness is next to godliness, right?" He indicated the sink.

Sean had had trouble with such everyday tasks since his recovery. He washed up and went out the door with Fu.

"What did you say about my son?"

"I said he was quite the killer."

"Football?"

"Yeah, that, but he put the hurt on Frankie Robich bad last night."

"What do you mean?"

"Sent him to the hospital."

"Who's Frankie Robich?"

"A stand-up guy. Works at Bendix. Or used to. Might be a vegetable."

Hon opened the passenger door and Sean got in. When Fu got in the driver's seat Sean continued.

"What do you mean sent him to the hospital?"

Fu spoke to Hon. "I's telling him about his kid. He didn't know he's got a real Mike Tyson on his hands."

"More like that EF guy, what's his name? One who bites ears off and shit?"

"Yeah. Maybe that."

"What are you talking about? What happened?"

Fu started the truck and waited until he had pulled back out into traffic to respond.

"I didn't get it all. Something about a beef in front of the Subway. Cracked the guy's head open."

"Who?"

"Robich. Like I say, your boy's a killer. You ought to be proud. Followin' in his father's footsteps."

Fu gave him a wicked grin. Hon cranked the Sirius. Fu just kept grinning, but Sean reached out and turned off the radio.

"The fuck," Hon said, starting to reach out for the radio again. Sean put a firm hand on her arm.

"Give it a break for a minute. I want some answers."

Hon brought the .45 up with her other hand. "I don't give a shit about your answers."

"Hon, hon, patience," Fu said, gunning the engine and flying around a pokey Beetle. "Word's just out, that's all. It's Braden, man. Nobody has to tell you 'bout somethin'. It's in the water like."

"What's in the water about me?"

"You flew the coop a shitload of years ago and now you're back saying you was the one killed Carol Slezak."

"Okay, so why are you taking me back to New York? Don't you want justice for her?"

Fu snorted. "Man, come on. Get serious. She's fuckin' dust. She doesn't need no justice. Save your fuckin' justice for someone who needs it. Me, for instance. Three tours and I'm on the fuckin' night shift moldin' plastic trays. That sound like justice to you?"

"Answer my question. What do you care if I turn myself in?"

"I care 'cause it's unpatriotic. G. G. Trask the retard sliced that bitch and they caught him red-handed, confessed an' everything. Now you're gonna come along and say that's wrong. Fuckin' unpatriotic, right, hon?"

Hon didn't say anything for a few seconds. She looked like she was stewing over not having the radio. Sean was about to ask another question when she piped up.

"She's not a bitch."

"Oh, fuck. Here we go again. Okay, okay, hon. She's not a bitch, you're not a bitch, there ain't a single bitch in the whole world 'cept the ones with four legs. Satisfied?"

Hon didn't say anything. Sean wondered about the contradiction between the misogynist shit Hon seemed to enjoy and her PC reprimand, but he changed the topic instead of going there.

"Stallings put you up to this?" Sean had seen the powder blue pickup stalking him before he got to Stallings's office, but he knew too that Stallings knew all about him when they met.

"Stallings? The DA? Man, you have been fuckin' out of it. 'Bout the only thing I'd do for that asshole is send him through the fuckin' stamper out at the job."

"Then who?"

"I told you it was a people's choice kind of thing. Nobody wants somebody comin' around sayin' some guy doin' life is fuckin' innocent. It's just not right. Ever heard of the fabric of society? Well, somebody like you comes along and it's like goddamn scissors. So we all took a vote and I volunteered to clear the brush, so to speak."

Hon lifted the .45 and waggled it for emphasis. "And one thing we haven't mentioned is we're not taking you on some overnight. You stay outa Braden or we're gonna just forget all about that carrot shit, go right to the stick."

She reached over and blasted the radio again. End of conversation. Sean tried to imagine some sort of town meeting in which he was voted out of Braden, but that was ludicrous. Even he, the outsider, the naïve one, knew things didn't work that way. There was some one person, maybe a couple, who wanted him gone again. The only one who fit that profile was Alan. Alan had been ready to drive him to New York and he certainly seemed capable of setting up this current abduction. But Sean couldn't quite square these crude operatives with the Alan he saw on the campaign posters, the one who came to see him at the apartment, the one Risa was married to and the father now to Kevin.

They had S-curved through the Delaware Water Gap and were on a six-lane stretch of Route 80 in western New Jersey. Sean looked out at the thickening traffic and the rolling hills to the north and realized that this was the first time he'd been in a car, well, a carlike cab, in probably over eleven years. Staring at the movement out the window, hoping to make the spitting rhymes and thumping bass coming out of the speakers background, he tried to remember the last time he had ridden like this. He remembered Carol driving him home, but he didn't think that was the last time. He remembered Risa once in the passenger seat screaming at him to stop, that he was too drunk to drive. And he remembered a horrible moment when he had strapped a four-year-old Kevin in his car seat, knowing he shouldn't be going near the wheel, getting in the front seat and passing out, only to be found an hour later by Sim, Carol's father. Sim had slapped him awake with Kevin crying in the backseat.

Sean started to sweat in the grip of these dark memories and felt ill. As if she knew what he was thinking, Hon rolled down the window and let wind rush mix with the misogyny. Sean's breathing slowed and the scene in front of him changed. At first he thought it was going to be another onset of the murder and he braced himself. Things went dark, but they had a different quality this time. He could see he was traveling a road very similar to this one and he wondered if he were just falling asleep. But the vision, or whatever it was, pushed through and he could tell there was the fragment of a memory knocking.

He was in a car and all was lit by the dashboard light. His vision was blurry, and the cars flying by out the front window seemed like searchlights coming at him, fireflies going away. It seemed as if he had been sick, his hands sticky with some kind of substance. His pant legs were stiff but he couldn't see why. He heard a voice talking to him for a long time but couldn't make out the words.

Then he looked over at the driver's seat and saw a stern, snarling figure, made even more threatening by the blue light coming from below. He was saying, ". . . and stay there," but not looking at Sean. Sean squinted into the memory, trying to clear his fogged vision. What was he seeing? Who was this?

A few more minutes passed before he realized who the driver was. It was Alan. Not the campaign poster Alan, but Alan with shaggy hair and a mustache, an Alan he couldn't remember seeing before. Sean swam in this memory now, trying to hear what Alan was saying. But his ears pounded with something else and suddenly the whole thing vaporized.

"Motherfucker!" Fu laid on the horn and twisted the steering wheel so violently Sean thought they were going to roll. Hon stuck her gun hand out the window and pointed the .45 at an SUV they were passing.

"Move the fuck over, asshole!"

The driver saw the gun, ducked, and swerved right. Fu looked over, horrified.

"Stow that, soldier! What the fuck you think you're doing? Jesus Christ!"

Fu was apoplectic. Hon pulled the gun in, not the least bit contrite. Sean heard more than one loose screw flying around in Hon's brain pan. Fu floored the pickup, saw an exit ahead, crossed three lanes, and took the ramp. He came to a stop sign, took a hard right, went a quarter of a mile down a two-lane past a development in the works, then took another right until he found a service road behind the development. He pulled in and stopped. He got out of the cab, went quickly around the front of the truck, ripped open the passenger door, and hauled Hon out.

She didn't go easily. She put a good kick into his thigh and swiped at him with the .45. He clamped her wrist, gave it a wrenching twist, and had her on the ground with his foot on her ass in a second.

"You stupid bitch! It ain't enough we got a car that screams different? You gotta point a fuckin' piece at Mom and Pop back there? Jesus fuckin' Christ. We gotta take back roads now. How the fuck are we going to get to goddamn New York on back roads?" He plucked the gun from her hand.

"Let me go!"

He did and Hon jumped up as if she were ready for another round.

"Get in the car. For chrissake. I gotta think."

Sean had thought about running, but then he remembered that Fu had his pills. Hon's act had scared the shit out of him, both while it happened and in the aftermath. She was pure reaction, hotwired by some training or personal defect, beyond reason or even thought. She got back in the cab and sat next to him. He could smell an animal body odor he'd never smelled before. He wondered if she knew he was there.

When Risa made it back to The Kitchen it was nearly lunchtime. Howie Francis, her beer distributor, was bringing kegs in from his truck.

"You going for a swim the other day?" he asked as Risa held the door for him.

"What?"

"When I saw you down by the bridge. Looked like you was going for a swim."

"Not hardly." Risa vaguely remembered seeing Howie's truck as she followed Sean.

Bell had set up a long table by the front window, and when Risa asked about it, Bell gave her a look before she answered. "Third Friday? Cluckers Club?"

"Oh." Risa made a mental note to either be back in the office or out of the restaurant when the group of retired men, the Cluckers, showed up with their ridiculously lame jokes and magic tricks. They were an institution her father had courted, had even thought funny. She didn't feel the same, especially not on this day.

Warren Mastic was at his usual spot, twirling his soda water, but today his daughter Eileen was with him. Eileen was a year or two younger than Risa, a loan officer at the bank, and the second best woman golfer at Cresthill. Her daughter Star, only seventeen, was the best.

"Thanks for corralin' Pa Wednesday, Risa. I'm sorry. I got tied up."

"I'm sorry he didn't stay tied up," Risa said, wondering where a joke had come from on this day.

Eileen laughed. "Yeah, he's getting slippery. Right, Pa? You're getting slippery."

Warren didn't hear or didn't realize he was being talked to.

Eileen turned back to Risa. "You got a second? I'd like to talk to you about something."

"Sure." Eileen didn't make any move to go anywhere. There was no one near them at the bar.

"Did I ever tell you what Star did about a year, year and a half ago, with Pa?"

"No, I don't think so."

"She got me to buy her a small little handheld tape recorder and she interviewed him for hours. She had been reading that *Tuesdays with Morrie* book. At first she was going to do a project for school, like an oral history of Braden through Pa's eyes. But then we all were realizing that he was getting the A disease and Bill told her, 'Why don't you just let him talk on anything, whatever he can remember, and then we'll have that.' So bless her soul, she did. Like I say, spent hours and hours with him, and now we've got this great archive I guess you'd call it of what Pa knew, what he saw."

"That's terrific," Risa said, seeing one of the first Cluckers come in wearing a straw fedora, seeming to be bursting with new yucks.

"I was thinking about that when I heard Sean was back in town."

Risa turned back to her quickly. Finally somebody willing to talk to her directly. "Yes?"

"There's one thing on that tape Pa says about Sean."

"What?"

"He knew Sean well. You remember that? I think Sean worked a summer with his crew and he liked him. I remember him saying how sad it made him to see Sean, well, going downhill."

"That's what he said on the tape?"

"No. He said he saw a strange thing one morning. You know he was on the county road crew for, I don't know, fifteen, seventeen years before he got the job in the shed. And in the summer he liked to do the early morning shift, go in about four, go out, get dropped off, walk down one side of a country road, up the other, picking up trash. He said he liked being by himself, when it was cool, liked the exercise.

"On the tape he says it was one of those mornings he saw Sean coming down out of the woods near The Ding Dong, looking like he was drunk again. Pa was on the other side of the road, but he figured he'd go over and see what he could do. He'd been wanting to talk to Sean for months about his drinking. You know Pa had a problem back when. Anyway, before he could get across the road, a car pulls up, a guy gets out, goes to Sean like he was expecting he'd be there, sort of helps him up and shoves him into the passenger seat of his car."

"When was this?"

"Star tried to pin him down, but he wasn't sure. He thought it was one of the last summers he was on that road crew, so it would have been, or could have been when Sean left."

"Who was it who picked him up?"

"Star asked him that and he said he didn't get a good look, didn't recognize the car. But he said if he had to place a bet on it he'd say it was Sean's best friend. He couldn't remember the name when he was talking to Star. He was starting to go and a lot was slipping, but I always assumed it was Alan."

"Alan wasn't around then."

"He wasn't?"

"That summer he was in Washington."

"Oh. Well, it probably was someone else. But Pa says on the tape that it stuck with him because Sean comes out of the woods, out of nowhere, and this car pulls up like it was arranged."

Risa couldn't imagine anything being arranged for Sean in those last days in Braden. She knew little about where he had ended up most nights, but she knew they had to be random flops, outdoors, even. When he did make it home, in the morning, he often reeked of earth and sweat. All that was so chaotic. He never could have arranged for someone to pick him up in the wee hours.

And it really couldn't have been Alan in the car. Not only was Alan away but he had put distance between himself and Sean and Risa ever since they told him they were going to get married and have a baby. For the first couple of years after that announcement, the three had tried to keep up a semblance of their high school friendship, but Alan had been much too wounded to pretend he enjoyed being around them. He introduced them to one woman he had met in Washington, but all concerned could tell that relationship was going nowhere. And when Sean began his slide, losing jobs, losing his dignity, Alan seemed disgusted. When he got hired by a law firm in Washington, he saw Sean and Risa only occasionally. No, Alan was out of the picture. She didn't know who else there would be who would be in cahoots with Sean.

Risa weathered the Cluckers Club, several members of which seemed less obnoxious to her this time. She wondered if they all knew about Sean and weren't up to their usual brand of *Hee-Haw* humor in the face of such serious news. When they had left and the lunch crowd faded, Risa was about to try Alan again when Henry came in. Risa was by herself near the front window putting the tables the Cluckers used back where they belonged.

"Have you seen Sean this morning, Risa?"

"No. I guess you haven't either."

"He didn't take the bus."

"I know."

"He did talk to Stallings, though."

"Talk? What did he say?"

"I don't know. Stallings called Doris and told her in no uncertain terms that we should not run any story on Sean or his claims."

"That's good."

"Yeah."

"Maybe Stallings convinced Sean he was way off base and Sean went back on his own, or got a ride to Scranton," Risa said without any conviction at all.

"Could be, but don't you think Stallings would have said that to Doris?"

"I don't know. The bottom line is you're not going to do a story, right?"

Henry puffed out a sigh and tapped a manila folder he had under his arm. "I went through G.G.'s confession. It's pretty solid. Do you want to read it?" He held out the folder. Risa hesitated, then took it. "There's only one hole I can see in the confession, in the case."

"What's that?"

"Nobody really knows when Carol was killed."

"Yes they do. Come on, Henry. All those doctors and experts. They had it down to what, a six- seven-hour window?"

"Yeah, you're right."

Henry gave in too easily. Risa could see Henry was more conflicted than he was letting on. Risa looked down at the twenty or so pages of the confession. She didn't know what to hope for. Did she want G.G. to be guilty? Somehow that didn't seem right. Did she want him to be innocent? That would mean Sean was guilty. She certainly didn't want that.

When she looked up, Henry was staring at her as if he had just handed in homework he knew didn't measure up. Risa had the feeling G.G.'s confession wasn't going to settle anything.

The radio was off in the cab now, and Sean sat in the middle of a Fu/Hon cold war. Hon had been reprimanded but was not cowed. She sat with the .45 on her lap, absentmindedly flicking the safety on and off until Fu gave her a look and she stopped. Fu looked like he could explode any second, but his constant lookout for cops kept him quiet.

They had taken back roads paralleling Route 80 for a while but they were slow, and Fu kept saying he couldn't be late for work. When he figured they were far enough away from the scene of Hon's gun pointing, he pulled back onto the interstate and joined the rush heading east toward the city.

After they passed Paterson and started seeing signs for the George Washington Bridge, Fu's anxieties started to poke through. He asked Sean where his apartment was and Sean said he really didn't have an apartment, just a room in a rehab halfway house.

"Well where the fuck is that?"

"Harlem. Just below Morningside Heights."

"So how do we get there?"

"By car? I don't know."

"You don't know?"

"I was on the streets. I never drove anywhere. I hardly ever took a bus or a subway. I don't know shit about the city."

Hon piped up. "Just drop his ass at the other end of the bridge, let him find his own way."

This was probably counter to their instructions, but Fu liked the idea. He didn't want to get lost in New York, and fucking Harlem sounded like niggerville. Niggers in the unit, in a deployment, were fine, but not out on the fucking street while he was driving a powder blue pickup.

Traffic was practically at a standstill on the George Washington Bridge. Sean wondered if the fidgeting Hon might whip out the gun again to get things moving. They took the first exit off the bridge, spiraled down to the Henry Hudson, and Fu started to panic when he was caught in the southbound flow of traffic. He managed to get them off the highway at 125th Street and stopped by the girders near a parking lot for Fairway.

"Your money," Fu said to Sean. Sean had wondered if this was going to be part of the deal, make sure he didn't have anything to return to Braden on. He opened his wallet and pulled out a ten and two ones.

"That's it?" Hon asked. "How were you going to get back to New York?"

Sean showed her his round-trip ticket. She took it, tore it up, and threw the confetti out the window. Then she opened the door and stepped out.

Sean turned to Fu. "My pills."

Fu looked at him for a long moment, his eyes softening. Good cop, Sean thought. "Just keep your ass here in fucking Gotham and you'll be fine. Braden's way fucking off limits, got it?"

Sean nodded yes. Fu took the twelve dollars and pulled the pill bottle out of his jeans pocket. It was cracked, a small chip of plastic had broken off the bottom, and the inside of the bottle was powdery. Fu looked it over.

"Sorry, man. Musta been when I had to deal with the bitch." He started to give it to Sean, then folded it back in his palm. "Don't got any Percs or Vics, do you? I'll trade you."

"No, just this. Keeps me from drinking."

"I know, but you got pains, don't you? You sure? Want me to check your bag for you?"

Sean started to unzip his bag and Fu stopped him. He gave Sean the pill bottle and indicated he should leave the truck. He seemed deflated, maybe scared about the trip back. Hon didn't share Fu's anxiety. She was sheltering the gun from view and glaring at Sean as if he'd just told her she looked like Miss Piggy.

"You ever show up in Braden again, we look bad. And we don't like lookin' bad."

"Thanks for the advice. And for the ride."

Hon got back in the cab, slammed the door, and blackened her glare. Fu pulled out, turned around one of the girders, looked like he was going to drive up the off ramp, stopped with a squeal of tires, circled back, and went north under the highway.

Sean watched until they were out of sight, until he was sure they weren't circling back. He looked down quickly at the broken pill bottle. The pills were all intact, though some had left residue on the inside of the bottle. He took a sock out of his backpack, put the bottle in the sock, and put both back in the backpack. He took out another sock and retrieved a twenty-dollar bill from the three hundred or so dollars he had left. Fu, he thought, had been a victim of his nervousness. Had he checked for painkillers he would have found Sean's bankroll.

Sean walked over the cobblestones to Broadway. It took him two blocks to find a pay phone and then another half a block to find a store that would change his twenty and give him quarters. He called the reception desk at the halfway house. He was thankful when he got Don, the newly minted social worker who was something of a pushover.

"Hi, it's me, Sean Collins."

"Sean. You're late. You were only signed out until last night."

"I know. Some complications. Look, I'm going to be staying for another couple of nights."

"Staying?"

"Yeah. I'm still out in my hometown. I want to see my son. And—"

"Sean? What's going on?"

"I said. Things are going well. I just need a couple more days here. I'm staying with some friends and—"

"Sean, you're calling from New York."

"What?"

"Caller ID. The number. You're at a pay phone in New York."

Sean hung up. He walked quickly away from the pay phone, wondering if this caller ID could tell them where he was exactly, if cops could come and get him. But then he slowed his pace, realizing that he wasn't wanted, hadn't broken any laws or parole. They just wanted to help him, to keep him off booze, to help him get his memory back.

He stopped then, realizing fully where he was, what had happened. He'd been kicked out of Stallings's office, kicked out of Braden. The buildings on Broadway hulked over him, the train above on the elevated tracks screeched as it pulled into the station. He had been out on his own for two days and had weathered the horror, a near suicide attempt. That was in Braden. He didn't know if he could resist that suicidal urge in the city.

He felt himself sweating now, fear rising. Fu and Hon scared him, but not as much as the vicious memory and what he might do to himself, to Kevin's future. He saw the stairs up to the subway, knew that the number 1 train would take him close to the Port Authority Bus Terminal. He was filled now with the sense that he wasn't safe where he was, in the city. He couldn't do anything here to help himself.

And there, in Braden, was Stallings's fucking indifference, his haughty certainty about G.G. Sean had been rattled by that at first, but now the injustice of the system smacked him full face. He had personal reasons for wanting Stallings to take him seriously, but there were more political ones as well. A guy who's comfortable keeping a railroaded innocent like G.G. in prison for life needs to be exposed, at least made to own up to his lethal indifference.

He started up the stairs. There were others to go to in Braden. He could go to the sheriff, make him listen. He heard a downtown train pulling into the station. There was no doubt about what he had to do. He took the rest of the stairs two at a time.

19

Risa got only a couple of paragraphs into G.G.'s confession before she had to put it down. He hadn't begun to detail the actual murder, but he had talked about Carol, about her kindnesses toward him, about how she understood his love of chopping brush. It was this evocation of the caring Carol that got to Risa.

Carol had taken care of her mother and father from such a young age that when she was a teenager, when she and Risa would do silly high school stuff, it always felt to Risa as if Carol was just doing these things to play at being normal. She would often say that she had to "get back to reality," when she meant she had to go home.

After they graduated from college, in the fraught months between Sean's father's suicide and Kevin's birth, Carol was an almost constant presence. She seemed to understand intuitively when Risa needed her help, when she needed to be left alone. Carol herself was on a high, having found the love of her life, as she put it, in a graduate student at Syracuse, thinking about a life together with him. Risa met him once when he visited Braden and he seemed nice enough, but with little spark. If you asked him about his work, he'd come alive. If you asked him about all the snow in Syracuse, as Sean had once, he drew something of a blank.

Sitting in the office at The Kitchen, Risa felt a sadness about Carol's death she hadn't felt in years. Despite what Sean said, she couldn't believe Carol would take Sean into her bed. Carol had been very happy with whatever his name was, Dan something, and she knew what Risa was going through with Sean. She had been as attentive to Risa as she apparently had been to Sean. Risa remembered that horrible week when Sean was nowhere to be found. She had called Carol several times, gotten no response, and figured, as did everybody else who knew Carol well, that she was in Syracuse visiting her boyfriend. In fact it was he who alerted the sheriff's office that Carol might be missing, doing so only hours before the town cops found her abandoned car.

Risa picked up G.G.'s confession again and skimmed the first few pages. Stallings had said the motive was sex, that G.G. had mistaken Carol's friendliness for flirtation, and that G.G. didn't know about normal sexual relations, could only imagine some sort of violence. Stallings had even trotted out a psychiatrist who had examined G.G. to give the supposed motive some scientific gloss.

Risa's eyes rested on one line on the fourth page. "I wanted to get her up in the woods so nobody would see us, so I told her I found some kittens when I was clearing brush and they was abandoned. There weren't no kittens, but I knew she liked cats so I said that. She wanted to go up and help them out."

Risa was about to turn the page when something about the kitten ruse stopped her. Had she heard this in the courtroom? She couldn't remember. It must have made sense to her then the way it made sense to her now, as emblematic of Carol's Florence Nightingale personality. But something else was hidden in that account, something that nettled.

Bell came to the office door and said she was leaving, that all the prep for dinner was done.

"You okay?" Bell asked, seeing Risa's faraway gaze.

"Yeah."

"I hear he's left again."

"I guess so. I don't know."

"And how's Kevin?"

"He's okay."

"Will Neese was just in, said he thinks Kevin should get a medal."

"I don't want to hear that kind of stuff. No, please."

"I understand. I've got breakfast tomorrow, but I've got a doctor's appointment at one."

"Everything okay?"

"Yeah. Just my once-a-year breast smashing."

"Hate that. I'll be here by eleven."

Bell left, and Risa followed her out to the bar. Walt Stoddard, the owner of The Ding Dong, was there nursing an afternoon beer. Risa had known him forever and always thought his head needed a Stetson to go along with his crop of long hair, handlebar mustache, and a voice that seemed to have its origins deep down in some saddle.

"Missing a good tap, Walt?" This was their standard opening when visiting each other's establishments. Walt only nodded and got to the point.

"All I'm hearing true, Ris? Sean and all?"

"I don't know how far it went, but yeah."

"It went all the way to Sean saying he killed Carol. He playin' games or—"

"No games."

"Sane?"

"I guess so. He's sober and seems to have his head on straight except for that one thing."

"You believe him?"

Risa knew she couldn't say flat out that she didn't, not to Walt. He had made a stink about G.G.'s arrest and confession but had been howled down by Armey and Stallings. "I don't know, Walt. I'm confused."

Walt nodded and shook his head. Risa imagined that Sean's

arrival and revelation were a bitter vindication for Walt. Doubly bitter in that he had always liked Sean.

"Let me know if there's anything I can do," he said as he pushed a five across the bar and left quickly. Risa had the feeling she was somehow guilty herself.

She spent the next few minutes absentmindedly tidying up the bar when a thought hit. Cats. Carol didn't like cats. She was allergic to them. That didn't mean that she wouldn't have responded to G.G.'s asking her to help with orphaned kittens. She most likely would have, but didn't G.G. say something about her liking kittens?

Risa went back to the office and found the passage: "I knew she liked cats." It was completely possible that G.G. had just misunderstood Carol, or that he had liked cats and Carol didn't want to hurt his feelings. All these things were possible, but the words swimming in front of her eyes now looked different, the pages felt different in her hands. Doubts rose.

She turned back to the first page and began to read again. Now the words weren't so much about Carol as they were about G.G., about the people he was with when he made the confession. She looked at the names on the first page. Sheriff Armey and John Stallings were there. A stenographer. But there was no lawyer for G.G. He started off the confession saying he didn't want a lawyer. What was Risa going to find besides the cat information? She sat and continued reading.

Ten minutes later she was rattled. The one doubt about the confession had become many. All it took was seeing the whole thing through a different lens, walking in G.G.'s shoes. Maybe Walt's appearance had done that to her. The vivid, gory details became too vivid, too gory, almost poetic, from a man who everyone knew was a near illiterate. The motive for the murder was nonexistent. The only thing that rang true was his concern for Carol, and Risa could see Stallings and Armey working that angle constantly, reminding him several times that he needed to tell the truth for Carol's sake.

She finished her reading and was walking into the bar area when the phone rang. She saw a New York phone number and hesitated. It could be a lot of people calling, suppliers, salesmen. But she knew it was Sean.

"Hello." She heard bus noises.

"Is Risa there?"

"Sean? It's me. Where are you?"

"New York, but I'm getting on a bus to come back in a few minutes. I know I shouldn't call you, but I don't know who else. Is it okay?"

"Yes. Why did you leave if you're coming right back?"

"I was forced to. Some guy and his girlfriend forced me to go with them, dropped me off in the city, warned me not to go back."

"Some guy?"

"He had a light blue pickup and a Fu Manchu mustache."

"That's Jerry Landis and Patty Dane. One's more psycho than the other."

"That's them."

"If they said to stay away . . ."

"I don't give a shit. I can't stay here, in the city. Stallings wouldn't listen to me. I'm going to go to the sheriff and make him listen."

"Sean . . ." Risa stopped herself. She wanted to tell him what she had just been doing, what she had found in G.G.'s confession. But she realized that would make him think she believed him. She hadn't gone that far.

"What?"

"Stay there. Let me talk to some people here, maybe find you a lawyer. Then you can come back. Landis is really dangerous."

"I'll take my chances there. I'm dangerous to myself, Risa.

I told you what happened yesterday. I've gotta get someplace where I can make somebody believe me and do what's right."

"'What's right'?" Risa was stalling. She was the one he needed, the one he needed to convince and to help him get what he wanted. But that was the last thing she wanted to be or do. She wanted Sean back whole and blameless.

"I've gotta go. I've gotta find someplace to—"

Risa heard a buzz and some clicks, then a half a word from Sean and the line went dead. She waited for the phone to ring again, and when it didn't she called the number on the ID. A woman answered and said there wasn't anybody near the pay phone who looked like Sean.

Risa was pure reaction now. She knew what she was going to do. She was going to meet Sean's bus and she was going to protect him, from Landis, if she had to, from himself. She dialed Alan's cell, got his voice mail, left a brusque "Call me," and hung up. Sean would need a place to stay. She thought of a dozen friends who might possibly put him up for a day or two, but she didn't want to put them in jeopardy if fucking Landis was looking for him. Then she had a thought.

She called Henry and reached him at his office. She told him about Sean's call. Henry whistled at Landis's name.

"He likes guns and that Patty's still in combat."

"I know. But he's coming back. I've got to . . . Could he stay in your tool shed?"

"My tool shed?"

"Is it still there? I remember—"

"It's still there. There's even a cot. Jesus, Risa."

"I know. He's got a plan. He's going to go to Armey. It'll just be for a night. If Armey throws him out on his ear, maybe I can convince him to go back."

"I'm going to be in Harrisburg tonight. There's a committee meeting and I'm not going to drive back until tomorrow."

"That's okay. I'll see he gets taken care of. Is it locked?"

"No. Is there something like harboring a criminal here?"

"Do you think he killed Carol?"

"No."

"Then you're not harboring a criminal, right?"

"Right."

"Thanks. Obviously nothing about this to anyone."

"Obviously. I'll leave the back door to the house open so he can use the bathroom. There's nothing in the fridge."

"I'll take care of that. You're sure you're okay with this?"

Henry hesitated. "Yeah. I'm sure."

"Henry. I read the confession."

"And?"

"You read it over again, right?"

"Yeah."

"That's not G.G. talking. I don't think he killed Carol."

"You don't? So Sean . . ."

"I can't believe that either."

"So, who?"

"I can't imagine. But think about that on your way to Harrisburg. Something's off here."

They hung up and Risa turned to see Milt Norris sitting at the bar, his ever-present smile present.

"I realize I'm a little early for a beer, but I'm gonna have one anyway. A Miller. You won't tell on me will you?"

"Course not."

As Risa drew the beer, she thought about the last part of her conversation with Henry, about the possibility that Carol's murderer had not yet been found. She thought about the nature of a town like Braden and was chilled by the thought that maybe for years she had been serving breakfast, dinner, or a beer to the man who killed her best friend.

The Miller foamed over the top of the glass until Milt good-naturedly told Risa she might want to think about shutting off the tap.

20

Risa had gone home, grabbed a sleeping bag, some cold leftovers, and a flashlight. As she was about to leave the house, Alan called. Risa skipped any greeting.

"Did you get my messages?"

"No. Not until just now," Alan said. Risa could hear the hum of conversation behind him. "We didn't have coverage up there. What's up?"

Risa knew this was nonsense, that if Alan had wanted to call her he could have found a way.

"What are you doing with Landis?"

"Landis?"

"Crazy Jerry Landis. You may not want to be connected to him, but I'm connecting you. He forced Sean to leave town, took him back to New York."

"How do you know this?"

"Just answer me. What are you doing with him? You know what a wingnut he is."

"I don't need this, Risa. Sean's had his shot with Stallings, he's gone, case closed. Let's move on, huh? Lilly's pestering me. Have you got this photo op at the restaurant Wednesday with Tomlin taken care of?"

Risa at first didn't know what he was talking about. "We'll work something out."

"What's that supposed to mean?"

"Just what I said. I'll figure it out. Tell her not to worry."

"You sound pretty casual about this. It's going to happen like that, Risa, blink of an eye. He's going to be on a tight schedule. We've got to have precision on this one."

"I said I'd have it ready, Alan."

"I didn't hear a lot of conviction. Let me just explain something. The national scene's getting pretty murky. There are some thirteen, fourteen House races that were longshots but are now possibles for the good guys. And you know we're one of them. That's why Joe's coming. That's why we're getting phone calls from people in the West Wing. Joe's going to be talking about how the party has its feet on the ground, understands what folks like those in Braden need. He's kicking off a little tour with us. So this thing's got to come off like clockwork. I haven't asked you to do a lot lately, but this one's a biggie and I'd appreciate it if you worked up a little enthusiasm."

"Call off your dogs and I'll get some enthusiasm."

"I don't have any dogs and Sean's gone. Now, can I put Lilly on to talk to you?"

"No. Tell Lilly if she bugs me in the least little bit I'll dump a bowl of spaghetti on Tomlin's head as the cameras roll."

"Jesus Christ, Risa. Don't take your goddamn frustrations out on Lilly."

Risa hung up. Frustrations? It was so much deeper than frustrations now.

The bus was late and Risa worried she might be spotted if she sat in her car across the street from the candy store. But she didn't move. The argument with Alan had receded, but the phoniness of G.G.'s confession buzzed around her. In the hours since she'd read his spoon-fed words, she'd tried to make the false confession proof Sean was right about what he did to Carol. But she just couldn't go all the way with that. She heard air brakes behind her and saw the flat nose of the bus fill her rearview. She felt the tingle of the illicit.

Sean came around the front of the bus, his Yankees cap on, not looking at her but crossing the street heading for her car. In a second he was in the front seat.

"Thanks, Ris."

They looked at each other, full of questions, and Risa had the feeling this was Sean's real homecoming.

"I can imagine, but how did Landis get you to leave with him?"

"He had a gun."

"Jesus. Sean, I think Alan was behind that."

"I wondered. He know you're picking me up here?"

"No, but he'll find out. I'm taking you to a tool shed behind Henry Saltz's house. He's in Harrisburg for the night. I've got a sleeping bag for you, some other stuff." She shook her head, put the car in gear, and started moving ahead. "You shouldn't have come back. Landis is—"

"I need you to do me a favor. Another favor." He took a crumpled piece of notebook paper from his pocket. "Could you call this lawyer in Pittsburgh and see if he can come here and represent me? He's the one who thinks G.G. was falsely convicted."

Risa made a turn, looked down at the paper, then out at the street. "Yes. Of course. Sean?"

"What?"

"I don't think G.G. did it. I read his confession. That's not him."

"Right. Absolutely. That's one of the reasons I'm back here. That and the treatment I got from Stallings. I felt like I'd gone into the saloon, ordered a sasaparilla, and got thrown out on my ear. I'm not going to make that mistake again. I'm going to be prepared. There's too much at stake here to have that asshole stonewall me."

"You think this lawyer can help?"

"He said he could. We talked a month or so ago. I don't know why I went to Stallings without him."

Risa pulled into an alley, went past a couple of garages, and then stopped one property away from Henry's. The alley opened to a grassy incline that led to a stand of trees. On the other side of the alley, the weathered boards of Henry's toolshed backed up to the property line.

Risa and Sean got out and walked to the shed. A mixed-breed dog came from the corner of the house, barking, wagging its tail. Risa tried to hush her.

"I think her name is Gina."

"It is," Sean said, taking a note off a nail on the door. "And I'm supposed to feed her in the morning, and there's an electric fence."

Gina calmed down. Sean opened the tool shed door. Henry must have straightened things up a bit in the musty place. A cot was opened, and gardening tools, most rusted, were stacked haphazardly in the far corner. The only ventilation seemed to come from a small window in back. They stepped inside and Risa closed the door behind them, shutting Gina out.

"This do?" she asked.

"It's a palace."

Risa spread the sleeping bag on the cot. "I forgot a pillow." She flopped the flashlight on the sleeping bag, then took out some containers of food. "These should keep even in this heat."

"Thanks."

Risa fidgeted for a few seconds. "I can only go so far, Sean. I'll call the lawyer, but I can't go where you're going. I can't believe you—"

"Don't say it. You have to think about Alan. You have to think about Kevin. Help me with the lawyer and I'll take care of myself."

"Alan."

"I know I'm really fucking with his campaign but . . ."

"But what?"

Sean held Risa's gaze but seemed as if he didn't want to go further, to take her where he had gone.

"Back then. I know how I got to New York now. When Landis was driving me in, I sort of spaced out and all of a sudden I could see it. It was night, I was loaded, of course, and I had this sticky stuff on my hands, on my pants. I'm guessing it was blood."

"Sean."

"Sorry. You don't want to hear this?"

"Not if . . . if it's more of Carol."

"It's not. Not really. I don't know if it was blood. But I'm sure of one thing. Two things. We were heading into New York and Alan was driving. He looked a little different. His hair was shaggy almost and he had a mustache. I don't remember seeing him like that except in this one memory. But it was him. I'm sure of that."

Risa felt her breath speeding up. She had seen Alan with facial hair only once, at Carol's funeral. And him driving Sean to New York? That might fit with what Warren had seen. But she resisted any conclusions.

"He was living in Washington then."

"I know. But . . ."

Gina nosed the door open and came in, tail wagging, flooding the room with light. Risa turned quickly, waiting to see if anyone was behind the dog. Then she turned back to Sean.

"I better go."

"Just a sec. Face the truth about me. Please. I did a horrible thing. I'm going to pay for it. It won't do me any good if you, the one person . . . if you deny it."

"It wasn't you, Sean. Even if you did it, it wasn't you. You were blacked out. I saw you back then, saw a blackout or two. You weren't yourself. You were somebody else. Somebody else might have killed Carol, not you."

Sean shook his head. "You don't know the depths of this, Risa. I hate myself deeply for what I did. I wish I could wake from this terrible dream, but I won't be able to until I'm dead."

Risa fought tears now. "Sean. I didn't want to declare you dead. Alan kept saying it was just a business decision, just a piece of paper, but it was you. I was killing you. I spent years searching, even when Alan didn't know. I said I was going into New York for a show and I'd walk the streets." She shook her head and swiped at the tears spilling over her eyelids. "I told myself I wasn't going to do this."

"I think you kept me alive, Risa. I don't know what else it could have been. Lying there in the gutter I must have carried enough of your love to keep me going."

"It was always there."

They moved into a hug as if it hadn't been over a decade since the last one. When she felt Sean's familiar chest, Risa let the tears come.

"Help me stay alive, Risa. Help me do what I have to do."

She pulled back, wiping her eyes, half nodding but showing her reluctance at the same time. She reached up and kissed his cheek as she had before, an answer to his plea. Then she looked him in the eye and knew she wasn't going to lose him again, that she would do everything in her power to prove him wrong.

21

Sheriff Armey's voice came rattling through Alan's BlackBerry as Alan was riding down Route 81.

"What the fuck's up with Sean Collins, Alan? I hear he's back."

"Not anymore. He left. He went back to New York."

"When?"

"This morning."

"Not what I heard. I haven't been on top of this one 'cause I been pukin' my guts up the last couple of days. But he was driving around with your wife an hour or so ago."

"My wife? Who says?"

"One of my spies. People keep their eyes open for me."

"How did your spy know it was him?"

"He's wearin' a Yankees cap. Who the fuck wears a Yankees cap out here and lives to tell about it?"

"That's your ID? 'Cause I've got it from the horse's mouth that he's gone for good."

"He talked to Stallings this morning. Tried to. John give him the boot."

"I know. But he left shortly after that. Your spies might want to get their eyes checked."

"Bullshit. I was gonna call Risa, ask her what's up, but I thought I'd do you the courtesy. What do you mean 'the horse's mouth'? What horse you smootchin'?"

"Guess your spies don't know everything, Jack."

"He's tryin' to say G. G. Trask didn't kill the Slezak girl. You know that, right?"

"I'm on top of it. Trust me."

"I don't want that bullshit floatin' around. John already called Doris, told her he'd have her head if she put that shit in her rag."

"I'm with you, Jack. Why're you yellin' at me?"

"'Cause your wife's chauffeurin' him around town."

"Can't be, but I'll check into it. Chemo's a bitch, huh?"

"I turned my guns in. Throw up five, six, seven times an hour you feel like stickin' a Colt muzzle in your mouth and blowin' your brains out."

"You'd get a little more accuracy if you stuck it up your ass, wouldn't you?"

"Funny."

After they hung up Alan speed-dialed Risa, but she didn't pick up. He didn't want to leave a voice message. Lilly was in the front seat. She looked up from a text message.

"You might have a busy couple of days coming up."

"Don't I already have them?"

"They might want to do a sort of group meeting in Washington with you and four or five other key races."

"Who?"

"Congressional leaders and the White House."

"Fuck. Frank, you ready to drive to Washington?"

Frank, as always, nodded without smiling. Alan stared at his BlackBerry. He knew Jack Armey's network didn't fail him often. Could Sean have made it back already? And could Risa really be helping him? While he was thinking about this, Mel Carney called to say that everything with Frankie Robich was taken care of.

"He's no problem, but his brother, father of that kid Kevin decked on Scrimmage Day, still isn't too happy. Name's Richie. He's shop foreman over there, not some punk like his brother. I got a number for him. You might want to make a call."

"Thanks, Mel."

Alan took down the number.

"Mel, anybody say they've seen Sean Collins around today?"

"He's gone, Alan. I told you. He's gone."

"Yeah, but you might want to do some checking around."

"You don't trust me?"

"I trust you. I don't trust Sean's sanity, that's all."

"He's cracked, all right. I'll see what's going on."

Alan could hear Lilly's charm-school voice in the front seat and figured she might be talking to Washington. He hoped she was right about things being busy for the next few days. Especially a trip to Washington. He didn't want to be around Braden.

Risa could tell something was off as soon as she got through the back door. Kevin was sitting at the island in the kitchen, not on the phone, not texting, not smiling.

"Sorry, Kev. I got caught up. You must be starving."

"Why do you say that?"

Now Risa was certain there was a problem.

"Well, your practice. It must have been tough. I went by and looked for you today."

"At practice? You didn't see me."

"I know. When you don't have numbers, I can't tell who's who."

"I wasn't there."

"You weren't where?"

"At the practice."

"Really, why?"

Risa had taken the meal box she had picked up at the restaurant out of the paper bag and was starting to put the food on a plate. Kevin stood up and began to pace. Risa had seen this before and knew it was a signal of something deep troubling her son. She had always found this move of Kevin's remarkably similar to one Sean used to make when he was sober and wanted to make a point. He had always said he could think better on his feet.

Kevin stopped pacing and looked at Risa, anger rising. “Coach told me to go home after about fifteen minutes.”

“Why?”

“He said I was being too aggressive.”

“Too aggressive. Football?”

“Half-speed drill. I blindsided a kid.”

“And he told you to go home for that?”

“He said I needed some time off.”

“Did you tell Dad?”

Kevin gave her a strange look, as if the question was somehow alien. He shook his head no.

“Is it the fight you had, Kev?” Risa instinctively moved closer to him, but he backed up a little and she stopped.

“No. It was something else. I couldn’t think right.”

“What?”

“We were in the locker room, getting our pads on. Stevie gets like all serious and stuff and said he heard . . . what he said . . . He said he heard my old man was back in town.”

Risa was caught off guard and couldn’t help showing it.

“Kevin.”

“I told him he was full of it. I told him my ‘old man’ was dead.”

“Kev . . .”

“That’s right, isn’t it?”

“No, it’s not. And you know that Kevin. You were old enough. We told you he was being declared dead because we didn’t know.”

“You said it was just like he was dead.”

“Maybe, but . . .”

“That’s what you said.”

“Okay, Kevin. But he’s not dead.”

"So where is he?"

"Stevie's right. He was back here. He just showed up."

"When?"

"Two days ago."

"And you didn't tell me?"

"We were . . . I was waiting for the right time."

"Waiting for the right time? Stevie knows, half the guys on the team know, and I don't?"

"I'm sorry."

Kevin's arm whipped through a half circle so quickly it was a blur to Risa. She didn't flinch until Kevin's balled fist slammed into the wall beneath the kitchen clock and the sheetrock crumbled. Kevin's face was beet red with rage as he pulled his scraped knuckles out of the wall. He glared at Risa as he massaged his hand, then turned and headed for the stairs.

"Kevin," Risa called, following.

Kevin turned around menacingly, as if he might punch another wall. "Get away!"

He turned for good this time and stormed up to his room. Risa watched him go, then turned to the hole in the wall. Chunks of wallboard still dangled from the edges of the rupture and red flecks of blood dotted the yellow paint and chalky white of the sheetrock. She looked around the kitchen, almost expecting the flung chair to reappear or Alan to be on the phone saying he wasn't connected to whatever was going on. Things were coming apart. She couldn't cradle her son, soothe her husband, grieve for Sean. She looked back at the hole and thought for a minute that she was being sucked into its darkness.

22

The heat was dropping a bit, but it was still close and dusty in the shed. Sean had eaten and written in his journal, gone into Henry's house and used the bathroom, and then lay on the cot in the shed, thinking he should go to sleep. But he was too wired. He hadn't undressed yet. He imagined being in his underwear and Landis and his girlfriend showing up and him having to run in his skivvies.

He wondered how soon it would be before he'd call a room this size his home. He rolled to his side and in the dim light cataloged the gardening tools in the corner and on hooks on the wall. His eye stopped on a tool he couldn't at first identify. It looked like a knife, but as he squinted at it Sean realized it was a short-handled sling blade used to cut brush.

He was staring at this when, in an instant, the murder scene was upon him, as if it had leaped from the shadowy sling blade. It was as horrible as ever. And it was expanding. He was lurching toward Carol, the machete murderously solid in his hand, Carol's face already deformed almost beyond recognition. He realized he was in the grip of this vision, but for a long minute he was frozen, as if strapped to a gurney, and the images seemed plastered to his eyeballs. Then, when he seemed to lift the machete, probably for another blow, when Carol's full, bloody body was the only thing he could see, he managed to swing his feet over the side of the cot and sit up.

He made it to the door and went out into Henry's backyard.

He heard the swish of a neighbor's sprinkler, followed the sound through shrubs in back of the tool shed, saw the sprinkler undulating in the growing moonlight, waited until the spray moved away from him, walked through the soaked grass, grabbed the sprinkler as he had done countless times as a kid, and drank.

He ran away from the spray and went back through the shrubs, but he found himself in a different yard. He knew the way back to Henry's, but he didn't want to return to the shed until he was sure he could control the memory. This attack had been comparatively mild, but the shed still seemed dangerous to him. He began to walk toward an open space, a little moonlit hump. The weedy field was cool and mosquito free. He sat on a small stone facing the moon, which was rising lopsidedly over Braden.

The scene in front of him, with its shadowy blue grasses and its cricket soundtrack, was dreamlike. He leaned back and lay on the weeds, looking up at the stars. He felt the memory leave him completely, but a restlessness struck. He wanted to walk. The next thing he knew he was crossing Saffron Park. Then he was in front of the hotel. Then he was standing in front of a billboard staring at a can of Coors that seemed to be rocketing into space. He could taste the beer, and for the first time since he woke up in the hospital, since he started taking the experimental medicine, he imagined having a drink, the taste of it, the lift. He couldn't take his eyes off the billboard can for a long time, but when he did, when he started walking again, he was sweating with fear.

Now he needed to get back to the shed, reassure himself that he had his pills, and get some sleep. He thought he was taking the route Risa took, but in the dark of the alley he wasn't sure he had made the correct turn. The night was still. He had the sense that something was following him, not a person, a need. He moved ahead, still not seeing familiar signs of Henry's yard and his shed. He stopped. It was like his drunk days. In a town of ten thousand people, he was lost.

"To tell you the truth, I didn't believe him."

"You didn't?" Risa held out hope.

"It was too easy. I don't get the real perpetrators calling me, saying they want to confess. I told him he better make damn sure he knew what he was talking about. G.G.'s only going to get one shot, if he even gets that."

She had reached the lawyer, Charles "call me Chuck" Hamilton, after she had settled down, when Kevin was still up in his room. She had given him a quick rundown of what had happened with Sean. He didn't sound like any crank to her.

"He wants you to represent him. I think he's going to try to turn himself in again."

There was a pause on the line. "Hmm. I'll have to think about that, talk to some of my colleagues here at the clinic. Maybe that'd be the best way for G.G. to get his day in court. Can I call you back at this number?"

"Yes."

"They've got their own set of rules over there in Braden. I'm going to need somebody who knows what's what to help out. Would that be you?"

"I don't know. I still can't believe he would do something like that."

"Contrary to what I said before, I believe him now. It sounds like he's recovered more than when he talked to me and he's got the confirmation from the reporter."

After Risa hung up, she waited fifteen minutes before going up to Kevin's room. She knew now that she was going to have to tell him why Sean had returned, so he wouldn't hear that from friends, but despite what Chuck had said, she planned to make it sound more tentative than Sean was making it sound.

She knocked lightly on Kevin's door. He didn't answer. She

opened the door and saw him asleep on his bed, on top of his covers, in a T-shirt and boxers. She wondered if he had cried himself to sleep the way he had when Sean first left, when Alan hadn't yet come on the scene, when he would ask five, ten times a day where his daddy was and when he was coming home. Risa wanted to go to him now, lift his legs, pull the sheet down and cover him up, protect him. But he was too big for that, and if the night had taught her anything it was that Kevin was in many ways out on his own now.

As she snapped off Kevin's light, Alan called. He sounded as if he'd done some Johnnie Walking, as he called it, and was calling to say that he was going to spend the night near Scranton.

"I'm home tomorrow about noon and I'll be home right up to Tomlin's visit."

"Kevin found out about Sean."

"How?"

"Stevie. He had a bad practice after that and the coach told him to go home. He got mad at me and put his fist through the kitchen wall."

"What did you say to him?"

"Nothing. It was what I didn't say that got him mad. We should have told him."

"Shit. You want me to talk to him?"

"No. He's asleep."

"What did he do in practice?"

"He said he was too aggressive."

"What?"

"That's what I said. He said he hit some kid in a slow-speed drill, something like that."

"Half-speed. Shit. I'll call Coach."

"Better wait until you talk to Kevin."

"I want him out on that practice field Wednesday."

I don't ever want him on that field again, Risa thought to herself. "Wait until you talk to Kevin. Okay?"

"Yeah." He paused. Risa imagined him taking a drink. "Anything you want to talk to me about?"

Risa didn't like the tone of this. There was one big thing she wanted to talk about, whether Alan had driven Sean to New York, but she knew her case wasn't fully prepared. She felt if she broached the subject he'd tear her to shreds. Then she realized what was behind the question.

"Sean's back in town. Landis's threat didn't bother him," she said.

"And you saw to it he got bedded down in Henry's little shack out there, right?"

"Do you want to talk about this now?"

"No, but if it only took me three phone calls to find out what the fuck was going on, it's going to take Errol Roberts maybe five, six, and then he'll have a field day with the fact that my wife's aiding and abetting some deluded drunk."

"How can you talk about Sean like that? Jesus, Alan. Have you forgotten all we had together? We meant so much to each other. Can't you remember that?"

"You two running off and getting pregnant keeps getting in the way. What, he called you and you went running? Or did you call him and plead with him to come back? Either way, your message is loud and clear. You don't give a shit about this campaign."

"What do you think this is, Alan, freeze tag? Everybody stop right where you are until the campaign's over? You make it sound like I imported Sean just to piss you off."

"You didn't have to chauffeur him around."

"He's Kevin's father. And in case you forget that, there's a nice fat hole in the kitchen wall to remind you."

"Maybe that nice fat hole means he likes the father he's got, the one he calls Dad. Ever think of that?"

Risa knew she'd been outlawyered. How many times had arguments gone Alan's way just because he was the better debater? But maybe this time Alan was right too. Hadn't Risa pushed Kevin to accept Alan as his father, call him Dad?

"Don't you think it's better to keep in touch with Sean, know what he's thinking, than to ignore him?"

"They've got phones in New York. I've gotta go into a meeting. I'll see you tomorrow."

Risa thought she heard the rattle of ice cubes as he hung up. She could see leather-faced Lilly clucking over Risa's inability to get in line. In an instant she realized that she was now in the midst of her own campaign. She just couldn't imagine what victory would look like.

23

Alice Drummond pulled her car into her driveway, which ran along the side of her house to a barnlike garage in back, and the motion-sensor light on the front of the garage turned on. Alice could see that her husband Mark's car wasn't in the driveway. Had she forgotten something? Was this bowling night? Was Mark working the night shift, filling in for someone? Or had he finally had it, packed it in, left?

He had said that morning that he would be there to help with the groceries. Alice had left her job at the Wal-Mart in Bloomburg, driven to Hazelton, and done a two-week shop. Now she had a trunk full of bags and no husband to help her haul it all inside. That was like him these days. It was probably deliberate, she thought, probably one of his fucking "punishments." They had been married two years, seven months, and a year into the marriage Mark had started to get jealous. For no reason Alice could see. Alice was a very good-looking twenty-four-year-old, slim, still muscled, with long dark brown hair that she wore in a ponytail most often. She turned heads. But she didn't know what Mark's beef was. He was no slouch in the looks department himself.

Alice got out of the car and opened the trunk. Crickets sang in the wooded area that ran beside the driveway. The plastic grocery bags, with their handles sticking up like ears, looked like a gaggle of egg-shaped animals waiting for her under the trunk light. She grabbed as many as she could take, estimating she would have to make at least three trips into the house, went along the side of the car near the wooded area, and headed to the back door.

The sound then was nothing but a whisper, a crunch on the gravel driveway behind her, drowned out almost by the ratchety cricket noise. Alice had just barely registered it when a hand came from behind her and clamped on her throat. It was so sudden and unexpected that Alice clung to the grocery bags for a second, not fully aware of what was happening.

Then the strong hand drew her back quickly to a huffing male body and pulled up under her chin so that her jaw clamped shut. Breath had left her and she struggled to draw air into her nostrils as the hand pulled with a force she thought would break her neck. She tried to wriggle free, letting the grocery bags fly out and thump around her. She felt a face at her shoulder and a growled whisper.

"No, Carol."

The hand pinned Alice's neck to this growling face as she felt her lungs plead for air. She thrashed wildly and rolled an ankle on a loose watermelon. Her weight was too much for her attacker. They went down together. She tried to grab for his head, then looked down and saw the silhouette of a knife coming toward her. She managed to get her arm up in time to block the thrust.

She felt the gash across her forearm, tried to scream but was too choked to get anything out, and dug her sneakered feet into the gravel for leverage. When she pushed back against the body underneath her, she felt her shoulder give way, the bone's popping out of its socket audible. Enraged by the searing pain, she twisted even harder and suddenly the man's hand lost its grip.

"Help!"

The sound was loud and echoey to them. The man seemed frozen for an instant. Then he kicked out as Alice rolled onto her dislocated shoulder and screamed in pain. He freed himself from the weight of her body and crab-walked on his back until he could roll away from Alice and run. She heard him crash through the brush. She tried to scream again for help, but the pain radiating out from her shoulder was so intense all she could do was throw up.

A car turned a nearby corner and its headlights swept over the driveway. But the car didn't stop. Alice couldn't move an inch without the pain returning its flames to her whole body. With her good arm she searched her pockets for her cell phone and then remembered she had left it on the front seat. She felt she was going to be sick again but she couldn't willfully roll over. She flopped her head to the right and saw a can of corn still rocking in an indentation in the driveway. Beyond that she saw something she had definitely not bought. A baseball cap.

When she turned back, she triggered a shift in her collarbone and the black bolt of pain that went with that was so deep and unbearable that she passed out, thinking, "Why, Mark? Why?" before she was gone.

24

Kevin was in the kitchen when Risa woke at seven thirty and went downstairs. He was pawing a bowl of cereal, staring at the small TV on the counter. He didn't acknowledge Risa's entry.

"Hi, hon."

"Hi."

"What are you doing up so early?"

"Going to practice."

"But I thought you said . . ."

"Coach said I can watch."

"We need to talk first, Kevin." Risa moved around the island and turned off the TV. Kevin didn't look at her.

"No, we don't."

"Don't you want to know details?"

"What details? Who cares?"

"Kevin, come on. You're . . . you're in shock about this."

"No, I'm not. No big deal. Parents lie to their kids all the time."

"I didn't lie to you."

"No?"

"No. I was going to tell you."

"What, saving it for my birthday, a present or something?"

"Don't be sarcastic. I was looking for the right time."

"Yeah, well, thanks, but Stevie found it."

"Do you want to hear about what happened to him, where he's been?"

"No. He wasn't here, that's all I know."

"There was a reason."

"Yeah, he was a drunk. You know how low on the totem pole a juicehead is? Jesus. Couldn't he be a smack junkie or something exciting like that?"

Kevin tipped the bowl to his lips, threw his head back, and slurped the excess milk. He got up quickly and put his bowl and spoon in the dishwasher.

"It's a disease, Kevin."

He didn't look at her, didn't say anything, and went out the back door before Risa could even react. She made a small move to follow him, but she knew whatever she said to him in the driveway would be weak, unconvincing.

When the phone rang a few minutes later, she hoped it was Kevin. But it wasn't.

"Risa, it's me, Henry. I'm at Memorial."

"What? What's happened?"

"Do you know Alice Drummond?"

"Not really. I know her mother."

"She was attacked last night in her driveway."

"Attacked?"

"Somebody came up behind her as she was taking groceries into the house. A man. He tried to choke her, had a knife."

"Is she okay?"

"Yes, but she's got a badly dislocated shoulder and a knife wound that was strong enough to fracture her forearm."

"My God."

"The attacker got away . . . but he left something."

Risa realized that Henry was not calling with general information, that there was another reason for the call. She was wary now. "What?"

"A Yankees baseball cap."

"Sean?"

"Alice said the only thing her attacker said was something about a Carol."

"A Carol, like the name?"

"Right."

"This happened last night?"

"About eleven. Sean wasn't with you then, was he?"

"No."

"Doris called me around three this morning. Risa, it was like when they found Carol's body. Doris called, said get back here now. I checked out of the hotel and got here about an hour ago."

"The police?"

"Sheriff's taking the case. Drummond and her husband live just outside the town line. Armey's here in the hospital. He looks like he should be a patient."

"They know about Sean?"

"Yeah. At first they thought it was the husband, Mark. But he's got an alibi. Then they thought maybe he set it up. He and Alice have been having problems. His first cousin on his mother's side is our friend Jerry Landis, but if Landis had been involved she'd have a bullet through her head. Armey knows Sean spent the night in my shed."

"He used a knife?"

"The attacker? Yes. A big one is what Alice said."

"You think Sean . . . ?"

"If you go through the field behind Ralph and Vicky's house and into that wooded piece behind the old shopping center, it's only about a half-mile walk."

Risa knew the field Henry was talking about and now saw Sean walking through it in the dark, his Yankees cap on, some sort of knife in his hand. She shivered at the thought and tried to temper it with her memory of Sean's hug. He had said she couldn't understand what he was going through, with the flashbacks, but maybe he was talking about something even deeper than that. Maybe he was this Janus-faced man who had come back to Braden not for redemption or to turn himself in, but to stalk new prey.

"Did you see him this morning?" she asked warily.

"I haven't been home. I have to write this story." Henry sounded shaky, as if he were trolling the same dark waters of suspicion she was.

"I better go see him."

"Be careful, Risa."

"I will."

They hung up and Risa stood with the phone in her hand for a long minute. In the times she had seen Sean since his return, the times she had been able to look him in the eye, she had been struck by the collapse of time, by the presence of the Sean who had not yet gone off the rails. But what lay in store for her now? A new confession? The hard-eyed lies of a psychopath? She didn't fear Sean, the Sean she knew. She feared the one she hadn't yet been introduced to. If that one was there, in the shed, what would she do? Run? Call the cops? She didn't know.

Risa took these questions with her as she changed clothes, found her keys, went to her car, and started to drive to Henry's house. Halfway there she realized she had left her cell phone at the house, but she didn't go back to get it.

Sean didn't know what time it was, but he figured it was much later than he usually woke up. He had come out of a very deep sleep but didn't feel all that rested. In fact he felt almost hung-over with a dry mouth and a headache.

He remembered the giant Coors can on the billboard and laughed, wondering if just the image had gotten him drunk. He remembered part of his walk in a moonlit Braden then, remembered it as if it had been a dream, one with pieces and not a whole. He was warmed by the memory until he wondered if that would be his last walk in freedom.

He didn't move for a long while, his hands jammed between his legs. He realized he was still fully dressed, lying on top of the sleeping bag. He looked toward the back of the shed and saw the swing-out window open. He guessed he must have opened it sometime in the night, but he didn't remember doing so. He sat up and felt light-headed. He was about to stand when the shed door creaked open. Risa, backlit by the morning sun, stood in the doorway.

"Hi." Sean said, shading his eyes.

Risa took a couple of steps into the shed and stopped. She gave him a long, searching look before she spoke. "Just wake up?"

"Yeah, a few minutes ago."

Risa came a few more steps into the shed, but when the door started to close she stood where she was and nudged it to keep it open. Sean couldn't see her features well, but he could hear uncertainty in her voice.

"You look like you slept in your clothes."

"I must have. I woke up in them."

"I just spoke to Henry."

"Yeah."

"He was in Harrisburg and had to come back for a story. Alice Drummond, Joyce Chandler's daughter, was attacked over on Grove Street. She was taking groceries into her house and a man came up behind her and grabbed her."

Sean stood up and scowled at this. Risa was not just delivering news. "Yeah?"

Risa took a step back. She wanted Sean to catch on, to figure out where she was going, but she didn't know what his response was going to be.

"He had a knife."

Sean instinctively looked from Risa to the wall where he had seen the sling blade the night before. It wasn't there. Risa followed his gaze. He turned back to her.

"She all right?"

"I think so. She fought him off. She's in the hospital, got a dislocated shoulder."

"Good."

"Good?"

"I mean good she's okay."

They stood for a moment, Risa waiting, Sean squinting. The direct sun was drawing sweat beads from his cheeks and forehead but he sensed he shouldn't move. Risa seemed to have more to say.

"They didn't catch the guy, but they found something he left behind."

"What?"

"A Yankees baseball cap." Sean didn't need a road map now to see where they were going. He turned and looked at his backpack leaning against a sawhorse leg. He was sure he had put his Yankees cap on top of the backpack. But it wasn't there. "You don't have yours?"

"I guess not. I thought it was here."

Sean couldn't hold Risa's gaze now. He wiped the sweat from his face. He was reassembling his walk through Braden, made it up to the moment he was lost, then memory petered out. From his work with a therapist he knew not to panic when a memory wouldn't come, to just relax and let it arrive when it would. But Risa's stiff stance and her clipped questions didn't help him relax.

"You were here last night?" Risa asked.

"Yes. I went for a walk, but I was back here later."

"When?"

"I don't know. I don't have a watch."

Then he remembered going into Henry's dark, messy house to take a piss. Was that after he came back?

"Me?" Sean asked, his voice low and weak.

"The guy said something about Carol. A Carol at least."

"Shit. I just walked around, Risa. I know I should have stayed in the shed here, but I had another attack, a small one, and I wanted to walk it off. I went to Saffron and, uh, there was a billboard with a . . ."

Sean thought about the Coors sign and made a swift move that sent Risa back a step or two. He dove for his backpack, yanked open the zipper, hauled out a sock, plunged his hand into the sock, and pulled out his pill bottle. He shook out a pill and got it down after a couple of dry swallows.

As he was doing this, Sean turned and saw the questioning look on Risa's face. He closed the pill bottle and put it on the sleeping bag.

"Sorry. I need those. Sobriety pills. An experiment."

Risa was staring at him now. "The back of your shirt and pants are dirty, like you've been rolling around."

"Really?" He tried to look at the back of his jeans. "I lay down out back there, to look at the stars." When he turned back to Risa she was waiting for him to say something more, to show he caught what was going on. "So the finger points to me, is that what you're saying?"

"I'm not saying anything, Sean. I'm asking. Henry called. He was worried because of the cap and the knife and . . . He said when Doris called him it was all reminiscent of when she called him about Carol's body years ago."

Risa waited for this to sink in, waited for Sean to hold her gaze. She was looking for signs of deception, but she could see he was more confused than anything else.

"I don't know," Sean said finally. "There's kind of a blank. I know I was walking around, but . . ."

"Were you wearing your Yankees cap?"

Sean shook his head no. "I remember a sprinkler, the moon, a Coors billboard."

"And then you woke up here?"

"Yes. Just now. Just before you came. Do you think I could have done that, to her?"

Now Sean looked Risa in the eye and held her gaze. She didn't know what to think. Faith and reason warred in her. She had an abiding belief in Sean's goodness, but she was facing a man who had spent over a decade drunk, who had suffered deep brain trauma, and whose memory, though healing, was still a fragile one-winged bird.

"It's not about what I think. Stallings is going to have to come after you now."

Sean absorbed this. "Yeah. I guess." He looked around the tool shed. "So I must have come back, gotten my hat, the sling blade, and headed out again."

"Henry said it's just about a half a mile from here."

"Half a mile? You'd think some of a trip like that would be up here." He tapped his temple.

Risa agreed, putting that point on the positive side of the ledger. "Right."

"But, I've had a couple of times when things were just a blank. I went to a restaurant with some people from the halfway house and didn't remember a thing about it the next day."

"I think you should go back there Sean. Back to the halfway house. They know you, know what's wrong with you. Let Stallings come and get you. You know, maybe somebody's setting you up."

"Who? Who knows I'm here? Just Henry, right?"

"No. Lots of people. Alan knew about your coming back right away. The sheriff."

Sean shook his head. "No. That's too far out. Setting me up."

"Yesterday I would have said something like Landis kidnapping you was far out."

Sean was slump-shouldered now, as if he were standing before a judge. "It could have been me."

Something beyond both faith and reason flooded Risa now. She thought of Carol, not Carol the victim, but Carol who had tried to soothe Sean. She had understood his illness better than Risa had. Now it was Risa's turn to come to his aid. She went to him and put her arms around his waist. He didn't respond.

"Get your stuff. Leave the sleeping bag. There's a ten o'clock bus you can catch."

"Shouldn't I just go to Stallings, get it over with?"

"No. There might be more to this than we know. Don't make it easy for him. You need a lawyer. You need help. Come on."

Sean returned the hug briefly, and then started to pack up.

Sean was getting his shoes on when Gina began barking loudly in the front yard.

"I'll see what that is," Risa said. "If I don't come back right away, head for the grove. I'll pick you up there."

"The grove?"

"Behind my parents' old place. It's still out of sight. Go in the back way. You remember how?"

Sean, struggling with a shoe, nodded as he looked up. "Risa?"

"What?"

"Thanks."

Risa left the shed and walked around the side of Henry's garage. As soon as she had a view of the front yard she knew something was wrong. Gina was doing a little circle dance, barking and looking at the front door of the house. And then she saw a sheriff's cruiser parked at the curb. She slowed and peered around the corner of the garage. A deputy stood on the small concrete porch, waiting. She knew him. He was the youngest of the Hanson kids. David. He didn't see her.

Risa stepped back and looked toward the tool shed. Sean was just coming out of the door, looking for her. She waved for him to run. He didn't get it at first, then did, and took off.

Risa turned back just as the deputy came toward her, head down. She could handle him. She had caught him once, behind the restaurant, in an embrace with a woman not his wife. He hadn't been able to look her in the eye since.

"David. Whew. You scared me."

"Sorry. What are you doing here?"

Risa had no cover prepared. "Henry wanted me to look at his messy backyard, see if it had any hope. You?"

Hanson hesitated. "I'm looking for somebody who I think is staying in Henry's tool shed."

Risa looked toward the backyard as if she might see somebody there. Then turned back. "I didn't see anyone. Who're you looking for?"

"I, uh, don't know if I'm authorized to say."

"Mystery, huh?"

"I guess so."

"I bet it'll be all over The Kitchen in fifteen minutes. I'll just find out there." Risa had thrown in The Kitchen reference to make sure Hanson remembered their moment out by the trash bins.

"It's your ex-husband, Risa. You knew he was back, didn't you?"

"Yes. But I thought he had left again."

"Seems he hasn't."

"Who says?"

"That I don't know."

"And he's supposed to be in Henry's tool shed?"

"That's what they told me."

Risa figured enough time had elapsed. "Well, I didn't see anybody back there."

"Henry really wanted you to look at his backyard?"

"That's what he said. I wonder if he wanted me to see Sean."

"Maybe. Let me take a look."

He started for the tool shed. Risa moved away slowly, and then after he'd passed, followed him. The shed was empty. The sleeping bag on the couch was rumpled, however, as if somebody had slept there. Hanson went toward the cot, blocking Risa's view of it.

"Somebody's been here." He reached down, picked something up off the sleeping bag, examined it, and turned to Risa. He held the pill bottle in his hand. "No name on it." Hanson put it in his uniform pants pocket.

"What does the sheriff want with Sean?"

"I don't know. I was just in my car over by the stadium and I got the call. Go to Henry's, see if Sean Collins is there."

Risa turned and walked out, hoping Hanson would follow. She didn't know if there was anything else in the shed that might tell him Sean had been there. Hanson came out of the shed and they walked together to the front.

"He may need those pills. He's recovering, a recovering alcoholic."

"Yeah?"

"I saw him yesterday. He said he needs those to stay sober. Do you want me to take them?"

"You? Why?"

"He might come and try to see me."

"If he does, call us right away. And if he needs these, tell him where he can find them."

Risa realized she had made a mistake. She didn't know how to undo it. She could see Hanson was enjoying having the upper hand. They reached the cruiser.

"Where's your car?"

"Didn't bring it. Walked over."

"Want a lift?"

"No thanks. I need the exercise."

"Speaking of that. Kevin hurt?" Hanson said, about to get in the cruiser.

"Hurt? What do you mean?"

"I saw him sitting out practice this morning. Wondered if he was hurt."

"No. Coach just wanted—"

"Him to rest? Good. He deserves it. He plays hard. That boy's going to be the key. Know what I mean? The key."

It seemed Hanson wanted to stay and talk Bulldog football. Risa only nodded and started to walk away. Why hadn't she said something like those were her pills or something smart? Hanson got in the car. When Risa heard him start up and pull away, she looked back. All she saw was Sean's pill bottle moving down the street.

25

When Sean made it to the grove he found a comfortable spot at the roots of a hemlock, a natural seat. The branches had grown a lot but still started only a few feet from the ground and provided dense cover for anyone sitting inside. Sean saw a couple of relatively fresh butts around the grove and imagined teenagers still found shelter from the storms of adolescence here the way the Three Amigos had.

His thoughts darkened as he realized where he was, how he had so badly messed up his homecoming. And now, if he had in fact attacked that woman, he must be sicker than he thought and should be locked up immediately. Locked up or dispensed with. He began to sweat, thinking that suicide might once again be the answer. There was Kevin to think about, but there were his unknown victims out there to consider as well. He was spiraling into an acceptance of this black fate when Alan came into the grove. He was dressed in a business suit, but he knelt down in the dirt and pine needles and spoke to Sean.

"Look. I'm going to get you out of here."

"Risa told you where I was?"

"This isn't about Risa. It's just about you and me."

"You're taking me to the bus?"

Alan looked around as if somebody might be nearby. "You're too drunk for the bus."

"I'm not drunk."

"Once a drunk, always a drunk. I'm going to take care of you."

"Alan. I need to get on that bus, get back to the halfway house."

Suddenly Alan was only inches away from Sean, his breath sour through his whisper.

"Stay right here. I'll be back to get you. Understand?"

Sean turned away from the foul breath. "Yeah. I understand."

Alan didn't respond, and when Sean turned back, there was no Alan. Sean realized quickly that there had been no Alan to begin with. He had seemed real, but he wasn't.

Sean inched toward panic. The woman on the bus. Now Alan. Was everything in between fiction as well? Was there anything real in what he was seeing? Risa, just appearing like that under the bridge. How could that have actually happened? Where was the anchor? Back in New York? That all seemed real, but who knew? How could he test things?

The pills. He reached instinctively for his backpack to reassure himself the bottle was safely in the sock. But as he began unzipping the backpack he remembered that he had taken one of the pills in front of Risa. And then he could see the pill bottle nested in the folds of the sleeping bag. Had he put it back? He tore at the zipper and pawed through the backpack. The pill bottle wasn't there.

The world accelerated. He saw himself banging through barroom doors, lurching toward the bartender, demanding shots and downing them in rapid succession. Had he lived something like that? No, he'd seen it on a TV show. The cop show. The bald guy did that, relapsed like a motherfucker. Sean's throat went dry and sweat now covered his face. He started lying to himself, saying the only reason he had been able to make the trip was that pill bottle, that medicine, that he wouldn't have dared come away from his support without it.

He stood quickly and banged his head on a low branch. He

couldn't think. Was the bottle still in the shed? Where was the shed anyway? How had he gotten from Henry's to this place? Where was he?

The bottle ballooned now, a piece of plastic he needed more than anything in the world. He looked around the grove, his panicked vision blurry at first. Which way? He saw Risa's parents' house through the branches. He had come in from the right. He turned right and started out of the grove. When he was almost out he remembered his backpack, went back, searched through it again just to make sure, zipped it up, and hunched his way under the branches to the light of day.

After Risa had walked a couple of blocks, she retraced her steps, went through Henry's yard and back to her car in the alley. She thought about going directly to the grove and picking up Sean, but she wanted to go home first and get her cell phone before she drove Sean to the bus, in case the lawyer called.

Alan's car was in the driveway. She pulled in behind his and saw his silhouette through the kitchen window. She would have to go in and make some excuse why she was going right back out again. Alan practically assaulted her when she entered.

"Where have you been? Your cell phone's here. I've been trying to call you."

"Sorry. You're back early."

"Where's Sean?"

"I don't know."

"Armey's looking for him. He assaulted Joyce Chandler's daughter last night."

"You don't know that."

Alan glared at her. "You talked to him this morning, didn't you? Where is he?"

"I don't know. I did talk to him. I don't know where he is now. I know he said he can't remember any attack."

"Attack. Attempted fucking murder is what it was."

"Henry called. It sounded horrible."

"And so you went over and alerted him and he took off."

"I went over and talked to him. He walked around town last night. He . . ." Risa realized that to say more would bring up the Yankees cap, the knife, the stains on the back of Sean's shirt. She had to go on the offensive. "When your thugs drove Sean into New York, they triggered a new memory for him."

"Who'd he kill this time?"

"Nobody. He remembers you driving him into New York."

"We road-tripped plenty of times. All three of us."

"Not that. Later, when he was a pass-out drunk."

"Bullshit. He said he doesn't remember shit from then."

Risa saw an opening. "Could have been around the time of Carol's murder."

"What do you mean, around the time?"

"Just that."

"I was in Washington, remember?"

"Only an hour and a half away."

"What would I be doing driving him into New York?"

"I asked myself the same question. Especially when I heard that Warren Mastic saw Sean get in a car early one morning with a guy he thought was Sean's best friend."

"What the fuck does Warren Mastic have to do with this? He's fucking gone."

"He wasn't when he told his granddaughter about what he'd seen. It must have stuck with him, like there was something fishy about it."

Alan put his fist to his mouth and paced, thinking, as if he were in the courtroom. "You're all over the map here, Risa. You're making me out to be some kind of criminal."

"I'm not making you out to be anything. I just want to know what went on."

Alan seemed caught, ready to spill some sort of beans, and Risa, suddenly, wasn't sure she wanted to hear what he was going to say.

"All right. I did. I drove Sean into New York."

"When?"

"Around the time of Carol's murder."

"What were you doing in Braden?"

"I wasn't in Braden. I'd been in Cleveland for a wedding, a friend of mine from Yale, Karen Rogers, remember her? I had to be back in Washington on Monday so I drove all night. But when I got near Braden, I thought I'd stop in at my parents', get some shut-eye, and then go on. Just before I got to The Ding Dong, about a mile before, where the creek crosses the road, I saw somebody stumbling around near the roadside. I stopped and couldn't believe it was Sean."

"You just saw him by chance? You weren't looking for him?"

"Looking for him at five in the morning? I was just looking for a place to sleep."

"And it was just coincidence?"

"Right. What are you looking for here?"

"The truth. Two minutes ago you said you didn't drive Sean into New York. Now you say you did. And you say you just happened on him in the wee hours. You're the lawyer. Tell me if you wouldn't question that story."

"Well, I might, but I wouldn't get anywhere. It's what happened. Period."

"So you drove him into New York."

"I drove him into New York. I confess. But I think I should stop there. You don't want to hear the rest."

"No. We'll just leave it at that."

Alan's BlackBerry sounded and he looked at the screen. But he didn't answer. He looked up at Risa.

"You promise me you'll keep what I tell you to yourself?"

"No. I don't know what you're going to tell me. You're going to have to trust me."

"All right. If this thing takes me down it'll be your ass too. Remember that."

"Got it."

"He had blood on his hands, and one pant leg, his right, was soaked in blood up to the knee. He was as drunk as I've ever seen someone who was still vertical. He hardly recognized me at first. I got him in the car and asked him about the blood. He didn't seem to know what I was talking about at first. I asked him if he had fallen, if he was hurt. I couldn't see any gashes or anything that would produce that much blood. He looked at his hands for a long time, you know, like drunks do. Then he turned to me, I'll never forget this, he turned to me and said, 'I killed someone.'"

"He said that directly, like that?"

"Yes."

"He didn't say, 'I killed Carol'?"

"No. 'I killed someone.' We were driving by then. I was going up the Front Street extension. I was going to take him to your house. But I stopped. I pulled the car over and tried to get him to tell me more. But he was gone by then, passed out. I must have stayed there ten minutes trying to decide what to do. To this day I don't know why I didn't drive him over to the police station or up to the barracks and let them deal with it. But he was my friend, he was your husband. We were once so tight. Even though we hadn't seen each other for a while, I still felt the . . . I don't know what you'd call it. The loyalty. Before I knew it we were on Route 80 headed for New York. He'd sort of come to every now and then, say he needed a drink, and then look over at me and say, 'I killed her.'"

Alan stopped at this, staring for emphasis.

"So, you were the one who took him to New York?"

"Yes."

"And you never told me?"

"I never told anyone. I'm sorry I have to tell you now. If he hadn't come back here I never would have told you."

"Those years we were searching for him, you never said, 'I took him to New York'?"

"We searched New York."

"But you never told me."

"Would you have wanted to hear that he was a killer?"

"I would have wanted to hear that you took him to New York. What did you do when you got there?"

"I took him to a hotel down near the Village, a place I knew about from—"

"Let me guess. Yale days."

"Right. And I hate that tone."

"What happened at the hotel?"

"He was sick. I got him some booze, cleaned him up, gave him all the cash I had, and left. I had to be in Washington by one or two or something. I don't remember what it was. I couldn't think about anything else. I kept checking for two, three days after, but there were no reports of any murders. I figured he was just hallucinating."

"And smearing himself with blood."

"I don't know, Risa. What would you have done?"

"I wouldn't have taken him to New York and dumped him on the street."

"He was in a hotel."

"He was sick. You said it yourself. He couldn't take care of himself."

"Yeah, well, you want to look at it in hindsight, fine. Look at this. He's still alive, he's a free man for now. He hasn't spent the last ten years behind bars."

"You're saying you saved him?"

"I'm saying I didn't know what the hell to do. And then when they found Carol's body, I . . . You saw me at the funeral.

I was a wreck. I went to New York and scoured the place, but he was lost."

"Lucky for you, huh?"

"Lucky?"

"Say he'd showed up back here a couple of days later, turned himself in like now, and told them his good friend Alan had taken him into New York even though he confessed to a murder and had blood on his hands and pants. Stallings, Armey, they'd be interested in that, wouldn't they? Not to mention the state bar."

"You're forgetting something."

"What?"

"G.G.'s confession. They had that before Carol's funeral, remember? What am I going to do, waltz in with this circumstantial evidence, a suspect I can't even find, and indict myself in the process?"

"Sounds like a stand-up sort of thing to do. For me, maybe. For Kevin."

"Fuck, Risa! You don't think I had you in mind in all this?"

"I'm worried you did."

"What do you mean?"

Risa shook her head and looked down, trying to decide whether to answer him. Her thoughts were all pinned to the image of Sean's front-seat confession. Sean had said his hands were sticky, but she hadn't let him go further. Now here was Alan with corroboration. She took this as the solid evidence of Sean's guilt in Carol's murder that had been lacking in the last few days. She knew that now, here in the kitchen, she had been taking out the shock of this on Alan, abusing the messenger. But she couldn't help herself. She kept up the abuse.

"Nice to have Sean out of the way so you could help the damsel in distress, wasn't it?"

"Jesus Christ, Risa. Jesus fucking Christ. Are you serious? Do you really think I'd do something that . . . that lowdown?"

"I think you kept the fact you drove Sean into New York quiet for eleven years. You had him declared dead, for chrissakes."

"No, you did."

"You helped. You pushed for that. And all the time you knew where he was?"

"I didn't know where he was. But you know where he is now, don't you? And now I'm guessing you know he attacked that girl last night. Don't you? I told you. I went back to look for him. You know we had them search everything they could in New York, Philadelphia, Boston."

Risa shook her head no, but that was a weak response. She was almost sick to her stomach absorbing the reality that Sean had killed Carol. Denial. Fucking denial. Now it was Sean and Carol in the woods, something going terribly wrong, Sean grabbing her throat, dragging her, and then. . . .

"Risa?"

"What?"

"I don't know. Where did you go?"

Risa shook her head. She thought about Sean, hiding behind her mother's house now. And she was looking at Alan, wondering if the things she'd just heard, the things she had just said, had cleared the air or caused irreparable damage.

"I'm here," she said finally.

"And are you with me on this?"

"With you on what?"

"There's no need to broadcast my role in Sean's disappearance, is there?"

Raw self-preservation. "I won't say anything. But I don't know about Sean."

"I'll take my chances there."

"I don't like the sound of that. Call off your thugs."

"I told you, I don't have any thugs."

Alan's BlackBerry sounded again, and this time he took the

call. He walked into the living room. Risa let the new revelation sink deeper. Sean the pianist, the kid with the wry sense of humor, blood soaked? She looked at the hole Kevin had made in the wall. She gagged on the connection.

Alan came back in the kitchen texting and suddenly for Risa he was a foreign body, someone who had ripped her husband from her.

"I've got to go," Alan said without looking up, heading for the door. Risa thought about stopping him, going over the details again, making sure she heard him right before she went off to meet with Sean. But Alan was out the door before she could say anything.

Then she realized that she had blocked him in. She grabbed her keys and her cell phone. She didn't want him to come back in and tell her she had to move her car. She didn't want him to tell her anything anymore.

26

Henry's morning had been so hectic that by the time Sheriff Armey got hold of him, pulled him into the corner, Henry couldn't think straight. Half the time he had been on the phone with Doris. She wanted to make the attack on Alice Drummond front-page news and she kept rasping commands at Henry every five minutes, pushing him to try to interview Alice, to run down Alice's husband and try to get some reaction from him, to get Sheriff Armey to "open his fucking mouth for once."

Though they wouldn't let any TV reporters in to see Alice, they let Henry interview her. But when he walked into the room he became rattled almost immediately. She looked much worse than he had imagined, her throat and jaw ugly masses of purplish skin, yellowing her face up to her cheekbones, her right arm heavily bandaged, her left in a sling, her eyes darting and still fearful. Her mother was sitting next to the bed, her father standing, looking like he was going to punch the nurse just to work out his rage.

Henry turned on his recorder and began, but his questions seemed to come from somewhere other than his voice box. He couldn't look Alice in the eye and he knew he was making a mess of the interview. Every time he even gazed in Alice's direction, Carol Slezak's slain body lay on the bed instead of Alice's wounded one.

When he left the room he felt he had escaped something.

He went downstairs to the lobby and saw a TV reporter from Scranton's Channel 3, Debbie Fins, talking to Stallings. He knew he should join that conversation, but when he started toward the two of them he got a look from Stallings that said keep away. That was when Sheriff Armey called him over.

Armey looked like shit. His Santa Claus paunch had shriveled, his face was drawn and ghostly, and his hair was coming out in patches. But his eyes still had some life and they fixed Henry with a glare he couldn't avoid.

"Fuckin' déjà vu, right, Henry? You and me. A body."

"She's not going to die."

"All praise to Saint whoever. You ain't a greenhorn this time, are you?"

"Veteran."

"Watch how you use that word, boy. You don't know shit about real war."

"Experienced. How's that?"

"Better but questionable. What the fuck you doin' with Sean Collins hiding out in your tool shed?"

"I . . ."

"He used your ass, Henry. What, he give you some sob story?"

"No."

"Risa. Risa give you some sob story? 'Cause you and Risa fucked up. Looks like he was just looking for a base of operation for his next sally. Don't it look like that to you?"

"You mean Alice."

"Course I mean Alice."

Henry hesitated, then nodded toward Stallings. "He told John he killed Carol. John wouldn't listen to him."

"Yeah, that's a fuckup. But you ever heard of the big lie technique, tell a big enough whopper and nobody'll believe you? John didn't realize how slick Sean is. John might have to pay for that one. But you, what're we going to do with you?"

Henry stared at Armey, frozen by the implied threat. "I don't know."

Armey got his face to form as much of a smile as he could. "Nothin', Henry. You just play ball from now on and we'll forget that harborin' business. You got it?"

Henry got it.

He made his call to Risa, then went to his office and tried to fashion something like a story from the bits and pieces and shitty interviews he had. The work kept looping him around to images of both of the women, Alice and Carol, and every time it did Henry was distracted, lost the thread of what he was writing.

He finally cobbled together an article and, after he had sent it, got a fine tongue-lashing from Doris. She said he was looking piss-poor under pressure.

"So who's the suspect?"

"Armey's not saying."

"I know. I can read. Who's the suspect?"

"I don't know."

"Oh, for chrissake. You high over there?"

"I don't do that."

"Maybe you should. Readers are going to be so fucking far ahead of us on this one. Everybody's buzzing about Sean Collins."

"Yeah. That's a good one."

"A good one?"

"A good possibility."

"I'm hanging up, Henry, try to make something of this piece of shit you just handed in."

Henry sat in his cramped office for another fifteen minutes hoping the fog that had descended on him in the morning would lift. It didn't. Risa seemed to be his anchor now. He reached her in her car and she told him the whole story, including the fact that Hanson had Sean's pills. Henry didn't think that was any big deal until Risa told him about his dependence, about what she'd seen earlier in the tool shed.

"Do you think he knows he's missing them?" Henry asked.

"I don't know. I'm on my way to find out."

"Where is he?"

Risa hesitated. "Maybe it's better if I don't tell you."

"Yeah. I think you're right. But keep in touch, okay?"

"Okay. Talk to you later."

Henry decided to go home, to take a nap, even though he knew he should be working the story. He managed to bike to his house and when he got there heard Gina barking in the backyard. He went in through the front door, then into the kitchen, and just as he looked outside he saw Sean go into the tool shed.

Henry went quickly out the back door. Gina stopped barking and came to him, wildly excited, happy to know her barking had brought her master to her.

Henry called out before he got to the shed. "Sean?"

There was no answer. Gina whined. Henry pulled open the tool shed door. His eyes adjusted quickly to the dim light but he could see no one inside. Had he imagined Sean going in the door? Gina used her nose instead of her eyes, however, and went to the cot, stretching out her front paws, giving little yelps. It was then Henry saw Sean's hand, then his shirt under the cot. He went closer.

"Sean? It's me, Henry."

Sean didn't move for a few seconds, then slid his way out from under the cot, dragging his backpack after him.

"What are you doing back here?" Henry asked as Sean stood, brushing himself off.

"I think I left a bottle of pills. Did you talk to Risa?"

"Yes. She said the sheriff's deputy found the bottle. He's got it."

"Shit." Sean shivered, his eyes flicking. "They came to get me."

"Right."

"They think I attacked that woman last night."

"They have a lot of evidence," Henry said, staring blankly.

"I don't remember parts of the night. I don't know if I did it or not."

As if he were waking up from a dream, Henry suddenly realized where he was, what was going on. Doris's call, the interview with Alice Drummond, the whole jumbled morning. Now, looking at Sean, he could see things more clearly.

"Do you still want to turn yourself in?"

"No. I need to get back to New York, to get my pills."

Henry knew he should work some subterfuge, walk in the house, call the sheriff's office. But he didn't. He wanted Sean to go, one less thing to deal with. He looked at his watch.

"If we go now, you can make the bus to New York. Do you want to do that?"

"I have to."

"They'll find you in New York."

"I've got help there. And Risa's working on a lawyer."

"So you want to get the bus?"

"You think they'll be looking for me, the sheriff, at the bus?"

"I don't know. I can take you over in my car. If it looks like they're there we can just drive on, maybe pick up the bus someplace else. But we've got to move."

Sean looked around the shed as if the bottle might be there, hiding. That simple search seemed to remind him of his vulnerability, of the haven that waited for him back in New York. He nodded to Henry's question.

"I should have fucking stayed there."

Henry loaded Gina in the backseat of his car, had Sean slouch down out of sight in the passenger seat, and drove the indirect, back route to the bus stop.

He went slowly down the alleyway behind the abandoned

hotel, across from the candy store and bus stop. When the nose of his car was far enough past the corner of the hotel and he could see the bus stop, he waited.

"Thanks for this," Sean said.

Gina paced back and forth on the seat behind them, eager for some sort of adventure. They had waited only a few minutes when the bus made its sweeping turn from Market and glided into its spot. Henry waited to see if there were passengers getting off or coming out of the candy store to get on. None did. Henry pulled out quickly and parked about fifteen yards in front of the bus. Sean got out and walked, head down, to the open bus door.

Sean still felt exposed as he stood in the front of the bus waiting for the driver to come out. He kept looking around for anything that looked like a sheriff's car. Henry was still parked in front of the bus. Sean thought about going back to Henry, asking him to take him to another stop, maybe all the way into New York.

When the driver bounded up the steps, he surprised Sean.

"Oh, didn't see you get on," he said. "Headin' back so soon?" Sean realized he was the driver yesterday as well.

"Yeah." Sean's eyes continued to look for cruisers as he paid for his ticket, got his stub, and headed back to find a seat. There were four or five other passengers, but they were all at window seats, not looking at him. He found a seat in the back but didn't sit down. He kept looking out the window, ready to run if some sheriff's deputy pulled up. He thought about being trapped in the bus and read the instructions on the emergency window across from his seat.

The bus driver said something to the passenger in the front and went back inside the candy store. Sean worried that it had something to do with him. He could see Henry's car, still parked in front of the bus. Should he leave the bus, go to Henry, make his getaway? He was about to start down the aisle when the driver returned, bounced up the steps, slipped quickly into his seat, shut the door, and started the engine. Then he looked in the rearview mirror and spoke loudly.

"Have a seat. We're on our way."

Thinking this a command, Sean sat. The bus did a U-turn, and as it did Sean could see Henry following the bus's progress in his side mirror, then pulling out and heading away from the bus. Sean was still tense as they turned down Market Street heading for the bridge. He knew he wasn't leaving for good. He would go back to New York, gather himself, and return.

The blast of a car horn to the right of the bus halted these thoughts. Sean turned to see what it was all about. The bus was crossing Front Street and he caught a glimpse of Landis's powder blue pickup stopped at the light, Landis laying on the truck's horn, Patty Dane in the passenger seat, waving her hand out the window. The pickup squealed a right turn and, fishtailing, raced after the bus.

When the truck was out of sight behind the bus, Sean swung around in his seat. The driver seemed oblivious at first, then must have caught the racing pickup in his side mirror. Sean threw himself across the aisle in time to see Landis pull up beside the bus, still blowing his horn. Dane was screaming up at the bus, shaking her fist.

As the bus took the ramp onto the bridge, the bus driver pulled a little to the right, to let the pickup pass. Sean could see a car coming toward them on the two-lane bridge. Landis gunned the pickup and Sean lost sight of it as it drew even with the bus. The bus driver kept his eyes straight ahead, trying to avoid scraping the concrete sidewalls. The car coming toward them was blowing its horn now, slowing. Landis cut in front of the bus, nearly rolling the pickup, darting between the scissoring car and bus. He pulled ahead of the bus and was almost on the other end of the bridge when he jammed on the brakes and the pickup slid sideways, blocking both lanes.

The bus driver had to brake hard to stop in time. The other passengers were yelling now, being jerked around by the violent stop. Landis jumped out of the driver's seat, brandishing a tire iron, striding toward the bus, Dane right behind him. She had something in her hand that could have been a gun. The bus driver didn't move to open the door, but when Landis started pounding on it with the tire iron, the driver threw the lever and the door opened.

Sean was frozen in the aisle, watching the scene play out as if it were on a screen. Then, when Landis popped up beside the driver and pushed him back in his seat, Sean came to. Landis swept his gaze over the bus until he spotted Sean. He came quickly down the aisle. Sean looked to his right, saw the emergency window, reached over, and yanked at the red handle. It wouldn't budge. Landis was yelling something. Sean jumped up on the seat, kicked the handle as hard as he could, but it still didn't budge. He grabbed the seat back in front of him, got leverage, and kicked again. The lever sprung up, letting the window flap out. Landis was only a few seats away now, coming fast, the tire iron raised. Sean threw his right leg through the window opening, pushed the window open farther with his hand, ducked his head, and rolled out just as Landis's tire iron came down on the seat back next to the window.

Sean fell to the pavement but was able to break his fall with his right hand and knee. Pain shot up from the knee, and when he tried to stand the knee buckled at first. Sean could see the car that had been going the other way stopped in the middle of the bridge, the driver getting out. Sean looked up at the window and saw Landis's leg poke out. He forced himself to stand and limp-walked toward the back of the bus. He saw Landis getting more of his body out the window. Sean turned and started to run.

The pain was hobbling, but Sean could practically feel Landis breathing down his neck, could imagine the thud of the tire iron. He reached an awkward stride and he went past the driver coming toward him, an overstuffed man in a white shirt and tie.

"What's going . . . ?" He saw Landis drop to the ground, the tire iron bouncing away from him, and stepped aside.

Sean turned as Landis got to his feet. Behind Landis, Sean could see Dane getting in the truck cab, backing it, turning toward the bus and Sean. Ahead of him, Sean saw about a hundred yards of pavement. Jumping in the river wasn't a choice: He ran as best he could, the pain in his knee lessening as he did so. He could hear Landis gaining now, yelling something, and he could hear the grind and squeal of the pickup. He knew he couldn't outrun the truck. He got to the bend in the pavement where the bridge became a ramp, went about twenty yards down the ramp, looked over the side as he ran, gauging when he could jump. The pickup noise was crescendoing now, and Sean, without hesitation, vaulted the sidewall. He felt himself floating for a brief second before the pathway to the water rushed up at him.

He landed on both feet and rolled. He stood in time to see Landis try to leap the sidewall. Landis caught a toe on the lip of the concrete and couldn't get his legs under him before he pinwheeled down and landed flat on his right side, bouncing off the pathway, the tire iron clanging down toward the river.

Landis rolled in pain but couldn't stand. Sean looked up to see Dane come to the sidewall, look down, assess the situation, and aim whatever was in her right hand at him. Sean heard a pop and an instant later a dull thud behind him. It was not like the movies. It took him a long two seconds to realize he'd been shot at. He saw Dane still pointing the gun at him and finally convinced himself he had to move. He dove for the cover of the bridge and made it underneath as a bullet zinged off the pathway.

He stayed under there, listening to the confusion above on the bridge, watching Landis struggle to get a breath. He heard the pickup peel out. He looked around at the stanchions, realized they were no cover, and decided to run west. He knew that there was a thick stand of hardwoods a quarter mile down the river bank.

Sean heard sirens as he breached the cover of the bridge, looked up, saw no one looking down, and then ran along the pathway beside the river until it became a dirt path. He was out of breath and slowed. When he looked back, he could see the top of the bus over the bridge sidewall, still parked at the other end, and then the lights of a cruiser as it came onto the bridge.

He picked up his pace. The dirt trail became no more than a rut as it plunged into the wooded area. Trash clung to the shrub branches that dipped into the water. Sean had to hack his way through parts of the path with his arms. He had his head down doing this when he crashed through some thick brush and nearly fell on a naked couple, on a blanket, surprised by the noise he made, untangling themselves in midfuck.

Sean didn't say anything but wondered if he should turn back, go up the hill, or continue near the river. The couple, in their twenties, he skinny and farmer tanned, she overweight and bathing-suit sunburned, watched in fear, trying to cover themselves. Sean mumbled an apology and charged ahead down the river path.

Winded and dizzy, he stopped after a couple hundred yards. All he could hear was his own huffing breaths. He thought about the bridge. Was that real? Had he really been chased and shot at? He heard a distant siren but that didn't prove anything. He felt himself slipping, unable to trust the truth of something as undeniable and solid as a fucking gunshot.

He could go back to the bridge, see things with his own eyes, talk to others. That would be a good test. But he risked an arrest doing that. And an arrest meant no pills. He kept moving. There had to be other ways to test this reality. Sean got his breathing under control and kept walking, away from the bridge. Other ways. Risa could help, maybe.

And then he stopped when a powerful feeling surged inside him. Death was a test. Die to this reality or this dream and the truth would bloom in front of him forever. He took a few more steps as if he could walk away from this thought. He knew there was something loony in this solution, a suicide's warped logic, knew he had at least one golden reason for remaining alive, Kevin, but oblivion's voice was muscular and insistent, and its lure filled Sean with the promise of revelation, perhaps even redemption.

Was he running away from the bridge now, he asked himself, or into the arms of a blessed eternity?

27

After she found out Henry was taking Sean to the bus, Risa went to The Kitchen, but she was close to useless. Her last thread of hope that Sean didn't know what he was talking about had been cut. He had killed Carol. He would have to come back and face that music. And Kevin would have his father's culpability to deal with on top of his return.

She called Kevin. "I need to talk to you, hon."

"Not now."

"No. Not now. At dinner. We'll have dinner at home. The two of us. Maybe Dad."

"Dad." Kevin said the word as if it were new to him.

"Kevin. I realize how hard this is. There are a lot of things you need to know. The more you know, the easier it will be for you."

A town police car went screaming past the restaurant. Risa couldn't hear what Kevin said. "What?"

"I'm having dinner with a friend."

"Who?"

"Ellen."

"Ellen who?"

"From the playground. She's making me dinner at her house."

This hurt. If there were ever a time when Kevin needed her and she him, this was it. And yet he was choosing someone else, a girl, over her. "Can't you do that another night?"

"She's got it all planned."

Risa could hear Kevin's voice receding, as if he were on a train, pulling away. She wanted to hold him, apologize, tell him the story, reason with him, laugh again. But he was going and she couldn't stop him.

"Be home early."

Kevin didn't answer that directly. "See you."

Risa hung up and stood staring at the wall of photos and plaques.

Bell came from the kitchen. "What the hell's going on?"

It took Risa a second to remember the cruiser. "I don't know."

They heard more sirens in the distance and Bell went outside, with Risa following. They could see a sheriff's cruiser now streaking down Market Street.

"If my hip didn't feel like a rusty pipe I'd go see what was up," Bell said.

Risa was flooded with the same sort of dread she had had on Scrimmage Day. She started to move forward instinctively. A couple of others were heading the same way she was, with the same curiosity. A kid on a bike whizzed past them. When Risa got to Market, she almost stopped, afraid of what she might see. She'd once seen an accident on the old bridge with the car hanging over the side, the injured driver dangling over the water.

The bus was the first thing she saw over the twirling cop car lights. She sucked in a breath and moved forward. An ambulance came down Front Street and John Headly jumped out, walking quickly down the pathway. Risa came to a knot of onlookers standing behind the cop cars. She asked a couple what had happened, but no one seemed to know. The bus was stopped and a few passengers were walking away from it. Risa didn't see Sean among them, though she knew that was the bus Henry was going to put him on. Had he not taken the bus?

Things spiraled as a state trooper cruiser car arrived on the other side of the bridge, John Headly raced back to the ambulance, and more onlookers arrived. Risa couldn't take it any longer. She went through the de facto barrier of the cars and started onto the bridge. She looked down and saw cops surrounding what looked like a dead body, others searching the area near the body. She looked at the body long enough to know it wasn't Sean. Then she reached one of the passengers, a slight woman in her twenties, still wearing iPod earphones.

"What happened?"

"This guy in this pickup come by the bus, stopped, the bus stopped, the guy gets out with that thing you use to change a tire, smashes the bus door, then comes on the bus lookin' for somebody. Some guy in the back jumps out the window, the guy follows him, and chases him until they both jump over the side. Then this woman in the pickup, she goes after him and starts shooting at him."

A trooper Risa didn't recognize came to them.

"You all witnesses? Come over here. Don't talk to anybody. Come over here."

He started herding them, and Risa turned to look back at the gathering crowd. Sean. Landis. It had to be. Her heart pounded heavily with the realization. Shot?

Suddenly Henry came through the crowd and onto the bridge.

"What do you know, Henry?"

"All the radio said was shots fired. Stay here."

"I think that's Landis," she got out before Henry took off.

He found the trooper, identified himself, looked over the sidewall, took notes, came back to Risa briefly.

"Landis was after Sean. Sean's on the loose."

"What?"

"Landis must have found out. He blocked the bus at the bridge, Sean went out the emergency window and ran. Landis fell off the ramp, hit the ground. He's in critical. His girlfriend took off with the truck. She actually fired shots at Sean."

"Where's Sean?"

"There was a lot of confusion. They don't know if he went east or west along the river."

"Why would those two try to stop him?"

"I don't know. I put him on the bus. I . . ."

Henry suddenly seemed frozen by the scene, by his task, his eyes going blank.

"Henry?"

He snapped out of his little trip and turned to Risa, his voice calmer. "I've got to get to the office, start working on this."

"How did they know he was in the bus?" Risa asked, but Henry wasn't listening.

She started walking with him. Henry grew increasingly agitated.

"This is going to be big. A shooting. Now we're going to have to say something about why Sean's here."

As they turned off Market, Risa looked back at the commotion. Alan, she thought. He knew where Sean was and probably knew he was taking the bus. Is he behind all this?

A helicopter ripped overhead and Henry looked up. "Jesus."

Risa's cell phone buzzed. Before she could say anything, Alan's voice came screaming through the phone.

"I just heard about what happened. Don't say a word to the press." And then he hung up.

Risa looked over at Henry. He was ashen.

"Come on, Henry. You've got to find out what's going on here."

"That's a press copter. Already."

"Come on."

Risa tugged his arm and Henry moved along with her. As if in some sort of sick dream, Risa saw Lilly Barkin coming toward them, seemingly clueless about what was unfolding only blocks away.

"Hi, Risa," she said.

Risa could only see Alan in her face, Joe Tomlin's trip, and growled back as she passed. "Fuck Wednesday!"

Sean had threaded his way through tangled brush for fifteen or twenty minutes when he heard a helicopter coming up the river from the west. The slap of the propeller blades made him duck, though he was surrounded by brush and the leafy cover of hardwoods. He looked up expecting to see a police helicopter but instead saw the letters WWRB on the fuselage and a cameraman hanging out of the side door, pointing his camera toward the bridge. He could hear sirens in the distance. He was beginning to believe all that was happening was real. At least the question was fading.

The pills. He tried to belittle their importance, but suddenly being on his own without them seemed impossible. He remembered when Sandy came to his bed and offered him the trial. He took the pills just to be compliant but . . .

"It's actually a couple of over-the-counter drugs that a pharmacist stumbled on and realized the combination had a powerful effect on the alcoholic's urge," she had said.

Remembering this, Sean stood, a plan coming to him. Find a phone, call Sandy, get the combination and, somehow, get the drugs he needed. A stop-gap measure, but his thinking had narrowed now to survival. He was back on the street, no money, no clothes other than what he was wearing, no place to sleep. But he did have his sobriety. He could figure things out. He had survived eleven years in some blind haze. Having his eyes open now, he reasoned, would make it that much easier to survive. He could do this.

After another mile or so working his way through the river

brush, the wooded area thinned and across a clearing he could see cars on Susquehanna Road. He couldn't remember what the terrain was like farther west, how much cover it afforded. The trees ahead were clumped and he went from one stand to the next when there was a lull in the traffic. He made about another half mile this way, seeing the back of what used to be a tire warehouse across Susquehanna Road. He heard a siren and saw what he thought was a state cruiser heading into Braden.

He didn't realize he was angling close to the road until he was almost at the back of a Citgo station. It was a sleepy old place and Sean wondered at first if it was still open. Then he saw a car pull in and an attendant, a teenager with his shorts down way past his waist, go to pump gas. Sean waited another ten or fifteen minutes and saw the same thing three or four more times. When Low Shorts was back in the office, Sean left the cover of the brush, went up quickly to the road, and walked to the station before another car passed. He made it into the office, but nobody was in there. There was a garage connected to the office, but nobody seemed to be in there either. Sean saw a phone, an ancient black model, on the desk and was about to pick it up when he heard a flush, and Low Shorts came out of the bathroom behind the office.

Sean had surprised him and he stood with his hand on his belt buckle for a second.

"What?"

"Sorry. Didn't mean to . . ."

"Need gas?"

"No. The phone. Can I use your phone?"

Low Shorts was gangly, his face pockmarked by zit remains, his blue eyes going from Sean to the phone and back to Sean as if doing so might answer some question.

"Not supposed to use it. Your cell don't work?"

"Uh, no. Just a quick call."

They heard the crunch of tires on gravel and turned to see an SUV packed with children and a mom pull up to the pump. Low Shorts gave the phone another look as he moved out of the office.

"Okay. No long distance."

"Thanks." Sean waited until he was out of the office, dialed Sandy's direct line, forgot to dial one first, redialed, and waited. The mom had gotten out of the car and was speaking to Low Shorts. He pointed toward the office and she said something to one of the kids who were spilling out of the SUV.

Sean recognized the mom. He couldn't remember her name. She was the younger sister of a guy in his class, a geek named Hunter Morris. Sean wondered if she would recognize him.

A familiar voice came through the line. "This is Sandy."

"Sandy, it's Sean. Collins."

"Sean, where the hell are you?"

"I'm . . . I'm in my hometown."

"In Pennsylvania?"

"Yeah." He turned his back to the door as a little girl and her younger brother came into the office looking for the bathroom. Sean heard them, turned, and pointed to the bathroom.

"You were just in New York yesterday, weren't you? We're worried."

"I'm okay. I just . . . I just have to stay here for another day or two."

"Why did you go back? Did you get the information?"

"Yeah but . . . Look I can't stay on this phone long. I . . . well, I lost my pills."

"Oh."

"Yeah. I took one this morning and I'm fine. But tomorrow. I know you said the medicine is a combination of over-the-counter drugs. I thought you could tell me which ones and I could get them."

"You lost the pills? You sure? You didn't just misplace them, forget where they are?"

"No. They're gone. Can you . . ."

"I don't think so, Sean. I think you ought to find a way to get back here. We'll take care of you."

"It's not like that. I can't."

The girl was knocking on the bathroom door. "Come on out, Jeremy. I really have to go."

"You don't sound good, Sean. Get on a bus and we'll help."

"I tried to get on the bus but they chased me off."

"Who? What's going on? Have you relapsed?"

"No! No. And I don't want to. That's why I need the pills, the what-do-you-call-it. The combination."

"People are chasing you?"

"Yes. It's all very confusing. I'm sorta stuck. I need those pills. Please, Sandy, trust me. I haven't relapsed, I'm not going crazy. My memory's coming back. It's just . . . Please trust me."

Sandy didn't say anything for a long minute. Sean imagined she was making notes the way she always did. Then she spoke evenly. "Stay on the line. I'm going to call Dr. Price."

"Why?"

"He has to give his approval. You know that."

"Don't go. Can't you tell me now?"

"Stay right there, Sean. I've captured your number. If we get cut off I'll call you right back." And she was gone.

The boy came out of the bathroom and traded punches with his sister before she went in. Sean, waiting, turned to see Low Shorts and the mom coming toward the office. He turned his back to the door. The line to Sandy sounded dead.

"What's taking so long?" the mom said as she and Low Shorts came into the office.

"I don't know," said the boy.

Low Shorts went to a beaten-up register and got it to open

on the second thump. He made change as the girl came out of the bathroom.

"It stinks in there."

"Jenny, stop," the mom said, counting her change.

"She's right. It does," Low Shorts said.

"Thank you. Come on, kids." The mom herded the two out of the office. When she was gone, Sean turned back toward the door. As he did, Mom turned back, still walking, looking inside the office as if she wanted to get another look at Sean. He turned away again and Low Shorts was staring at him.

"Somebody's getting some information. Be done in a sec." Sean prayed for another car to come, and just as Low Shorts sat at the grimy desk, Sean's prayers were answered.

"What is this, a parade?" Low Shorts mumbled as he left the office.

With the commotion gone, Sean could hear better. It sounded like he was still connected. Then suddenly Sandy was back.

"Sean?"

"Yeah. I'm here." He grabbed a pen next to the register and tore a corner off a daily calendar on the wall. "Go ahead."

"Dr. Price says I can tell you, but he wants you to come back as soon as you can."

"I will."

"And he says if I tell you, it'll jeopardize your place in the study."

"What does that mean? He won't give me the pills?"

Sandy waited as if she were gathering herself. "Sean, you don't need the pills."

"What are you talking about?"

"Do you know what a placebo is?"

"No."

"It's a . . ."

"I know what a placebo is. Those pills aren't placebos. Don't try to tell me that."

"You're in the control group, Sean. I didn't know that until just now."

"There's a mistake. Do you know how powerful those pills are? You put a beer in front of me and I won't think twice about pouring it down the drain."

"I know. But it's not the pills, Sean. It's you."

"Bullshit. Do you know how many years I tried to stop? When my kid came. When I lost jobs. When I—"

"But you're different now."

"I still have the disease. You know that, for chrissakes. What are you always saying?"

"I know. But you believed the pill could keep you sober and it was that belief that changed you, made you able to do it."

"Fuck. Sandy, can you check again please? Maybe there's another Collins in the study. I know I was taking a drug. I could feel it."

"There's no doubt, Sean. Come back here and we'll get you through this."

Sean saw Low Shorts coming back to the office. He didn't want to break the connection to Sandy, to his lifeline. Low Shorts was almost in the office.

Sean had no choice. He hung up.

Low Shorts stopped in the doorway and looked at Sean as if he'd caught him with his hand in the till. "What's up?" he asked, backing up a step.

"Nothing," Sean snapped and pushed past him. When he got a few steps from the office, a car blew past on the road. Sean suddenly realized he had to hide again. He walked west down the road until he was out of sight of the Citgo. He saw no cars coming either way. He leaped a runoff gulley and went quickly into the woods.

Henry had been standing in the middle of his dinky office for ten minutes, listening to his cell phone buzz, his landline sound, and the messages being left. The bridge incident had been like a match to a chain of firecrackers, and the accelerating pops, the calls from reporters as far away as Harrisburg and Philadelphia, the commands from Doris, were in the process of blowing his eardrums out. Forget deer-in-the-headlights stuff, Henry was mummified by the assault. He knew he had to get going, but every time he tried to sit, to take down numbers, to make calls, to look over his notes, Carol's battered body immobilized him.

He shivered to think that many of the calls from other reporters were due to the fact that they had made connections already, that they had somehow figured out that Sean's escape had something to do with Carol's murder, and that connection was leading them to him, the reporter who had covered the murder. He didn't know how that could have happened, how they could have connected the dots so soon, but if they weren't calling about that now, they soon would be.

Suddenly he lashed out, kicking a file cabinet, hurling an empty Coke can against the wall. Why the fuck did he have to go through all that again? Sean. Sean was the problem. If he'd stayed dead, stayed curled in his booze in New York, Henry would never have had to think about that sight again. And yet here he was with the phone going nuts and that body being launched at him over and over. He sent a trash basket spinning into the corner, wheeled his desk chair in a violent circle, and then sat. His landline sounded and he grabbed the receiver, ready to vent on whoever was on the call.

"Henry Saltz, please."

"Yeah."

"Henry?"

"Yeah."

"It's Debbie Fins, Channel Three."

"What?"

"Going nuts, huh? Look, I'm up in Scranton. We're heading down in a few minutes. Can you just help me out? I'm hearing this thing on the bridge has something to do with that assault on . . . Alice Drummond. Something about the guy who's in the hospital is related to Alice. You know anything about that?"

"No."

"Henry, come on. We've got to do a little pool reporting here. I'm not your competition. You're going to have to do some sharing here soon. The weather forecast for Braden looks like a shitstorm followed by more shitstorm. I know you want to hang on to your story, but let me tell you from experience, ain't gonna happen. We work together and we can keep a lot more of it than you can alone."

Henry hung up. He saw Doris was calling his cell phone and answered.

"Henry, for chrissakes, where you been?"

"Working the story."

"Well, you don't fucking let me go to voice mail when you're working the story. You take my fucking calls."

"Yeah."

"What have you got?"

"Just what I told you from the bridge."

"That's it? Everybody's got that now. Who knows about Collins saying he killed the Slezak girl?"

"I don't know."

"What did Stallings say?"

"I haven't talked to him yet."

"Why not?"

"Won't take the call."

"Are you shitting me? He was out on the bridge."

"Not when I was there."

"Jesus, Henry, find him. And find Risa. Tell her to keep us exclusive. Alan's probably got her zipped up anyway. Can Landis talk?"

"I don't know."

"Say 'I don't know' one more time and you can forget about

coming to my Christmas party. It's 'I'll find out.' You heard troopers found the pickup?"

"I'll find out."

"Henry. Snap out of it. Don't make this like the first time. You don't have to go look at some body all hacked up. You just got to talk to people, do a little sleuthing. Come on, son. I need you."

"Yeah."

"And don't talk to any other goddamn reporters. If the fucking *New York Times* calls you, you refer them to me. We got boots on the ground. They're punching their GPSes trying to figure out where the fuck Braden is. This is called an advantage, Henry. Use it. Get your ass moving."

She hung up as the landline sounded again and Henry let it go to the message.

"Henry. It's Alan Benson. Call me on my cell as soon as you get this."

A few seconds later Henry saw Alan's number come up on his cell phone. He had really heard only one thing Doris had said. He went to look for Risa.

28

It was late enough in the afternoon that Sean thought about just staying where he was until nightfall, in the woods surrounding a sad-looking picnic ground. But he kept moving, darting across the open space and walking parallel to Susquehanna Road. He wanted motion to replace thought. He still couldn't believe that he had been given a placebo, but there was no way to argue the point. He was going to have to go without the pills no matter what.

He had six dollars in his wallet, and he thought about throwing that away, making sure he couldn't walk into a bar and order a drink. He stared at some crushed beer cans near a fire pit in the picnic ground and felt a pull he hadn't felt since his near death in the subway. He kept walking.

The woods thinned again and he had to keep moving closer and closer to the road to keep in deep cover. Then the woods ended altogether and a grassy slope stretched out in front of him as far as he could see. He looked around, trying to get his bearings. Across the road was a gentle incline of about ten yards that led to some deeper woods. He crouched as a car passed and felt an ache in his thighs. He knew he could reach the woods and probably be safe there for the night.

He heard the gurgling of a small creek and realized how thirsty he was. He stood and saw the creek, really just a dribble in the August heat, near enough that he could make it there and back before a car passed. Crouching in a run, flattening himself on the bank of the creek, he got a few good mouthfuls and made it back before an RV hummed by. That foray gave him confidence, and when the RV was gone, he dashed across the road, up the incline, and into the woods. The knee he had landed on coming off the bridge throbbed. He found a shielded open space and sat down, hugging his legs to his chest.

It was only when he sat that he realized he had seen something down the road, something familiar. As he was running, he thought it was a road sign, maybe a diamond-shaped curve arrow. But it wasn't that. It was rounded on the top. And he knew the sign, had seen it many times before. He lay on his back and looked at the whispy clouds above, starting to catch some of the pink of sunset. He felt his tired bones melting into the soft earth. He could go to sleep right there. Was it safe? His thoughts started to splinter and he could feel the slide into sleep starting.

Then suddenly he jerked up to a sitting position. It was the sign for The Ding Dong. That's what he had seen down the road. Shit. He was less than a quarter of a mile from the watering hole that had been his de facto home for the last few months he was in Braden. He had wandered away from the bridge and ended up in the one place he didn't want ever to be in again. He looked quickly around. Was this it? Was this the place he had seen for months now, the woods in which he killed Carol?

Sean closed his eyes and got the jumble in his head down to one thought: Don't drink. He opened his eyes, calmed to a degree. He took a couple of normal breaths. And then a scene of simple horror came to him. He saw a man, his ragged pants falling off him, shuffling down a blasted block of dilapidated houses on feet so swollen he couldn't tie the laces of his mismatched shoes. He could both see this man and feel him from the inside. The man saw the remains of a tossed-off sandwich poking out of a brown bag near the curb, reached for it, was thrown off balance, and sat heavily. Then he managed to rake in the sandwich and shoved it all in his mouth, tasting a meat he couldn't recognize along with the grit of dirt. When he had swallowed this he pulled a pint of Georgi out of his pants pocket, swigged the little that was left, and then sent the bottle skittering down the sidewalk so that a passerby had to dodge it.

"Hey, asshole," somebody said, but the man didn't hear. The burn of the booze was flaming in his throat, telling him it was time to get more.

When Sean came out of this memory, he swallowed hard, welcoming the smooth flow of saliva down his throat. The light was low. He didn't know how long he'd been in this trancelike state, but he knew what he'd seen and felt was something that had happened to him. Had he recovered another memory? He was certain he had.

Then another scene from his years on the street slid into his consciousness, this one a vivid recollection of a silent hand out begging from a sitting position, a dollar bill resting on his outstretched palm, being blown away when he couldn't get his frozen fingers around it fast enough.

The trickle of memories soon became a gush. He was in a dank room fighting with a skinny, stringy-haired woman over a beer can that had dropped and spewed foam. He was showing a cop his phony ID. He was waking up in a city-run flophouse to a man with an empty eye socket going through his pockets. He was alone at the end of a subway car, the other passengers moving away from him, a black teenage girl telling him he smelled like shit.

When the barrage of memories dwindled, it was nearly dark. Sean knew he should be glad his memory was coming back, but he wasn't. What good was memory if it was going to cough up scenes like that, or an absolute horror show like Carol's mangled corpse? And what lay ahead? Would he one day have a vivid recollection of trying to kill Alice Drummond? He had come back to Braden to settle things for himself, but he had only fallen farther into the chaos of his jumbled brain.

He was up and walking before he realized he was doing so. He wanted to get away from himself. The lines between reality and a dream blurred again.

A hot light, pointed at him from about fifty yards away, brought him back to earth. He stopped, not bothering to crouch. The strong beam was on him fully and didn't move. He saw that he had come out of the wooded area and the light was coming across an open space. He heard a car pass and realized he was closer to the road than he thought. He heard the thump of bass from some music coming from the direction of the light. He squinted and shaded his eyes enough so that he saw the humped backs of car tops in the open area in front of him. A parking lot. He knew suddenly that he'd come to The Ding Dong.

And he had come the way he had come so many times in the past, on foot, staggering usually then, going in through the back door, hoping he'd get served or someone would bring him a go cup out back. That light in the back had been a beacon for him then, a sign the place was still open and it was not too late to get a drink. If it was off in those days it meant he'd have to go knock on G.G.'s door in the extension out back and get him to give him a drink. G.G. would lecture him, but when Sean started to shake, G.G.'d give in.

Now the light was nothing like a beacon. It was a blaring siren, a white hot temptation asking, "Whatcha gonna do, boy?" Did Walt still own the place? Could he just walk in and sit at the bar, order a beer? The thought scared him. He hadn't had a thought like that since he'd been on the medicine. He could walk by bars, hear the music, the games, the glass clinks, even smell the woody welcome, and keep right on going, not even wanting to detour. But now he was imagining Walt's bristling mustache asking him what it would be tonight. He began to sweat as he saw the oval top of a shot glass only a foot away from his face.

He backed away from the light, stumbling over a root, turned, and walked quickly away. The music faded, but it seemed that a voice, a gruff accusatory one, was crawling all over his back saying, "What's your hurry?" The waning moon had risen enough to give the woods a bit more light. He walked until The Ding Dong light was gone and there was just the silence of the woods and the occasional whine of tires on the road. The trees were sparse, mute. His breathing slowed. He didn't know exactly where he was, but he figured he had to be somewhere near where he had encountered Carol, strangled her, dragged her away.

He had not managed to walk away from himself. His limbs ached and his head pounded. He saw clearly that any future he had would forever be yoked to his terrible past. Redemption was for people who had stumbled. He'd fallen hard, a spill you don't rise from. Stallings, jail, a public condemnation? What would that do? There was a more surefire solution.

He sat on a rock staring at the nature-mulched earth in front of him. There wasn't any reason to run anymore, either from the law or himself. Worrying about what would happen to Kevin was just an excuse, a piece of cowardice. He had his evidence, knew how dangerous he was still. What was he waiting for?

His stare lost focus. The darkness at his feet became a brown blob. He was lost to the world for minutes, or an hour. He couldn't tell. And then out of the soup below him a small yellow patch broke through the dark. He brought himself back to a focused gaze and saw among the dead leaves the yellow thing poking out. He reached for it and when his thumb and forefinger gripped it, he knew what it was, knew it had been put there for him. He pulled and the half-buried object rose, ripping up through the leaves. He reeled it in until the length of it hung limp in his hand.

It was a nylon cord. Though it had been buried for a while, it was still strong. He tugged it, testing. It was the right size for his needs, the right strength. If he was in a dream, it would be the perfect test. He didn't have to look above him for a branch. He knew one would be there.

Sean smiled to himself. He saw a logic to all that had happened in the past few days. And the conclusion of it all was resting in his palm. It was so perfect. He had come full circle, in a way. This cord, this lifeline, was an old friend, reassembled for his benefit, still the exact same color it was when his father had used it. Finally, Sean thought, I'm home.

He looked up and saw the shadowy outlines of a sturdy branch. He stood and gauged the height of the branch, and then all became easy, automatic. He looped the cord over the branch, tied a bowline, pulled hard on the cord and found the branch immovable, tied the cord around his neck and stood on the rock.

There was no Kevin coming to him this time. There was a certainty and a peace. He thought about a prayer, some final word, but before he could think of anything, his right foot slipped and his left foot followed. There wasn't the yank he had expected. The cord bit into his flesh and then a searing pain radiated from his jawbone to the back of his neck and up to his head. He was able to get several short breaths before the cord blocked his windpipe.

Then the darkness around him was filled with starbursts that gave way to a powerful set of headlights coming toward him, a subway bearing down to finish the job it had started. And in the path of that certain death Sean's world narrowed to one indelible thought: truth was about to be revealed.

29

"No. I'll have a beer."

Risa, behind the bar, looked back at Henry. "Beer? You sure?" Risa had never seen Henry with a drink of any kind.

"I'm sure. A beer, please."

Henry had stumbled into The Kitchen after Risa had spent hours of anxiety and frustration trying to get news of Sean. The restaurant and bar had been filled with rumors, supposed sightings, and the occasional cold shoulder from those who held Sean responsible for the chaos in town now. Outside, cruisers passed every few minutes, news vans clogged the narrow streets, and helicopter shadows ran along the building walls.

On top of this, Alan kept calling, refusing to say more than his first admonition: "Don't talk to anyone." Risa finally stopped answering his calls. But she didn't talk to any of the reporters who tried to interview her, even the locals. She made a call to Chuck Hamilton, the lawyer, who said he was prepared to come to Braden if Sean was found.

"I'm going to need your help," Hamilton had said. "I need to be absolutely certain Sean's got it right about the Slezak woman." Risa said she thought he did have it right but she would do what she could to make sure. She had settled the question of Sean's guilt for herself, but a more difficult question had been with her for hours. Alan. She could understand why Sean's return had put him in a tizzy, that his campaign was in jeopardy because of Sean's presence. But it seemed like more than the campaign was at the root of Alan's actions. Alan was clearly hiding something about the night he drove Sean to New York. Could he have really been sitting there in the front seat with Sean, hear Sean say he had killed someone, and drive him into New York? And if that wasn't true, what had gone on? And whatever had gone on, was it so damning that Alan felt he had to send a murderous duo after Sean?

Risa opened a Coors Light, colored water as one of the barflies called it, and gave it to Henry. "When you were covering Carol's murder . . ."

"I don't know if I want to go down this road, Risa. I've got a shitload to do between now and ten o'clock tomorrow."

"Okay. Just this one. When you were covering Carol's murder, did you ever talk to Alan about it?"

"Alan? I don't think I even knew him then. He wasn't living here."

"He visited every now and then."

"Yeah. But what would he have had to do with Carol's murder?"

"Nothing. I just wondered." She delivered this with a walk-out-of-the-room-but-leave-the-door-open look. Henry got it and took a swig of his Coors.

"I guess I should call Alan, huh?"

"He might talk to you. He's not talking to anybody else."

Henry was picking up the game. "What do I ask him?"

"I don't know. Sean and Alan were good friends, or had been. Sean was so wasted he killed Carol. How did he get to New York?"

"Alan?"

"Good idea."

Henry didn't need any more dots connected. But he didn't seem all that eager to leap. He started to go for his wallet, but Risa stopped him.

"On the house. Henry, they're going to find Sean soon. He can't stay hidden around here. I want to know the whole truth about what happened with Carol. I've got Kevin to think about. This is his father. I want him to know what really happened. Help me dig out the facts, okay?"

Henry didn't look up to the task, but he nodded yes as he went out the front door.

Bell came from the office.

"Man, if I hear another helicopter I'm going to get my ground-to-air and pop one of them. How're you doing?"

"Peachy. We got everything covered for tonight?"

"I don't know. Those reporters decide they all want the meat loaf special we'll be in trouble." She paused, gave Risa a concerned look. "I've got a shitload of questions I'd like to ask you."

"If it's about Sean or Alan or whatever is going on here, save your breath. I have no idea."

Bell reached out and put a hand on her shoulder. "Just wondered if maybe we should substitute ribs for the meatloaf."

Risa tried a thank-you smile. "Sounds like a good idea."

Risa spent the next hour and a half trying to operate normally while plotting what she could do to clear her head of the suspicions she had about Alan. She remembered a Yale reunion book he had in his study. Maybe this Karen Rogers whose wedding he was supposedly at wrote in that book. Maybe she is still single. Or maybe she talks about how great her wedding was eleven years ago, and how it went on into the night, and how they were all sorry when Alan Benson left early.

A camera crew came in at one point, and Debbie Fins followed a little later. Risa headed for the office. She had the door ajar and heard Debbie near the end of the bar, asking Bell if Risa were around, if Bell knew where Alan was.

"Seven places at once, honey," Bell said and ended the conversation.

Alan himself called again and Risa took the call this time.

"You didn't talk to anybody, did you?" was his opening.

"The whole world. Just finished my tenth interview."

"You can joke about it, but we've got to do some serious damage control, Risa."

"We wouldn't have to if you'd turned Sean in ten years ago."

"Fuck."

"Or maybe if you hadn't sent that psycho after Sean."

"Or maybe, just maybe if Sean had kept his fucking ass out of Braden we'd be going about our business instead of hosting a fucking media feeding frenzy."

"How did you end up on that road the night you picked up Sean?"

"Shit, Risa."

"Simple question."

"Which I answered."

"With a tangled, complicated story."

"Story? You think I'm lying?"

"I think there's more that needs to be said."

"Well, not over the phone."

"So there is more?"

"Jesus Christ, no. What? You don't want to believe Sean killed Carol?"

"I can believe that. I just don't know how, blind drunk, he managed to arrange for a car service."

"I gotta go."

"To be continued, Alan."

"Just don't talk to anyone, okay. For me."

He hung up.

Risa fumed. Alan had done practically everything he could to make her suspicion mushroom. She started to clear her desk, to get a piece of paper and write down what she knew, what she wanted to know. As she pushed the pink message slips away, she caught the name Slezak on one and pulled it out of the pile. It was in Bell's handwriting and it said, "Tracey Slezak, Carol's sister," with a Pittsburgh area code phone number. Risa took the message and found Bell behind the bar.

"Carol's sister called?"

"Yeah."

"What did she want?"

"I don't know. She asked for your cell number but I thought, no, can't do that."

Risa saw Debbie Fins leaving her table, coming toward her. Risa shook her head and went back into the office. She dialed the number. She tried to remember what she could about Tracey. She thought she was a teacher but she wasn't sure. She was in Pittsburgh, and Risa thought she'd remembered that Tracey had gone to college there.

"Tracey? This is Risa Tuvic."

"Hi, Risa. I'm watching our six thirty news. They just had a story on that thing on the bridge into town."

"So you know about all this?"

"Not really. But I had to call you. My aunt Roe, who lives in Anson and goes to shop over in Braden, said she heard a rumor."

"About what?"

"About your husband."

"My husband Alan?"

"No. I'm sorry. Your, I guess, ex-husband. Sean?"

"Yes."

"This was before the bridge thing. Roe said Sean was back in town and that he was trying to turn himself in for, you know, Carol's murder. Is that right?"

"It is Tracey."

"Why's he doing that?"

"It's kind of a long story, but he's recovered memories and one is of having killed Carol. He says it's driving him crazy."

"You think he really did it?"

"I do."

"Not G. G. Trask?"

"Probably not."

"Me neither."

"What do you mean?"

"It just didn't sound right. You know how G.G. is. I was so torn up at the trial I couldn't hear straight, think straight. But when they read the confession, that didn't sound like G.G. at all."

"I know."

"They questioned Dan, but . . ."

"Dan?"

"Carol's fiancé. When she was gone, everybody thought she was up seeing him. He was in his lab with a partner, so he had an alibi. He thought it might be this kind of stalker guy, but after G.G. confessed I don't think the police did anything about it."

"What stalker guy?"

"Not really a stalker. Just some guy who was sort of smitten with her. He was a freshman when Carol was a senior. She never said anything to me about it."

"Do you know his name?"

"No, but maybe Dan does." Tracey paused and then offered an opinion. "Excuse me for saying this, but I don't think your hus . . . your ex killed Carol. He was drunk all the time I remember, but he wasn't a bad guy."

"But people do things when they're drunk they wouldn't do otherwise."

"I know, but Carol was trying to help Sean. She even . . . Well she was trying to help him."

"She even what?"

"She sort of . . . I don't know if I should say it. I mean, Dan doesn't even know."

"She slept with him."

"Yes. Did he say that?"

"Yes."

"But it wasn't like really. It was more like when a baby gets up in the middle of the night and you take him into bed so he can sleep. Carol brought him home and he was going to sleep on the couch. But he ended up in her bed. I don't know what went on, but Carol wasn't ashamed of it. She thought he might be getting better."

Getting better. That hit Risa harder than when Sean had admitted he'd been with Carol. Tracey's image of a child needing midnight comfort was too accurate. Sean had been a child, one Risa didn't want to deal with, didn't want to comfort in bed. She had a child, a real child, she needed to take care of. But Carol had taken her place as nurse, as mother. Was she seeing some sort of improvement that Risa hadn't been able to see? Risa wrestled her guilt to a standstill.

"Tracey. Was Alan involved? Was he helping Sean too?"

"Alan? Alan Benson?"

"Yes."

"I don't think so. I don't remember him being around. I mean, I was younger and there was my mother and Carol was about to get married. It was . . . Oh, they had a fight."

"Who?"

"Carol and Alan."

"Really? About what?"

"I don't know. I remember Carol hanging up the phone and saying out loud, 'Fucking Alan.' The reason I remember is because she said that right in front of Mom. I was shocked. It was the first time I'd heard that word in front of my mother."

Risa could imagine Alan and Carol fighting over a lot of things. And she could imagine young Tracey seeing it as more than it was because her sister had used the f-word.

"Are you still in touch with Dan?" Risa asked.

"Not in a few years. He got married. It was tough on his wife. I have a number. I don't know if it's still good or not. Do you want it?"

Risa didn't know what she would want to talk about with a lab mole who was in Syracuse at the time of the murder. But Tracey had splashed a little doubt on her certainty that Sean was the killer, so she said yes and took down the number. Risa then filled Tracey in on some of the things they weren't yet reporting about the bridge incident, gave her her cell number, and they hung up.

Risa sat thinking for a minute and then stood quickly, oddly energized. She had another piece of what went on. She could see Carol helping Sean, see her selflessness. Maybe she thought she was helping Risa as well. And she had an argument between Alan and Carol. That could mean something. She reached for the office door when it pushed open by itself and Kevin stood there.

"Ooh. You scared me."

"Sorry, Mom."

"I thought you were at . . . what's her name?"

"Ellen. I was. This news. What's going on?"

"Come in. Close the door. What do you know?"

"They said that nutzoid and his girlfriend tried to kill my father and he got away and he's out there somewhere."

"Yeah. That's about it."

"And the sheriff's looking for him?"

"Yes."

"'Cause of that attack on that woman last night?"

"Yes."

Kevin sat and stared at the chain of scabs on his knuckles. Risa could see the rage that had led to those scabs had been trumped by the incident on the bridge, by his father's new notoriety. Now Kevin's problem wasn't just his. It was the town's, it was the sheriff's, it was on TV. She knew he wasn't ready for this. Not in the least.

"Do you know why Sean, your father, came back in the first place?"

Kevin nodded, but kept his eyes glued to his knuckles. "He killed your friend when he was drunk."

"Who told you that?"

Kevin looked up and met his mother's eyes. Risa saw a sorrow in them she had never seen before. And a maturity. She realized Sean's return was going to be even more difficult for Kevin than his departure.

He spoke softly. "Dad. Dad told me."

30

The blackness was without bottom. A void that neither opened nor closed. Time and light had no place there. And yet he understood that he still existed, that his brain still functioned. He moved ever so slightly, and the profound dark was jarred and began to cough up shapes, small indications that all was not lost.

He felt a pain under his chin and tried to swallow. The cough that came sent the inky world around him skittering and his vision filled with the dark forms of the woods. He was back and something beyond thought and feeling told him he was alive, that what he was looking at and feeling was real.

Sean tried to move but he still didn't have the strength. It was as if he were being told to stay where he was, to think, to puzzle out something, to wait, to remember other moments when he had been prone. He was on the street, sprawled, snoring himself awake as a cop kicked his bloated feet. He was curled on the floor in a cold room. He was on subway tracks wrestling a cop. He was face down drunk in dark woods.

He attempted another swallow and got the same coughing result. He felt the nylon cord around his neck, reached up and tore it loose. But when he tried to get it over his head he felt the weight of the branch the cord was still attached to. He turned, but in the dark he could see little. He yanked the cord and the branch, splintered and broken away from the tree trunk, dragged toward him.

Sean was able to get the cord over his head now and lay there, breathing hard, figuring out that the supposedly sturdy branch had broken, that he had been saved, that he was alive and real. And he remembered the last seconds before all went completely blank, the feeling that something was about to be shown to him. He guessed his salvation was the lesson he was to take from his brush with death.

Then a voice, sudden and rushing, came to him. He slid backward, sure the voice was only feet away. But he couldn't escape it and, within seconds, Alan, younger, with the same facial hair he had in the front seat memory, was inches from his face, hovering, talking fast.

"I'm going to go get my car. I'm coming back for you. You understand?"

The memory was so vivid that Sean nodded yes, felt the slurred thinking of a nearly passed-out drunk.

"You sure?"

Sean didn't answer, but he knew he had before. And he knew he had been in the same woods he was in now. It wasn't the horror of Carol's bloody body, but there was the low growl of something horrible around the corner. His near-death at his own hand had opened new channels of memory. He stayed where he was, expectant and full of fear.

Alan shook him and then left. The night was silent again, but foxhole silent, as if any second something would come over the rim of his consciousness and slam into him as Alan had just done. He wasn't frozen to the spot. He knew he could get up and leave, but he knew that was the coward's way out, a bottle of sorts, numbing.

Sean felt things opening, deepening. He didn't jump back when he heard a grunting and a mumbling nearby, a scraping and dragging sound mixed with the voice. He looked all around him and saw nothing. The sound moved away. It wasn't now, he knew, but it had happened and he had roused himself and followed the sound. He didn't resist the memory now, felt the staggering steps he had taken, saw himself lurching through brush, then falling to the muddy earth, unable to move.

He had come closer to the sounds and he looked up to see a thin, growling figure, kneeling, his torso and arms rising and falling, rising and falling. And something in that falling was causing a thump on the ground he could feel in his chest.

Then it stopped. The figure dropped something heavy and was gone as if he'd never been there.

And Sean, in a sudden rush of clarity, knew what was going to come next. He knew he was going to rise after several minutes of numb incomprehension, slide himself forward, nearly run into some mass on the ground, struggle up to a kneeling position, and look down on the indelible image of Carol's lifeless, mangled body. And after that he was going to pick up the weighted handle of a machete and bring the blade close to his face for drunken inspection. He knew now that those minutes above his friend's body had been the first to make it through his cauterized brain years later, cut through and fool him into thinking he had been the kneeling figure rising and falling.

He had had enough. The horror that had soaked the images of Carol's body in the past now became a deep, deep sorrow and grieving. He cried without knowing he was crying. He lay back and rolled to his stomach and buried his face in his hands until he had no more tears to shed and the sleep of the innocent took him to a dreamless peace.

31

It's Washington, Risa," Alan said as he was packing. He had been home only half an hour and had been on his BlackBerry most of that time. "I stay here to deal with some crisis, quote, unquote, which is not my doing and turn down a press parade at the Capitol and I pass Go and do not collect shit? It's his problem, not mine."

"It's mine too. And Kevin's," Risa said. Having left the bathroom to make her argument for Alan staying, she was in her bra and panties and felt exposed, vulnerable.

"Don't play that card," Alan said.

"What card?"

"Come on."

"No. What 'card' am I playing?"

"Kevin. The emotion. His father back."

"That's not a card, Alan. That's reality. We're not pieces to be moved around on your board. Kevin's been through a shitload the last few days. He—"

"He's got you."

"You've been the only father he's ever known, really."

"Yeah, well now he's got two."

"How can you be like that?"

"You got sucked back into it, why shouldn't Kevin?"

"Sucked back into what?"

"Sean. What have you been doing to help me in all this?"

"I shut up, for one thing. I didn't tell them you took Sean to New York."

"Well, that was good for both of us."

"What? Shutting up or taking Sean to New York?"

"Don't start that again. Don't make it seem like I . . . like I wanted to get him out of the way."

Alan went down the hall to his study. Risa wondered if it was time to ask the new question she had for him. He had come back to the house after she and Kevin had been home for about an hour. They had walked up from The Kitchen together, talking about Sean. There had been a stream of phone calls from reporters and then friends who had seen TV news reports, but the only one Risa had taken was from Henry, who said Doris was insisting they publish his damning interview with Sean whether they had found him or not.

Kevin was radically changed from the wall puncher he had been only a couple of days earlier. He peppered his side of the conversation with numerous "Yeah, Ellen said the same thing" comments, and Risa guessed Ellen must have been partially responsible for the change. The fact that Landis, whom Kevin knew of, had chased Sean, and his girlfriend had shot at Sean, made things different for Kevin. He wasn't taking pride in his father's escape, in him being a fugitive, but it made what he thought was black and white—his father had left, had killed a woman before he left, and was a bad man—into something more shaded.

Alan came back in the room with some files to pack.

"What time are you leaving tomorrow?" Risa asked.

"Eleven, something like that. But I have to be down at Front Street early. We're going to do a couple of interviews."

"About Sean?"

"Yes, about Sean. Why the surprise?"

"Because you said you weren't going to talk about it and because you didn't say anything when you came in."

"Well, we just sort of worked it out. One's with Henry and one's with that Debbie Fins. We can control both of those."

"How's that?"

"Influence, Risa. You don't want to know."

"I'm afraid you're wrong. I do want to know."

"Then why haven't you been interested up to now? Why have you been dragging your feet on this campaign? Now that it's about Sean, you're all ears, right?"

"Well, yeah. And there are questions I can't answer. That helps."

"I hope you're not back to why I was out on that road when I picked Sean up."

"There's that. But the one I'm interested in is new. What did you and Carol argue about just before she was killed?"

"Carol?"

"You argued with her over the phone."

"Says who?"

"Her sister, Tracey. She called today. She doesn't think G.G. is guilty. And she has trouble believing Sean killed Carol."

"But she thinks I had an argument with her so . . . I killed her?"

Risa had come close to thinking that but had never said it to herself. She stared at Alan now as he glared at her.

"You had an argument, didn't you?"

"I don't remember that. I was in Washington, for chrissake."

"Except when you were home picking up Sean and taking him to New York."

"I don't remember an argument with Carol. I was coming back from a wedding when Sean stumbled toward my car. You want to call more witnesses, or should we send this one to the jury?"

Risa turned her back, unhooked her bra and slipped it off, picked up a nightgown and put it on, turned back, and started to get in bed. Alan was down to his boxers.

"You want me to sleep here or go downstairs?"

Risa got in bed and pulled the sheet up. The air conditioner cycled on.

"I want to believe I have the whole truth."

Alan continued to stand. "And you don't feel you have it now."

"No, I don't."

Alan reached for his pillow, started toward the door, then stopped.

"This isn't some take-out-the-garbage difference of opinion, Risa. It's going to still have bite when the truth comes out, when you see I was telling the truth all along."

"When prodded."

"Right. Think a marriage can withstand prodding and thinking a partner's lying?"

"I don't know, Alan. I've been wondering if a marriage can withstand a campaign. Do you realize how this running around for votes has changed you?"

"Do you realize what good I've been doing out there on the trail?"

"For Alan Benson?"

"For the people of the Twenty-third District."

"You can't turn it off, can you? You're just programmed now."

Alan walked to the door, signaling an exit line, and he delivered it forcefully. "Focus. I'm focused and I'm going to stay focused until we've won the seat."

He left, closing the door behind him, and Risa found herself almost laughing at his attempted dramatics, but almost crying at the hole that had opened up between them. Alan hadn't been able to answer her question to her satisfaction. She could see in his eyes that he remembered the argument with Carol perfectly. If it had been just a tiff between friends, why would he deny it?

And she had heard Alan say what she had been unable to

even think: "So I killed her?" She couldn't go that far. She could believe Sean in his sickness could have committed the act, but she couldn't believe Alan, sober and ambitious, would have had any reason or wherewithal to kill Carol.

She turned off the bedside light and slid down under the covers. The air conditioner hum was like some anxious drone under her thoughts. Alan. Sean. Kevin. Alan. Sean. Kevin. The words accelerated and she rolled to get away from them and then Sean was with her. He was so real she gasped. He smiled but said nothing. She felt his arms pull her toward him. He was light and soft and comforting. His breath sent all thoughts floating away. His body said she didn't need tears. Think, Risa. Think. And within seconds, she was asleep.

"Sean. Get up."

The voice was familiar enough but he couldn't place it. He was still on his stomach, his face turned to one side. He saw a pair of shiny boots scuffed with new mud and a pair of dilapidated sneakers. There was a new light in the woods, an early morning with promise. He rolled and looked up to see Deputy Hanson, whom he didn't recognize, and Walt Stoddard, whom he did. It was Walt who had spoken.

"Morning."

Sean got to his feet and as he was doing so realized he had a full bladder and had to pee immediately. He turned away from the two men and hobbled a few yards off on his stiff, painful knee. "Just a minute."

As he peed, he rewound the breakthrough of the night just passed and felt as if he might lift off the ground. He had been there. He had seen what he had seen. But it wasn't he who had strangled Carol, dragged her to higher ground, hacked her lifeless body. It was somebody else. He zipped up and turned back to the men. They weren't sharing his triumph.

"Hello, Walt."

He'd always thought of The Ding Dong's owner as a father of sorts, a wise touchstone with sparkling eyes and a cheerful grin. But there was no crinkly smile now.

"Sean, you all right?" Walt nodded toward Sean's knee.

"Better than the guy who was chasing me."

"You can say that again. He's dead."

Hanson cleared his throat. "You're going to come with me, aren't you?"

"Who are you?"

"Dave Hanson, Sean."

"No shit. You had a growth spurt. Got a badge now, huh?"

"Yup. You're willing to come in, talk to us, right?"

"Who's us?"

"Sheriff Armey. The DA."

"I already tried to talk to him."

"I guess he wants a second chance."

"So do I."

"How's that?"

"I better explain it to him. How'd you find me out here?"

Walt answered. "Kid at the Citgo down the road put two and two together when they stopped to talk to him. I made it eight when they came to talk to me last night. Figured you might go back to your old quarters."

"My old quarters?"

"You used to crawl up here late at night, before you took off."

"Yeah, I guess so. Those nights are a little hazy."

"Carol was the one who told me. Said she would check on you after work."

Sean acknowledged this with pursed lips and a sigh. "Yeah."

"So I applied some outdated logic to the whole thing."

"What was that?"

"A criminal always returns to the scene of the crime."

Sean looked up. This wasn't the Walt behind the bar with the new one about the gopher who got his dick caught in the bear trap. Walt's blue eyes were icy with disgust. Sean suddenly realized where he was, the hole he had put himself in. Walt was the face of Braden now. For months Sean had imagined scorn as the proper reaction to what he was going to confess to, scorn and disgust such as Walt's. But the world had turned for Sean overnight. There was no need for a confession. There was no reason for the scorn. But for the moment only he knew that. And he realized that the lesson he had learned in Stallings's office, that blind justice could be deaf as well, now applied equally to both his confession and his retraction of that confession. He might be, in other words, fucked.

Walt was looking at the nylon cord and fallen branch, "Goddamned kids," he said.

He walked away and left Sean with Hanson. Hanson radioed headquarters, gave his position, said he was bringing Sean in. He didn't call him a suspect, but his eyes did. Sean could only remember Hanson as a runt kid who was part of a minibike crew that threw water balloons at cars going over the bridge, cars that couldn't turn around and chase them.

He limped down the hill and out of the woods with Hanson behind him. When they reached the road, he saw Walt in the distance walking on the shoulder toward The Ding Dong. That receding figure was suddenly judge and jury, Walt's rejection a sentence passed. Sean realized in a flash how difficult it was going to be to convince the Walts in Braden of his innocence once he got in Hanson's cruiser.

"Just a minute, Dave."

"What . . . ?"

Sean hobble-ran after Walt and called to him when he got within shouting distance. Walt turned, saw him coming, then turned back and kept walking. Sean caught up with him near The Ding Dong road sign.

"Walt, listen to me. I know what you've heard, but I didn't kill Carol. I know that now."

Walt kept walking and gave Sean a withering look. "Don't make it worse. Own up to it, for chrissakes."

"It's my memory, Walt. It's all screwed up. Or it was. Things are coming back now. I was there. Out in the woods. I saw the guy do it, kill her. But I didn't realize what was happening. Or I was too polluted to know. But I saw him, saw the body."

Walt stopped. "You're sounding like a fuckin' worm, Sean."

Sean could see Hanson, in the car now, coming toward him. Another cruiser came over the rise behind Hanson's car and was bearing down on him as well. He looked back at Walt, who was as stolid and impassive as a cigar store Indian.

"I'm going to prove it somehow, Walt."

"Fuck off, Sean. Go do what's right. For Carol."

What was right for Carol? Turning himself in, taking the rap? Or finding out the truth, maybe getting other pieces of memory to fall in place, finding out who really did it? The second cruiser was coming fast, Hanson slowing as he trundled along the shoulder. Sean took one last look back at Walt. Walt's eyes offered absolutely no hope.

Sean turned and sprinted as best he could up the incline and into the trees. Over the rasping of his breath he heard Walt calling, Hanson shouting, car doors opening and closing. But he didn't stop. He knew he was not going to be able to run for long, that the woods he was going into weren't all that deep, but he had to try to get away, to put distance between himself and the Sean who had come back to Braden a couple of days ago. That Sean had been bludgeoned by the horrors he'd seen and his deep guilt, a suicidal basket case, it seemed now. Leave him behind. Let the Hansons chase after him. The Sean high-tailing it through the woods now was the Sean who might, just might, be able to finally bring justice to Carol Slezak.

32

"Risa, it's me. Henry. They caught Sean but he got away. Out by The Ding Dong."

"What?"

"Now he's saying he didn't kill Carol."

"Didn't?"

Henry told her what he knew, what Sean had told Walt before he took off for the woods. Risa tried to swim up from a heavy, dream-drenched sleep. "They sent a bunch of cops in to find him, but he had a good head start."

"Didn't do it? He said he didn't do it?"

"Right."

"Why? Why did he change his story?"

"I don't know. Doris still wants me to write the article."

"To hell with that, Henry. He wouldn't change his mind if he didn't have some good reason. Something's happened. Wait until he can tell you."

Henry started to say something, but Risa hung up on him. She called Chuck Hamilton and woke him up. He was not happy to hear the news.

"This is what I was saying. I've seen it so many times. Guy wants to confess, then he gets cold feet. Shit."

"I don't think it was cold feet."

"You wouldn't. Wives, girlfriends. You're probably the reason he's backing out."

They hung up and Risa tried to think clearly. But the word

"innocent" kept getting in the way of any plans, any strategy.

She could only think to tell Alan in person. She checked on Kevin but didn't wake him, then left for Alan's headquarters. She didn't quite know why, but she didn't know where else to go. She barely had the sand out of her eyes, Braden was steamy in the early morning sun, and the world seemed to have reversed itself once again.

Sean called fifteen minutes after Risa left the house. The landline rang and a groggy Kevin heard it but let the answering machine pick up. The message gave Risa's cell number. Sean remembered the number and hung up.

He was at a phone booth by the side of the road near the long-ago-abandoned railway station. He had been followed when he fled, but the cops who came after him were slow footed and the ones who followed them were legally blind. They had missed him twice by only a few yards. He had then made it through the woods and had found the phone booth after traveling parallel to state Route 124 for a mile or so. He didn't see any cruisers—not any townies, sheriffs, or troopers. He took a chance going to the exposed phone booth, found three quarters in his pocket, used one to dial the old number he and Risa had, and got her answering machine.

He called the cell number. Risa's voice mail picked up and he told her he was at a phone booth and needed to speak to her. After he'd hung up he kicked himself for not telling her where he was. He was about to dial again when the phone rang.

"Did you just phone me?"

"Risa?"

"Sean, where are you?"

"Out by the old railway station. They caught me but . . ."

"I heard. Got away. Henry said you told Walt you didn't kill Carol."

"I did. I mean I did tell Walt. A big piece of the puzzle came in last night."

"What?"

"I was in the woods, where I guess I had gone a lot. Walt said Carol used to check on me up there after work. Well, I was there, at night, and I know Alan came to me, woke me up, told me not to move, that he would get a car."

"Alan? Came to you? When was that?"

"I'm almost certain it was the night Carol was killed, because that memory dovetailed with another one, seemed to be in the same time frame."

"What was the other one?"

"I heard somebody dragging something. I followed the sounds. It was very dark, but I could see shapes. I saw somebody, a thin guy, kneeling over this thing, I didn't know what it was, and he looked like he was pounding it. He left and I went over to it . . ."

Risa rushed to fill in the blank. "It was Carol. And that's the memory you had before?"

"Yes."

"You didn't kill her?"

"No, Risa. I didn't. I tried to tell Walt. He didn't believe me. I hear myself saying it and it sounds so phony. I say I killed her and then when I get caught I say I didn't, but I know what I'm seeing is the truth. The streets have come back to me and the killing has too. I don't know what's going to happen, but above all I want you to know the truth."

Nothing Sean said sounded phony to Risa. But what he was saying opened a black question. "Do you think it was Alan?"

"I can't imagine it, but he was there."

"You're sure it was Alan?"

"I'm sure. They kept saying this in the clinic, that it's all still up there in my brain, like it is for everybody. It just needs some reason to get out. I almost killed myself last night, Ris. That must have opened something up. It's real to me now, as real as you and I talking here."

"Almost killed yourself?"

"I'll tell you later."

"Alan had an argument with Carol right around that time. I talked to her sister."

"He wasn't in Washington, at least that night."

"He said he just happened to find you on the side of the road."

"He told me he was coming back."

"And I never could figure out why he seemed so unsurprised that you were bloody and saying you killed someone."

"Still. Murder?"

"You don't have to be drunk to go crazy. I'm going to go see him."

"And do what?"

"I don't know. I can't just let him . . . He's supposed to go to Washington this morning. I can't just let him leave without . . ."

"Maybe you should wait."

"Are you sure he was there?"

"Absolutely certain."

"I called Hamilton. He was really pissed. He's not going to help. Let me try to find somebody else. Think you can stay hidden till dark, then come to my house?"

"Do you think that's the best thing to do?"

"Yes. Call me first if you can, to make sure."

"Okay. Where do you live?"

"Wanda Malinowski's old house. You remember it?"

He said he did and they hung up. Risa got out of her parked car and walked toward Alan's headquarters. What was it, only four days earlier when she had made the same walk, dreading Scrimmage Day? That seemed like an innocent time now. A much darker pall hung over her steps. Alan. Carol. Could she have been living with, sleeping beside Carol's murderer all these years?

Fueled more by a burning need to get answers than a rational assessment of what she should do, she pushed open the headquarters doors. She didn't know the young volunteer at the front desk. "Hi, I'm Alan's wife. Is he back there?"

"No," the bright-eyed girl chirped. "He just left."

"For Washington?"

"Yes."

"But it's . . . when did he leave?"

"A minute ago. They're parked out back."

Risa tore out the door, went down the alleyway, and found Alan talking to Debbie Fins, who had a microphone in hand, a cameraman behind her. They were laughing about something when Risa approached. Alan saw her coming and stowed the laugh.

"Hi, Risa. You remember Debbie Fins?"

Risa nodded but didn't come close enough for a handshake. "Can I talk to you?"

"Sure. We're done, aren't we, Debbie?" He was at his slick best. Debbie seemed to have been charmed.

"Yes. Thank you, Alan. I'm glad you went exclusive with me. I'll be sure people know the full story."

"I appreciate that." As he always did, Alan reached over and shook the cameraman's hand before he shook Debbie's. They moved away and he turned to Risa, aware that Debbie was still within earshot. "What, honey?"

Risa moved away and Alan followed. When they were about ten yards away, Alan turned his back to Debbie and frowned at Risa. "What's up?"

"You know they got Sean and then he got away, right?"

"Yes."

"I just talked to him. He called."

"What did he say?"

"He said there's been a marked improvement in his memory." She waited to see his reaction to this, but Alan only gave her a glassy stare.

"I heard. Now he says he didn't do it. Right?"

"Right. He also knows now that you were there earlier on the night you took him to New York. You found him in the woods and told him you'd be back to pick him up."

Alan flushed. He spread his arms as if he were addressing a jury and wanted to dramatize a point. "Goddamnit, Risa. You came over here to tell me that? You don't think I've got enough on my mind? You want me to deal with the hallucinations of an old drunk?"

"That's exactly right. Were you there? Did you tell him you'd be back to pick him up?"

Alan made a disgusted shake of the head. "Did you hear what I just said? I don't want to deal with this now. Period."

Risa peered over his shoulder, then back at him. "Watch what you do. You're on camera."

Alan whipped his head around in time to see the cameraman lower his lens. Alan moved quickly to Debbie and the cameraman, had words with them, got apologies and promises not to use the shot, and came striding back to Risa.

"So, are we clear on this? No more questions about that night."

"Fine. Let Stallings take care of it. That's what you're thinking? He'll do what's right for you."

"For me?"

"You scratch my back, I'll scratch yours."

"You're over your head, Risa. You're making all these amateurish assumptions about how things work. Stallings will give Sean a fair shake."

"With Alice Drummond's attack in his face? I doubt it. Sean saw the killer with the machete. Saw the body after the killer left. That was what he had been seeing all along. The body after the killer left."

"And who was the killer?"

Risa surprised herself. "We'll leave that for Stallings to hear."

Alan turned around to make sure there were no cameras rolling, then barked down at Risa. "This a game to you?"

"Sort of. Your rules."

"Yeah, well, my rules say this is all a bunch of bullshit. Sean's fucking with you, fucking with the whole goddamn system. Lost his memory, my ass. He's back here for something else. I hope Stallings hears his goddamn new story and kicks his butt back to the fucking streets of New York where he belongs."

"Will you answer the question, then?"

"What question?"

"Why you were out there in the woods with Sean. Why you told him to wait, that you were going to get the car. Why you drove him to New York."

"And you know what the answer is going to be to all those questions?"

"What?"

"You. You were the reason."

"Me?"

"Yeah. He wasn't right for you. You knew that back in high school. You knew you and I were perfect for each other. But he poured honey in your ear somewhere along the way and got you pregnant and then he started fucking up. And you know how that tore at me? Can you imagine? I tried to warn you. Remember I came by one night when he was on a bender and told you how bad things looked from the outside."

"I don't remember that."

"Of course not. Mr. Good-for-Nothing had you and you were blind. So what the hell was I supposed to do?"

"Mind your own business."

"But you were my business. Don't you understand that? Sean was a detour. It was you and me. How many times did we say that or think that in high school? I was going places and you were going with me. Remember? So Sean had to go. Especially when he started staying away from you, treating you like shit."

"So, what, you greased the skids for him?"

"For you. It was all for you."

"What was all for me?"

"What I did. And I'm fucking proud of it. Look where you are now. Look where Kevin is now. You think you would have had what you have now if you'd had him around?"

"What did you do?"

Alan turned again to see if Risa's raised voice had carried to the little knot of people by the car. It hadn't. He turned back.

"Sean wanted to get drunk. I made sure he stayed that way. I didn't want him to pull some sort of recovery shit, keep you and Kevin on a string, then fuck up again and send you all into a tailspin."

"You kept him drunk? You were in Washington."

"I put a lot of miles on that Honda."

"What are you saying? You would drive here from Washington to get Sean drunk?"

"Keep him drunk is what I said. Just bring out the true Sean so you and all the world could see it."

"Let me get this straight. What would you do to keep him drunk?"

"We were drinking buddies. Let's put it that way."

"One-beer-Alan was a drinking buddy?"

"Somebody had to make sure he kept going. He didn't care who was pouring the drinks. He kept his mouth shut. He was one sick animal who needed to be cut out of the herd. You couldn't see that, but I could."

"Cut out of the herd? How long did this go on?"

"Couple of months. He was ready. He was already going by the time I figured out what to do. I kept out of sight so nobody would know what was going on. Then the time was right and I knew I had to act."

"Take him to New York?"

"Right. And make sure he stayed there. I almost lost my job because I was spending so much time in New York. Then his brain went to mush and I knew he could do it on his own."

"I can't believe I'm hearing this."

"When you do believe it, look at yourself and give me the credit I deserve. Your good friend Carol? She almost fucked it up."

"How?"

"She'd go out and try to take care of him, sober him up. She said it was for you, but she didn't know what she was talking about. I was the one who had your interests at heart."

Risa stared at the face of delusion, her heart pounding in her chest. It was all so clear now. Alan had held Sean's head underwater until he nearly died, then carted him to New York to finish him off. He had been in those woods the night Carol was killed. He had told Sean he was going to come back with the car. He must have run into Carol and killed her before getting the car and taking Sean to New York.

"You killed her, didn't you?"

"Of course not."

"I don't believe you. What happened?"

"I told him I'd be back. When I returned, he wasn't where he'd been. I went up and down the road and found him. He was all bloody. I knew it was the time to get him away from you forever."

"You killed her, you son of a bitch. You've been lying about this for days now. Go the whole way, Alan. Come on. She got in your way. She was fucking up your plans. You just went crazy."

"No."

"He had blood all over him and you didn't stop, find out what happened?"

"It didn't make any difference. He was leaving. I was getting rid of him. What if I had turned him in and there'd been a case and he stayed around and you stayed with him? What good would that have done you? Or us?"

"He saw you kill her, and you got him out of there. You couldn't kill him right there so you took him away, for a slow death, right?"

"I swear, and this is the last time I'm going to say anything to you about this, ever, I did not kill Carol. I went to New York and heard about the murder three days later, like everybody else. Case closed. I'm staying in Washington tonight."

He started to walk away and Risa lunged for him, caught his jacket sleeve.

"No. You're staying. You're going to Stallings."

"Let go, Risa." Aware of the people waiting for him, Debbie and her cameraman packing up, Alan pulled Risa's hand away slowly.

"Alan. You're forcing me to make this public."

He turned to her and put both hands on her shoulders, trying to make it look like a warm gesture.

"You do any such thing and you will live to regret it. That's not a threat. It's a statement of fact. You live with what I just told you and you keep it to yourself and one day you're going to come to me and say, 'You were right.'"

He turned and started to walk toward the car. Risa followed, growling.

"You going to send Landis after me too?"

Alan kept walking. "He's dead."

"You can find somebody else. Maybe his girlfriend."

"Get away, Risa, you're making a scene."

Risa looked over at Debbie Fins. She and her cameraman

were staring at the unfolding drama. Henry was coming up the alleyway. Risa started toward them, enraged now.

"I've got a news flash for you," Risa shouted as she walked. Then she felt Alan's hand clamp on her arm and spin her around.

"You go another step, you talk to them over there, and I promise you someone close to you will get hurt badly. That is a fucking threat."

Risa thought for a second he was going to hit her. Kevin. He was talking about Kevin.

She freed her arm and snarled at him. "You're not getting away with this." She didn't move.

"Get in the car."

"Like hell. Shove me in. Go ahead. Maybe they'll get a shot of that."

She glared at him. He looked over at the three still standing wide-eyed. He looked back at Risa as if he'd like to spit in her face.

"It was for you, you ungrateful bitch. All for you. You fuck with me now and I will have your ass."

He straightened his suit jacket, nodded to Debbie Fins, got in the car, and was gone before Risa's breath slowed. She looked over at the reporters. They were waiting. She wanted to stomp over to them and spill all she knew. She could hear Alan's car squealing around a corner. He had threatened Kevin. He'd never be able to take that back.

Risa walked toward Debbie Fins. Henry was with her. She couldn't talk to them now. She needed something more than her hunch to go public, and she needed to make sure Kevin was safe. The cameraman started to raise his camera, Debbie pointed her microphone. Risa waved them away.

She kept walking and Henry caught up with her.

"What was that?"

Risa felt the burn of suppressed rage sear the back of her skull. She couldn't think. She could only hear Alan's threat pound over and over. What could she do to prove her case? She had to have time.

"Don't even come close to printing that story, Henry. Come to my house tonight."

He nodded, started to say something, and she cut him off with a wave before walking away. Her thinking started to clear. DNA evidence. Witnesses. She'd have to be the one to find the fucking proof.

He did it for me? She saw Alan's naked body above her in the bed. She thought she was going to be sick. But she kept on walking. There was too much to do.

33

After he talked with Risa, Sean went back across the road into the woods and hunkered down in thick bushes. The pissy rain was on and off. He counted three cruisers that went past, none slow enough to be looking for him.

Risa had believed him. That single thought glowed through all that had happened over the past four days. And hadn't it been that way throughout their long history together? Even when he didn't believe himself, when he doubted his world enough to drown himself in the bottle, he knew somewhere down in his troubled thinking that Risa was on the shore pulling for him.

When he had begun to recover his memory in the hospital, he had told himself that remembering lovemaking with Risa was dangerous. But in the silent woods now, with his memory seeming to improve by the hour, he let himself travel to their joyous times in bed, the beauty of her skin, the mystery of deep union. He said a prayer of thanks and, without even thinking about it, crossed himself for the first time in decades.

After an hour or so he realized he was starved and that he hadn't eaten in more than twenty-four hours. He remembered a mom-and-pop convenience store that used to be on the other side of the railway station. He felt in his pocket, found that he still had the bills, and headed toward the store.

The store was a sad blond brick relic. There was only one car in the parking lot. He waited for a while but no one else pulled into the place. There was a faint whiff of bacon in the air and, after a few more minutes, Sean succumbed.

Half the shelves in the place were empty. A bearded bear of a man behind the counter nodded as Sean entered, grabbed a can of beans and a bag of popcorn, and headed for the cooler case. DON'T BREAK THE SIX-PACKS, a sign read. He saw loose cans and bottles of forties on the lower racks. He forced himself to look to the right, to the soft drink section. But he stared at the Coke and Pepsi for only a few seconds before bringing his gaze back to the beer. There was no craving, but there was no question either. He opened the cooler door, wrapped his hand around a forty of something called Silver Bullet, and pulled it out. He saw a counter with plastic utensils, got a fork and a spoon for his beans, and went to the front.

The bearded man was watching him now through thick, taped-up glasses, scratching his stomach. Sean put his items on the counter.

"That it?" the man said. Sean nodded, keeping his head low. The man began to punch the register. "Guess you don't recognize me, Sean, with my beard. Randy Nowak."

Sean remembered a kid in high school named Randy Nowak, but he hadn't looked anything like this guy.

"Sorry. Yeah. The beard got me."

Randy looked up at Sean and gave him an enigmatic smile. He was reaching for a paper bag when he did this, then looked down. "Outa bags. Be right back."

"I don't need . . ." Sean started, but Randy was headed for the back and disappeared through a door. Going to make a call? Sean looked down at the *Philadelphia Inquirer* Randy had been reading, dropped on his stool now. Sean could see a picture of the bridge out of Braden and what he thought was his name in the subhead of the story. He pulled out four dollar bills, ready to take off, when, as if coming back from a drowse of some sort, he saw the Silver Bullet sitting next to his popcorn and can of beans.

What was he doing? He'd heard people in group claiming something like "The bottle just jumped into my hands." Now it seemed the bottle was there on the counter all by itself. And it was talking to him. No words, just a murmured come-on full of why-nots. Sean could feel the twist of the screw cap, the first chug, something he hadn't felt in months and months. Fuck it. It was their fault. If he'd had the real drug he'd be fine, but they fooled him. So it wasn't him, it was them.

He began to sweat. How many times had he heard the relapsed blame someone else for their fall? Well, now he understood what they were saying. You give everything over to a higher power and if you take that first drink it's not your fault. It's that higher power's fault.

Randy's return made Sean jump. He was carrying an armful of paper bags and stuffed them into a cubby below the counter. He put one on the counter.

"Five seventy-five, Sean." As he said this, he looked down and saw the *Inquirer.* He looked up. "That fucking Landis was an animal. Good riddance."

Sean barely heard him, his eyes glued to the sweat forming on the forty. "Yeah." He put his four dollars on the counter. Randy hesitated, then picked up the bills.

"Need a couple more here, Sean."

"Couple more?"

"Dollars. Comes to five seventy-five."

Randy didn't seem to be neutral when Sean looked up at him. He was giving a straight total, but Sean had the feeling he was being pointed about something, testing Sean. And then Sean knew he had to get out of there, away from the newspaper, away from the beer.

"Skip the beer. I'll just take the others."

"Sure." Randy punched the register again. "Now you got enough. Do me a favor, would you? Put the beer back."

Sean couldn't read Randy. Was he trying to stall things, keep Sean there until the cops came? He didn't wait to find out. He grabbed the popcorn and beans and took off. Outside, he turned right, away from the railway station, went a quarter mile up the road until he was out of sight of the store, then crossed the road and doubled back, heading into the woods. He was still trying to avoid the cops with this maneuver, but he felt as if he were running from an object without legs, a tall, sweaty bottle that was out to get him, that was right behind him.

After he got the pull top open, he wolfed down the beans and then the popcorn. He wished he had bought the Coke. But he felt better. He could think. Alan? What was Risa saying? What could he remember other than the raw fact of Alan being there talking to him? He could see Alan getting him drinks and go cups. That seemed right. But what did Carol have to do with it?

He heard dogs in the distance and wondered if they were bloodhounds on his trail. He shivered. He wanted it to be dark, to get to Risa's, to see her eyes and know that all was going to work out.

When Risa got back to the house, she was still shaken. The ugly scene in the parking lot, Alan's vicious threats, were on a loop tape. Kevin wasn't downstairs, and she hoped that maybe he was at practice. As much as she had come to dislike everything about goddamn football, he would be safe there. She went upstairs and found him still in bed, awake, reading a graphic novel, looking pale.

"You okay, Kev?"

"No. I'm sick. I took some Advil."

She felt his head. He didn't have a fever but he looked way under the weather.

"Did you get something to eat?"

"Yeah. But it didn't go down well. I feel like I might throw up."

"You want me to call the doctor?"

"No. I'm just going to stay here. I'll be all right."

Kevin had always been a trouper about being sick, never wanted to stay out of school. Risa had always found his stoicism touching, a boy trying to mimic a man. Now it was doubly touching, her warrior son, pride of the Bulldogs, laid low by a bug, sloughing off a doctor's visit.

Then his vulnerability worried her. She imagined some Landis-like attack and shuddered to think Kevin wouldn't be able to defend himself. Should she not go to The Ding Dong as she had planned?

"Kevin, some things have gone on that we have to think about."

"I saw the *Inquirer* online. There's an article about the bridge thing and Landis and my father. Ring Tone said they caught him this morning, but he got away."

"That's right but don't believe everything you read."

"I don't."

"There are big changes coming. Your father's return has opened up a lot of things. I don't know the whole truth yet, but I can tell now from what I know that things are going to change."

"What things?"

"Things between Dad and me."

"What things between you and Dad?

"I don't want to go into it now. But it's serious. And it's not about you."

"You're getting a divorce?"

Kevin saying it made it real in a way thinking about it couldn't. But that was just the half of it.

"Yes."

"In the middle of his campaign?"

"I don't know when."

Kevin looked as if he might be near tears. “Is it true my father attacked that woman?”

“No. I’m sure now he didn’t do that.”

“Everybody says he did.”

“Everybody’s wrong.”

“And he says he killed your friend Carol.”

“Not anymore. He knows now he didn’t.”

“That’s screwed up.”

“It is. We’ll find a way out of it, though.”

Kevin looked up at his mother. She could see the little boy still inside the adult body.

“Do you still love him?” It was as if he were five again and asking where his father was. The bald question was one she hadn’t dared ask herself, but now she couldn’t avoid it. Her answer came easily, without need for thought.

“I do, Kev.”

Kevin blinked rapidly a couple of times, as if trying to make sense of what she said. Then he nodded and got out of bed.

“Kevin, are you okay?”

“Yeah. I’ve got to go to the bathroom.”

“I mean about what I just said.”

“It’s your life, Mom.” There was nothing accusatory about this. It was a statement of fact, it seemed, and not one that came from Kevin’s own personal hurt. Risa thought that moment might be the first truly adult one she’d seen in Kevin’s life. He stayed near the doorway for a second to see if Risa had more she wanted to say. But Risa only nodded, her tears spilling down her cheeks, and Kevin left the room.

Risa struggled with whether she should leave Kevin alone. Was Alan’s threat real or toothless? She only had to think about the attack on the bridge to tip the scales in favor of real, but she couldn’t imagine him doing anything to Kevin. She couldn’t say why, but she felt her next move had to be in the direction of the scene of the murder. She had the feeling the very space there would offer up some answers. She knew she should be trying to find a lawyer, digging into the case, seeing what other dots connected Alan to the crime. But the pull to be near The Ding Dong was too much. She decided to go see Walt.

As she was leaving the house, she saw she had a voice mail.

"Hello, Risa. This is Dan Marcus, Carol Slezak's, uh, fiancé. Tracey called and told me what's going on. Kind of hard thinking about all that again. The guy who sort of harassed Carol was named John Goetz. If you Google him with Syracuse University you see some stuff. I'm pretty sure he didn't have anything to do with the murder. He was just some kid in love. Let me know if there's anything else you need."

One more nail in Alan's coffin, Risa thought as she drove. It wasn't likely that some random suspect was going to pop up. Alan had been on the scene as the murder happened. He had been in the middle of a sick, ruthless scheme at the time. There was no reason to doubt he had added a murder to his deeds. Risa's only question now was how to bring those facts out into the open.

She detoured to the old railway station and slowed as she went past. She saw the phone booth Sean had called from, but no Sean. She took a shortcut and was soon in The Ding Dong parking lot. She climbed the rain-slicked grassy incline to the scene of the killing and in a few minutes was standing where she imagined the murder occurred.

It was just a small clearing in among some hardwoods, but after a minute of standing there it became populated with a drunken Sean, with Alan telling him to stay there, with Carol coming on the scene to check on Sean, with Alan returning, arguing with Carol, choking her, then dragging her to the open spot and hacking her with G.G.'s machete. Carol was dead long before she was cut. Did Alan use the machete to cast suspicion on G.G.? Risa guessed so, but that put the murder in the realm of a premeditated one, something more grim and unimaginable.

She left the spot quickly and went to The Ding Dong. There were only a couple of lunchtime drinkers at the bar, no one at the tables, and, at first, no one behind the bar. Then Walt came out of the kitchen. He didn't seem pleased to see her.

"Hello, Risa." He gestured to a table and they sat.

"I need your help now, Walt. You said to ask if I did."

"Don't ask me what I think you're going to ask me, Ris. I'm sick to my stomach over this. You know what happened, right? Sean tried to weasel out."

"His brain, Walt."

"No. This memory shit fries my shorts. I know drunks, blackouts, hell, even brain injuries. I just don't buy he seen one thing last week, another this. I don't think it works that way."

"Forget about Sean for a minute. Do you remember Alan being around here at all then?"

"Benson?"

"Yeah."

"No. Why should I? He was what in college or . . . no, down in Washington."

"Right. But he was also here occasionally pumping Sean with drinks, hoping he could get Sean away from me. He was with Sean in the woods the night Carol was murdered. If you gave me even decent odds, I'd say he killed Carol."

"Risa. You all right? This is Alan, your husband. Where you get this from?"

"From Alan, from my husband. He admits to everything but actually killing Carol."

"Boy, you sure you got that message right?"

"Yeah."

Walt looked over at the bar and got up. "Be right back." Risa saw him shaking his head as he poured two beers and returned. "Alan? Carol? I don't see it. What's the motive?"

"She got in the way. She was trying to help Sean. Alan was trying to get him out of town, away from me."

"Shit. That don't sound like Braden, does it?"

"Neither does Jerry Landis."

"Yeah. Now that was really fucked up."

"Alan was behind that. He sicced Landis and Patty Dane on Sean."

"That one I might believe. There's been a lotta talk around about how Alan's got stars in his eyes and don't want anything to get in his way."

"Same as eleven years ago. Carol didn't say anything about Alan that you remember, I guess."

"Nope. She was helpin' Sean, takin' care of him out back. You know that, right?"

"Yeah. I do now. You didn't see Alan at all then?"

"Shit. That was so long ago. I might have. You asked around, some of the regulars then, Arnold, Mike, Sonny, Gisela?"

"No. I asked Henry, but he'd only been in town a week or so."

"Yeah, that's right. Who else?" Walt sighed. "There was somebody around who went to college with Carol."

"Really? I just . . . Who?"

"Not sure. I remember her gettin' pissed at some guy come in the bar. It was tough to piss Carol off. I told her I'd throw him out, but she said that wasn't necessary. I told the cops about it, but they were on G.G.'s ass. I don't know if they looked into it."

"You see him, know what he looked like?"

"No. But didn't you say Alan . . . ?"

Risa wasn't ready to abandon her belief that Alan was involved, but the combination of Dan talking about a stalker and the image of Carol pissed at somebody new in the bar couldn't be ignored.

"I'll ask the others."

"Yeah. But Risa, do yourself a favor. Try to take off your

rose-colored glasses. Drunks can fuck up real, real bad. Even nice guys like Sean. Carol was tryin' to help him. An' I seen it with my own eyes many, many times. Guy wants to stay drunk, he's gonna lash out at anyone takin' that bottle away from him. Keep that in mind."

Risa said she would, but as she walked to the parking lot her crowded brain found it didn't have room for much more than suspicions about Alan. Braden, she said to herself, needed to take off its rose-colored glasses.

34

Doris had been barking at Henry all afternoon. She wanted him to write up his interview with Sean for a special she was going to put out. She made it seem as if this one story was make or break for *The Statesman.*

"We got our asses scooped by the fucking *Inquirer*, Henry. The *Inquirer.* They're fucking closer to the gallows than we are. We don't get something meaty in print in twenty-four hours, we'll all be having cocktail hour at the unemployment office. Get me that interview by six. That's o'clock and that's this evening."

Henry told her he was working on the piece, but what he was really doing was trying to figure out what had happened between Risa and Alan. Debbie Fins had said there was a big fight between them. He wanted to call Risa and ask her what was up, but she had been adamant about not wanting to see him until nighttime. He found a photograph of Carol's funeral and saw Alan with his arm around Risa's shoulder. Were Alan and Risa fighting over Sean, over something that happened back then?

As the afternoon wore on, Henry was feeling more and more trapped. He was ping-ponging between Risa's impassioned plea and Doris's growling commands. He was brought back to his first weeks on the job when the enormity of a real murder had thrown him completely. Doris had ridden him then, hard, forcing him to get on his bike and get the story. He had skimmed the surface, but he had gotten some reporting on paper. Doris always said it was because the body he'd looked at was so ghastly.

This time it was the mystery of it all. The case, in the course of five days, had gone from a neat package in a file drawer to a ragged, unkempt mess hopping around his office, a new discovery every day. You could watch stuff like this on TV and get excited for the cop or the investigator, pick through the clues with them, find justice. But that's not what it was like for Henry, in the real world, on the inside. It was hell and, he thought, might spell the end of his career. He began to hope *The Statesman* would in fact meet its demise, preferably before he had to turn in copy.

When she got home, Risa heated some soup and took it up to Kevin, but he was sound asleep and she didn't wake him. The phone rang a few minutes later.

"Hi, it's me," Alan said. His voice sounded bright, normal. Risa was too surprised to say anything. Was he close? Was this a continuation of the threat? "You see us?"

"See you what?"

"Somebody from the office was going to call you. We went to the White House. They had us do a grab conference with the Speaker. You can see me right behind her. It was just on national."

Risa hung up without another word, as if she'd just gotten an obscene phone call. She had spent hours imagining Alan killing a friend in cold blood and then he had come through the wire like a dancing puppet blabbering about some photo op. He called back immediately and left a message, one Risa erased without listening to it. Then she kicked herself for doing so. That might be evidence she had just destroyed. Could the phone company retrieve those? As she was reeling through the messages, she hit the one from Carol's fiancé, Dan. She scribbled down the name he had given her, John Goetz, sat at the kitchen table, and went online as she ate the soup she had made for Kevin.

She started to look up John Goetz and Syracuse University, but her thoughts drifted. Why was she following this lead? Why wasn't she doing something about her suspicions of Alan? Why wasn't she trying to get Sean a lawyer? She felt the weight of everything. It was getting late. Sean should be coming soon. And Henry. But what could she tell either of them?

She looked out the window and saw a cruiser parked across the street. The light outside was starting to dim, but she thought she could see Dave Hanson at the wheel. He was probably waiting either for her to leave or Sean to show up. Then the landline rang. She got up and answered.

"Ris?" It was Sean.

"Sean. Where are you?"

"Same place. I'm getting ready to come over."

"Come through the back. There's a sheriff's car out front. Henry's going to be here too. We can tell him the story. I talked to Alan."

"What did he say?"

"It was horrible. He said he had gotten rid of you so he and I could be together."

"What?"

"He kept you drunk, when Carol and everybody else were trying to help you."

"Fuck."

"I'm sure he killed Carol."

"But he didn't confess, did he?"

"Not to the murder. Sean? Things might be dangerous. Alan threatened me by saying Kevin might, I don't know, be a target."

"Kevin? Where is he?"

"He's here. He's down with some bug. He's been sleeping all day."

"What does he know?"

"Everything. And he asked if Alan and I are finished."

"What did you tell him?"

"Alan threatened Kevin, Sean. In no uncertain terms. I didn't tell Kevin that, but when he asked, I told him Alan and I were . . . were finished."

Sean let this sink in for a few seconds. "I'll start out . . ."

Risa thought she heard him say "now," but a noise like a truck backfiring sounded in the background and then the connection went dead. The talk of Kevin sent her up to his room again. He was still sound asleep.

The first shot shattered the phone booth glass behind Sean and sprayed shards over his back and neck. He ducked and turned in time to see the spark of the second bullet and hear it clunk into the metal trim. He tried to get the folding door open from a crouch, but it was rusty and resisted. He looked back to see Patty Dane walking unsteadily toward him, the .45 in front of her face. He knew he was trapped, didn't try the door.

He had seen a couple of cars go by as he was talking to Risa but hadn't noticed one nondescript Ford pass, then stop fifty yards up the road. Patty was shaking with rage.

"Get out of there, motherfucker. I want a clean shot."

"Hold it. Stop." Sean couldn't think what to say. He couldn't think period. His heart was going so fast it was lapping itself. Patty looked like shit turned over with a shovel. Her hair hung in scraggly lumps, and as she came another step closer he could see her face was a mass of red blotches. She might have been royally drunk to boot.

"I want you the fuck out of there."

Sean opened the door, calculating how he might be able to dive back for cover if she shot again. Rather, *when* she shot again. He prayed for inspiration, or a car to come down the road. Patty was making no attempt to conceal the execution.

"Patty. Why are you doing this? I had to come back."

"You killed him."

"Who?"

"The best fucking soldier who ever put on a uniform. You killed him!"

"It was an accident. He was chasing me. He . . . he slipped. You saw that."

"Fuck you. He was the best fucking . . ." She looked like she was going to cry.

"But why were you chasing me? What did I do to you?"

"We told you not to come back and you disobeyed orders. You know what we do to people who disobey orders?"

"Who told you to run me out of town?"

Patty choked up, and as she did she fired the .45. The unaimed bullet whistled off into gravel by the road. Frozen by the shot, Sean didn't think about running until it was too late. Patty leveled the gun again.

Sean blabbered to keep her from shooting. "It was Alan, Alan Benson, right. He's the one. If he hadn't—"

"Fuck Alan Benson. He's a fuckin' pussy."

"Right. He sent you to do his dirty work. He's to blame—"

"He didn't send us shit. It was that other pussy and I'll get him next."

She was weak and rattled, and Sean could practically smell the booze from ten feet away. She was drifting and he thought she might just fall down asleep. But the gun wobbled menacingly. He didn't think he could run fast enough to get away, but he could keep her distracted long enough for a car to come by.

"Who? What other pussy?"

"The fucking reporter."

"The reporter? Henry Saltz? What did he . . . Why did he?"

"How the fuck am I suppose'a know?" Her speech was slurring now. The gun could go off any second without Patty willing it.

"Henry put you up to—"

"Shut up! Fuck Henry. Fuck everybody else. You killed my baby. You—"

"Wait, wait! What's it going to do to kill me? It's not going to bring your baby back."

This startled Patty, as if it were a revelation, as if she had thought Landis would return if she just mowed down a couple of people. "He's—"

"He's gone. He's not coming back."

Patty's face shattered like the phone booth pane she had just shot out. Her crying was primal, an outburst of twisted love. "You fuck! Why did you say that?"

Sean was ready to run now. He could see the dawning realization smack Patty back to what he thought was a less-drunk reality, and he was fully in her more clear-headed sights. She moved the gun and Sean dove for the ground.

But instead of shooting at him she snapped to attention and made an awkward, drunken salute with her gun hand. Then she moved the barrel of the gun to her temple and fired. She flopped to the ground like a thrown fish and in an instant her dead eyes were on the gravel, on the same level as Sean's stunned face, staring at nothing.

The gunshot rang in Sean's ears. He could see she was dead. How had she found him? Where was he? What was happening? He heard a tire screech and saw a pickup stop across the road. He couldn't move. Patty still clutched the gun. A man was coming out of the pickup now, yanking a shotgun from his cab window, cocking it. For a second Sean thought this was Landis. The man seemed to know him.

"Sean. Don't move."

The man was leveling the shotgun now.

Sean forced out words. "She shot herself."

The man kept his eyes on Sean. "I know who you are, Sean.

I know they're looking for you." The man's voice was tinny through Sean's gunshot-numb ears.

And then the word "Henry" came to Sean. He looked down at Patty, her eyes still glued on eternity. She had said Henry had been behind their kidnapping him. That couldn't be right. Why?

"Sean. I'm gonna call nine-one-one. I can use this gun. Don't try anything." He pulled a cell phone out of a belt holster and flipped it open.

Henry and Alan were working together? Could that be it? Sean knew he was in shock, but he could feel himself thinking clearly. Was that the way things worked in Braden? Everybody in cahoots?

And then, as if he had leapfrogged a dozen possible connections, the memory piece he'd recovered the night before came screaming at him. The thin guy, his hand with the machete rising and falling. That wasn't Alan. That was Henry. There was absolutely no reason why it should be Henry, and Sean couldn't see a face, but he knew beyond a doubt it was the greenhorn reporter.

"Henry," he said out loud.

"It's Phil, Sean. Phil Cosgrove . . . ," the man said, then spoke into his phone. "There's been a shooting on state Route 124."

He stopped to listen. Sean looked back down at Patty. Henry Saltz. What had Risa said? Henry was doing something, helping her. What did she say? It was just before the shooting started. He was . . . going to Risa's house!

"Let me make a call," he blurted out. Phil was talking low into the phone, still training the shotgun on Sean. He heard Sean's request and shook his head no.

Sean could see Henry and Risa together. What was Henry up to? He had murdered Carol. What else was he capable of? Alice Drummond? Suddenly Sean's world collapsed to this image of Risa, unsuspecting, Henry ready to pounce. Without thinking,

Sean turned quickly, used the phone booth as something of a shield, and gimped as fast as he could, first down the road, then across the pavement and back into the woods. He heard Phil shouting, heard what sounded like a warning shot. But he didn't stop.

As he crashed through the now nearly dark woods, he tried to think straight, figure out the best route to get to Risa's house. He kept seeing Henry and Risa together. And he began to see Kevin there as well. The pain in his knee was like blows from an ice pick. But seeing Henry again lunging over Carol trumped the pain by a longshot.

35

After she hung up with Sean, Risa looked out the kitchen window again. The cruiser was gone. She thought it would still be better for Sean to come in the back way. As she sat back down at the computer, she started to think about whether Sean should tell his story to Henry or just turn himself in.

The computer screen had gone to black. She hit the space bar and the Google results for John Goetz and Syracuse were there. She had to take a second to remember what that was all about. The stalker. She had lost interest in that possibility, but she was curious if there was any mention of him. She could imagine some freshman falling in love with a girl like Carol. And she could imagine Carol being sweet to him, gently trying to get rid of the pest.

The first result was a report or a paper written by a John H. Goetz about Syracuse's history as the Salt City. Risa clicked on the link, but it said the paper was no longer available. She went back to the results and found a report of a restraining order that had been issued to a John Henry Goetz. Risa did the math and found that it was issued about thirteen years earlier. She figured this must have been the stalker.

On the second page of the results there was a link to an article in the *The Daily Orange*, the student paper, about editors for the next year being elected, with John Goetz winning the student affairs editorship. She clicked on the link and got the full front page of the paper. A grainy photograph of the new editors accompanied the article. There were seven of them, three women, four men. Risa scanned the picture, then went to the caption to see which one was John Goetz. She looked back up and found him behind two women, smiling, his hair longish and curly. Something about him looked familiar, but he probably just had that sort of bland face you might think was a hundred people you know.

Her cell phone rang again. It was Bell. She had heard about the argument in the parking lot with Alan. Risa began to tell her what happened, but while she was talking her eyes drifted back to the laptop. Syracuse as the Salt City started to tangle up with the Henry in John Henry Goetz and the combination got overlayed on the picture of the newly elected editors.

"Bell, I'm sorry. I've got to go. Call you later."

She folded the phone slowly, staring at the laptop, not sure she wanted to look at the photo again. But she enlarged the photo in the browser, which increased its graininess, and she gave John Goetz a long look. The words "Henry" and "Salt City" continued to dance together.

For a long minute she resisted what she knew she had come to. She was looking at Carol's stalker. She was looking at a young Henry Saltz. A young Henry Saltz who had moved to Braden only weeks before Carol's murder. Risa stood, her growing comprehension warring with her resistance. His face hadn't changed that much in thirteen years. And Walt had said something about Carol knowing someone from college.

She wandered into the living room wondering what to do with the discovery she'd just made. The evidence, such as it was, was circumstantial. There was a stalker in Syracuse who had been warned to stay away from Carol. That stalker got a job in Braden. Carol was in Braden. Carol was killed. There was nothing directly connecting Henry to the murder.

But there was his silence. Why hadn't he said from the beginning that he knew Carol before he moved to Braden? If he was guilty of the murder, the answer was obvious. If he wasn't, if he just happened to move here a week or so before Carol was killed, he might realize he would be a prime suspect if he said he had known Carol in Syracuse. Someone would look into his record and the conclusion would not be hard to make, that he had killed the object of his obsession.

Risa raced through what she knew about Henry, what he'd told her, what she'd guessed. Could he have really gone out to the scene of the crime and reported on the case if he had committed the murder? That couldn't be possible. Then something small but telling smacked her in the face. Henry's dog. Gina. Short for Regina. As in Carol Regina Slezak.

"My God." Risa was stupefied, unable to take all the pieces she had and put them together. Eleven years. The meals she'd served him. The place he'd had in Braden. It was impossible to think . . .

Risa heard a tapping coming from the kitchen. Sean, thank heavens, she thought as she left the living room and moved toward the back door. She was about to enter the kitchen when she saw that it was Henry tapping. She stopped. He leaned down and peered through a lower pane, showing himself, letting her know who was there. Risa saw his youthful, open face harden as he saw her standing, frozen, staring at him.

She forced herself to move and went to the door. Out of the corner of her eye she could see the laptop open on the kitchen table, the photograph of the editors large on the screen. In one move she opened the door, turned her back to Henry, and reached over to close the laptop. When she turned back, Henry was through the door and close to her.

"I left my bike in the garage. Nobody saw me come in."

"Oh, right." Risa turned away. She couldn't look at him and think.

"Doris is livid. I didn't hand in the article." Risa turned back. Henry was even closer. "The *Inquirer* scooped us and she's really pissed off. Did you read it?"

"No."

Henry looked at her for a long moment, more probing, Risa thought, than she'd ever seen him before. She had always thought of him as a strange reporter in that he had trouble looking people in the eye. But he was looking her in the eye now.

"This has really upset you, hasn't it, Risa?"

"Yes."

"Me too. Can you tell me what you and Alan were arguing about this morning?"

"Just about Sean, whether he was guilty." Risa was losing her nervousness. This was Henry in front of her. She had never feared him. Maybe there was an explanation for the coincidence she'd just uncovered.

"It seemed like more than that," Henry said.

His voice was soft and questioning. Risa could almost imagine him a puppy, cocking his head. His features, as he stood beside the island in the cone of light from the hanging lamp, were delicate. She saw no reason to retreat.

"Did you know Carol had a stalker when she was in Syracuse?"

"No." Henry's face gave no hint of surprise other than a small eyebrow raise at the new information.

"Her fiancé told me. The guy might have followed her to Braden."

"Who? The stalker?"

"Right. John Goetz."

Now Henry's face darkened some. "Really? Followed her to Braden?"

"I don't think the police ever followed up on the lead."

"I didn't hear anything about it. I think if he was a real suspect we would have heard, don't you?"

"Yeah. Probably a dead end." Suddenly Risa felt she needed to get Henry out of the house so she could think, call somebody, do something.

"Why did you want me to come tonight, Risa?"

"I'm not sure. I was really upset then. I'm sorry."

Henry nodded and started to turn toward the door, thinking. When he turned back quickly, Risa had all she could do to stop herself from jumping back.

"But what about the machete? It was definitely G.G.'s machete."

"Right. How could a stalker from Syracuse have G.G.'s machete?"

Henry didn't turn to go this time. His eyes lost some focus, and when he spoke his words came out in packaged, eerie chunks.

"Of course he could have stolen it. That's what G.G. said at first."

"Right."

"If he moved to Braden to be close to her, he would have gone to The Ding Dong. Anybody who's ever gone to the men's room at The Ding Dong knows that G.G. had his machete propped by the mops. He could have seen that."

"I guess so." Risa could feel a shift, the image in front of her not syncing with the voice coming out of Henry's mouth.

"And she might have talked to him. She might have been surprised that he was there, but she wasn't going to do anything, just talk to him that time."

"That time?"

"Before she had called the cops. He had been too forceful in his love."

Risa caught the shift in tone, and followed suit. "But they were talking, right? John Goetz and Carol were talking at The Ding Dong."

"That's right. I mean, like normal. But what she was saying was so weird, so wrong."

"What was she saying?"

Henry pulled back a little. Risa thought he might be coming back to himself, that her question was too on the mark.

"Something like . . . like the worst thing she could say. And he thought it was a joke at first. He'd come all the way down to Braden and the very first time he saw her she said . . ." He shook his head.

"Said what?"

"She said she was going to get married. He laughed because that was so strange. So weird. How could she marry someone else?"

Risa could feel her pulse quicken but Henry was calm. "You can't be married to two people," she said, with all the sympathy she could muster.

"But she didn't know that."

"No."

"That's why that machete was there. He went to the bathroom and there it was, like an answer. All the time he was taking a piss he could hear the machete talking to him. 'Just wait,' it was saying. 'Just wait your time.'"

"Wait."

"Yes." Henry gave a half smile with this, a detached half smile that didn't really fit his face. "So he waited. He took the machete and went outside and waited. It was like always. He had to wait for her a long time. He was always outside her apartment or her class, waiting. But he knew there wouldn't be more waiting. He was going to remind her they were married. Remind her, that was all."

Henry scowled as he stopped talking. Risa could see him reentering the black memory, something even more disturbing for him.

"Do you think he reminded her that night? John? Did he remind her?"

Henry looked up at her so suddenly she gasped. He didn't notice.

"He had to! He had a job. He was settled in. How could she leave him there again? That's what he said to her."

"In The Ding Dong?"

"No. When she came out. He thought she'd go to her car, but she didn't. He thought she was avoiding him. She walked up into the woods. That was really strange, don't you think?"

"Yes."

"But he caught up with her. She wasn't going to just disappear in the woods and get married. He ran and caught up with her and he tried to explain but she was angry and she wouldn't listen. She kept talking. So he had to stop that talking, right? The words were ugly. She was telling him to leave her alone. When they were married? Why? She just didn't understand and so he made her stop talking. That was easy. You don't have to argue with someone. You can just hold them tight where the words come out and they stop talking."

"Henry?" Risa had had enough. She couldn't take what she suspected was coming next. She wanted to get Henry out of the house. She wished the cruiser was outside. Henry didn't respond to her. He was talking to himself now.

"She didn't like it, but she stopped. And once she stopped, she realized what he was saying. And that's when they were finally together. He listened to the machete and they were together. He had stopped the words and then he had to make sure she wouldn't go off and leave him, get married. After a while he could tell she was never going to leave him again. He found her keys and they just drove off together."

This last came out in a whisper. There were tears behind the words, but they seemed more tears of joy to Risa than sad tears, terrified tears.

"And they're together still?"

"Yes. It's been disturbing for him recently. But yes."

"Disturbing?"

"People talking about him behind his back. Saying, like, she married somebody else."

"That couldn't be."

"No, but they were saying it. He got angry and came back to show them, and he got all confused. There was this one he thought was Carol. He forgot she was still right there with him."

Alice Drummond, Risa thought. "He's okay now, isn't he?"

Henry stared past her and she had the feeling the Henry she had known for years, the bodily one, was gone. She started to think about how she was going to get him to the police, or maybe the hospital. If he'd broken with reality, she might have to deal with this other Henry, with John.

"Do you want a ride home?"

Henry continued to stare past her, black bullets shot into some void. Risa wondered if the other Henry had left, had had his time in Henry's consciousness and left.

"I really need to get some sleep. I have to do a lot in the morning and I bet you're tired after all this . . ." she said, looking up at the clock.

He didn't answer. His right hand shot out like a snake, his long fingers wrapped around her throat and lifted her, slamming her head into a cupboard behind her before she even realized what was happening. A scream that formed in her chest was choked off by the pressure on her windpipe. Her ears rang as Henry pushed on her throat, jamming the base of her skull on the cupboard, the scissoring on her neck excruciating.

Henry leaned in as he pushed, his free hand groping for the knife rack just out of his reach. He was growling a whisper in Risa's face but she couldn't hear the words. Her senses were shutting down from lack of oxygen. His palm on her windpipe felt like metal. Starbursts in her vision winked out as a curtain of darkness descended. She knew she was still kicking, but it seemed like someone else. She needed a breath desperately but she couldn't even open her jaw. Things were closing down rapidly. She couldn't see. She could distantly feel her head being thumped against the cupboard and that briefly brought her vision back.

He was within inches of her, his face as calm as an evening lake. And then suddenly he flew away, reeling back, his hand leaving her throat as suddenly as it had come. She slid to the floor, the island and the kitchen beyond tilting left, then right. A huge gulp of air made it down her windpipe and she thought her lungs would pop like a balloon. She thought her neck was broken.

But she heard a commotion and was able to look to her right. There were struggling bodies, one in boxers. Sound started to come back and she heard the grunts that went along with the struggle. She had a brief glance at a kitchen knife moving wildly around the bodies before the struggle vanished out the doorway into the living room.

A scream made its way out of her mouth. She flopped to one side and crawled toward the doorway to the living room. She saw the bodies more clearly now. It was Kevin. He and Henry were clawing at each other's throats, the knife on the floor near Risa.

"Stop!" she managed to get out as she crawled toward the knife. Kevin got the upper hand and hurled Henry as if he were some blocker he could just flick away. Henry stumbled to the floor, knocking into Risa. Kevin pounced and landed a solid punch to the side of Henry's face. Henry's head snapped around, but he kicked out and momentarily got Kevin off him. Then Kevin was on him again and started landing punch after punch until Henry curled like a porcupine protecting itself.

But Kevin was deep in a rage now and didn't stop. He stood and kicked Henry hard in the back of the head. He reached down and grabbed the kitchen knife. Risa managed to get to her knees.

"Kevin! No! Stop!"

Kevin threw the knife away but he was not down from the adrenaline rush yet. He gave Henry a hard kick to the kidneys. Henry threw up and curled tighter.

Risa stood after a couple of attempts and pushed Kevin back. "Don't."

She stumbled into the kitchen and found her cell phone on the island. She dialed 911, and when she got an operator, she tried to talk but it felt like there were razor blades in her throat. She took the phone in to Kevin. Still boiling, he managed to get the information out.

Risa stood unsteadily, her body jangling, looking down at the fetal-positioned Henry, asleep it seemed in his own vomit.

"They're coming," Kevin said, folding the phone, not willing to leave his place behind Henry. "Are you all right, Mom?" Risa could only nod yes. "I was just coming down to get an Advil. Why was he doing that?"

Risa couldn't answer. Tears were welling up now. Kevin had saved her. Nobody had been able to save Carol, but Kevin had saved her. She wanted to go to him, but he was still in the battle, still boiling. They heard a grunt and looked down.

Henry opened his eyes, saw the puddle of puke in front of his face, and recoiled. Kevin tensed. Henry looked up at Risa as if she were a stranger. Then he looked around the floor and up at the glowering Kevin. When he turned back to Risa, he watched her for a long few seconds. Risa was shaking now with the shock.

"What happened to you, Risa?" Henry asked, in his own voice.

But Risa still couldn't speak, still had the razor blades in her throat. And then the room tilted and she couldn't make it tilt back right. She saw Kevin moving quickly toward her, but she knew she had to sleep, and before Kevin reached her, she toppled to the floor.

36

Trying to take a back route to Risa's house, Sean got lost and had to stop for a minute. His knee was buckling now with every step, but he was able to make good speed just the same. Henry kept him going. He was as certain of Henry's guilt as he'd been of his own only a few days ago, and he realized that should have given him pause, made him wonder if he could be certain of anything ever again. But this was different; he wasn't seeing one thing and making assumptions. He'd seen Henry's vicious attack and he knew Henry had to be behind the assault of Alice Drummond.

When he caught his breath, he realized he was only a yard over from Risa's. He went through a row of shrubs and thought he saw the back of Henry's head in the kitchen window. Then the head was gone. There was a security light on, so Sean circled in its shadow and went through the back door to the garage.

When he looked through the kitchen door windows, Sean couldn't quite make sense of what he was seeing. Risa was sprawled unconscious on the kitchen floor, Kevin, it must have been Kevin, was in his boxers holding a kitchen knife out like a sword, and Henry was standing, staring. Sean thought he heard a siren in the distance.

He pushed open the door and Kevin jumped.

"Kevin, it's me. It's all right."

"Who?"

"I'm your dad." Kevin was shaking. "It's okay. What happened?"

"Yeah. That's what I'd like to know," Henry said evenly as he looked from Sean to Kevin. Henry's face was scratched and his clothes disheveled, but he seemed oddly calm.

"I don't know. He . . . Mom . . . I came down and he was choking Mom. He had a knife. I . . ."

"Is she okay?" Sean moved slowly, not sure if Henry had another weapon, if he was going to do something. He went closer to Risa, saw bruise marks on her neck, but could tell she was breathing normally. The sirens were getting closer now. Sean looked up and saw Henry pull something out of his pocket. He lunged at Henry and grabbed his wrist as Henry grasped a minirecorder.

"What, Sean?" Henry said, stepping back. Sean took the recorder but couldn't read Henry, what he was going to do next.

"What happened, Henry?"

"I haven't got a clue. I was talking to Risa. I came over. I was going to see you. We were talking. She was telling me something. Then all of a sudden, I mean just like that, I was on the floor throwing up."

"He was choking her!"

Henry looked at Kevin with what Sean thought was sincere incomprehension. "Who was, Kevin? Who was choking her?"

"You!"

Henry looked from Kevin to Sean. "Somebody was here, that's for sure." He slowly pulled a notebook out of his back pocket. "I've gotta get this down."

Sean and Kevin looked at each other. Kevin wasn't ready to accept what Henry was saying, believe it wasn't some act, but Sean was. His bullshit meter hadn't left zero. He heard tires braking outside.

"You were choking Risa the way you choked Carol, isn't that right, Henry?"

"Carol?"

"You killed Carol. You did that, didn't you?"

"No, Sean, you did. You told me that. You were there."

"I was there, but I saw you do it."

"Come on, Sean." He looked back down at Risa. "Jesus. Is Risa all right?"

"No," Sean said. "You tried to kill her."

"Me? No. I'm her friend."

Sean would remember forever the look Henry gave him then. It was the look of someone who had just been introduced to the darkest side of his being and didn't catch the name, couldn't quite connect the dots.

Risa was coming to. Sean went to her.

"Risa, you okay?"

Risa's eyes came open and she tried to swallow. Her hand went quickly to her throat, to the stabbing pain. The kitchen door opened and Dave Hanson came flying into the room, stunned, unable to figure out where to begin. He finally turned to Henry.

"What happened?"

Henry stood where he had been all along, now with a pen poised over his notebook.

"I don't know."

37

Gina barked incessantly while the investigators went through Henry's house after his arrest. The dog seemed to have some sense that things were off, that her owner wasn't going to like what these men and women were doing to the house, and that she needed to keep reminding them they were trespassing. They finally dragged the dog into a cruiser and let her bark her fool head off there.

What Gina might have been trying to protect was a cache of more than two thousand handwritten, unsent letters from John Goetz to Carol found neatly filed in a closet in the otherwise messy house, some fourteen or fifteen years of a one-sided correspondence between a besotted, deluded young man and the woman he thought he had married in a ceremony late one night in the woods behind The Ding Dong.

Tom Adsit, a local lawyer who had become fascinated with the case and who readily agreed to represent Henry, went through the entire correspondence and told everyone in town that the letters were all the evidence one could wish for of Henry's insanity. The most recent letters talked about Sean's return and Sean's absurd suggestion that he, not John, had "married" Carol on that fateful night. John vowed to protect Carol from this intruder and detailed some of the things he had done to that end—hiring Jerry Landis and Patty Dane, staging an attack that would get Sean in trouble—but the letters showed that

Sean's appearance threw John for a big loop and had him clashing with Henry often.

Henry had stayed Henry while they took him from Risa's house to the courthouse. He was confused about why they were taking him in, said he had to call Doris because there had been an attack on Risa, as he scribbled notes in the backseat of the cruiser. But once they put him in a small windowless cell, he became John Goetz. Dave Hanson would tell everyone he talked to that when Henry went through the door to the cell and turned around, he was "Mr. fucking Hyde."

"Just like you see in some goddamn movie, like he'd put a mask on. We told him to snap out of it, told him we knew he was just playin' to get off, but he wasn't playin'. He was fuckin' gone."

In the next few days, John Goetz would have only one concern. He would tell them anything they wanted to know, he would do whatever they wanted him to do, as long as he could be assured Carol could stay with him. When Armey first heard John voice this worry, the sheriff answered that he thought she could stay. But that was too vague. John became agitated and demanded certainty. Armey gave it to him.

He was docile after that, and three days after he was arrested they took away the suicide watch. Tom Adsit at first couldn't get him to speak, but after he read the letters and told John that Carol wanted him to speak, John opened up and told Tom the whole story of his love affair with "the woman I was always meant to be with."

On the eighth day of his incarceration, John asked for a pen and paper. He wrote a bizarre letter to Carol, full of odd, poetic-sounding code words, and seemed to be ecstatic about their enduring union while at the same time being troubled by what he saw as exposure of their heretofore secret love.

He then managed to find his carotid artery with the pen point and sat still as blood pumped from the wound. When they found him he was lying on his cot, the letter to Carol a blood-soaked pillow they had to peel off his cheek.

Alan was in a Washington hotel room, his coat off and his tie loosened, and had just poured a drink for himself and an old acquaintance from his days in the capital, Marni Tate, when Lilly Barkin called. Marni sat on the edge of his bed, her long legs prominent. She had been gushing over Alan's success, his growing stardom in the party. He almost didn't take Lilly's call when it came in, but Marni got up to go to the bathroom and Alan answered.

"What's up, Tiger Lilly?" A joke between them. Lilly told him about Henry and the attack on Risa. The news didn't broadside Alan the way it would everyone else in Braden. He had suspected from the beginning that Henry had murdered Carol. "Suspected" was probably too mild a word. After he had gotten Sean in his car on the night of the murder, he had driven past The Ding Dong and had seen a thin man he would only later come to know as Henry getting in the driver's seat of Carol's car. When, days later, he heard about Carol's murder, he had two pieces of information to deal with: Sean's confession in the car and Henry getting into Carol's car. Sean had by that time completely forgotten the whole night, the drive to New York. He was awash in the booze Alan had been almost literally pouring down his throat. After G. G. Trask was arrested, when Alan knew who Henry was, there was no upside for Alan to tell what he knew. There would be too much else to explain.

But he felt he had to feign surprise, even with Lilly.

"My God. Henry?"

"Yeah."

"I'll get a car. I should be there in three, maybe four hours."

"No. Stay where you are. Risa is adamant. She doesn't want you to come home or come to the hospital."

"Why not?"

"I don't know. She can't talk well. She just said to tell you that. I went there and they gave me the bum's rush."

"But I have to. I can't just let my wife be attacked, be in the hospital, and not go. How would that look?"

"We'll release a statement."

"She can't talk?"

"He did something to her vocal cords. She'll be all right, but she can't talk now."

"Tell her I'm coming. I don't have any choice."

"Bad move. What if she doesn't let you in? How's that going to look? I think we should do what she wants."

"To hell with what she wants. Listen to me. She's done everything she can to sabotage my campaign. Keeping me out of the hospital would be the icing on the cake. You just tell her she has to think of somebody other than herself right now, got that?"

"Look, Alan. She'll come around in a day or so. She's in shock. Here's my plan. We'll say you're huddling with advisers and can't be reached. You don't answer the phone for twenty-four hours. Then when she sees things clearly, you come flying to her aid."

"How am I going to be unavailable?"

"Where are you?"

"The Sheraton."

"You check in under your own name?"

"I, uh . . ." Marni came out of the bathroom, smiling, sitting back on the bed. "No. I didn't want any reporters to bother me."

"So that's how you're unavailable. I'll pass the statement by you later. I'm afraid we're going to have to distance ourselves from Stallings. He's got a major fuckup to deal with and he's going to pay for it. So let us work on this. Just hunker down. This will blow over. We're getting great feedback in the district from the grip-and-grin at the White House."

"Okay. Good work, Lilly." He hung up and glowered.

Marni lost her smile. "Is everything all right?" she asked.

"Fine. To hell with her, then," Alan said, more to himself than Marni. "I'll find a way around this."

"Around what?" Marni looked at him with caring, concerned eyes, eyes that would understand what he was talking about, that knew the value of his goals.

"My wife. She's a problem. Maybe you've got some advice."

"I'll see what I can do. Tell me."

Alan took a long gulp of his drink and began.

G. G. Trask had more trouble believing that he didn't kill Carol Slezak than he did believing they were letting him go. There was tangible evidence of this last. A lawyer came to see him and talked about a court appearance, and then there was the court appearance, and then he was holding a bag with his clothes and personal belongings in it and Walt was driving him back to The Ding Dong.

Walt tried a couple of ways to help G.G. see that he was innocent, but he couldn't dent eleven years of G.G.'s certainty of his own guilt.

"I don't want to do no brush cutting no more, Walt. I've got to get rid of that machete."

"They took it, G.G. It's not there anymore."

When they got back to The Ding Dong, G.G. surprised Walt by pulling a book out of his bag, a tattered paperback without a cover. He told Walt that a friend in prison had been teaching him to read better and that it only took him a month or so to read a book now.

"Then I go back and see what it all meant, you know, what the story was."

"I wish you'd been able to reread that confession, G.G."

"Why?"

"You might not have signed it."

"I don't understand all this, Walt. They found my machete up there. Who else could have done that?"

Walt didn't push the point. He drew two beers and put them on the bar.

"Well, let's just call it a miracle you're back. To your health."

He picked up his glass and raised it. G.G. stared at the other beer, then shook his head.

"I don't think I better, Walt. That night I did that to Carol, I had one too many, know what I mean? I remember Carol laughed at me because she thought I was acting silly. Think that's why I done what I done, cause she laughed at me?"

Walt gave G.G. a long look and tried to imagine Stallings and Armey stuffing G.G.'s head with a false confession.

"Maybe, G.G. Maybe that was it."

Kevin's first practice back was his last ever in a Bulldog uniform. After calisthenics and some mirror drills, the linebackers and offensive linemen squared off in the dreaded one-on-ones that Kevin had, in the past, loved. The trick in the drill, for the linebackers, was to keep the lineman from getting in low and driving you, to stand him up by grabbing his shoulder pads, and then, when you saw the direction the ball carrier was taking, shed the blocker.

Kevin had wanted to go back to football after the attack on his mother in part just to feel normal again. The calisthenics had felt good. The mirror drills made him feel light on his feet. As he stood in line for his turn at the one-on-one, he could feel the adrenaline begin to pump, hear the pad pops of the players in front of him, see that he was going to be paired up with Will Tamarinsky, a tough, 220-pound senior, a fireplug who could lift you off the ground when he got in under your arms.

At the snap of the ball, Tamarinsky got low and Kevin thought he was finished. But suddenly Tamarinsky became Henry and Kevin used some reserve tank of arm strength to straighten Henry up and to hurl him back into the ball carrier. The linebacker coach was in Kevin's face in a second.

"That's it, Kevin! That's textbook, son. You all see that? That's what I want out here, that's what I want."

Kevin looked around at the players behind him, at the whole practice field, and wondered where Henry was hiding, when he would come out again. When Coach later tried to dissuade Kevin from quitting, he told him to use "that unfortunate incident" as a motivation. Kevin obliged and was motivated to quit.

Sean had watched the practice without telling Kevin he was going to do so. He saw the ferocity of the hit and, combined with the YouTube video of the Scrimmage Day hit, wondered where that particular form of violence had come from. Sim, Kevin's grandfather, had size and muscle but never used them to do more than carry a full keg up a flight of stairs.

As Risa had on Scrimmage Day, Sean wondered if the conditioning in the football program itself had given Kevin the ability to use his body to hurt others, or if football just brought out something that had always been there. He had believed himself capable of the worst violence and though he hadn't actually done what he thought he'd done, he would never be able to exempt himself or anyone else from the possibility of a sudden onset of violence.

When Kevin came back to the house and said he had quit and why, Sean prayed that Kevin's heroic act wouldn't echo darkly in his life. Sean knew something about those sorts of obstacles and didn't wish one of them on his son.

The open manhole in Sean's new life was drink. Or rather, on paper, it seemed that way. But after having left the forty of Silver Bullet on the counter at the convenience store, Sean found himself back where he had been when he thought medicine was keeping him from the bottle. Only he didn't have either the medicine or the belief. He just lacked the desire. A doctor back in New York who was working on brain trauma and memory and was fascinated by Sean's case couldn't really explain why Sean might no longer want booze, but he wondered if the damage to Sean's memory centers might have wiped out some crucial mechanism whereby the brain remembers drink as a pleasant experience and forgets the downside.

By the time Sean was examined, he had very little interest in his medical condition. He was more concerned about Risa's state. She had recovered from her physical injuries but was having a hard time coming to grips with what had happened, with, as she said, "the suddenness of it." And with the deception. She made a decision shortly after getting out of the hospital to bury what she knew of Alan's horrible acts at the time of Carol's murder. She knew she could torpedo his campaign, but she didn't want to go public, to have Alan deny and dissemble, and so she stayed quiet while he squeaked out a victory and took off for Washington.

Gradually Risa began to see the horror and the violence as perhaps a necessary component of what she called her rebirth. As counterintuitive as it sounded, she wondered if that hand of death on her throat had in some twisted way led to a new life for her. The Sean she had fallen deeply in love with as a senior in college was back to stay. Alan was gone. Kevin, in some ways, was back as well. When he told her he had quit football, she cried. She tried to make sure he wasn't doing so for her, but she didn't really care why. She knew she could put that Scrimmage Day hit in some scrapbook of forgettable moments and not have to fear years of going to games wondering if her son was going to hurt somebody.

In the winter Risa began handing The Kitchen over to a grateful Bell. Risa and Alan's divorce had gone through, Sean had a couple of job offers he was considering, and all Risa really wanted to do was paint. It had been almost impossible for her to go into The Kitchen at first. She knew from reports that the place had been filled with nonstop buzz about Henry, Sean, the attack, and Kevin's rescue of his mother for months after the events. She wanted to talk about the late autumn light in the backyard, the dun wash of stripped hills across the Susquehanna at sunset, the curve of Kevin's hand as he poured a glass of milk.

And she didn't need The Kitchen for conversation. She had Sean. Once she got her voice back, she and Sean began to make up for eleven years of lost talk. As they had in college, they began planning trips in after-dinner "fantasy sessions," as they called them. Twenty years older than their college selves, they dreamed about less exotic locations and finally booked a trip for the three of them to Italy.

Part of their talkfest was Sean's rapidly recovering memory. He found that he hadn't spent his entire eleven years in New York on the streets, that he had been in various programs under false names, that he had been helped often by a functioning heroin addict, a woman who used him to make her buys and who in return made sure he didn't starve or freeze to death. She had OD'd a few months before the frozen Sean ended up on the subway tracks.

It took Kevin and Sean a while to find common ground. Kevin, who had been so succinct with Risa when she had first told him about the crack in her marriage to Alan, nevertheless took his time accepting Sean as his father. A turning point came shortly after Kevin quit football and he ran into Alan. It was an awkward chance meeting, with Kevin still calling him Dad. Alan, in no uncertain terms, had let Kevin know he was disgusted with Kevin's decision to, as he said, "leave the Bulldogs high and dry at linebacker." He went on to compare Kevin's move to Sean's "blowing off an opportunity to play for Joe Paterno."

At dinner that night, for the first time since his father had returned, Kevin called Sean Dad.

They were in The Kitchen. It was one of the last nights Risa was going to be working and she had told them to sit at the table under one of Sim's pictures so she could, as she passed by, see "all three of my men together."

"Ellen wants me to go on this trip over spring break," Kevin said. "To New Orleans, with a bunch of kids from school, to help rebuild some of the Lower Ninth Ward. What do you think?"

"You talked to Mom about it?" Sean asked, still a little tentative about making unilateral parent decisions.

"No."

"Are you going because of Ellen or because of the good people of New Orleans."

"Both."

"Can't lose, then, can you?"

"I don't know. To tell you the truth, cities sort of scare me."

"Because of what I went through?"

"Maybe."

"I've never been there, but they say New Orleans is pretty laid back as cities go. And Kev, my experience was extreme. Maybe we should go into New York one day and look things over. I don't want you to be afraid of things you don't have to be afraid of."

"Sounds good. Let's not take the bus, though, huh?"

Sean smiled at his son's little joke.

Risa came to the table. "Dessert for you two?"

Sean put up his hands. "Nope. One-eighty-three at the gym today."

"Hey, at least you were at the gym. And you, Kev, you worrying about your weight?"

"Nope. I'm worrying about the decision, quote, unquote. Key lime or chocolate raspberry. What do you think, Dad?"

There was a moment of silence as Sean and Risa waited to make sure they had heard what they had heard. Kevin tried to read the silence, his father's wide-open loving look, his Mom's tears. "I know I called Alan that, but it's all right to call you Dad, isn't it?"

Sean's eyes spilled over now. He looked at Risa and then back at Kevin.

"It's perfect, Kev. It's perfect."

Touchstone Reading Group Guide

INTRODUCTION

Sean Collins is a recovering alcoholic, trying to put his life back together after years on the streets. He is also recovering from amnesia and is haunted by graphic memories of a dead woman named Carol—a woman he used to know. When he discovers that Carol really was murdered and that the accused murderer might have given a false confession, he fears that he is to blame. He returns to his hometown of Braden to turn himself in.

Sean's ex-wife, Risa, has not only remarried but had Sean declared dead after he went missing eleven years earlier. When he returns to Braden, it turns her world upside down. Is her ex-husband, the father of her son, a killer? Is her current husband, Alan, Sean's erstwhile best friend, the man she believes him to be? Who really killed Carol? The answers will surprise everyone.

TOPICS & QUESTIONS FOR DISCUSSION

1. At the opening of the novel Risa is plagued by a sense of looming disaster, which is borne out by events. Have you ever had similar intuitions?
2. Risa is alarmed by her son's violence during his football game, and again during the fight with Frankie Robich. Is Kevin's aggression understandable, given the context of both incidents, or is Risa right to be worried?
3. Sean and Risa both worry that Kevin may inherit the suicidal tendencies of Sean's family. Alcoholism is also believed to have a genetic link. Do you believe the right upbringing is enough to counteract these kinds of tendencies, or is nature stronger than nurture?
4. Sean accuses Braden's law enforcement of bullying G. G. Trask into a false confession. What were their motives for doing so? Do you think they ever truly believed G. G. was guilty?
5. Alan and Carol were drawn into Risa and Sean's relationship by Sean's addiction, and both betrayed their friendships. While Alan was actively hindering Sean's recovery, Carol believed she was

helping. Put yourself in Risa's place: How would you feel about Carol's attempts to fix her husband?

6. Who is a more convincing suspect: Alan or Sean?
7. Did you see the twist coming? When did you first suspect that Henry was involved?
8. How absolute is the division between Henry Saltz and John Goetz? Do you believe that Henry truly is unaware of John's actions?
9. Both of the book's villains are motivated by love gone wrong: Alan's for Risa and John's for Carol. How does this affect your feelings about their guilt? Do the motives for their actions change anything?
10. Were you surprised by Risa's decision to leave Alan and re-commit to Sean? Compare the two men: Alan, reliable but a liar, and Sean, a wild-card in recovery. What would you have done?
11. Sean is granted forgiveness by both Risa and Kevin. Does he deserve it?
12. At the novel's conclusion, G. G. Trask still believes he killed Carol. How do you predict he will deal with this guilt?

ENHANCE YOUR BOOK CLUB

Sean suffers from amnesia, a condition widely depicted in film. Have group members come prepared to discuss their favorite depiction of amnesia and its consequences. Some suggestions that may be of interest: *Unknown White Male,* a documentary; *Memento*, a thriller involving anterograde amnesia; *Eternal Sunshine of Spotless Mind,* a surreal love story involving chosen amnesia.

Braden is a football town much like Odessa, Texas, depicted in the book *Friday Night Lights* by H. G. Bissinger (which inspired the film and TV show). Discuss the books and/or the adaptations, and consider what role school sports plays in your own town.

Henry Saltz suffers from dissociative identity disorder (DID), also known as multiple personality disorder. Consider another novel featuring DID as the group's next read—for example, *Thr3e* by Ted Dekker or *Sybil* by Flora Rheta Schreiber.

Author Doug Magee is a photographer and screenwriter as well as a novelist. Check out his website, DougMagee.com, for more details as well as discussions and giveaways!

A CONVERSATION WITH DOUG MAGEE

What method do you use to plot out your books? Are you ever surprised by the turns the narrative takes?

I don't outline my books extensively. I usually know where the story will begin, where it will end, and some plot points in between when I start to write. So that does give me a number of surprises as the writing progresses. In *Darkness All Around,* for instance, Alan became much more actively involved in Sean's disappearance from Braden than I had originally thought.

Memory and its vagaries play an important role in your novel, demonstrated in Warren's age-related wandering, Sean's amnesia, and Henry's dissociation. Was there a real-life incident that led you to explore this theme?

Yes. I'm getting old! No, there was no one incident that prompted the exploration. I'm fascinated by the mind's plasticity, by aberrations in brain chemistry that lead to odd perceptions, and by the way in which our minds easily lead us astray.

Both of your mysteries take place in small towns. What is it about small-town dynamics that you find so compelling?

Technically, as a writer, small towns reduce the number of variables in the story, making it easier to handle plot and character. But even in big cities you can find neighborhoods and areas that act like small towns. What most fascinates me about these settings is what people don't say to each other. These things are often not secrets, per se, but omissions, assumptions, and even politenesses. There seems to be a lot of communication in the town of Braden, but I suspect a lot of people knew G. G. Trask was innocent before Sean returned.

Do you ever feel guilty for putting your characters in such dire straits?

No. That's my job. Their job is to find a way out.

***Darkness All Around* depends on three medical conditions: alcoholism, amnesia, and dissociative identity disorder. What kind of research did you do to get the details right?**

I don't depend a lot on detailed research when writing fiction. I think too many specifics can actually take the reader away from the more emotional aspects of diseases. Also, over the years I've been exposed to people suffering these conditions and made many mental notes about them as I went along.

Kevin's aggressive actions during his football game worry Risa, and his football training leads him to put Frankie in the hospital. Does Risa's concern reflect your own opinion of sport-sanctioned violence?

I played high school and college football. I wasn't very good but I enjoyed the game then. All three of my sons are basketball players and I'm happy about that. Football's emphasis on violence was something I accepted when I played the game but now seems to me an unnecessary danger.

You have written nonfiction and screenplays as well as mysteries. Does your writing process change at all from one to the next?

It does. Fiction for me requires a very steady, day-by-day, workmanlike approach. I actually write to a word count. Screenplays are done more in bursts. Nonfiction is often a process of writing, research, more writing.

You state on your website that you are opposed to the death penalty. How do your personal politics inform your fiction?

I don't want my fiction to carry messages, but neither do I want it to traffic in stereotypes about our criminal justice system just for the sake of fulfilling a formula. I believe a lot of people see through the standard rhetoric surrounding punishment in our society, understand that things aren't as black and white as some would have us believe. So I like to have my characters, at least some of them, reflect this skepticism.

Which character was the most difficult to write? Which was the easiest?

I think this is a writing cliché, but for me the hardest characters to write are the protagonists, the easiest are the minor characters. Risa, in *Darkness All Around,* was difficult because she was a woman and she was being whipsawed by circumstances so much. A character like Walter or Fu or Hon is much easier to brushstroke quickly.

Who are your influences as an author? What do you read when you're writing?

I'm a recent convert to mystery and suspense fiction. I was an English major in college and concentrated on early-twentieth-century fiction, D. H. Lawrence, Beckett, James Joyce. But I'm happily going through Chandler, Hammett, Richard Price, Dennis Lehane, and others now, and when I'm writing I love to have Robert B. Parker along as a sidekick.

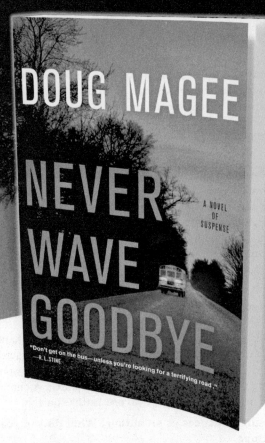